continued . . .

The Rhetoric of Death

2011 BARRY AWARD NOMINEE FOR BEST PAPERBACK ORIGINAL
ONE OF *DEADLY PLEASURES* MAGAZINE'S BEST BOOKS OF 2010

"[A] superb historical debut . . . With an experienced writer's ease, Rock incorporates details of the political issues of the day into a suspenseful story line." —*Publishers Weekly* (starred review)

"Rock brings firsthand knowledge of dance, choreography, acting, police investigation, and teaching to what is hopefully the beginning of a mystery series . . . [A] fascinating historical mystery . . . Plenty of derring-do and boyish mischief sprinkled into the plot make this a fun read, and Charles's thought-provoking struggles as he questions his vocation lend added depth. . . . sure to satisfy those eager for a great new historical mystery."
—*Booklist* (starred review)

"Rich with historical detail . . . meticulously researched. [Rock] captures a city and time that is lively, dangerous and politically charged, and makes it sing . . . [Her] fine eye for historic detail and well-drawn characters will continue to engage readers."
—*Kirkus Reviews* (starred review)

"Rock is an exciting new discovery. Her plotting holds your interest, her characters are real, and her attention to details of the time period is extraordinary. Highly recommended for fans of historical thrillers and readers who enjoy Ellis Peters, Edward Marston, and Ariana Franklin." —*Library Journal* (starred review)

"Rock balances perfectly the differing claims of detection, romance, suspense, and historical detail. As a mystery, as a kind of coming-of-age novel, or as a docudrama on early Jesuit pedagogy, *The Rhetoric of Death* works remarkably well. . . . Very entertaining." —*Commonweal* magazine

The Whispering of Bones

Judith Rock

BERKLEY BOOKS, NEW YORK

THE BERKLEY PUBLISHING GROUP
Published by the Penguin Group
Penguin Group (USA) LLC
375 Hudson Street, New York, New York 10014

USA • Canada • UK • Ireland • Australia • New Zealand • India • South Africa • China

penguin.com

A Penguin Random House Company

This book is an original publication of The Berkley Publishing Group.

Library of Congress Cataloging-in-Publication Data

Rock, Judith.
The whispering of bones / Judith Rock. — Berkley trade paperback edition.
pages cm
ISBN 978-0-425-25366-3
1. Collège Louis-le-Grand (Paris, France)—Fiction.
2. Jesuits—Fiction.   3. Murder—Investigation—Fiction.
4. France—History—17th century—Fiction.   I. Title.
PS3618.o3543w57 2013
13'.6—dc23
2013003498

PUBLISHING HISTORY
Berkley trade paperback edition / November 2013

PRINTED IN THE UNITED STATES OF AMERICA

10 9 8 7 6 5 4 3 2 1

A View of Paris from the Point de la Cité by Theodor Matham / Private
Collection © The Bridgeman Art Library; *The Great Siege Tunnels* © Eric James / Alamy;
Priest © Yolande de Kort / Trevillion Images.
Cover design by Danielle Abbiate.
Interior text design by Tiffany Estreicher.

For Shannon Jamieson Vazquez, editor,
who sees deeply, corrects unsparingly, and gives new books
to the world with excitement, love, and commitment.

ACKNOWLEDGMENTS

There's always more to know, always more mistakes to catch, and more possibilities to see. John Padberg, S.J., Patricia Ranum, and Catherine Turocy have patiently and enthusiastically helped me make the Charles du Luc books historically accurate and revealing. I am especially indebted to Patricia Ranum's new book, *Beginning to Be a Jesuit*, about the Jesuit Novice House in Paris in the 1680s. Heartfelt thanks also go to Caroline Jacquier at the Mazarine Library in Paris, for her tireless help as I researched this book. As always, the eagle-eyed team of early readers has corrected, suggested, and encouraged. And the art people at Berkley Books have once again outdone themselves creating the beautiful cover.

Chapter 1

Two Jesuits leaned into the wind, black cloaks streaming behind them. As they passed beyond the city wall and made their way south on the rue St. Jacques, the wind caught the wide brim of the older man's hat and sent it flapping through the brilliant light like a wakeful bat. His young companion loped after it along the cobbled road.

"My thanks, *maître.*" Père Auguste Dainville, thin and long-legged as a heron, pulled the returned hat down over his feathery white hair. "That's three times now," he said. "My hat is seeing to it that you get your exercise."

Maître Charles du Luc, a twenty-nine-year-old former soldier still undergoing the long Jesuit training for priesthood, smiled affectionately. "It's a good day for running, *mon père.*"

He offered his arm again and Dainville took it gratefully. The new school term had recently begun at Louis le Grand, the Jesuit school in Paris where they both lived and worked, and Dainville had just returned from his summer stay in the school's country house at Gentilly. Charles was dismayed at how much more fragile the old priest seemed. Dainville was his confessor.

Soon after Charles had come to Paris, something over a year ago now, the old man had seen him through a bleak time of decision and penance, and Charles had grown very fond of him. When Dainville had asked him at breakfast to be his prop on this short pilgrimage to the Carmelite church's ancient crypt, Charles had gladly said yes. But now, as the old man stumbled on a loose cobble and Charles steadied him, he wondered whether they should be taking this walk at all.

"According to Saint Ignatius," Dainville said, "true Jesuit obedience is like becoming a staff in an old man's hand." He gave Charles a sideways smile. "When the staff is also young, and able to run and fetch things for the old man, surely the obedience is even more complete."

Charles's smile was somewhat wry. "My thanks, *mon père*. As you know, I've rarely been praised for obedience."

"With God all things are possible. Tell me, how are you finding your latest stage of training, your theology study?"

Charles tried and failed to suppress a sigh. "It has begun well enough, *mon père*."

"Well enough," Dainville repeated musingly, watching Charles from the corner of his eye. "But I think you are not pleased enough."

"I'm trying to be."

"Many Jesuit scholastics starting theology feel as you do, you know." Dainville was silent for a moment. "But it's very hard. Until now, you've been active and engaged with the world, teaching, working on our theatre productions, helping with the students' almsgiving. And suddenly you must sit down and listen to lectures. Not to mention keeping yourself up at night wondering what in God's name Saint Thomas and Saint Augustine—but especially Saint Thomas—are talking about. Ours is indeed a hard discipline."

"I know these studies are essential if I'm to be a priest, *mon père*. But . . . I feel exiled from the world."

"Of course you do." Dainville eyed Charles again and then shook his head dolefully. "And, of course, you don't even have directing the summer ballet to look forward to."

Charles felt himself flush. "Well, the rector did say I'll be directing the ballet next summer. For which I'm very grateful. But it's—" Hearing how very ungrateful he sounded, Charles clamped his mouth shut.

"But," Dainville murmured, "it's only October."

"Yes. And I keep dreading the months between."

"Who would not? You won't have even the *slightest* reprieve until then. Week after week shut up in the college, no reviving variety . . ."

Charles, suddenly suspicious, bent a little in an effort to see Dainville's face beneath the hat brim. "Actually, I *will* go out occasionally. I'll still be helping Père Damiot with the students' weekly almsgiving for the congregation of the Holy Virgin."

"Oh! Will you?" Dainville looked up at Charles, his eyes wide with pleasure. "That's very good news. So you will get out occasionally."

Charles began to laugh. "And I'll be going twice a week to read Saint Augustine's *Confessions* with Père Quellier at the Novice House. So I'll hardly be exiled from the world. You've well and truly caught me, *mon père*."

"It's so pleasant to cast oneself as the star of one's touching inner drama," Dainville murmured, his eyes on the dusty road. "You do it very well—perhaps that's why you're so good at producing our ballets."

Charles's face was burning. "*Mea culpa.* I suppose I not only keep feeling like a sullen schoolboy, I've been acting like one."

Dainville laughed softly and squinted against the light at a range of tile roofs visible above the wall on their right. "You'll think I'm changing the subject, but I'm not. Our Saint Ignatius arrived from Spain on this road, you know. It's the pilgrim road to Saint Jacques of Compostela, and in his time those buildings were a pilgrim hospice. It would be just along here that he had his first sight of the roofs of Paris in the distance."

"I suppose it would be," Charles agreed.

"Tell me, *maître*," Dainville said in his teacher's voice, "why did our beloved founder come to Paris?"

"To enroll in one of the Paris colleges—Montaigu, wasn't it?"

"Correct. And why did he enroll?"

"To learn. He'd been a soldier and a courtier and was little schooled."

"Just so. And what class did he put himself in when he arrived?"

"In the basic grammar class."

"*Habes*," Dainville said triumphantly. "You have it, indeed! He needed to learn Latin for what he felt God was calling him to do. So, at nearly forty years old, that dignified Spanish noble-man sat on a bench with mere boys and learned his Latin." Dainville looked expectantly at Charles.

"And if Saint Ignatius could so humble himself with igno-rant boys, surely I can give myself to further learning with my fellow scholastics," Charles said, answering the unasked ques-tion, and added, "Perhaps I can even do it with a good grace."

"Very well reasoned," Dainville said innocently, as though Charles had come to that conclusion on his own.

Charles bowed ironic thanks. He did some arithmetic in his head. "What do you suppose Paris was like when Ignatius came?"

Dainville cocked an eyebrow at him. "Even I cannot remember back a hundred and sixty years. But I remember clearly how different it was when I was young. It was a good deal smaller. And far more dangerous. For instance—"

Hooves thundered over the cobbles and Charles pulled Dainville to the side of the road as a red-wheeled carriage flew past them.

"There was far *less* danger from carriages then," the old man said, waving away dust. "But some things have changed for the better. As I've said, Paris is certainly safer now." He shook his head. "When I was young, people hardly dared go out at night. Even in broad daylight, there were murders in the streets!" His expression darkened. "Just fifteen years ago, a nephew of mine, a Jesuit, disappeared in broad daylight. He was never found. He and I weren't close; somehow I never took to him. But still, he was my sister's son. Of course, when he disappeared— murdered, we all assumed—Lieutenant-Général La Reynie had not been in charge of policing all that long. Before him, we had no police worthy of the name. I tell you, that man deserves an assured place in the heavenly city for what he's done for Paris!"

Charles smiled, relishing the thought of telling that to La Reynie. He knew Paris's police chief better than he sometimes wished he did. But on the whole, he agreed with Dainville's assessment of the man.

"Were you born in Paris, *mon père?*"

Dainville nodded and was quiet for a moment. "My family was Robe nobility—all the men were in the legal professions. My father was a very successful Paris notary who had bought his notarial position and made it pay extremely well. He meant for me to be a lawyer and later a judge in the *Parlement*. But when he set me to studying the law, I rebelled."

"*You?* You rebelled against your father?"

"I wasn't always eighty," Dainville replied tartly. "Yes, I rebelled."

"What did you do?"

Dainville eyed him. "If I didn't know something about your own youth, I wouldn't tell you. But you're no innocent to be corrupted." They both burst into laughter. When they had mastered themselves, Dainville said, "What did I do? Most things rebellious sons do, including several duels. Finally, the third time I was caught dueling, my father decided not to help me, but let me take my chances at the courts in the Châtelet. Fortunately for me, my dueling opponent's shot and mine both missed, so no one had died, and the judge at the Châtelet who heard the case knew and respected my father, and let me go with only a heavy fine. Which my father set me to earn by clerking for a year there in the Châtelet courts."

"And then?"

"And then, when the fine was paid, I refused to go back to my law studies and my father disowned me. Left me with what I stood up in and nothing in my purse. So I presented myself at the Paris Novice House."

Charles eyed him dubiously. "You had discovered a religious vocation?"

"I had discovered what it was to be very hungry." The old man grinned at Charles. "And I knew nothing about the rigors of a Jesuit novitiate. All of which the Novice House rector quickly realized. He told me to go home to my father. Which I could not do. So I spent a while living by my wits."

Charles gaped at him.

"And do you know what happened?" Dainville's face shone with remembered delight. "I discovered that having nowhere to lay my head was very unpleasant for my body, but very clarifying for my soul. I began to find room for God. When I presented myself again at the Novice House, they had to shave my head to rid me of fleas and lice, but they let me in."

"That is a humbling story, *mon père*." Charles regarded his confessor with a mixture of love and awe, trying to imagine the gangling young novice Dainville must have been, with a shaved head and reeking of the herbal mixture used on lice. "Thank you for telling me."

"Don't take my young self too seriously," the old priest said, laughing a little. "*I* did enough of that."

Ahead of them, the long gray north wall and crow-studded tower of the Carmelite church came into view. Ready to be out of the wind, Charles and Dainville quickened their steps to the north door, the only one that opened outside the convent walls. After the dazzling autumn light, they stood for a moment, blinking in the dim nave. Though Notre Dame des Champs had once been part of a very old Benedictine priory, it had been redecorated for modern taste, and marble and gold gleamed in the shadows. The walls were hung with paintings whose colors were sharp and vibrant beneath the softly glowing glass of the old windows.

Charles and Dainville went up the side aisle, up a few steps, and then to the left around the altar, where a small door stood open on steps plunging into near darkness. Charles went first, Dainville gripping his shoulder for safety. Even Charles had to keep a hand on each wall for balance, the stairs being worn and polished smooth from centuries of devout climbing up and down.

When the two Jesuits reached the single candle flickering in its sconce outside the blue and gold Lady chapel beneath the nave, they stopped for a brief prayer and a rest for Dainville. Then they started the forty-foot descent to the crypt. The first flight of stairs had been straight, but now they wound like the inside of a shell. As on his one previous visit to the crypt, Charles found himself fighting rising unease as the walls seemed to close behind them and the air grew dead and chill. He was almost glad to hear someone climbing toward them as they reached the stairs' final twist.

"Wait," he called to the unseen climber. "There's no room to pass. Can you go back down?"

The steps halted abruptly and then retreated. When Charles and Dainville rounded the curve, a man was waiting patiently at the bottom. Blackly silhouetted against the antechamber's only candle, which was mounted on the wall behind him, the man's slender outline showed a plain brimmed hat but lacked a wig's long curls or the lace of shirt cuffs. An artisan, perhaps, Charles thought, as the man bowed his head deferentially and turned sideways pressing himself against the closed door to the left of the stairs to let them pass. They murmured their thanks. As they ducked under the low archway that led to the crypt chapel, his steps receded briskly above them.

The chapel was a bare and stony place, long and narrow and swathed in shadows under its arched stone ceiling. By the light of the few candles burning in wall niches, Charles helped Dainville to the single prie-dieu snugged against the wall, halfway to the small main altar. When the old man was settled, kneeling on the prayer desk's thin cushion, Charles went farther forward and knelt on the stone floor. He bowed his head and began the prayers belonging to the Hours of Our Lady.

"Mary who never forsakes us, look on us with the eye of pity . . ." He was immediately distracted by his knees complaining at the Carmelites' failure to put another cushioned prie-dieu in the chapel. Having learned that if he waited quietly his body would probably stop wanting what it couldn't have, Charles opened his eyes and gazed at the altar and its small wooden statue of St. Geneviève, patron saint of Paris. Her painted colors were faded and there were gouged places in the hem of her gown where gems had been ripped out. She'd lost an arm, and she stood a little hip-shot, as though easing her slight weight off a tired foot. But she was smiling. Charles smiled back, noticed that his knees had gone quiet, and reapplied himself to his prayers.

He didn't go as far into prayer as he sometimes did, and the deep, luminous Silence that sometimes visited him didn't come. Still, he rose from his knees with satisfaction enough, bowed to St. Geneviève, and turned toward the prie-dieu. But Dainville wasn't there. Charles looked blankly around the empty crypt.

"*Mon père?*"

His voice echoed unanswered. Surely the frail old man had not started up the stairs alone. Charles hurried down the crypt, pulled the heavy door open, and stumbled into near blackness instead of flickering candlelight.

"Père Dainville, where are you?"

Fearing that Dainville had found the candle burned out and fallen, and was lying somewhere hurt on the floor, Charles began feeling his way around the antechamber. The stone walls suddenly disappeared beneath his hands and he fell through the half-open door on the chamber's far side and caught himself on his hands. He got up and called out to Dainville again, but there was only silence. Cautiously, he went farther into the dark room. Then he heard a thin thread of breath from somewhere beyond the door. He started toward the sound, but something rolled beneath his foot and he tripped over what felt like blocks of stone, nearly falling again. Reason finally made itself heard—if he injured himself he'd be no good to Dainville when he found him—and he felt his way back to the chapel and took a candle from a wall niche. With a sinking heart, Charles carried the candle back to the other chamber. The light showed him Dainville lying on his back near the wall, half cushioned on a pile of rags.

"Oh, no," Charles groaned, and knelt beside him. The left side of the old man's face drooped like a tragedy mask, his mouth twisted and his eyelid half open. "*Mon père*, can you hear me?"

Dainville didn't move, except for the small rising and sinking of his chest. Charles put a hand on the withered neck, searching for the beat of blood. He found it, but it was weak. Fighting panic, desperately afraid that the old man would die here and now under his hand, Charles got to his feet and set the candle on a fallen block of stone, so that he could lift Dainville into his arms. Then he realized that the stairs were too narrow for carrying him like that.

"What were you doing in here? Couldn't you have waited for me?" he asked Dainville pointlessly, as he took off his cloak and tucked it as tightly as he could around the thin body. When Charles straightened, he saw that part of Dainville's cloak still lay fanned out along the floor. He tried to gather it closer, but it caught on something. When he jerked it free, he cried out, in spite of his years as a soldier. A hand and part of a black sleeve showed at the edge of the pile of rags. The hand lay palm upward, seeming to reach toward him in silent appeal.

Chapter 2

Mastering himself, Charles leaned to touch the hand. The flesh was cool, but perhaps that was only because it lay on stone that held the cold of endless winters. As quickly as he could, Charles moved Dainville to the lower edge of the rag pile. Then he pushed the rags aside, uncovering the body of a young man, hardly older than his students at Louis le Grand. The man lay on his back, unmoving. Charles felt for breath and the beat of blood, but expected none; the way the man's head was twisted and angled on his shoulders showed that the neck was almost certainly broken. A broken neck might happen by accident, especially on the crypt stairs. But no one breaks his neck and then hides himself under a pile of rags.

Charles signed a cross over the body and turned toward the antechamber. He could do nothing for the dead, but there was still hope for Dainville. Leaving the candle where it was—he didn't want the old man to wake in darkness, if he woke—Charles took the worn stairs three at a time. Holding his side and wet with sweat, he burst from the top of the stairs into the church. A small slender nun in the black and white Carmelite habit, busy with candles at the altar, turned serene gray eyes on him. Charles mopped his face with his sleeve and fought for enough breath to speak.

"What is it?" the nun said anxiously. "Please, sit down here on the altar step."

Charles shook his head. "I need help," he panted. "My companion—very ill—stairs—" He gulped air and tried again. "I can't carry him up alone. The stairs are too narrow."

"Our priest is in the sacristy. I'll get him."

Before Charles could say what else was needed, she was gone, and he let her go. Speed couldn't help the dead man, but it might help Dainville. She was back almost at once, a burly friar with a face like an amiable bull close behind her.

"I'll help you bring your man up," the friar said, and strode toward the stairs.

"Thank you. I'm coming." Charles turned to the nun. "One more thing. There's a dead man, a young layman, down there, in the room across from the chapel. Your abbess needs to know." He decided to leave the news that the man had likely been murdered for the abbess's ears.

The nun's eyes widened, but she said calmly, "Yes. I'll go for her." She crossed herself, reverenced the altar, and hurried toward the cloister door.

The friar's slapping sandals had stopped in the doorway to the stairs, and he was staring at Charles. "A *dead* man?! In the well chamber? Are you sure?"

"If the well chamber is across from the chapel, yes, I'm very sure." Charles urged him down the stairs. "If he's someone who comes here regularly, you may recognize him. Let's go."

The friar went, still talking over his shoulder. "So many people come, I doubt I'll know him. What killed him?"

"His neck's broken."

"Oh, dear. He must have fallen over something." The friar turned to watching his feet and the steps. "That chamber's full of rubble, workmen have been in there. I tell the abbess the room should be locked, but who can tell an abbess anything?" He shook his head. "She's not going to like this. Not one little bit."

Charles bit back saying that the dead man hadn't liked it, either, and they descended the rest of the way in silence. When they reached the well chamber, Charles saw that Dainville hadn't moved. He pointed to the dead man, and the friar bent over him and then straightened, shaking his head.

"Poor young man. Never seen him that I know of." He sighed and signed a cross over the body. "Well, let's get the live one up. Prayers over this one will have to wait."

Charles lifted Dainville by his shoulders, the friar gripped him around his knees, and they made their slow way up the narrow stairs, Charles ascending backward. When they struggled through the door at the top, the abbess was waiting for them. She swept a glittering black glance over Charles and Dainville and nodded crisply at the nave's front bench. "Put him there." She watched them lay Dainville gently on the bench and then nodded at Charles. "I must speak with you before you go. And you, *mon frère*," she said to the friar, "please go down and stay with the dead man until I come."

"First I must get Père Dainville home," Charles said, positioning himself to lift Dainville into his arms. "After that, I will return, but—"

The friar, looking askance at Charles's refusal of the abbess's order, gathered his skirts and fled to the crypt.

The abbess made a small impatient noise at Charles. "Do you really wish to create a spectacle—and make Père Dainville's condition worse—by carrying him through the streets like an armful of hay? We have an old sedan chair that will probably hold together long enough to get him to Louis le Grand. Our gardener and his helper are bringing it as quickly as they can. Sit for a moment and cushion his head, while you tell me about the dead man."

Seeing the wisdom of waiting for the chair, Charles sat and drew Dainville's head onto his lap. "My thanks for the chair," he said, stroking the old man's hair off his forehead. He looked up at her. "You know Père Dainville?"

Her lined square face softened. "Yes, he comes often to pray, and also to look at what remains of some very old paintings on the well chamber wall. There's a lovely one of Our Lady. I've grown very fond of him. I'm very sorry to see him like this." She smiled slightly. "Forgive me, I have not even told you my name. I am Mère Catherine Vinoy."

Charles bowed as well as he could from the bench. "And I am Maître Charles du Luc. I wondered what Père Dainville could have been doing in that chamber." He was quiet for a moment, wondering sadly if Dainville might have meant to show him the paintings before they climbed the stairs. Then, pulling himself back to what was needed, he said, "So. The dead man. What I didn't tell the sister or the friar is that I suspect he's been murdered."

The abbess drew back and crossed herself. "Dear Blessed Virgin, are you sure?"

"No dead man hides himself under a pile of rags. Only his hand and a few inches of sleeve were showing. I think Père Dainville saw it and the shock brought this apoplexy on him."

"As it well might," she said grimly. "Is he long dead?"

Charles shook his head. "Cool, but not very." Forestalling her next question, he said, "No one else entered the crypt chapel when we were there, but there was a man waiting to climb up as we reached the bottom of the stairs. I assumed he was coming from the chapel. He waited calmly enough for us to pass."

"Could you recognize him again?"

"No. He was outlined against the candlelight. I think he was youngish, by the way he moved. And by the outline of his clothes, not a man of quality—no wig or lace or long coat skirts. And he didn't speak." Charles frowned. "If he had come out of the well chamber, surely I would have heard that old door open and close. Because it was closed when the man was standing in the antechamber."

"Unfortunately," the abbess said wryly, "you would not have heard it. Extensive repairs are about to start in that chamber. I've just had the door well oiled to prevent annoyance to those in the crypt chapel when the work starts."

"So I wouldn't have heard anyone going in or out of that chamber while I was praying."

"No. Well, there's no point in regretting my efficiency," she said, with a fleeting smile. "I will send for the police *commissaire.*"

They both turned as the north door opened and a man in coarse brown breeches and jacket came in, pulling off his wide, battered hat. From where he stood, he made the abbess a rough bow.

"We've brought the chair, Mère Catherine," he called. "Do you need us to carry the father to it?"

"No," Charles said, "I'll bring him."

He gently lowered Dainville's head to the bench, rose, and lifted him in his arms. The old man's bones were sharp and his weight was alarmingly slight. Charles looked bleakly at the abbess.

"If Père Dainville—if he—" Charles found that he couldn't say the words. "When the police find the killer," he said grimly, "I pray he will not go to the scaffold with *two* deaths to his account."

Outside, the faded red sedan chair, probably new about the time Louis XIV's father was born nearly ninety years ago, waited like a once-handsome man caught in unforgiving daylight. The thing looked like a good gust of wind might be the end of it. Charles hoped its brittle wood and cracked leather would indeed hold together until they reached Louis le Grand. The gardener and his fellow who were going to be the "baptized mules," as chair carriers were called, ran their eyes unhappily over Charles's bulk and length.

"Will you have to go inside, too?" the gardener asked.

"Yes. To hold him. Can the chair—and the two of you—carry us both?"

"I suppose *we* can carry you both. Whether the chair can, only God knows."

The gardener held Dainville while Charles folded himself into the leather box built around the chair's two facing seats. Then they settled Dainville on blankets piled on the chair's floor, with his head and shoulders resting against Charles's knees. The gardener shut the door. "Up!" he called, and the grunting "mules" hefted the chair by its wooden poles and wobbled with it to the road. Charles disengaged one hand from supporting Dainville and closed the box's moulting velvet curtains to keep out prying eyes.

Holding Dainville tightly against the chair's swaying and bouncing, Charles prayed that the apoplexy would pass and leave him unmarked—or at least not badly marked. His praying ended abruptly as the back of the chair thudded onto its short rear supports and left the rest tilted upward like a sinking ship. The rear "mule" was groaning and cursing.

"Ah, *merde!* Aaaaah, *non!*"

Charles shoved the curtains aside as the front carrier set down his poles and the chair leveled out. "What's happened?"

No one answered him, and he stuck his head as far out as he could without dislodging Dainville. They were just inside the city wall, stopped in front of the Dominican monastery among the St. Jacques gate market stalls. The gardener was helping his fellow hobble to the steps of a house, and market sellers, customers, and passing pedestrians were calling out the usual Parisian mixture of advice and commentary while carriages and carts made their way around the chair. A little girl in a dark blue skirt under a stained white apron pinned to her bodice stopped to stare.

"*Maître!* Maître du Luc!" She ran to the chair's window, her thick curling brown hair tumbling from her white coif, and dropped her empty bread basket unceremoniously on the cobbles. Marie-Ange LeClerc was just turned ten, the daughter of bakers who rented one of Louis le Grand's few remaining shop fronts. "What are you doing in a chair, *maître?*" She gripped the window's edge to peer inside. "Your 'mule' stepped in a hole and twisted his ankle and—" She broke off, suddenly seeing Dainville. "Oh, no, what happened? Poor Père Dainville, is he dead?"

"No, but he's very ill." Charles looked again at the two carriers arguing beside the road. "Marie-Ange, are you finished delivering bread?"

She tilted her head at the gate of the Dominican monastery behind her. "The monks were the last."

"I need your help. I want you to sit here where I'm sitting and keep Père Dainville from falling sideways—you can do it, he's very light. Then I can help carry the chair and we can get him home."

She nodded eagerly and Charles eased himself out of the chair, keeping one hand under Dainville's head. Then he helped Marie-Ange inside, and resettled the old man against her knees.

"Hold his shoulders as tight as you can." He started to close the door.

"Wait, my basket, *Maman* will kill me if I leave it!"

"I'll get it." He shut the door, grabbed the basket, and went to the back of the chair. "Let's go," he called to the gardener, as he hung the basket over one of the rear poles. "I'm your new 'mule.'"

The gardener stood openmouthed for a moment, then shrugged and went to the front poles. "Lift when I say 'up,' then. Ready? Up!"

The rue St. Jacques quickly began sloping down to the river, which made carrying the rear of the chair somewhat easier, but the old war wound in Charles's left shoulder was soon throbbing from the weight. It took all his agility to keep step as the gardener dodged the usual array of dung, spoiled and discarded market produce, a small flock of stubborn milk goats, and a weaving passenger chair on wheels pulled by a man and pushed by a woman from behind. A passing carriage driver's whip nearly knocked Charles's hat off, and a baying dog chased a cat between his feet.

"Hold up," he shouted, as they finally reached Louis le Grand's postern door. Sighing with relief as the chair came to rest on its supports, he hurried to its door and helped Marie-Ange out. As he stooped to gather Dainville into his arms, something smacked against his back and raucous laughter came from across the street. Leaving Dainville in the chair, Charles whirled furiously, blocking the door from whatever was being thrown.

Two students in short black University gowns stood jeering at him across the street. "So Jesuits are taking chairmen's money now," one of them called. "Your piles of gold aren't enough for you?"

"You gutless sons of gelded pigs!" Marie-Ange picked up the rotten fish they'd thrown at Charles and hurled it back with deadly aim. As it hit one of the students—with a satisfying *splat* square in the chest—the college postern opened and a portly, elderly lay brother in the brothers' short black cassock and canvas apron surged into the street. Heedless of traffic, he put himself between Marie-Ange and the students, who had started toward her.

"You leave her alone, you hear me?" Frère Martin shook his big fists at them. "Bothering a little maid, shame on you, you milk-livered whelps!"

The students, who seemed to recognize Martin, backed up. The brother nodded with satisfaction and advanced on them. Charles caught him by his cassock.

"Let them go, Frère Martin, I need your help here!"

"Oh, it's you, *maître*, I didn't really see you. I heard Marie-Ange and came to see that she was all right." He smiled at the little girl. "I take it you threw the fish, *ma petite*—and a very nice aim you have!" He swept a puzzled glance over the sedan chair and the waiting gardener. "But Père Dainville went out with you, *maître*, where is he?"

"Here." Charles turned back to the chair and gathered Dainville in his arms, then straightened.

"Oh, blessed Mary! Ah, his poor face—struck!" Martin exclaimed, using the old word for apoplexy.

"Yes, I'm taking him to the infirmary." Charles nodded toward the Carmelites' gardener. "Will you please give this man something for carrying the chair and find someone to help him take it back to Notre Dame des Champs?"

"Of course!" Calling to the gardener to wait, Martin, whose usual job was watching the postern door, hurried back through it toward the main college courtyard.

Marie-Ange picked up her basket and ran to open the postern wider for Charles and Dainville. "Will you come and tell me how he does, *maître?*" Her round face was furrowed with worry. "I'll pray for him."

"Please do. Thank you for your help, Marie-Ange. I'll come when I can." She pushed the door closed after him, and he lengthened his stride through the street passage. He was half running by the time he reached the main courtyard.

The last classes of the afternoon were in session and the vast main court, the Cour d'honneur, was mostly empty. A bored courtyard proctor taking his ease on a stone bench looked up when he heard Charles crunching across the gravel and then leaped to his feet in dismay.

"What's happened, *maître?* Is it Père Dainville?"

"He's ill, *mon frère.* Please find the rector and ask him to come to the infirmary."

The proctor ran toward the main building, and Charles strode through the archway on his left. The infirmary stood beyond the student court, in the midst of a small physic garden. The year's last sweet and pungent scents rose as his cassock skirts swept past fading herbs and flowers to the infirmary door. He carried Dainville into the small vestibule and shouldered open the door into the Jesuits' infirmary. The long room with its two rows of beds was full of late-afternoon quiet but empty of patients.

"Frère Brunet!" Charles made for a bed at the far end of the row, near the tiny chapel and the infirmarian's chamber. "Are you here?"

He put Dainville down on the bed and was untying the old man's sash with shaking hands when Brunet hurried in from the vestibule.

"I was upstairs in the student infirmary. Who's ill, *maître?*"

He bustled down the room to the bed. "Oh, dear." Shaking his head at Dainville's twisted face, Brunet pushed Charles gently aside. "See to his shoes."

With deft fingers, the infirmarian finished untying the sash, set it aside with its long wooden rosary, and peeled Dainville's cassock off him, leaving him in his long white linen shirt. Charles unbuckled the priest's worn black shoes and dropped them on the floor's rush matting.

"Now, *mon père*," Brunet murmured, lifting Dainville's knees so he could pull the blankets up, "we'll just get you under the covers and nicely warm, that will be better, won't it? There you are." He pulled the blankets up to Dainville's chin, put his forehead to Dainville's to check for fever, and laid his fingers against the old man's neck. "His blood's not beating as strong as I'd like. Tell me exactly what happened."

He listened wide-eyed to Charles's account, exclaiming in horror at the murder. "Whoever killed that boy bears the guilt for this as well, and I hope he hangs!" He stared down at the old man. "Père Dainville would have been—maybe still will be—eighty on Saint Martin's Day. But that's a month away."

Charles swallowed hard. "May I watch with him?"

Brunet eyed him. "Don't you have a class to teach? Or somewhere you should be?"

"No class," Charles said, ignoring the rest of the question. "I've started my theology study."

"Have you?" The infirmarian's face was as sympathetic as if Charles had said he had gout. "Well, I know you have to, going toward your priesthood as you are. Yes, stay with him while I make a tisane. I might be able to get it into him with a spoon." He went to a tall cupboard beyond the bed. "Theology," he muttered, shaking his head as he reached in. "Always something *there* to fight about. Me, I'm glad to be just a lay brother.

But Jesuits are supposed to find God in all things, even in theology, I suppose . . ." His words trailed off and he leaned deeper into the cupboard. "Ah. Got it." He turned with a pottery cup and a small, stoppered clay pot in his hands. "I'll be back as quick as I can, *maître*."

Charles pulled a stool to Dainville's bedside and sat holding the old man's hand, for his own comfort as much as for Dainville's. Worry choked his prayers and seemed to be squeezing his heart. He turned his confessor's dry, thin hand over and found himself thinking that the tangle of lines in the palm was like a map. A map of all Dainville had done, of the twisting path that had led to faithfulness. Hoping that his own life would be as faithful, he watched the shallow rise and fall of the thin chest and willed it to go on.

Tears stung his eyes. He thought of the young man lying dead in the deep crypt at Notre Dame des Champs and wondered who would weep for him when the terrible news came. And he thought of the man at the foot of the crypt stairs, so blackly outlined against the single candle flame, and wondered if he'd just come from praying—or killing.

Chapter 3

The door from the vestibule opened and Louis le Grand's rector came in. Charles let go of Père Dainville's hand and stood up as Père Jacques Le Picart hurried down the row of beds.

"How is he, *maître?*" The rector was wiry and gray-haired, and peasant Normandy still sounded in his speech.

Charles shook his head, trying to pick through his scattered thoughts for an answer, but Frère Brunet emerged from his chamber with a steaming cup and a spoon and forestalled him.

"He's none too good, *mon père,*" Brunet said. "Apoplexy, they call it now. Struck, I call it." He sat down on Charles's stool, stirring the tisane, and the soft fragrance of chamomile rose from the cup. "Struck by a murderer, so Maître du Luc says."

"*What?*" Le Picart rounded on Charles, his sea-gray eyes horrified. "He was attacked?"

"No, not by the murderer's hand," Charles said. "We went to Notre Dame des Champs to pray in the crypt. While I was still praying, Père Dainville went into the well chamber across from the chapel. I found him there, fallen onto a pile of rags. The dead man had been mostly hidden under the rags, but his hand and arm were visible. I think Père Dainville saw that and the shock brought on this apoplexy." Seeing Le Picart's next question on his face, Charles said, "The body wasn't yet cold."

Le Picart stared at him. "Are you telling me that the man was killed while you two were in the chapel? But surely you would have heard a quarrel or a fight. Did you see anyone?"

Charles told him about the man silhouetted at the bottom of the stairs, and what Mère Vinoy had said about having oiled the chamber door hinges in preparation for the upcoming work in the chamber.

"So you told the abbess."

"I told her what I knew and she said she would send for the police. She also loaned a sedan chair for bringing Père Dainville home."

Le Picart smiled briefly. "She's a good woman. And an impressive administrator. She makes me wish we had nuns in the Society of Jesus. Though one could wish she'd been less impressive and had left the door hinges alone." His smile faded as he watched Brunet spooning sips of the tisane into Dainville's mouth and gently wiping away what spilled. "Do you want to bleed him, *mon frère*? Or send for a physician?"

"Neither." Brunet scowled at Le Picart as though the rector were holding out the bleeding basin and the lancet. "You know I don't believe in bleeding. The poor man is already so frail and you want to take his lifeblood from him?"

The rector held up his hands in submission. "No, truly I don't! I only wondered."

"Hmph. As for a physician . . ." Brunet eyed his patient. "We'll see." His suspicion of University-trained physicians and their harsh remedies—and high fees—was well known at Louis le Grand and, most of the Jesuits felt, had probably saved not only the budget but lives.

"Use your judgment," Le Picart said. "I'll sit with him awhile."

To take his confession, if he regained consciousness, Charles thought sadly. Or to give him last rites, if he continued to sink.

Brunet nodded and got up from the stool. "He's not going to drink any more now. Sit here, *mon père*. I must go to check on a boy upstairs, and then I'll be back."

"You, too, must go, *maître*," the rector said to Charles. "In the midst of all this unhappy news, I've neglected to tell you that you have a visitor waiting in the *grand salon*. A cousin of yours, he says."

"A cousin?" Charles said in surprise. He had many cousins, but none—so far as he knew—visiting Paris. All his family lived in the south. "Did he give his name, *mon père*?"

"He is Monsieur Charles-François de Vintimille du Luc. You must not keep him waiting longer."

Charles groaned inwardly. This cousin had never been a friend, and there were few people he wanted less to see.

The rector's nose twitched and he frowned. "I keep thinking I smell fish. Fish gone bad."

"Oh." Charles reached behind himself, trying to feel the center of his back. "I'm sorry, *mon père*. I forgot. A University student threw a fish at me outside our postern. I'll go and clean it off." He looked down at Dainville. "Will you let me know if—if he's worse?"

"Of course. Go now."

Charles bowed and took his leave, worry over Dainville vying with dismay at the news that his unbeloved cousin awaited him. As he let himself out of the infirmary and walked through the windy garden, he could hear the voices of Louis le Grand's day students, exulting over their release for the day as soon as they were beyond the various college gates and postern doors. As he entered the boarding students' court, a Jesuit scholastic shepherded a group of boys through the archway from the Cour d'honneur. Two of the boys had been among Charles's favorite students: Walter Connor and Armand Beauclaire, both good in rhetoric and even better at dance—in spite of the havoc Beauclaire's peculiar inability to tell right from left could create onstage. Now they dropped back from the scholastic and their fellows and stopped to make flourished bows to Charles, grinning from ear to ear. Seeing that their shepherd hadn't noticed and kept walking, Charles sketched an equally silly bow to the boys and waved them on, smiling with pleasure at seeing them.

Dusk was falling and Louis le Grand's uneven roofline was sharp against the sky, bristling with round and square towers that seemed to have been dropped haphazardly on the roofs' blue-gray slate. In its hundred and twenty-four years, the college had grown from a private townhouse with a grand courtyard to a checkerboard of graveled and turfed courts surrounded by three-, four-, and five-story buildings, the newest of brick and the oldest half timbered. The high walls of blackened stone were honeycombed with archways leading from one court to the next, and Charles's way led beneath two more arches, one round and one pointed, before he reached the main court and the main building's back door. He climbed the back staircase to his chamber, removed his cassock, and saw that the fish remains were beyond simple wiping. He put on his clean cassock, consigned the fishy one to the laundry, washed his hands, reknotted his sash, and carefully readjusted his shirt collar to show the correct edge of white above the cassock's high black collar.

Hoping your cousin will go away if you make him wait long enough? His chiding inner voice was right as usual. Telling himself that the sooner he saw his cousin, the sooner he'd be rid of him, Charles went resolutely downstairs and to the doorway of the *grand salon*. The high-ceilinged reception room was the only room at Louis le Grand with any claim to elegance. Its red and gold carpet was worn but not threadbare, and several good paintings in wide, gold-leafed frames hung on the wall. The pair of tall beeswax candles on the heavily carved side table were not yet lit and the room was dim. For a moment, Charles thought he'd gotten his wish and his cousin had left. Then he saw him across the room, peering at a small, red chalk drawing of St. Ignatius, one of the school's treasures.

Unmoving and unnoticed in the doorway, Charles watched him. Most du Luc men were named Charles, after an illustrious ancestor. And most looked like this cousin, Charles-François de Vintimille du Luc, a former soldier turned galley captain. Short and thick bodied where Charles was more than six feet tall, dark where Charles was Viking fair, he seemed top heavy under the curly black wig cascading over his shoulders. Charles wondered if the wig was meant to draw attention away from his cousin's empty left coat sleeve—Charles-François had lost his arm at the battle of Cassel in 1677. Charles had come through that same battle unscathed, though he'd taken a musket ball in his shoulder just a few days later at the battle of St. Omer. Ten years was long enough to forget most things, but seeing his cousin's neatly pinned-up coat sleeve brought memories slamming against Charles's eyes.

"*Bonsoir, mon cousin,*" Charles said, walking away from his memories and into the *salon*.

Charles-François turned from the drawing. "I wondered how long it would take you to gather enough courage to walk through that door."

"I was admiring your wig," Charles shot back. And grimaced

because, as usual, they were throwing words at each other almost before they'd said hello. He tried to put warmth into his voice. "Have you come to bring family news, Charlot?" Charles-François's face reddened at the nickname, though Charles had only used it from habit. Five years older but a head shorter, Charles-François had been called Charlot, "Little Charles," by the family ever since Charles had shot past him in height.

Charles sighed inwardly and tried again. "In her last letter, *Maman* said your ship was in the Mediterranean. Why are you in Paris?"

Charles-François's long nose was pinched with anger. "I came to see Amaury de Corbet."

Charles stared at his cousin. He hadn't heard that name in ten years. Amaury de Corbet was a young nobleman who had been with them at the Battle of Cassel, and who had later kept Charles from bleeding to death when he was wounded at St. Omer.

"I didn't know Amaury was from Paris," Charles said, trying not to let Charles-François see how hard the name had hit him. "I haven't seen him since I left the army. But that's hardly surprising. I barely knew him."

"Oh, he isn't *from* Paris. So you really don't know that after you used your little graze"—he glanced disdainfully at Charles's shoulder—"as an excuse to quit fighting, Amaury followed me into the Royal Marine? He was under my command these last ten years. Most of the time—except when he got drunk and talked about you and how nobly selfless and penitent you were to join your Society, damn you—he was the best officer on my ship."

"How did he know I had become a Jesuit?"

"That, I admit, is my fault. When he learned I'm your cousin, he asked about you and I told him," Charles-François said sourly. "Amaury might have talked now and again about leaving, but put a sword or a musket in his hands and he forgot all that soon enough. Until two years ago, when his father died. Monsieur de Corbet was a good military man, he'd been a commander in the Dutch war and after. And he'd told Amaury that if he went on about his damned guilt and left the military, he'd disinherit him. Not that he had so much, but without it, Amaury had nothing." Charles-François sighed in disgust. "But when Monsieur de Corbet died, Amaury started talking about you and sin and God so much it made me sick. But losing a father hits a man hard, and I tried to think it was just that. Until one fine morning a few weeks ago, when Amaury showed me an official letter granting him permission to leave the navy." Charles-François came so close that Charles could smell the reek of tobacco on his breath. "He left because of you. Because of you and what you did at Cassel."

Charles gazed blindly at the floor, seeing the horror of that sunlit noon outside Cassel's walls. The king's army had the Netherlands city under siege. Charles-François and Amaury de Corbet, each an officer with a small squadron of men, were near the front line of the siege encampment that day. Charles, sometimes sent out as a scout, had been passing on information to Amaury. Things were quiet and most of the soldiers were eating their midday bread and cheese. Two of Amaury's men started toward a pair of dilapidated cottages in a nearby muddy field, wondering loudly to each other if anything edible had been left in them. Musket fire burst from a cottage doorway. One of the soldiers was killed and the other wounded. The rest of their squadron charged the cottages, ignoring Amaury's orders when he tried to stop them. Charles's cousin and his squad joined the charge. Charles saw that Amaury—who was even younger and more inexperienced than the nineteen-year-old Charles—couldn't control his men. Trying to help, Charles grabbed his cousin, thinking that if Charles-François was stopped, his soldiers would stop, too. But as Charles tackled his cousin, another shot from the cottages hit Charles-François in the arm. After that, the world turned red and stinking. The cottages were full of refugees and one of the women had a musket. All of them were slaughtered—several women, a half dozen children, and one old man. Charles and Amaury had been able to do nothing.

Or were you too afraid to do anything? Charles's inner voice said, as it had said more times than he could count. Wrenching himself away from the memories, he realized that his cousin was talking to him again.

"—so I'm telling you, if you know what's good for you, you're going to help me get Amaury out of your Novice House!"

Charles squinted in bewilderment at his cousin. "What does the Novice House have to do with this?"

"Have you lost your ears as well as your balls? I tell you, Amaury has gone mad enough to think he wants to be a Jesuit. He's in your Paris Novice House!" Charles-François rocked forward onto his toes, his round dark eyes bulging with anger. "And if you don't help me get him out, I will personally see to it that every Jesuit on earth knows what a slinking"—he pushed Charles lightly in the chest—"damned"—he pushed him again, and Charles stumbled backward—"*coward* you are!"

It was as though Charles's life as a Jesuit had never been. He shoved his cousin roughly away and reached for the sword that hadn't been at his side since he walked through the door of the Avignon Novice House eight years ago. The du Lucs were minor nobles, and in the code of nobility, only blood could wipe away Charles-François's insult. Then the moment of rage passed and Charles stood rigid and silent.

But Charles-François read his face all too well. "Shall I lend you a sword so you can invite me into the street? No? You really did leave your manhood at Cassel, didn't you? Too bad it wasn't you the peasant woman killed. Before you tried to make Amaury stop his men from killing the king's enemies."

"*Enemies?* Those were terrified *peasants* you helped Amaury's men murder. Starving women and children trying to hide from war, for God's sake!"

"Anyone who shoots at the king's soldiers is an enemy and deserves everything he—or she—gets! But Amaury didn't deserve the guilt you left him with. You ruined him. Now you've taken him from his rightful place as a fighting man. Just like you took my arm and half my fighting skill!"

"God calls whom He calls," Charles said. "And in His own good time." He suddenly almost pitied his cousin. "However you judge what I did at Cassel, if Amaury has offered himself to the Society, that's the opposite of cowardice. Though I don't expect you to understand that."

Charles-François shook the stump of his arm at Charles, the pinned sleeve flapping like a small pennant. "What I *understand* is that if you hadn't pulled me in front of you to save yourself from that damned woman's shot, I'd still have two good arms to fight with!"

"If you hadn't urged on Amaury's men and your own to slaughter her and the rest of them, you'd still have two good arms. They were miserable refugees, Charlot, and I pulled you back to stop you trying to kill them—why can't you understand that? God knows I've always been desperately sorry the shot hit you."

"You *hid* behind me, you were too rabbit-scared to fight *peasants,* even after they killed one of Amaury's soldiers and wounded another. If you'd had the balls to help us like you should have, Amaury wouldn't have slowly rotted inside all these years. He wouldn't be trying to hide in your damned Society now!"

Charles-François was shouting and spraying spit. "His men and mine only did their duty! He's guilty of *nothing* but listening to *you*. But you—you're guilty as hell itself!"

Charles folded his hands so tightly that he felt the small bones being pulled out of place. A door opened at the end of the *salon* and Père Montville, the Prefect of Studies in charge of day students, put his head out of his office. His round, normally pleasant face was dark with displeasure and he frowned from Charles to his cousin. "What is the meaning of this uproar, *maître*?"

Charles tried to keep his voice neutral. "*Mon père*, please forgive the disturbance."

"Please remind your guest that this is a religious house."

"Yes, *mon père*."

Montville withdrew into his office and shut the door.

Grinning, knowing that Charles would bite his tongue off now rather than react, Charles-François flicked a finger against Charles's chest. "Yes, *mon père*. No, *mon père*. Just a handsome little automaton carrying out orders, aren't you? And that's what your Society will make of Amaury." The grin vanished and the man's mouth twisted with hatred. "You make me sick! I meant what I said; I'll see that every Jesuit on earth knows what you are and what you did. Your Society's a military order, what use do they have for cowards?"

Charles shook his head wearily. "No, we aren't a military order."

But Charlot wasn't listening. "I'll go to your Superior General in Rome, if I have to. You've only taken first vows. They'll throw you out fast enough. You won't be able to hide your gutlessness any longer in your safe Jesuit nest, where you obey and don't have to think."

Charles lifted his gaze and looked at his cousin. "Most men carry out someone's orders. I decided not to carry out any more orders to kill. As Amaury apparently has also decided. God go with you, Charles-François."

Charles walked out the rear door of the *salon*, ignoring his cousin's shouted demand to come back, and walked straight into Père Le Picart.

"Forgive me, *mon père*—"

The rector was looking beyond him into the *salon*. "Who is shouting?"

"My cousin. He's angry."

"So I gather. Angry at you?"

Before Charles could answer, Charles-François was at his heels, pushing him aside.

"You don't know what a coward my dear cousin Charles is, do you?" he challenged the rector. "You have a *coward* in the pope's army. That's what you Jesuits are, aren't you?"

"No," Le Picart said quietly. "Not his army."

Momentarily silenced, Charles-François gaped at him. Charles said nothing. He was more than willing to let the rector face his cousin down, and he didn't care whether that was obedience or cowardice. Whichever it was, he wanted his cousin to go and take his fury with him.

"We were established to help souls, *monsieur*," Le Picart said with deceptive mildness. "To teach and counsel, to help the poor, and work in the world in all its variety. How can we help you?"

"You can give up Amaury de Corbet, who's in your Novice House! Because my cowardly cousin enticed him there. He—"

Le Picart took a step toward Charles-François and held up a sinewy hand. To Charles's surprise, his cousin's mouth snapped shut.

"Enticed him?" The rector looked questioningly at Charles.

"I haven't seen Amaury de Corbet since I left the army, *mon père*."

"Monsieur de Vintimille du Luc, I have nothing to do with the Novice House. But you may certainly go there and speak with its rector. I wish you a blessed evening and a peaceful night. You may go out the way you came in."

The rector and Charles-François stared at each other until, incandescent with fury, Charles-François strode back into the *salon.* Charles and Le Picart stayed where they were until they heard the street passage door open and slam shut.

"Well." The rector looked thoughtfully at Charles. "Why do I have a feeling he'll be back?"

Charles sighed. "Because he will, when he doesn't get what he wants at the Novice House."

"Come and tell me what all that was about. I think I should be armed with the facts when he returns."

Suddenly so tired he was weaving as he walked, Charles followed the rector to his office. "How is Père Dainville?" he asked, as Le Picart lit a small tallow candle and waved away its pungent smoke.

"There's no change yet." Le Picart settled himself behind his desk. "Frère Brunet thinks God may be about to take him. It will be very hard to let him go." He gazed sadly at the candle's small yellow flame. "Père Dainville has been a Jesuit as long as I've been alive. And a member of this house most of those years. I've rarely known a man so able to see into the souls of others. I doubt there's a better confessor in the Society."

Charles nodded, wondering whether Le Picart knew about Dainville's turbulent youth. "I'm grateful that he's been my confessor."

The rector nodded. "Now tell me about your cousin and his accusations."

Something close to panic swept through Charles. He couldn't tell the whole truth. He'd never told even Père Dainville about that terrible noon outside Cassel.

Le Picart was watching Charles in alarm. "Sit down, *maître*. You've gone as white as your shirt."

Charles put an involuntary hand to the edge of white linen showing above his cassock collar, as though the touch of something so ordinary might help him, and sank into the chair in front of the desk. "My cousin and I have disliked each other since we were children," he said carefully. "Some part of his anger means no more than that."

Le Picart waited.

"As you saw," Charles went on reluctantly, "he has lost an arm. We were both wounded in the Spanish Netherlands. He at Cassel, and I at Saint Omer a few days later. He's always blamed me for the loss of his arm."

"Why?"

Charles folded his hands together and fixed his eyes on the small, plain crucifix on the wall beyond Le Picart. "There was musket fire from some ruined cottages near the Cassel wall. A soldier was killed and another wounded. Their comrades ignored their very young captain's order to stand off—the captain was the man my cousin was talking about, Amaury de Corbet. The soldiers attacked the cottages. A peasant woman had fired the shots. A little group of peasants, refugees from some village, had found a musket somewhere and hidden in the cottages. I tried to help de Corbet stop his men, but my cousin and his own men joined the attack. I was trying to hold my cousin back when another shot from the cottages hit his arm. He thinks I tried to hide behind him and that's why he was wounded." Charles fell silent.

The rector sighed and crossed himself. Charles was afraid that if he moved, his control would shatter. He had never told this story to anyone. And he'd still kept back the worst part.

"Is there more?" the rector said gently.

"A few days later, I was shot at the battle of Saint Omer and de Corbet saved my life. But I didn't see him again after that." He finally allowed himself to look at Le Picart. "Do you think I might be able to see him in the Novice House? When I go there to study with Père Quellier?"

The rector's cool gray eyes searched Charles's face. "Given that Monsieur de Corbet saved your life, I imagine that Père Guymond—the Novice House rector—would allow you to see him briefly. Are you going to tell Monsieur de Corbet that your cousin is searching for him?"

"No. And if my cousin comes here again, I won't tell him I've seen Amaury."

Le Picart nodded. "Good. If Monsieur de Vintimille du Luc goes to the Novice House as angry as he left us, it's certain that he'll be turned away in short order. Even if he masters himself, it's unlikely that de Corbet will be allowed to see a layman this early in his novitiate. So don't worry about him." The rector's eyes were still on Charles, and full of concern. "This has been an afternoon of shocks for you and I know that you missed supper. Go to the kitchen and get something before you return to your chamber."

"Thank you, *mon père*." Charles stood up. "But Père Dainville—will you—"

"I will let you know if there is a change." The rector stood, too, and came around the desk to put a hand on Charles's sleeve. "I'm going back to sit with him. I think that whatever happens, he will be at peace. It is your own peace that should concern you now."

Nearly undone by the compassion on his superior's face, Charles made his escape, his secret coiled like a little snake in his heart.

Chapter 4

Charles forced down the bread and warmed-over mutton stew the kitchen brothers gave him and went to his chamber. The city's bells were ringing Compline, the last of the day's hours of prayer, and when he opened his chamber window, the bells' clamor beat in his body as though the sound struck his ribs as well as his ears. The wind had died, leaving the city chilled, but he stayed at the window and shut his eyes, murmuring the first few Compline prayers.

"God, come to my assistance . . . make speed to save me . . ." But Père Dainville's stroke-twisted face and the smooth young face of the murdered man in the Carmelites' well chamber kept coming between him and the words. He prayed for his confessor's recovery, for the murdered man's soul, and that the killer would be found. But it seemed to him that his prayers refused to "rise." Not that he really thought God was "up," but often when he prayed, he felt that what he offered or asked broke free of himself and went—somewhere. *Help me*, he begged silently. And then, *forgive me*.

But those prayers, too, went nowhere. The image of

Dainville and the murdered young man were pushed out by older memories. Cassel's walls rose again in his mind, and he heard the peasants' shots, saw Amaury de Corbet's soldiers fall, saw their enraged comrades charging the war-ruined cottages. He saw the woman with the musket, wide-eyed with fury and terror in the first cottage's doorway, felt his cousin fall against him as her shot hit home. He saw himself finally reach the cottage door where Amaury stood, ashen and sick. The woman who'd wounded Charles-François, all the children but one, and an old man lay dead in their blood. The earthen floor was slick with it. Charles shouted at the soldier who had his musket trained on the little boy, but the soldier fired. The jubilant men moved on to the next house. Sick with horror, Charles leveled his musket at their backs. And then let the barrel drop. The men were his fellow soldiers. If he shot them, he would die. Either there and then, or soon after by hanging. So he stood still, listening helplessly to women screaming in the second cottage. He hadn't hidden behind Charles-François, or caused his cousin the loss of his arm. But Charles-François's assessment was right—he was a coward.

Except for the partial account he'd given Le Picart, he'd never told anyone about that day at Cassel, not even his confessors. His mother knew, but only because she'd pieced together things he'd said during the fever that came after his wound. She'd reassured him over and over that he hadn't fired his musket because the men were the king's soldiers and he was loyal. But she was wrong. He hadn't fired his musket because he'd been afraid. When he began to recover, he'd prayed constantly for forgiveness. Just before he'd entered the Jesuit Novice House in Avignon, his mother had told him flatly that he'd never hear God's forgiveness until he stopped shouting accusations at himself.

He raised his head. The bells had long since stopped and the rue St. Jacques was quieter than it was in the daylight. The lanterns hanging from the sides of buildings had been lit and cast small pools of light on the cobbles. A little way up the hill, an upper window opened in a house on the other side of the street and a woman leaned on the sill, her white coif gleaming in the lantern light. She was singing, though too quietly for Charles to hear the words. But he recognized the melody, because he'd heard it in the streets. He remembered its words, too, about the pleasure of seeing a lover, and about love's danger. He leaned his elbows on the windowsill, thinking about his own youthful love, Pernelle. He'd chosen God above all else. And she had also made her own choices. But a deep place in his heart would always belong to her. They had let each other go for many reasons, good reasons, but love songs still wrung his heart. *How long are you going to stand here spinning yourself another drama? Don't you have work to do?* his critical inner voice said. Charles sighed and swung the small-paned window shut. Then he picked up the malodorous tallow candle from the stool beside his bed, nodded as though in greeting toward the small painting of Mary and her Child that hung nearly invisible in the shadows, and went into the tiny study that opened from his sleeping chamber. He shut the door behind him, as though that would keep his needling inner voice out.

The study was like his sleeping chamber, with whitewashed plaster walls, beamed ceiling, bare floor, no fireplace, and little furniture. He put his copper candlestick beside a thick book on the table that served him as a desk, sat down beneath the painted crucifix over the chair, and eyed the book with distaste. He liked studying. Or he *used* to like studying, he thought sadly, shifting on the hard chair's thin red cushion, trying to get comfortable. Half seriously, he wondered if it was too late to just be a lay brother. Lay brothers didn't have to read St. Augustine. And if he were a lay brother, he could work in the stable, take care of the horses. One of the things he missed most about his father's—now his brother's—house and fields and vineyards far away in the south, in Languedoc, was being around horses.

But he knew he couldn't be a lay brother, not even to be around horses, because during the summer he'd come to know even more deeply—beneath complaining and fears and even beneath his terrible secret—that he wanted to be a priest more than he'd ever wanted anything. *Anything?* the needling inner voice replied, having apparently wormed its way under the door. *More than Pernelle? Yes*, he told it. *More than I wanted Pernelle. So shut up.*

That silenced the voice, and Charles opened the book. But instead of reading, he leaned back in the chair, trying to let the day's shocks and fears recede. The study's closed window did little to muffle the occasional sound of carriage wheels echoing off the buildings that lined St. Jacques. In a space of quiet, he heard someone shout, someone else shout back, and running feet pounding downhill toward the Seine. Then a loud group—University students, judging by their garbled Latin drinking song—came out of the little rue des Poirées across from Louis le Grand and turned toward the taverns in nearby Place Maubert. When quiet settled again in the room, he watched a mouse come out of its hole beneath the window. She—Charles felt sure it was a she—watched him warily, whiskers twitching, and edged cautiously toward his feet. Irrationally glad to see another creature, he leaned over to see what she might be after and saw that she was stalking crumbs from the cakelike *sable* Marie-Ange had given him yesterday when he passed the bakery. He'd eaten it at his desk last night, in an effort to sweeten reading St. Augustine. The mouse snatched a tiny piece from the floor and sat up, turning it in her paws and watching him, bright-eyed and unafraid. Charles, too, sat up, opened his book and tried to find as much contentment in St. Augustine's *Confessions*.

But the clamor in his mind returned, growing louder than the bells had been, and soon blinded him to what was on the pages. Finally, he took his candle and went to the prie-dieu in his sleeping chamber. He put the candle in the sconce beside the prayer desk and knelt. The little painting of Mary and her Child on the wall in front of him glowed in the candlelight. He gazed at Mary, who sat on a bench in a small room, with the Child on her lap and an open window at her back. She was smiling down at her son, and Charles thought again about the murdered boy in the well chamber. *You know what will happen to your son,* he told her. *How do you bear it?* She went on smiling at the laughing baby as though darkness would never fall over the green hills beyond the window, or over the Child, or in her heart. *Will Père Dainville live?* Charles asked her. She was so quiet that he seemed to hear the fire in her grate crackling and murmuring. For the first time since he'd come to the college, he felt that she didn't hear him, felt shut out of the room in the painting. He put his head down on the ledge of the prie-dieu, exhausted and forsaken.

He fell asleep there and woke sometime in the dead of night to stumble to his bed.

When the college's five o'clock rising bell pealed, he greeted God's new day with a groan. He mumbled his waking prayer and crossed himself, straightened his bed covers, found his cassock in the dark and pulled it on over his knee-length linen shirt, and was kneeling at the prie-dieu before he was more than half awake. Mary and the Child were remote and silent. He prayed, lit his candle from the passage sconce, washed his face with water from his copper pitcher, and cleaned his teeth with a linen rag and the thick paste his mother regularly sent him. Then he shouldered the small satchel he would need for his classes and started through the dark maze of uneven passageways to the back stairs that led to the chapel and Mass. Père Thomas Damiot, the young priest who lived just across the passage and was one of Charles's closest friends at the school, was already on the stairs. They smiled a greeting at each other but didn't speak, breaking the night's silence before Mass being frowned upon. Charles, yawning, stumbled off the bottom step. Damiot grabbed his arm to keep him upright and gave him a questioning sideways look that Charles pretended not to see.

On most mornings, when Charles went into Louis le Grand's chapel, the sight of the rosy, open-armed angels reaching down from the painted ceiling of the chapel's false dome lifted his spirits, no matter what else was happening. But this morning, he kept his eyes on the floor as he followed Damiot to a bench toward the back of the nave. As Jesuits, students, and people from the neighborhood gathered for the first Mass of the day, Charles knelt on the stone tiles and prayed for Père Dainville. When that prayer was finished, he stayed on his knees, not praying, but thinking about going to the Novice House later and trying to see Amaury de Corbet. And about what they would or wouldn't talk about. Then the priest celebrating the Mass came in, everyone stood, and Charles tried to give himself up to the mystery of God coming to meet him in the bread and wine.

When the Mass ended and the neighborhood people were going out the west door into the rue St. Jacques, a loud woman's voice made Charles and Damiot turn to see who was being so heedless of reverence and courtesy. Two women were halted just inside the door. The better-dressed one was shaking a finger in the other's face.

"Of course you may not! You spend enough time in church. And you have work to do! Why else are you living in my house, I'd like to know?"

The scolded woman, whose face was half hidden by a scarf draped around her throat and head, turned sharply and disappeared into the street. The other woman, suddenly aware that everyone was watching her, drew her long cloak of silky gray wool closer and stalked after her companion.

Charles and Damiot went with the rest of the Jesuits and students out the chapel's always-open north door, into the Cour d'honneur. The sun had still not reached the rooftops, and the college's age-blackened walls were crusted with frost. Charles pulled his cloak collar tightly around his neck as they crunched across the gravel toward the fathers' refectory.

"Have you heard what happened to Père Dainville?" he asked Damiot.

The priest nodded. "On the way to supper last night, Père Montville told us he'd been taken ill. Apoplexy, he said. And that you were with him."

"He'd asked me to go with him to the Carmelites' crypt chapel—he's grown very frail, you know, and needs help now. But he wasn't only taken ill," Charles said grimly. He told Damiot about the murdered man. "I think seeing him is what brought on the apoplexy."

Damiot crossed himself and gave Charles a long look. "I've known men who seem to attract mosquitoes and fleas, but until you, I've never known a man who attracted dead bodies. Though it's a talent that seems very useful to the head of our

Paris police," he added dryly. "Lieutenant-Général La Reynie has had more than a little reason to be very glad of you." He raised an ironic eyebrow. "Though that cannot be said for some of our Jesuit superiors."

Charles was in no mood for Damiot's humor. "If Père Dainville dies, whoever killed the man in the crypt will have two deaths to pay for. And I would gladly help La Reynie scour Paris for him! Though you're right about the superiors. I'm not likely to have the chance to help La Reynie this time."

"I wouldn't mind helping him, either," Damiot said, earning a startled glance from Charles. "Though what help I'd be is open to question." That drew a bark of laughter from Charles, who could not imagine the fastidious Damiot in tandem with the blunt police chief.

"So you've been told in so many words that you won't have the chance to help La Reynie again?"

"It's unlikely I'd get permission, now that I've started theology study," Charles said lightly, sidestepping the question.

They went through the archway into the fathers' court, where the fathers' refectory and most of the Jesuit living quarters were.

"Why am I sure there's more to it than that?" Damiot said quietly.

Charles sighed. "Because at heart you're the village witch." He'd rarely been able to deflect Damiot from anything he wanted to know. Or already, somehow, did know.

"The college *is* much like a village," Damiot said, smiling. "And you must know that it's bad luck to keep things from the village witch."

"If I tell you, will you put a spell on my Saint Thomas book so it won't open? All right, the rector told me last summer that there's been too much gossip in the college about things I've done. He cautioned me to call no more attention to myself. You're not the only one who knows something about what I've done with La Reynie, and the rector wants no more talk about that."

The ironic eyebrow went up again. "For his own sake, I would imagine, as well as yours. Which is administratively understandable. But unfortunate, because from what I've heard—and seen—you're quite good at finding killers."

"However," Charles responded, "that talent is not in demand in the Society of Jesus. And, it seems, neither are scholastics who make themselves conspicuous. So La Reynie is on his own. And he'd better catch the man," he added darkly.

They had reached the refectory, where cloaked Jesuits were going to and from the frugal college breakfast of bread, cheese, and watered wine, taken standing and in silence. But near the bottom of the stairs to the door, a small group of Jesuits was talking quietly. Père Joseph Jouvancy, the rhetoric professor whom Charles had worked with last year, stood with three college administrators: Père Montville, Père Donat, the rector's third in command, and Père Le Boeuf, the dour college provisioner. Maître Louis Richaud, an unpopular, sour-faced scholastic at the same stage of training as Charles, hovered nearby, trying to listen without seeming to.

Père Jouvancy's face lit with welcome when he saw Charles. As he gestured to him, Montville turned also. "Ah, *maître*," Montville began, but Jouvancy was already in full spate.

"My *dear* Maître du Luc!" the little rhetoric professor cried, beaming at Charles. "We do miss you sorely in the rhetoric class. The boys as much as I."

"Not more than I miss being there, *mon père*. The saintly church fathers are not nearly such good company."

"As my saintly self, you mean?" Jouvancy grinned at Charles.

"I'm already planning next summer's ballet and I am *so* thankful that you'll be working with me! I'm calling it The Ballet of Seasons! And with the leaves so lovely just now, I've been thinking that Autumn should wear—"

"*Mon père!*" Donat, a dull-witted stickler for every slightest rule and formality, glared at Jouvancy. "Remember, I beg you, what we are discussing here!"

"Hmmm?" Jouvancy glanced at him. "Yes, we're discussing the ballet. Now, *maître*, as I was saying—"

Damiot, who had drifted unobtrusively in Charles's wake and was listening, choked with stifled laughter. Montville rolled his eyes and stepped closer to Charles.

"*Bonjour, maître,*" Montville greeted him loudly, drowning Jouvancy's words. Red-faced, portly, and usually in high good humor, Montville was uncharacteristically sober and impatient. Lowering his voice, he said to Charles, "The rector asked me to tell you that he and I have already been to the infirmary, and Père Dainville is much the same." He looked warningly at Donat, who had edged around his bulk and was staring malevolently at Charles, whom he seemed to dislike this morning even more than usual. "The rector also reminds you," Montville said in Charles's ear, "to speak as little as possible of what happened yesterday. The less gossip here about the poor murdered man, the better." He tilted his head very slightly toward Donat and the stiffly silent Le Boeuf, who was regarding Charles as though he were a column of kitchen expenses that refused to add up correctly. "As the presence of two of our companions here should remind you," Montville went on, "the less gossip about your involvement with yet another death, the better."

"But, *mon père,*" Charles couldn't help saying, "I'd never seen the man before. I'm hardly 'involved' in his death. And it was almost certainly Père Dainville who found him first."

"Yes, yes, but there are those who won't bother with that distinction. So remember the rector's caution, because—" Suddenly realizing that Charles was looking beyond him and no longer listening, Montville frowned and turned sharply.

The scholastic Richaud, who had crept close to Montville to overhear what he said to Charles, skittered backward. In the last several months, Richaud had taken to reporting Charles to the rector for fancied infractions of the rules. Now Charles watched with unconcealed satisfaction as Montville upbraided the other scholastic. But his satisfaction turned to wariness as Donat and Le Boeuf protested against Montville's "unjust chastising" and took their martyred favorite up the stairs to breakfast.

"And there you have it, Maître du Luc," Montville murmured, watching in disgust as the trio disappeared into the refectory. "Those three are the heart of at least half the college gossip. And too many of their rumors are aimed at you." He eyed Charles. "I'm not the only one in authority here with hopes for your future. So heed the rector's warning. And mine." Fetching a sigh from the depths of his formidable belly, he made his ponderous way out of the courtyard.

Charles let his breath go and looked around for Damiot. His appetite for breakfast was gone, but he knew that if he didn't eat, half an hour of classes on the church fathers would make him wish he had. Damiot was talking to another grammar professor, so Charles started toward the refectory door on his own. But Jouvancy suddenly appeared beside him. Charles expected Jouvancy to say more about the ballet, but he didn't.

"I saw all that," he said soberly, glancing toward the refectory door. "Don't let those three worry you. Père Montville and our rector think very well of you. And you know that I do."

"That's kind of you, *mon père*," Charles said. "I'm grateful."

"You may not be, when you've heard what else I'm going to say to you." They reached the top of the stairs and Jouvancy drew Charles aside. "I'll be as quick as I can. So listen. You have much talent, which leads you to put your nose where it needn't go. Or where others don't want to find it. Oh—I know, I know, don't bother saying it. You don't mean to cause trouble. But you do cause it. And why? Because you are good at too many things. That is more often a curse than a blessing. One who is good at too many things tends to think he knows best."

"I don't think that," Charles said hotly. "I only—"

"You 'only' think I'm wrong. And that you are right."

Charles's face burned and he held his tongue.

"I'm going to tell you a story about Père Dainville when he first came to the Novice House. No, I wasn't there, of course. But the story has been told to most of us older men. For our own good. Now it's your turn. When Père Dainville entered the Society, he was not very amenable at first to obeying his superiors."

Charles could easily believe that, remembering what Dainville had told him about his life before the Novice House.

"After a somewhat turbulent first year of his novitiate," Jouvancy said, "our Père Dainville began to see the benefits of obedience. Finally, he said to his novice director, "Well, *mon père*, it is inexpressibly comforting to understand that *I*, at least, am not God!"

Charles smiled in spite of himself. "Did you make that up for my edification, *mon père*?"

"It is true, I promise you! And one day in time to come, if I am not much mistaken, you will tell it to some other young man of ours."

They went into the silent refectory, whose bare floor, walls of snow-white plaster, and high ceiling made it seem colder than the courtyard. Charles took a glass of watered wine from the side table, cut himself slices of bread and cheese, and began to eat. Richaud, Donat, and Le Boeuf, standing together and eating on the other side of the big table, pretended not to notice him. Charles ate quickly and drained his glass. Then he gave thanks; returned the empty glass to the side table; nodded to Damiot, who had just come in; and escaped outside. But two bent, elderly Jesuits were coming slowly up the stairs, and he went back and held the door open for them.

"But did you *hear* her this morning?" one of them said, loudly aggrieved, as he climbed. The irreverence!"

"Shhh. I think everyone in the chapel must have heard her," his companion replied, and Charles realized they were talking about the two women who had argued after Mass.

"Why on earth her husband left her the business, I cannot fathom," the first man said, shaking his white head. "I tell you, a self-respecting cleric can hardly go into the shop now, she's selling such blasphemy!"

"Oh?" His companion leaned closer. "More obscene books from Holland?"

"Those, no doubt, but even worse, she's got *Descartes* displayed *downstairs*—not to mention that poor, bitter-tempered Pascal! How that man could be so blind to God's good gifts I cannot fathom. And we taught Descartes—how he could—"

"Well, Pascal and the Jansenists are at least Catholics . . ."

The two men made their way through the door, and Charles closed it thankfully as the college clock chimed the half hour. As he went briskly down the stairs, Damiot caught up with him. "Where do you go now?" he said.

"I go to Père Remy, here in the fathers' courtyard, for the Saint Thomas Aquinas class."

"How do you like the class? And how many of you are there?"

"There are eight of us starting theology. As for the class, it's all right. Except that because of my height, I'm assigned to the back bench, and Père Remy is hard to hear. Which is not going to make Saint Thomas any clearer."

Damiot grimaced in commiseration. "Yes, Thomas can be obscure enough without that. And after Thomas, what do you do?"

"I have my first session on Saint Augustine at the Novice House. With Père Quellier. The eight of us go in pairs on different days. I go with Maître Richaud," Charles finished ruefully.

"You're fortunate. He's a great authority."

"Oh? Maître Richaud is?" Charles said innocently.

"That doesn't deserve an answer. So far as I know, Maître Richaud is an authority on nothing but sheets." Until now, Richaud had been a *cubiculaire*, overseeing student chambers and shepherding boarding students through their daily schedules. "Well, keep your heart up, *maître*, Père Quellier is worth a little suffering."

"I hope so," Charles said with a sigh. "May all your students be bright today."

"Hmmph. That is tantamount to hoping that our Lord will come back to earth before dinner. Which one may hope for without expecting it." But Damiot strode eagerly toward the Cour d'honneur and his first Latin grammar class of the day.

As Charles crossed the court to an old timbered house where the scholastics' classes were held, the frost was melting on the courtyard's north wall, and the sun was finally high enough to chase shadows. Glad to be going inside, he pushed open the ancient house's weathered oak door. The smell of old wool met him, from generations of cassocks perpetually damp in Parisian weather, and under it the smells of tansy and rue, evidence of diligent lay brothers fighting a century and more of fleas.

Charles was the last to arrive in the classroom. As he took his seat on the last of the four short benches, the class bell began to ring and Père Valère Remy moved from his chair to the lectern.

"Please stand," Remy said, his soft voice nearly inaudible and his hunched shoulders rising and falling in what looked to Charles like a sigh of resignation.

The eight scholastics rose to their feet, Remy offered up a not very hopeful prayer for the grace of learning, and the scholastics sat down again.

Remy surveyed them. His angular face was pale and lined, and his large brown eyes looked oddly vulnerable. "I begin," he said, "by reminding you once more that you studied philosophy earlier in your scholastic years because philosophy is the beginning of theology, the foundation of the thirst for a systematic knowledge of God. Never forget that, because you will need all the philosophy you learned in order to grasp what Saint Thomas and I attempt to teach you now." That dire reminder given, he swept a doubtful gaze over the class. "As I said at our last meeting, Saint Thomas lived for several years at the Dominican monastery just up the hill from us and was a revered teacher at the University. Not, of course, revered by everyone, since rivalry at the University four hundred fifty years ago was much what it is now. Thomas had a gift of divine clarity. He made for us a very useful system for understanding God, nature, and humanity. He is called the Angelic Doctor for good reason." Remy cocked an eyebrow at his students, and the ghost of a smile came and went on his face. "You would think his Dominican brothers, who still live just up the hill beside the wall, might enjoy some of that same clear thinking. But apparently not, since they are on the point of taking us to court over our brotherly request that they stop siphoning more than their share of water from our common springwater pipe."

The students smiled and nodded dutifully, the water dispute having begun back in June and being common knowledge.

"But we should have patience with them for failing to measure up to Saint Thomas, since most of *us* are lesser beings than our own Saint Ignatius was. So. In the first article of the *Summa Theologia*, we find . . ." Remy's voice dropped into its usual learned murmur.

Charles checked the point of his quill, rearranged his paper and the square of board under it, and tried to be grateful that they were studying only selected parts of Thomas's *Summa Theologia*, which was the saint's four-thousand-page "summary" of theology. Straining to hear the lecture, Charles began making notes and trying not to look out the window every few sentences to see from the sun how much time had passed, and how soon he could go to the Novice House and ask to see Amaury de Corbet.

Chapter 5

Charles was first out of the room when the class was dismissed. But he had to wait for Maître Richaud, who was last out, his measured pace and bowed head proclaiming—as it was meant to—his great humility.

"Shall we go, *maître?*" Charles forced a smile and started toward the Cour d'honneur and the street passage.

"I have to go and get another pen."

"Why?" Charles turned around.

"My quill broke just now."

"Please be quick," Charles said as mildly as he could, "or we'll be late. I'll be at the postern."

Richaud bowed his head and paced slowly away. Charles sighed and went on to the stone street passage that ran beneath the main building to the postern door. Frère Martin, the doorkeeper, was enthroned on a stool at the street end of the passage.

"A fine morning, *maître!*" he said. "I always love the bite of autumn air. Makes the brain work better, don't you think? I even guessed the riddle Marie-Ange brought me this morning when she came to ask after Père Dainville. Poor little maid, I didn't have any good news for her, they say he's just the same. But then she told me the September riddle from the *Mercure*— oh, not that the baker can afford to buy it," he said, seeing

Charles's surprise. "But its riddles are always passed around the *quartier*, you know. And I solved this one! Got a little cake for my trouble, too; she always brings me something."

"Well done," Charles said, smiling. *The Mercure Galant*, the news publication that reviewed the college theatre productions, was printed as a small, calf-bound book at the end of every month, and always included new riddles. "What was the answer?"

"Queen of Hungary water!" The lay brother's canvas-aproned bulk shook as he laughed. "And hard enough it was to follow the clues, I can tell you. But then maybe I had an advantage, because Frère Brunet uses Hungary water on my rheumatics, rubs it on my knees when I can hardly stand up. And it works, *maître*; remember that when you're as old as me! You can drink it, too, which is just as good for you, since it's mostly brandy!" He winked at Charles and glanced toward the courtyard. "Waiting for someone?"

"Maître Richaud and I are going to the Novice House."

"Ah. Him. I'll tell you in confidence that the lay brothers who look after the boarding students' lodgings are glad to see the back of him. And we're about to see the front of him," Martin finished, as footsteps echoed behind Charles.

"Fortunate us. A blessed day to you, Frère Martin."

The lay brother opened the postern and Charles was out the door like an arrow. Only to stop again and wait for Richaud to catch up.

"We have something of a walk, *maître*," Charles said. "Can you go a little faster?"

Richaud's flat black gaze under the slightly drooping brim of his black hat grew a shade more disapproving. "Jesuits are not supposed to make a spectacle of themselves in the streets."

"True. Jesuits are also supposed to be on time for their

obligations." The clock in the college tower began to chime. "We have exactly a quarter of an hour to arrive at the rue du Pot-de-Fer and find out where we are to meet our teacher. It would be rude indeed to be late on our first day."

Richaud grudgingly admitted that and walked a little faster, though still not fast enough to suit Charles. But since surging ahead of one's companion in the street actually did count as making something of a spectacle, he shortened his stride to match Richaud's. As they walked up the hill toward the rue des Cordeliers, Charles heard someone singing in the corner house, and his own steps lagged. It was the same song about the pleasure and danger of love, and the same singer. He looked up at the window where he'd seen the woman singing the night before, but no one was there.

"Le plaisir de vous voir est un plaisir extrême,
mais il est dangereux . . ."

An exasperated cry from within the house cut off the words. "Stop your noise! Customers are waiting!"

Richaud walked on, but Charles was looking at the long sign hung above the house door. At the feet of a saint with halo and staff, a black dog with a red ball in his mouth was pawing at the saint's robe, inviting him to play. Beneath the sign was a table piled with books, and the customers coming out of the shop had books under their arms. Richaud stopped and turned around.

"You said we were going to be late," he called disapprovingly. "And you shouldn't be listening to a woman singing," he added, when Charles caught up with him.

"I should put my fingers in my ears? And she's not singing now."

As they walked along the rue des Cordeliers and past the Sorbonne church, Charles wasn't thinking about the woman singing, but about a book he'd seen on the table beside the shop door. It was called *Conversations on the Plurality of Worlds*, by someone named de Fontenelle, and piqued his curiosity. He wished they were going to spend the rest of the morning talking about it instead of St. Augustine's *Confessions*. As they passed through the old St. Michel gate and out into the St. Germain suburb, Charles stopped and picked up a handful of turnips for a pretty street vendor who'd spilled them from her basket. Which, of course, earned him a frown from Richaud. But Charles saw out of the corner of his eye that Richaud's head swiveled in a near half circle to watch the girl's hip-swaying retreat along the road. Charles started to comment in retaliation for Richaud's chiding about the singer, but then he realized that it was the first time he'd seen Richaud show appreciation of anything, and he kept quiet. They walked in silence until they turned right onto the rue du Pot-de-Fer.

"There it is," Charles said. He pointed to the cross on the stone bell tower of the Novice House church, which showed above the neighboring roofs. Tall trees bright with autumn leaves leaned over garden walls along the street and gave the place almost the feel of country. They passed the church and stopped at arched double doors just beyond. Charles pulled the bell rope and a middle-aged lay brother opened the door, swept shrewd eyes over them, and stepped aside to let them in.

"I was told you'd be coming," the brother said. "Père Quellier will see you in his antechamber."

He led them along a gallery whose windows looked into a garden. At the gallery's end, a novice, wearing cloth slippers and a loose black robe to protect his cassock from dust, was industriously sweeping the floor at the bottom of a staircase.

For a moment, Charles wondered if he was Amaury de Corbet, then saw that he was the age Amaury had been when Charles last saw him—Amaury, like Charles, would be ten years older now, of course. The young man stepped aside, eyes modestly lowered, and the lay brother led Charles and Richaud up to the next floor, which had been the "noble floor" when the building was the private townhouse of the Mèzieres family. He tapped at an oak door halfway along the corridor.

"Entrez."

A lean, youngish priest was seated at a table in the center of a small anteroom. It was much like any other Jesuit room, with plain white walls, bare floor, beamed ceiling, and a wooden crucifix hung opposite the door. The priest's narrow, light eyes darted between his new students.

"Maître Richaud?"

As Richaud bowed, his satchel swung forward and hit the table, making it slide a little on the floor. The priest sighed audibly, pushed the table back into alignment, and turned to Charles.

"And you must be Maître du Luc."

Charles clamped his satchel between his arm and his side and bowed.

Something between approval and relief showed on the priest's face. "I am Père Quellier. Sit. Take out your quills and paper."

They sat, took what they needed from their satchels, put the satchels on the floor, and waited.

"You are here to learn something of Saint Augustine. So let us begin." He pointed at the thick volume before him. "The saint's *Confessions* were written in the fourth century after Christ. They are the extraordinary record of a man's search for God. Saint Augustine is far more forthcoming than most men about his longings and failings. In fact, you probably already know at least one thing he said." With what might have been the beginning of a smile on his thin lips, he eyed them. "Do you?"

Charles felt Richaud stiffen beside him and heard him give a disdainful little sniff.

"Maître Richaud?" Quellier said blandly, but watching him like a hawk hovering above a rabbit. "I think that you do know what the saint said. Tell us, please."

Charles turned politely toward his companion and tried to keep his face appropriately straight. He was fairly sure of what was coming. Richaud gave the teacher a sweet, sad smile.

"Yes, *mon père*, I do know something."

"Speak."

"The saint prayed—as, of course, we all must—for the gift of chastity." Richaud shuddered delicately. "But then he succumbed to the Enemy's urging and begged the *bon Dieu* not to give him that gift yet." He bowed his head. "He even had a child," he whispered. But the whispering was eager, almost hissing. "Saint Augustine fathered a bastard!"

The hawk struck, but very gently. "And the fact that the saint was imperfect in this way troubles you?"

The rabbit looked up in surprise. "Of course, *mon père*. Must it not trouble any Jesuit?"

"Perhaps. But other things should trouble him more, Maître Richaud. Like pride."

Richaud gaped at him. Charles, whose past gave him a great deal of sympathy for this part of Augustine's life, fixed his eyes on his paper. Quellier opened the *Confessions* and got down to business. He turned out to be a mesmerizing teacher, and Charles was startled when, at the ring of a small bell from somewhere in the house, he shut his book.

"That is all for now. Learn the passages I have given you

and we will discuss them when you return. In the meantime, take these words of Saint Augustine with you: 'The mind commands the body and is instantly obeyed. The mind commands itself and meets resistance.'"

Richaud gathered up his things. But Charles sat without moving, staring at the far wall and thinking how dismally his own mind had failed to stop him from thinking about the memories he shared with Amaury.

Quellier raised his thin eyebrows. "Maître du Luc? Have you something to say?"

"Oh. No. Forgive me, *mon père*." Charles quickly put his paper and quill into his satchel and stood up.

But Quellier wasn't through with him." Something about those two sentences has struck you."

"Yes, *mon père*. I have all too much reason to understand them. Thank you for giving them to us."

The priest nodded. "Until next time, then."

Charles waited for Richaud to reach the door and then said quietly, "*Mon père*, may I ask something?" Quellier nodded and Charles hurried on. "I have my rector's permission to request a short visit with one of your new novices. His name is Amaury de Corbet and I have just learned that he is here. He saved my life ten years ago in the army, and I have never properly thanked him."

Quellier stood up from the table. "Our new novices have been here less than a fortnight and are allowed few visitors. I must ask our rector. Wait here." He looked at Richaud. "Perhaps you would like to spend a little time in front of the Holy Sacrament, *maître*. Your companion will come to you there."

Jesuits frequently prayed before the reserved communion host in its small tabernacle in church or chapel and, to Charles's relief, Richaud accepted, though he looked suspiciously at Charles.

"The novices use the church gallery for prayer and it's best if no stranger—even a Jesuit stranger—disturbs them. I will send you the longer way into the nave."

He and Richaud left and Charles stayed in the dimly lit anteroom.

"'The mind commands the body and is instantly obeyed. The mind commands itself and meets resistance,'" he said out loud, amazed at how perfectly St. Augustine summed up his own experience. For ten years, his mind had been commanding itself to at least temper the terrible guilt he'd brought with him from the battle of Cassel, but it had gone on festering and aching. Whether it would help or hurt to see Amaury, he didn't know, he only knew he had to see him. He jumped, startled, when the anteroom door opened and Quellier reappeared.

"The rector says you may see Monsieur de Corbet. For a quarter of an hour only. Come."

When they reached the visitors' room, Quellier said, "Wait here and I will bring him."

Charles stood facing the door, his heart speeding as though he'd been running. The priest was back almost immediately, ushering a tall, very slender novice before him.

"He was just outside in the garden." Quellier took a small hourglass from a shelf, turned it, and set it on the table. "A quarter of an hour." He nodded to Charles and left them.

Amaury stood just inside the room, eyes on the floor, hands folded at the waist of his black cassock, his outdoor hat under his arm. "Hello, Maître du Luc." He raised his head and smiled. "I wondered if you knew I was here."

"I didn't until yesterday." Charles studied the face of the man standing before him. He wouldn't have known him again, at least not by his face. Ten years of weather and fighting had aged him far beyond the gangling, anxious youth Charles remembered. The eyes, though—those deep-set, brown-black eyes were what he remembered best. How full of anguish they'd been as Amaury tried and failed to control his men at Cassel. How wide with fear they'd been when he tore away half his own shirt and pressed it over the gaping wound in Charles's shoulder on the battlefield at St. Omer. How those eyes had dared him not to listen, dared him to die, while Amaury's voice vied with death for his attention with learned talk about wine until the wagon picking up the wounded made its slow way toward them.

"Maître du Luc?" Amaury said hesitantly, breaking the silence and glancing at the sand running through the glass on the table.

"Forgive me. I was—remembering. One reason I wanted to see you is to thank you for saving my life all those years ago."

Amaury nodded gravely. "Are you well?"

"I am. And you? Does it go well with you here?"

"Well enough. I'm older, of course, than most of my fellow novices. The senior novice in our chamber is twenty-one. He makes me feel like an old man."

Charles laughed. "As I recall, you're a year younger than I, so none of that, if you please! And the other two in your chamber? Are they as young?" Charles was vividly remembering his own novitiate and the scrupulously neat four-bedded chamber they'd shared for two years.

"We're only three in our chamber. The fourth didn't arrive. I suppose his family intervened. Or perhaps he lost his nerve."

Charles shrugged. "Both of those things happen."

A new silence fell as the two men studied each other.

Nerving himself, Charles said, "Charles-François told me you were here."

Amaury flinched. "He's very angry with me."

"But more angry with me," Charles said, half smiling.

"That's my fault. He knows it was because of you that I first thought of offering myself to the Society. Though the guilt of waiting so long to do it is all mine." Amaury looked beyond Charles at the crucifix on the wall. "I felt I had to wait until my father died. I told myself that was filial respect, but really, you know, it was only cowardice."

Charles flinched inwardly. Cowardice. There it was again, the word that seemed to bind the two of them together. "Is that why you followed my cousin into the navy? Because your father wanted it? I would have thought that, after what happened at Cassel, you would have wanted to stay as far from Charles-François as you could."

Amaury's face flushed. "I didn't follow your cousin." He sighed heavily. "After—because of what happened at Cassel, I told my father I wanted to leave the army. I thought he was going to kill me. He said that if I left the military, he would disown me, disinherit me, and make sure no one helped me to anything else. And I—I gave in to him. Then he got me into the Royal Marine. I was assigned to your cousin's ship, but he chose to think I asked to be under his command. Later, when I asked him about you and he told me you'd joined the Society, I knew you'd done it because of Cassel. That was the first step on my own way here. I'm very grateful."

Charles looked at him helplessly. "No. Cassel was *not* the reason—certainly not the most important reason—why I joined the Society. I joined because I read Saint Ignatius's biography while I recovered from my wound. I joined to help souls. I joined because I thought I could come closer to God than in any other way of living. I brought my guilt with me, of course I did, but guilt is not a good reason for becoming a Jesuit! We're not cloistered monks turning our backs on the world for our own salvation. You'll never make a Jesuit, if that's all you want."

Amaury drew himself up, and Charles had a startling glimpse of generations of unchallenged noble authority staring from suddenly cold eyes.

"I am giving my life to God in penance for what I failed to do at Cassel," Amaury said, his lips barely moving. "Who are you, *maître*, to tell me that's wrong?"

"Who am I? A Jesuit for eight years, that's who I am. And I'm telling you that being here will not wipe away what happened at Cassel."

Amaury's reply cut like a sword thrust. "I think that what you're telling me is that *you* have not been penitent enough for what happened at Cassel."

To Charles's horror, something of the momentary swell of insulted nobility he'd felt in the confrontation with his cousin Charles-François rose in him. He quelled it and managed a conciliatory smile. "I wish you only good," he said. "Here and everywhere. But, I beg you, think on what I've said."

Amaury's only reply was a look at the hourglass. "Our time has run out."

He bowed humbly, as to a superior, but his back was rigid with offense as he walked from the room, leaving Charles looking after him with regret that he'd given in to anger. And with deep misgivings about this new novice's vocation—for which the novice in question held him at least partly responsible. Charles left the visiting parlor with his own burden of guilt heavier than when he'd arrived.

Chapter 6

It was a silent walk back to Louis le Grand. Maître Richaud seemed as preoccupied and disinclined for talk as Charles was. When they reached the church of St. Étienne des Grès, just before Louis le Grand, Richaud stopped.

"Please, *maître*," he said ingratiatingly. "I am going to stop here and pray for a while. I will fast through dinner and join you after in the scholastics' common room."

Charles nodded and Richaud went slowly up the steps and into the old church, the picture of self-effacing piety. Shaking his head, but glad to be rid of the man, Charles went on to the postern and rang the bell. Frère Martin let him into the street passage and quickly shut the door. "*Maître*," the porter said, "Lieutenant-Général La Reynie's here. He wants you to come to the *grand salon*." Martin widened his eyes at Charles. "Me, I think it's about that dead man you found."

"Thank you, I'll go." Charles had been expecting La Reynie to come looking for him. The abbess had summoned the nearest police *commissaire* to Notre Dame des Champs, and the news would soon have reached La Reynie, the head of the police. Charles started to walk away and then turned. "How did you know about the dead man, Frère Martin?"

"Louis le Grand has the very best air for carrying news."

Martin shrugged and winked at Charles. "My village had the same air, can you believe it?"

Charles suspected that once Frère Martin knew something, the air wherever he lived would have that same miraculous effect. "Do you have any news of Père Dainville, *mon frère?*" The porter's smile vanished and he shook his head. "Just that he's mostly sleeping. But we know sleep heals, *maître*, so that's to the good."

"Pray God it is." Charles went heavy hearted through the side door from the passage. The main building's *grand salon*, where visitors normally waited, was empty. But the rector's office door opened and Le Picart looked out.

"Ah. I hoped it was you I heard, *maître*. In here, please. Monsieur La Reynie wishes to speak with you."

"Yes, *mon père*." With a sense of girding his loins, Charles crossed the *salon*. He'd helped La Reynie in the past, and he'd come to like and respect the man, even to feel warmly toward him. But having the head of the Paris police seek him out still made him uneasy. When he reached Le Picart's office, the rector was sitting behind his desk and Lieutenant-Général Nicolas de la Reynie, a big man in his sixties, faultlessly dressed in coat and breeches of finely woven black wool, stood stiffly in front of it. Charles could almost see the tension arcing between the two men. He could certainly feel their inheld anger.

Charles bowed first to his rector and then to the king's officer. "*Mon père.* Monsieur La Reynie."

"*Bonjour, maître.*" A muscle in La Reynie's cheek was twitching as he bowed slightly. "I trust you are well?"

"Very well, I thank you," Charles said warily. "And you?" The tension in the air made him feel as though they were trading conversation from a textbook of manners.

"I *was* well enough." La Reynie glared at the rector. "I had hoped—"

"One moment." Le Picart plucked the conversational bit out of La Reynie's mouth. "I will explain. *Maître*, we owe the honor of the *lieutenant-général*'s visit to your discovery of the dead man—may God receive his soul—in the Carmelites' crypt. Monsieur La Reynie has been trying to discover the man's name and wishes to ask you a few questions about what you saw yesterday. Brief questions." He leveled a chilly gray glance at La Reynie. "Before you go to your dinner and then to your studies."

"I am at your service, *mon père*," Charles said carefully. He knew the rector in this inflexible mood. It usually meant that Le Picart was protecting something or someone.

"*Mon père*," La Reynie said through his teeth, "I am hunting a murderer. Surely my questions matter more than anyone's dinner." He turned to Charles, almost but not quite turning his back on Le Picart. "Mère Vinoy, the Carmelite abbess, said that you saw a man at the foot of the crypt stairs. No one else reports seeing anyone come up the stairs. Describe the man you saw."

"As I told the abbess, I saw only his outline, And *mon lieutenant-général*, it seems very easy to go and come from the crypt unseen. I'm certain that no one saw Père Dainville and me go down."

La Reynie frowned and grunted. "Well? The man you saw?"

"He was silhouetted against the single candle there as he waited for us to reach the bottom of the stairs so he could go up. He waited very patiently—there was no sign that he was angry or disturbed. I thought he'd just finished praying in the chapel." Charles hesitated. "It would have been courteous to speak, but he didn't, though perhaps that was only his being a somewhat rough man, not a man of quality. I say that because from the shape of him, he wore no wig or wide cuffs or coat skirts. Just ordinary clothes. I'd say he was of middle height, and young, or at least not old, from the speed of his climbing the stairs after we passed." Charles held out his hands. "That's all I can tell you about him. Did you learn anything else from the body?"

"There were no other injuries. Though his wrists were somewhat chafed, as though he'd been tied. And he was a young man of quality. Expensive clothes and fine linen, well fed, soft hands."

"Do you know yet who he is?"

Instead of answering, La Reynie said, "I understand you've just come from the Novice House."

Charles glanced at the rector, who nodded slightly. "Yes, I had a class there, as Père Le Picart has no doubt told you."

"One of the few things he's told me," La Reynie said irritably. "Did anyone at the Novice House speak of a new novice who never arrived?"

"How did you know about that? The novice who didn't arrive was supposed to be the fourth in the chamber of the man I was visiting."

"Who is that?"

"Monsieur Amaury de Corbet, a new novice. I knew him slightly in the army and wished to welcome him. But you haven't said how you know that one of the novices never arrived."

The police chief smiled slightly. "Because servants are not only very useful, they know everything. I have a maid whose son lives at your Novice House. Not as a novice, he's only thirteen. He's one of several boys there who gets shelter and food and some teaching, in return for menial chores. I heard him telling his mother about the missing young man. I've spoken with the Novice House rector, Père Guymond, who tells me that the absent novice is a seventeen-year-old named Paul

Lunel, from Paris. When he didn't arrive, the rector made inquiries about him at the family town house but had no reply. The family—the mother and a brother—are away. Neither of them made any inquiry about young Lunel these last three weeks, which suggests that they assumed he was where he was supposed to be."

Charles thought about the smooth, softly rounded face he'd uncovered. That young man could well have been only seventeen. "So you're thinking that the dead man may be the missing novice?" Charles said.

"I am eliminating possibilities. A dead young man of quality where a dead man should not have been. A young man of quality missing from where he should have been. One never knows."

"And what are you going to do now?" Le Picart said, with a hint of impatience.

La Reynie took his time flicking imaginary dust from his lace cuffs. "Père Guymond is coming to the Châtelet this afternoon to look at the body." He looked up at Charles. "After that, perhaps I should speak with your novice friend."

"From what he said, I don't think he knows the missing novice."

"How can you be sure?"

"By the way he spoke of him. And also because Amaury de Corbet isn't from Paris, and is at least ten years older than this Paul Lunel."

The college bell sounded from the courtyard, ringing for midday dinner, and Le Picart stood up. "We must leave you now, *mon lieutenant-général*." The rector's smile was courteous, but without warmth. "I will pray for your success in discovering who the murdered man was and who killed him. God go with you."

"I am going, *mon père*." La Reynie showed his teeth in what

Charles had learned not to take for a smile. "As for *le bon Dieu's* plans for the afternoon, I couldn't say." With the slightest of bows and a roll of his eyes at Charles, he swept out of the rector's office.

Charles, swallowing laughter, started to follow him, but Le Picart called him back.

"I must speak further with you," the rector said. "If you miss your dinner, you may ask something from the kitchen, as you did last night." Le Picart went to the small window that gave onto the main courtyard and opened its casement of old greenish glass. The ceaseless noise of feet just outside, crunching over the courtyard's gravel to the college refectories, sounded like an army passing. "I could see," Le Picart said, his back turned to Charles, "that you were surprised by my coolness to Lieutenant-Général La Reynie. Though he didn't say it in so many words, he came hoping you would help him in this matter. I have allowed you to assist him in the past, for the good of the college and the Society of Jesus, as well as for other reasons. But I cannot and will not allow you to help him again."

"But—" Charles saw the rector's back stiffen and swallowed the rest of his protest.

When Le Picart turned around, the expression on his thin face was deadly serious. "Listen to me. I understand that if this murdered young man is indeed the missing novice Paul Lunel, then the *lieutenant-général* will have to ask questions in the Novice House. And though he represents the king's justice, he will not be able to find out things as easily as a Jesuit could." He paused and smiled briefly at the consternation on Charles's face. "Oh, no one would lie to him. Père Guymond, the rector, will want the killer caught as much as anyone does. But the obvious attention of the police is never welcome to the head of a Jesuit house. As I too well know."

Charles nodded, struggling inwardly with all the things he wanted to say. Le Picart hadn't said it outright, but Charles knew well enough that his being forbidden to help La Reynie was mostly because of the royal attention he'd drawn to himself so dramatically last summer.

"I told you when you returned from Versailles," the rector continued, as though reading Charles's thoughts, "that some of your brother Jesuits here in the college resent the scope—and the freedom—I've sometimes given to you, a mere scholastic. I am not sorry to have done so. What came of your actions in each case served the king's justice and God's, and also served the Society." He sighed and shook his head slightly. "Nevertheless, as a result, you and I are both under scrutiny, and not only by Jesuits inside these walls. I am under scrutiny by my superiors here in the Paris Province for what I allowed you to do. You are under the same scrutiny because a scholastic calling so much attention to himself is unseemly and raises questions about his future." His bleak gray eyes held Charles's gaze, and he nodded as he saw Charles take in what he'd said. "Furthermore," he continued, "this murder at Notre Dame des Champs has nothing to do with the college, even if the dead man should turn out to be a Jesuit novice."

"But if—" Charles heard his indignation and started over. "What I mean," he said quietly, "is that if a novice of ours has been murdered, and one of us can help to bring justice to bear, shouldn't that be done?"

"Of course justice should be done. And will be done by Lieutenant-Général La Reynie and his police. Not by you."

"Because of what Père Donat and Père Le Boeuf and Maître Richaud might do and say," Charles said flatly.

"Have you understood nothing? Hold your tongue and listen to me! Out of all of this last year's reports I sent to the head of our Paris Province about my men at Louis le Grand, the Provincial singled out yours for particular attention and concern. That is not a compliment, should you be so foolish as to think so. He does think, as I do—most of the time—that you have a promising future. He also thinks—as I know to my cost—that I allow you to overstep your bounds. He wants no more special privileges given to you. For the good of the Society's reputation and your future as a Jesuit. And for the good of mine as rector."

"I see," Charles said, chastened. "May I speak further?"

"If by 'speak' you mean 'argue,' the answer is no." The rector sighed and rubbed his face. "By our rules, you have the right to question an order, if you think obeying it would be an occasion for sin. About that, you may speak."

"Forgive me, *mon père*—and I do not ask your forgiveness as a matter of form. Of course you are not ordering me to sin. But if God has given me some degree of skill at helping to bring about justice, and I do not use that skill, is that not sin?"

"Perhaps. And so is clever theological argument to get what one wants."

"True. But this killer has not only taken a life, he is responsible for what has happened to Père Dainville. And Père Dainville may die."

"Père Dainville is old and fragile. What happened to him might well have happened anyway. What you want is vengeance, *maître*, and that belongs only to God."

"I want justice, *mon père*."

The gray gaze darkened. "You want your own will. Is this how you would repay Père Dainville for his efforts to help you grow as a Jesuit? To help you grow in Jesuit obedience? To help you subdue your noble pride?" He smiled bleakly at Charles's sharp intake of breath. "Oh, don't look so surprised, *maître*, it shows itself, believe me. Are you still so arrogant as to think that only *you* are capable of bringing about justice?"

Charles bit his tongue and forced his gaze to the floor. "I hope not, *mon père*."

"Then remember what you have chosen. Remember what you hope to be."

Charles held himself very still. That was the nearest thing to a threat he'd ever heard from Le Picart, and it was about the priesthood he so deeply wanted. "Yes, *mon père*," he said, to give himself time to think.

"Very well." Le Picart strode to the office door. "We understand each other," he said, as he opened it. "And now we have both missed a good part of dinner. Come, we'll go and beg from the kitchen."

Staying in the rector's presence after what had been said was not what Charles wanted, but he dutifully followed him out to the courtyard. As they turned toward the fathers' court, Frère Martin hurried breathlessly from the street passage.

"*Mon père!* I thought you were at dinner. There's a message for you!"

As Le Picart went to meet the porter, Charles waited where he was, but he could still hear what was said.

"It's that girl from The Dog," Martin said. "Marguerite? No. Rose, was it? I can't—"

The rector said impatiently, "Do you mean Mademoiselle Rose Ebrard?"

"That's it!" Martin sighed with relief. "I *knew* it was a flower. The girl from the bookshop. She's at the postern door, asking if you can see her at five o'clock instead of four."

"Tell her that will do. Get someone to bring her to my office when she arrives, and ask Père Montville to act as my companion while I see her."

"Yes, *mon père.*" Martin bowed and hurried back toward the postern and the girl with the flower name.

The rector came back to Charles and said, as they started walking again, "If you want to come with me to the infirmary and see Père Dainville before you go to your afternoon duties, you may."

Charles nodded, surprised. "Thank you, *mon père.*"

In the fathers' courtyard, they went past the refectory to the open door of the hot, busy kitchen beside it. Le Picart put his head in.

"Forgive me, *mes frères*, but two of us are very late for our dinner. Can you give us something here in the kitchen?"

A brother looked up from a bubbling cauldron at the hearth and wiped sweat from his eyes. "Of course we'll feed you, *mon père.*" He hurried across the stone floor, mopping at his face with his cassock sleeve. "No need to eat in here, go and sit, we'll bring your dinner."

In the crowded refectory, the midday meal was ending with small tarts that smelled of apples and cinnamon, and a middle-aged Jesuit was standing at the small lectern, reading from the life of St. Geneviève as the others listened silently. The rector's appearance brought everyone to their feet and silenced the reader, but Le Picart shook his head.

"I beg you, go on as you were. Business has made me very late."

He sat down in his usual place and gestured Charles to the table where the other theology scholastics were sitting. Charles had always been glad that worldly, family rank had no importance in a Jesuit house. However, as he went now to his table, he was glad that rank *within* the Society mattered enough to save him from eating in tense silence beside the rector, after the talk they'd just had. He sat down, nodding to the other scholastics. Most of them smiled vaguely and went on with their dessert, but the oldest of the group, Maître Placide Du Pont, looked at Richaud's empty chair and then questioningly at Charles. Du Pont, from Paris, was firm, unfailingly gentle, older than the others—older even than Charles—and had taken on the mild authority of the senior scholastic. In answer to the silent question about Richaud, Charles put his hands together as though praying. Du Pont shrugged slightly and took another tart from the dish. A kitchen brother brought leek soup, and Charles said a short silent grace and ate as quickly as he decently could, only half listening to St. Geneviève. As he ate, he considered what had happened in the rector's office. He'd seen a side of Le Picart he'd rarely met before. Not that the rector had been unfair. His concern for Charles's future was as real as his concern for his own position, that was clear. But Charles recognized immovable decision from which there was no appeal. He knew that if he went on protesting, or acted against the order he'd been given, he would in sober fact seriously endanger his Jesuit future. He sighed and nearly choked himself on his soup. As his coughing stopped, the scholastic beside him sighed, too, and looked sadly at his glass of watered wine.

The round-faced young man leaned toward Charles and whispered, "Isn't there *ever* any beer?"

"Shhh." Charles shook his head and tried not to laugh. The speaker was Maître Henry Wing, an Englishman and a late arrival from the Jesuit college of St. Omer on the Atlantic coast. St. Omer was small and poor and often sent its scholastics to Paris for their theology study. Since it was just across the channel from England, which allowed no Jesuit schools, many of its scholastics were English. This latest arrival—pudgy, pink, and fair, with peculiarly accented Latin—was very English.

The kitchen brother returned, snatched the soup dish, and put roast chicken with apples in front of Charles. The reader droned on about St. Geneviève saving Paris from the Vikings. The six other scholastics watched Charles like a circle of waiting vultures, silently willing him to eat quickly. No one could leave the table until the final grace was said, which would not happen until everyone in the room had finished. Charles kept his eyes on his plate and worked his way through his dinner. Finally, the reader finished, Le Picart and everyone else stood, and the rector said the final grace.

When the scholastics were outside, they made their way without consultation to their common room in the main building, where their living chambers were, for the midday hour of quiet recreation. The Englishman started to take the chessboard from the cupboard, but Du Pont smiled and shook his head.

"No," he said, "not chess just now. I have been thinking that we should finish the talk we were having yesterday at recreation. About women."

The scholastics settled themselves willingly enough on the room's hard chairs,

Maître Henry Wing spoke first, in his accented Latin. "Well, the last thing I said yesterday was that surely God made women, too."

Maître Owen Rhys, a red-haired Welshman also from St. Omer, whose Latin was even odder than the Englishman's, said, "Ye-e-es. He did. But only as an afterthought. Adam was first. So women are less important than men."

"And so the Mother of God is less important than you are?

Because you have the—um—dangly parts?" Maître Jean Montrose, from the part of France called Auvergne, was built like a cart horse and argued like St. Thomas.

The Welshman bristled, but Du Pont intervened. "Aren't we getting away from the question? The question that began our talk yesterday was how much time we should give to women penitents when we are priests."

"We should give women as much time as we give men," Charles said. "Or more, if more women ask our assistance. It would depend on one's assignment, would it not?"

"More time for women?" Richaud said from the doorway. *"More?"*

"You are late joining us, *maître*," Du Pont said mildly.

Ignoring that, Richaud sat down in the empty chair and drew his skirts close around him. His nostrils were pinched as though he smelled a woman at the table. "But you would want more time for women, wouldn't you, Maître du Luc? You like women. Perhaps too well. We're celibates—aren't we?" The question's questioning cadence hung in the air, and Richaud folded his hands in his lap with an air of satisfaction.

Charles gazed with distaste at Richaud's dirty fingernails, wondering why no one ever made him clean them. "Isn't hearing confessions and directing penitents part of the duty of a priest?" he said. "Both men and women confess and are penitents. When a Jesuit priest hears a woman's confession, there is always another Jesuit nearby, watching without hearing what's said. Where's the difficulty?"

Richaud licked his thin lips. "There *should* be another Jesuit nearby when one speaks at all with a woman. But there isn't always. Is there, Maître du Luc?"

"Life," Charles said lightly, "sometimes overtakes rules. Even our Lord told his disciples to harvest grain on the sabbath if they were hungry. Think on this, Maître Richaud. Are we supposed to hate half of God's human souls because we're celibate? Are we supposed to hate our Lord's mother?"

Wing slipped a fragment of tart crust, purloined from the refectory table, into his mouth and nodded enthusiastically. "Well argued, Maître du Luc!" he cried, spraying crumbs.

Du Pont sighed. "You are not to take anything from the refectory, Maître Wing. You are a scholastic, not a novice. You should know that."

Wing's pink face flamed. "Oh. Yes. I should. I mean—I do. But I'm always hungry," he said plaintively. "Because there's never any beer. Beer is very filling."

The others exchanged hopeless glances.

Montrose, the Auvergnat, brushed Wing's crumbs from his sleeve and said, "Returning to the point, I agree with Maître du Luc. The Society of Jesus exists to help souls. Not male souls. Souls."

Charles smiled at him. "So souls are male and female?"

"While they companion our earthly bodies, one might say so."

"But—to start a different question—that makes them sound as distinct from the body as my body is from my cassock," Charles said. "Saint Thomas said that the soul is what makes the body alive. Which means that if the soul becomes separate from the body, the result is death."

Maître Du Pont said, "But what about—" He turned sharply as the common room door flew open and banged against the wall. All of them stared at the young lay brother who stood there trying to catch his breath.

"Maître du Luc?" The brother looked uncertainly around the circle of scholastics.

Charles stood up. "What is it?"

"Frère Brunet says you are to come immediately."

Charles's heart contracted. "Père Dainville?"

"Yes, *maître*."

The lay brother barely had time to jump back from the threshold before Charles was in the passageway and running for the stairs.

Chapter 7

Charles reached the infirmary just behind Père Le Picart. Père Montville was at the foot of Père Dainville's bed, wearing his stole and laying out what he needed to give the last rites. Frère Brunet rushed down the row of beds to meet the rector.

"I thought he was better, *mon père*, truly I did! He was awake and knew me this morning, he even ate a little. So I sent the father sitting with him to eat something, and then I was busy upstairs in the students' infirmary and then in my room making a new tisane—"

"There's no blame to you, you were only doing what was necessary. Tell me what happened to him."

Brunet pulled himself together. "He went on much the same, but then I went upstairs again to see that dinner had come for my two patients up there. And when I came down, Père Dainville's poor face was twisted like a knot and I couldn't wake him. His breathing went on sinking and"—he held out both meaty hands in a gesture of defeat—"I sent for Père Montville and you."

They went to Pere Dainville's bedside, and Montville waited for the three of them to kneel. The rough gray blanket hardly rose and fell on Dainville's chest, and his face was pulled so far to the right that Charles hoped he was gone beyond feeling pain. Then Montville began the sacrament that would send the old priest anointed and shriven to the God he had served so well and so long. Charles joined in the prayers and responses, tasting his tears and wishing there were some sacrament for those who were losing Dainville and would have to go on without him.

The prayers ended and silence fell in the long room. A bar of afternoon sun had reached Dainville's bed and lay across his pale, ruined face. Charles put a hand on the blanket, as though touching it could give the old man strength for the work of dying, and also give himself some last comfort. The blanket's rise and fall grew smaller, the stillness after each breath grew longer, and when the stripe of sunlight had moved beyond the old face, there was only stillness.

Charles felt Le Picart stand up beside him and forced himself to his feet.

"*Maître*." Le Picart waited until Charles had wiped his face with his sleeve. "When the lay brothers have made Père Dainville ready, I would like you to take the first watch beside his body in the chapel."

"Yes, *mon père*," Charles said, surprised and grateful. "Thank you." He breathed deeply to steady himself. "What will happen now? Where will he be buried?"

"Not here. We've never had much room for a graveyard. He'll be buried in our church of Saint Louis. Do you have a theology class this afternoon?"

Charles shook his head.

"If you wish, you may go to the chapel for a while now. Your watch will begin at Vespers."

Charles bowed his thanks and looked for the last time at Dainville, whose twisted face seemed already relaxing into peace. Charles forced himself down the infirmary aisle and out into the garden. He looked blankly at the few autumn flowers and dying herbs, the familiar roofline and walls, and felt as though he'd never seen any of it before. *But that's what happens*, he told himself. He remembered going outside at home the night his father died. He'd looked at the stone house where he was born, the barn where the wine press stood, the vineyard spreading up the hill, the deep starlit sky, and for the first time in his life, none of it had welcomed him. Because the small, bald, irascible and earnest man who'd begotten him was gone from the earth. He hadn't expected Dainville's death to leave him as lost. Though Dainville knew more about him than his father had, much more about his wrestling in the dark depths of himself.

Perhaps cousin Charles-François is right, said the familiar, often acid voice that lived in his head. *You're a Jesuit because you can't get over needing fathers. Someone to tell you what to do . . .*

Shut up, damn you! Charles strode out of the infirmary court toward the chapel. As he crossed the Cour d'honneur, the college bell began to toll seventy-nine slow strokes, for the years of Père Dainville's life. Afternoon classes had just started, and the main court was mostly empty, but the proctors and a few others stopped as the bell tolled, praying briefly and crossing themselves. Père Joseph Jouvancy, the rhetoric professor whose assistant Charles had been, appeared in one of the rhetoric classroom's long windows and called out to him.

"Is it Père Dainville, *maître*?"

Charles nodded, and Jouvancy crossed himself and turned to tell his students. Wishing he could turn back the year and be there helping in the rhetoric classroom, with Dainville alive and at work somewhere in the college on an ordinary afternoon, Charles went into the chapel and knelt at the side altar dedicated to the Virgin Mary. The rue St. Jacques door opened and closed, quiet footsteps crossed the floor, and cloth rustled. Looking over his shoulder, Charles saw that neighborhood people were already coming in response to the bell. Prayers for Dainville had been asked at Mass, and now those who had known him were coming to honor his life and pray for his soul.

But Charles found it almost impossible to pray. He was grieving, but he was also shaking with anger. He was certain that Dainville had died because of how he'd come across the murdered young man—had been as good as murdered himself. That murderer had so far gone free, and it was clear that Le Picart was not going to let him do anything to find the man. He gripped the rail in front of him and looked up at the carved and painted Mary. Regal as a queen, she held her baby in the curve of her arm while the baby held a golden ball, symbol of the world, in the hollow of his plump hand. Charles told himself that if there was room for all the world in that small hand, there was room in his prayers for anger as well as grief. But try as he would, he could not form the anger into prayer. It stayed in his gut, burning like a torch.

Murdered! Charles flung the silent word at Mary, who went on gazing over his head. If Dainville had not come suddenly upon the body of the murdered boy in the Carmelite crypt, he'd be alive. Maybe he would have died in the next year or so, even the next month or two. But whoever had broken that young man's neck and hidden his body had shattered God's time. *When that man hangs,* Charles told himself, *I want him to know he's hanging for Dainville's death, too.*

The sound of heavy skirts whispered along the floor behind him, and he looked over his shoulder. He recognized the two women who'd argued in the back of the church after the morning Mass. Both wore long dark mantles, and scarves over their hair, one black and one a soft blue-violet. The taller one, with the blue-violet scarf, was wiping her eyes with a handkerchief.

"Oh, come," the other woman hissed at her. "He was old. Older than most people get to be. Time for him to die."

"It's not for you to say when it's anyone's time to die." The taller woman's voice was low-pitched and young.

"And it's not for you to contradict me who keeps you!"

Charles grimaced, recognizing the same harsh voice he'd heard that morning telling a woman to stop singing—probably the young woman who was with her now. Glad when the pair was out of his hearing, he turned back to the altar, but now his unwelcome inner voice was back.

Why do you go on thinking about the killer? Are you really so stupid? You've just been expressly told to have nothing to do with searching out the murderer. And threatened with what will happen if you disobey.

Charles set his teeth. *Lieutenant-Général La Reynie had known Dainville. I can remind him that seeing the body brought on Dainville's apoplexy,* he told the voice. For a moment, he thought the voice had sunk back into silence. But then it said, *Oh, so now you're a physician, knowing exactly what causes a man's death. You'll never give up thinking you know everything, will you?*

Doggedly, Charles began the prayers for the dead. All the while doubting that his praying did much good, and glad that Dainville likely needed prayers less than most of the newly dead. But he kept pushing the ancient words across his tongue.

Finally he rose and went to his study and St. Thomas Aquinas. Somehow, going on doing the next task, and the one after that, seemed like a small way to honor Dainville. To help himself pay attention in spite of his sadness, Charles read aloud.

"'Question: Is God simple?'"

He frowned at the page. The obvious answer was *no*, but Thomas never allowed the obvious answer. Charles read on.

"'Answer: It seems that he is not.'"

Surprised that Thomas agreed with him for once, Charles made his way through the learned opinions that came next. He finished St. Hilary's opinion and started on Boethius's, but his eyes kept closing and finally the book slid from his hands. He dreamed that the mouse was sitting on his desk, eating her way through his tallow candle and eyeing the book as dessert. Père Dainville was standing beside him, watching her and smiling. "You're wrong," the old man told Charles, his eyes shining. "God is simpler than the air. Only you can't see it because you are too simple-minded."

Charles woke as the bell rang for the end of afternoon classes. The sun was low, shining straight through his west-facing window, and he got up stiffly from his chair and went to look out. The window glass was cold to the touch, and people in the street were huddling into their cloaks as they walked. A slow-moving carriage drawn by a pair of black horses stopped at Louis le Grand's postern door and Charles craned his neck, looking nearly straight down, and saw Lieutenant-Général La Reynie get out and ring the bell. Charles was suddenly wide awake. Why would La Reynie come back so quickly, unless he had identified the dead man in the crypt? *What's the harm*, he snapped at the inner voice before it could comment. *I only want to know who it is. I have a right; I found him, I touched him.*

From the sun's angle, it couldn't be all that long until Vespers, which gave him another reason to go down. He grabbed his cloak from where it hung on the wall and hurried along the passage. If the rector was busy, La Reynie might have to wait in the *grand salon*, and Charles might catch him there. But when

Charles reached the *salon*, it was empty except for a lay brother in slippers, sweeping the carpet. The rector's office door was closed.

The college bell rang for Vespers, which meant that the vigil beside Père Dainville's body was beginning. Charles went quickly back through the *salon*'s anteroom to the side door, where he nearly collided with a woman just going out.

"Your pardon, *madame*," he said, stepping away from her and wondering where on earth she'd come from.

She smiled up at him. "No matter."

Her voice and the blue-violet scarf wound lightly over her dark brown hair told him she was the taller and younger of the two women he'd seen—and heard—twice in the chapel. He saw now that she was also very thin. As he made his small Jesuit bow, he thought that all her beauty was in her wide-set eyes, which were the same blue-violet as her scarf.

"I was looking at the painting there in the alcove beside the stairs," she said, as he held the door open for her. "The one of Saint Thomas."

Charles nodded politely, thinking that Thomas seemed to be following him everywhere.

She stopped in the street passage. "I do like the look of your Saint Thomas," she said thoughtfully. "I've never before seen a painting of a saint eating—a little cake, I think. He looks as though he liked his food! And he's holding a pot of honey." Her smile wavered. "A good reminder that there's sweetness to be found in spite of all the bitterness in the world."

Charles nodded, thinking that her mind was even more attractive than her eyes. "I've seen you once or twice in the chapel. And—forgive me, but I think I've also heard you singing as I stood at my window."

"Oh." She blushed and looked down. "I've recently come to

live with my aunt, Madame Cheyne, just up the street. She owns the bookshop called The Saint's Dog. Though everyone seems to call it The Dog. I am Mademoiselle Rose Ebrard."

Charles bowed again, remembering the door porter's message to the rector on the way to the refectory.

"Forgive me," he said, "I have not introduced myself. I am Maître Charles du Luc." He was puzzled at her startled look— a look of recognition, he would have thought, except that he was certain they'd never met before.

She busied herself for a moment with adjusting her scarf. "I've just been meeting with your rector, my new spiritual advisor." Her lips quivered and she pressed them together. "I had been meeting with poor Père Dainville. My father died shortly before I came to Paris," she said softly, "and Père Dainville was a great comfort. I will miss him sorely. I only saw him four or five times, but I grew so quickly to feel real affection for him. Though perhaps one is not supposed to feel that for a priest. He was so wise. And he welcomed me. Priests don't always welcome women, you know."

"I know. I hope that will change. But Père Dainville welcomed everyone," Charles said. "He was my confessor, too."

The sound of a smothered sneeze made them both look toward the postern. To Charles's surprise, Maître Richaud stood in the doorway of the porter's tiny room, rubbing his nose with his sleeve as his eyes darted between Charles and Mlle Ebrard. His short loud sniffs managed to convey extreme disapproval.

Charles sighed, suddenly sure that Richaud had been furtively watching and listening to Charles's talk with the woman. With deceptive mildness, he said, "What are you doing in the porter's room, *maître?*"

"I am helping a lay brother," Richaud said righteously.

"Frère Martin had to deliver a package. I was just coming in and offered to watch the door for him."

Which was probably true, Charles thought. And as luck would have it, that righteous offer had also provided him with the treat of catching Charles in a prolonged and unchaperoned talk with a woman. Foregoing things he wanted to say to Richaud, Charles turned to Rose Ebrard, "I must leave you, *mademoiselle*," he said loudly, for Richaud's benefit. "I am expected in the chapel."

"Is Père Dainville's body there yet?"

"It should be. I'm taking the first watch."

She hesitated and glanced at Richaud, who still lurked in the doorway. "May I follow you, Maître du Luc? I would like to go and pray for him."

"Of course," Charles said, feeling Richaud's eyes boring into him. "Come."

"He looks like a bad-tempered turtle," the young woman murmured as she followed behind him, and they smothered matching snorts of laughter.

Classes were over for the day. The only sounds as they crossed the big court, walking side by side now, were their feet on the gravel and the dry skittering of fallen leaves from the trees along the wall. Charles was uncomfortably aware that Mlle Ebrard was studying him covertly as they went. He found himself hoping that Richaud's suspicions were not going to be proved true for once. But her repeated glances at him were not in the least flirtatious. Charles knew flirting when he met it.

When they reached the chapel, two lay brothers had just finished setting up trestles at the front of the nave. Charles and Mlle Ebrard crossed themselves as more brothers carried in Père Dainville's coffined body and placed it on the trestles. She went to kneel behind the first row of benches. Charles waited where he was while the brothers lit tall candles at the coffin's head and foot, bowed to the altar, and withdrew. Maître Henry Wing, the English scholastic, burst into the chapel from the courtyard and stumbled over the threshold.

"Oops! I'm to keep the first part of the vigil with you," he said eagerly to Charles, who hushed him and showed him where to kneel before the coffin.

Charles knelt beside him. Grief assailed him and he bit his lip as tears came. The tears were as much for himself as for Dainville, but that was the way of grief. Dainville, after all, was gone to God. Or very shortly to God, Charles thought, since after a life like his, how long could it take to clean away his youthful sins? Surely the penitential time in Purgatory would be short for such a man. Charles knew that he was grieving over the empty place his confessor's death left in his own life and in the college. What other Louis le Grand confessor saw so deeply into hearts? Who at the college would know Charles as Dainville had? Who would companion his recurrent struggles with obedience? Who would repeatedly bring him to laugh at himself? Who would welcome his occasional hesitant account of the terrifying and longed-for Silence that sometimes visited him, and the heart-stopping sense of God's nearness it brought? He hid his wet face in his hands. *Oh, my father!* his heart cried. It was a cry of pure need, and he wasn't sure whether he was calling out to Dainville or God or his own father.

He straightened and drew a shaking breath, pulled out his handkerchief, and wiped his face. Then he folded his hands and began again the church's prayers for the dead. But he'd barely started when the bell rang for dinner and he felt his companion stir beside him. He glanced up and saw that Wing was looking anxiously at him, his pale blue eyes full of some question.

Wing leaned closer. "I'm hungry."

"We're here until Compline. After that, they'll give us something."

"Oh. That's a long time."

Charles gave Maître Wing a look that sent him back to at least the semblance of prayer and began his own prayers yet again. This time they took him beyond himself and into the quiet where his own needs and self fell away. Most of his own needs, anyway. Slowly, he grew aware that his body was clamoring urgently for the latrine. He tried to quiet the clamor, but it was no good. Ignoring his companion's hastily smothered startled yelp as he stood up, Charles bowed to the altar and made speed to the little courtyard off the Cour d'honneur.

When he emerged from the long, low wooden latrine building, Lieutenant-Général La Reynie was standing beside its screen of leggy rose bushes, his nose buried in a late yellow bloom.

Chapter 8

La Reynie looked up and snapped the yellow rose from its stem. "I was in the street passage, on my way out, when I saw you come out of the chapel. I need to speak with you." He patiently released the lace of his cuff from a thorn and put the rose in a buttonhole of his coat.

Charles glanced warily in the direction of the rector's office, though it wasn't even visible from the small court. "Did you find out who the dead man is?"

"Yes, I've just told Père Le Picart. Who is obviously not going to tell you. But I want you to know. The dead man is indeed Paul Lunel, the seventeen-year-old who never arrived at your Novice House."

Charles crossed himself. "God receive his soul." Then he remembered what Le Picart had said. "Where do you suppose he was those three weeks? Before he was killed."

"That is the next thing I have to find out. There are only servants at the Lunel house. They say they don't know where he's been. But I've learned a little more about him. As I told you, Père Guymond had no reply to his message that Paul Lunel hadn't arrived at the Novice House. The only family are Lunel's mother and an older brother, who were at the Lunel country house beyond Chaillot. The mother stays there most of the time, now that she's widowed. The servants say they sent the message there. Why there was no response, I don't know.

"Madame Lunel was known to be opposed to her son's vocation—she's something of a Gallican and fiercely anti-Jesuit. It was Paul Lunel's father, a judge who died last spring, who encouraged him. Père Guymond says that when the father knew he was dying, he was afraid his wife would try to keep the boy from becoming a Jesuit. The father sent Père Guymond a letter giving permission for his son to enter the Novice House and instructing him to pay no heed to Madame Lunel's objections. Why the boy waited until this autumn to present himself, Père Guymond doesn't know. Perhaps he was trying to reconcile his mother to his choice." La Reynie shrugged. "In any case, I am now obliged to ask questions at the Novice House, and also of any Jesuit I can find who knew Paul Lunel. I tell you frankly, *maître*, I need your help. You could ask many of those questions—and get an honest answer—much more easily than I."

Charles was shaking his head. "You've no reason to think that Jesuits will lie to you when you're trying to find the killer of a boy who was almost one of us. Besides that, though I tell you frankly that I *want* to help you, I can't. The rector has forbidden it. I cannot disobey him."

La Reynie stabbed his silver-headed stick so hard into the ground that the rose in his buttonhole dropped a petal. "You've disobeyed him before."

"In smaller things. But this time he's made it clear that my future as a Jesuit depends on obeying him to the letter."

"After what you did for the king in the summer, Père Le Picart should be nothing but glad for you to go on bringing the Society of Jesus to the royal notice by serving the king's justice!"

"Monsieur La Reynie, the Society is not the king's court. I

am not a courtier. I do not earn favor and trade on past success." He held La Reynie's angry gaze. "I *want* my Jesuit future."

"Do you? Or is it that you have suddenly grown more comfortable and less brave?"

Less brave. Cowardly. There it was again. A flare of anger—or was it fear?—burned through Charles. But he said nothing. They stood like two rams that had locked horns in a battle and couldn't get clear of each other. Finally, La Reynie's lips curved in a half smile, and he made Charles a mock bow.

"I used to be able to intimidate you. Or at least prod you into yelling at me."

Charles smiled a little, too, and the standoff eased. "I used to be terrified of you. When one is frightened of a large dog, one does tend to yell at him." Charles's smile widened as La Reynie's graying brows drew together. "And I haven't always been sure how much I cared about my Jesuit future. I'm sure now."

"So you've decided that your Society of Jesus is blameless and pure?"

"In exactly the same measure that you've decided the king you work for is blameless and pure."

"*Touché.*" La Reynie's brief laughter echoed around the little courtyard, and it was Charles's turn to make a mock bow. "Nonetheless," the *lieutenant-général* said, "this murder is a Jesuit matter and I need you."

Charles shook his head and made to turn away. "I've told you that I want to help you. But I cannot."

La Reynie's iron grip closed on Charles's arm and held him where he was. "Don't you care that this killer helped your Père Dainville to his death?" he said roughly.

Charles's self-control vanished. "Of course I care! I can hardly pray for Père Dainville because all I can think of is finding the man and hanging him with my own hands!"

"Then please, listen to me! If your rector hears that we've talked, I'll swear I kept you here by force."

Charles looked down at the hand on his sleeve, and La Reynie let him go.

"Say it, then," Charles told him. "But be quick."

"Your Novice House rector is telling me that I can talk to him but cannot question anyone else in his house. He is trying to claim that the novitiate is one of the old Liberties where the king's justice cannot enter."

"But he can't keep you out! The king's law runs everywhere in Paris now. Or so I've been told."

La Reynie cast his eyes up at the darkening sky in exasperation. "That's certainly supposed to be true. But I fight this kind of obstruction all the time. I think the abbot of Saint Germain would see every one of his monks murdered before he'd willingly let me in. The Novice House rector says my coming and going will deeply upset the running of his house and the formation of his novices and if I persist, he will instruct everyone there to tell me nothing and most of them will obey him. Which brings me back to you. The rector told me earlier today—before you joined us in his office—that you will be at the Novice House twice each week for your studies. And you know this new novice you mentioned, de Corbet. The dead man was supposed to live in de Corbet's chamber. No doubt there will be talk and speculation about the dead boy. I've already told you servants there are talking about him! If you keep your eyes and ears open, if you turn conversations to Lunel and learn something, how can Père Le Picart object? And if you tell me outside the college what you learn, how would he even know? I can easily make ways to see you on your way back from the Novice House."

"I won't go behind his back. And I'm unlikely to have much further conversation with Monsieur de Corbet. Novices are allowed few visitors." But in his mind, Charles was seeing the smooth curve of Paul Lunel's young dead face, seeing Père Dainville lying disfigured and helpless in the infirmary, both lives cut off by someone's malignant rage. "If I learn something—at the Novice House or here," he said, "I will tell Père Le Picart. He will tell you. He is not unwilling to help the king's justice find a killer; he is only unwilling for me to be involved. But that is all I can do." Charles nodded to La Reynie and started to walk away.

Behind him, the *lieutenant-général* said, "Too bad you are not your own man."

Charles stopped. Without turning around, he said, "I am the Society's man. Just as you are the king's."

"So we are two of a kind? Is that what you mean?"

Finding no answer to that, Charles went back through the thickening dark to the almost equally dark chapel. Maître Henry Wing flinched sideways and squeaked in surprise as Charles knelt beside him. Occasional whispers, the sounds of people walking clumsily as they tried to keep heels from clacking on the floor, and the rustle of cloth marked the coming and going of neighborhood people in the nave. Trying to take comfort from their presence and love for Dainville, Charles bowed his head.

But what La Reynie had told him refused to be pushed aside. Where had Paul Lunel been for three weeks? Had wherever he'd been and whatever he'd been doing gotten him killed? Charles doubted he'd hear much about Lunel at the Novice House. Gossip was not looked upon kindly in Jesuit houses. Not that that stopped it, but during the novice years, rules were unbending and their observance was scrupulously watched. Rules were certainly not lax later, but in small things, at least, some breadth of interpretation came with time and maturity. Unable to make his mental questions stop, Charles gathered his body to stillness, kept saying the words of the prayers, and waited for his mind to hush. Very slowly, the silence deepened around him, the sounds in the nave fell away, and even his grief was quiet, like a tired animal finally able to sleep. *Charles,* the Silence said. *Nothing is lost.* The voice that was not a voice poured through him like balm.

Then the supper bell rang from the courtyard, someone's sneeze echoed through the chapel like thunder, a bench scraped on the floor, and the street door began opening and closing repeatedly. People going home to their own supper, Charles realized, shifting his knees on the hard floor. He raised his eyes to the coffin. *Nothing is lost,* the Silence had said. What, then, of the emptiness death left? What was he to do with that? Unless the emptiness was a fullness he couldn't see? He let that thought wait in his mind, hoping against hope that there would be an answer. But there was not.

The thought changed shape like a cloud, and he found himself wondering what Père Dainville would have made of La Reynie saying that he and Charles were "two of a kind." Charles wasn't sure what to make of it. He knew that they shared a relentless need to find truth. Both of them had quick tempers, whose sparks quickly died, and neither suffered fools gladly. La Reynie had even offered once to take Charles into the police if he quit the Society of Jesus. But if they *were* two of a kind, what kind? Whatever the answer to that might be, it changed nothing. Including the fact that this watch beside his beloved confessor's body would not end until Compline rang, and his knees were already screaming at him.

Charles bent to bunch his cassock into thicker folds under his knees. As he straightened, a light, high-pitched giggle echoed startlingly around the chapel. Beside Charles, the English scholastic was staring up at the chapel's second-story-level gallery. Charles narrowed his eyes, trying to see in the dim light. He heard furtive footsteps and then the giggle came again. Something small fell from the gallery's balustrade and bounced on the stone floor. As Charles got angrily to his feet, the lay brother watching the chapel door hurried up the aisle toward him.

Others had noticed the sounds, as well, and scattered whispers came from the few people, mostly women, still kneeling in the nave.

"I can't leave the door, *maître*," the brother said softly when he reached Charles. "Can you go up there? Sounds to me like it's boys again. They tossed down a prayer book."

"I'll go," Charles said grimly. "If the little wretches run down the south stairs from the gallery, catch them and hold on to them. I thought we'd put a stop to this nonsense."

A month earlier, on the second night of the school term, five twelve-year-olds had decided to prove their bravery by spending the night pretending to be spirits haunting the chapel. Their giggling and running around the gallery had given them away to a Jesuit praying late, and they'd been caught. Four were seriously disciplined, and the fifth, whose idea it had been, had been expelled.

Now, wearily climbing the south stairs that led up from the nave, Charles wondered who was responsible for this new outbreak. From the pitch of the giggles, these were even younger boys.

"Come down!" he called as he reached the stairhead. "Have you forgotten that Père Dainville's body lies here?" Absolute silence fell in the gallery. Then there was a scuffle of feet toward the east end of the gallery over the chancel. "Enough!" Charles strode angrily toward the sound.

He rounded the gallery's curve, wishing he'd thought to

bring a candle, but sure that he must be nearly on the miscreants. The gallery's overhang cut off most of the light from the altar candles, but if the boys had escaped to the north aisle stairs, he would have heard them running. As he walked into deeper shadow, his hair prickled on his neck and a tiny whisper of breath sighed behind him. He whirled, but too late. Something hit him like a cast stone, pain ripped through the back of his left shoulder, and he cried out and fell.

For a few moments, he was aware of nothing but pain and the hot sickening feel of blood running down his back.

"*Maître?*" the lay brother called. "Are you all right?"

Charles's groan was inarticulate, but it was enough to bring the lay brother pounding up the stairs.

"What happened?" he cried, bending over Charles. "Bring a candle," he called over the gallery railing, "Maître du Luc's hurt! Where are those unblessed boys, *maître?*"

"It wasn't boys," Charles said faintly.

Someone came with a candle, and Charles groaned as hands prodded at his back.

"You've been stabbed!" someone said. "You're bleeding like a pig!"

The next few minutes were a chaos of questions Charles couldn't answer. "But did you *see* the man who stabbed me?" he finally managed to say, looking up.

Two lay brothers were bending over him now, and a man he recognized as a courtyard proctor was holding a candle. All of them shook their heads.

Charles breathed deeply against the pain. "The street door," he said, "who's watching it?"

"A proctor's there," said the man with the candle.

"Then the man's hiding somewhere." Charles tried to shrug off their hands. "Never mind me, find him!"

"Maître Wing, come up here and help us search," one of the brothers called down to the Englishman. "Bring a candle."

The brothers heaved Charles to his feet and one of them walked him toward the north stairs, which were on the other side of the altar and nearest to the courtyard door. The other brother called out to Wing to hurry.

When they reached the foot of the stairs, Charles saw that the women who'd been scattered through the nave praying for Dainville were gathered near the altar, in front of the coffin, and seemed to be arguing with someone.

"Stop your fussing!" an aggrieved male voice said to them. "I tell you, there's nothing wrong with him!"

The voice was Maître Richaud's, and Charles stopped. "What's happened there?" he called, but his voice was too weak to carry over the angry voice of a woman still arguing with Richaud.

"I've told you, I saw *no* one coming down those stairs," Maître Louis Richaud's voice went on. "But I wasn't looking, was I? I came from the courtyard to put a stop to the unseemly noise in here!" The women parted in haste as he pushed his way through them. When he saw Charles, he stopped, glaring. "I suppose you started this uproar?"

"No," Charles said through his teeth, "whoever stabbed me started it. I thought it was boys up there. But—" He caught his breath and leaned heavily against the lay brother.

Richaud snorted. "If they're hiding there, they'll be found." He frowned. "I heard someone say you've been stabbed. Surely you don't think one of our boys did that."

"Enough," the brother growled at Richaud. "I'm taking Maître du Luc to the infirmary."

"There's another man here who needs help," the oldest of the women said back. She pointed toward Dainville's coffin and the women with her moved aside. Beyond their wide skirts, a black shape was huddled on the floor and yet another woman was bent over it.

Charles's heart jumped into his throat. "Is it Maître Wing? Did the man stab him, too?"

"He's only fainted," Richaud said derisively. "I found him like that when I got here."

"I saw him faint," the older woman put in. "It was when he"—she nodded at Charles—"cried out—screamed, really—in the gallery."

The lay brother started Charles moving again. "Stay with him," the brother told Richaud. "If he doesn't come to himself quickly, bring him to the infirmary."

"He can come to himself somewhere else," Richaud snapped. "He can't stay here in front of the coffin!" With a put-upon sigh, he shooed the women aside, bent over Wing, and shook him impatiently by the shoulder. As the lay brother led Charles out the door, Wing stirred and mumbled behind them.

Chapter 9

"There were no students up in the chapel gallery," Père Le Picart said from his stool beside Charles's infirmary bed. "All the boarding students were where they should have been. And aside from the fact that I simply cannot believe a student would attack you, no one in the college—either student or Jesuit—has any weapon, you know that. The man who stabbed you surely lured you up there by moving from place to place and giggling and whispering like boys having a prank."

Charles, lying on his side to save pressure on his wound, looked up at the rector as best he could. "So the man just wanted to stab whoever came to find the students?" he said skeptically.

"Maître Wing thinks so," said Le Picart. "He thinks it's the same man who killed Paul Lunel and that he's going about, trying to kill Jesuits. He says that he heard someone running very lightly along the east end of the gallery, above the altar, almost straight above him. He thought the man was making for the north stairs and coming to kill him. That's why he fainted."

"But no one attacked him."

"No." Le Picart was quiet for a moment. "I've been told there were only a few people in the chapel, all women. And that you and Maître Wing and the lay brother watching the street door were the only Jesuits in the chapel. Correct?"

Charles grunted affirmatively.

"Anyone would know that the man charged with watching the door would be unlikely to leave it to round up a few students. So it would almost certainly be either you or Maître Wing who came upstairs to see to the supposed boys."

"But where in God's name did this man go?" Charles said. "How did he get away unseen? There must be somewhere that wasn't searched!"

"We searched everywhere. There was no one in the gallery; no one saw the man in the church. My guess is that he slipped out the north door to the back court and went over the wall by the stables." The rector smiled slightly. "Unless, of course, he was a demon."

"What?"

"Maître Richaud has been disciplined for putting it about that you were stabbed by a demon. For your sins, he says. Which is illogical of him, since a demon would no doubt be delighted by your sins."

Charles, outraged, tried to push himself up on his elbow.

"I was stabbed by a real man, with a very real knife. What if Maître Wing is right and this attack has to do with our dead almost-novice?"

"But why would it? Though you found him, you don't know who killed him. You can't accuse anyone."

"But the man at the foot of the crypt stairs—I saw him. If he was the killer, he may fear I can recognize him. That's at least possible."

"But he was only outlined against the light, you said. You couldn't see his features. And you said that he stood quietly and made no attempt to avoid you and Père Dainville."

Charles started to protest, but Le Picart frowned and put a hand on Charles's forehead. "Hush now, lie quiet. *Mon frère*," he called, "Maître du Luc is somewhat fevered."

"I thought he would be." Frère Brunet put his head around the doorway to his room beyond the infirmary altar. "I've been making him a *tisane*. I'm coming."

The rector sat quietly. Charles lay listening to Frère Brunet humming as he finished his mixing, the soothing sounds reminding Charles of his mother brewing medicine when someone in the household fell ill.

His eyes were closing when another thought jolted him awake.

"You'll have to reconsecrate the chapel," he said anxiously. "Since blood was spilled there. I'm sorry—"

"Shhh, *maître*, that's hardly your fault. You didn't spill your own blood. Yes, it will have to be blessed again. Meanwhile, we're using one of the small chapels. It's crowded, but it will have to do for a short time. Père Dainville's body has been moved there."

Charles sighed and shifted restlessly on the pillow. "Has Frère Brunet told you how long I must stay here?"

"No, he hasn't," Brunet rumbled, coming in from his room with a glass and a thick pottery bowl. "You're not going anywhere today or tomorrow, that's certain. The wound isn't so much—a slice, but not a deep one. The man's knife was sharp enough, but he didn't know much about using it." He put the bowl down on the table. Slipping an arm under Charles's shoulders, he turned him so that he could drink and held the glass to his lips. "Drink it all, it's *eau de melisse*, same as I gave you last night. Good for shock. Other things, too."

The sweet lemony taste was comforting and went down easily. "That's better than some of the things you've poured into me, *mon frère*."

"Don't complain. You'll drink what I give you and be glad!" He laid Charles down on his side again, put the glass down, and stirred the contents of the bowl. "Turn onto your belly," he growled. "This is going to hurt."

"The wound isn't his fault, you know," Le Picart said mildly.

"It's the one who did this I'm angry at."

Charles yelped as Brunet started peeling the bandage away.

"Sorry," Brunet said. "We've lost a novice—well, nearly a novice—and now some son of a pig—I'd guess the same son of a pig—has carved up Maître du Luc's back. Who's next? And what's that La Reynie doing about it?"

"Whatever he can, I assure you. He—Monsieur La Reynie—is furious."

"Good." Brunet poured something warm and fresh-smelling onto Charles's back, and it bit like a swooping falcon. Charles grunted. Brunet made an exasperated sound and stood up. "I forgot the fresh bandage. Don't move." He hurried into the room beyond the altar.

When he was gone, Le Picart said quietly to Charles, "Monsieur La Reynie is furious about the attack, but he's even more furious because the man attacked you."

"He said that?" Charles mumbled into the pillow.

"No. He said that he was going to Fontainebleau." The rector's tone was dark with disapproval.

Before Charles could ask why La Reynie had gone to the

palace where the king spent the hunting season, Brunet came back with a length of folded linen. He wrapped it briskly around Charles's back and chest and over his shoulder. Charles, gritting his teeth against the pain of being moved, suddenly wished that everyone would go away and stop talking to him. His head hurt and the light was too bright and everything suddenly seemed much too complicated to think about.

"There." Brunet laid Charles down again on his right side and put a hand on his patient's forehead. "Oh, dear. You're getting hotter. I think I'd better . . ."

Charles's eyes closed and the rest of the sentence melted into a dream in which La Reynie was dragging him painfully down the crypt stairs, asking why he'd let the demon hide so many bodies.

The rest of Thursday and Friday passed in intermittent shivering and sweating, and a confusion of dreaming and waking. Then bells were ringing, the infirmary was dark, and Charles was listening to the bells' clamor and trying to figure out what day it was. The burning in his back and shoulder had lessened and he was blessedly cool. He was drifting away from trying to think and back into sleep when a big hand enveloped his forehead. He grunted in surprise and tried to twist away.

"No, no, it's only me. Don't twist like that and your wound will be better pleased." Frère Brunet stood over him, nodding cautiously. "Your fever's much less, thank Our Lady for that grace. How do you feel?"

"Better. What day is it?"

"Hmmm?" Brunet was stirring something at the small table between Charles's bed and the next one. "Oh. It's Saturday. Saint Eata."

"Who?"

"He was English," Brunet said dismissively. "Years ago. I don't know why we bother with him."

"A martyr?"

"You might say so. Died of dysentery, so they say."

Charles grunted. "*That's* a horrible fate, even for an Englishman. Most martyrdoms are a lot quicker."

"Ah, had it yourself, have you?"

"I nearly died of it my first year in the army."

"Then that's three times—no, four times—you haven't died, *maître*. The dysentery, your army wound, that gunshot wound you got your first summer here, and now this stabbing. Not so much the wound itself this time, but the festering of it. I wouldn't push my luck any more, if I were you. God might be tired of saving you from yourself."

"What do you mean, from myself?"

"I don't mean what happened Wednesday night. But you joined the army yourself, didn't you? I mean, you're noble, so I hear, and you didn't join like so many do—because they've no money and nothing to eat. You just wanted to fight."

Charles said nothing, and Brunet advanced on him with the cup.

"This will help keep the fever away. The wound's festering is calming down nicely, but I want to make sure it doesn't come back. And you're going nowhere till I *am* sure."

Charles sipped at the bitter drink. "When can I get up?"

"When I say so. When your fever stays gone. I'll bring you something to eat shortly. Meanwhile, you finish that and say your prayers." He bustled away.

Torn between exasperation and affection, Charles watched the lay brother's broad back disappear down the room and out the door. Brunet was wrong, though, about the army; Charles hadn't gone into the army because he'd wanted to fight. He'd wanted to die, and not just any death. He'd wanted to die heroically in battle, a noble martyr to his family's refusal to let him marry his Protestant cousin Pernelle. His mouth quirked in a sad half smile. Of course, he'd been eighteen at the time, exactly the age for dramatic self-sacrifice. Well, if punishment was deserved for that, the terrible memory he shared with Amaury de Corbet had been ample penance.

Whatever he'd imagined he wanted at eighteen, he definitely did not want to die now. He wondered if La Reynie had found out anything more about Wednesday night's attack. He remembered Le Picart telling him something about the *lieutenant-général*, but now he couldn't remember what. He was still trying to remember when Brunet came back with bread, a steaming bowl, and watered wine. He put the tray down on the little table and helped Charles sit up.

"Here you are, *maître*." He put the bowl on Charles's lap and gave him a spoon. "Eat all of this; you've hardly eaten anything these last days."

Charles looked dubiously at the grayish mess in the bowl. "What is it?"

"Mutton broth with barley."

"It looks like baby pap."

"Babies have sense. Now eat."

"*Oui, maman,*" Charles murmured, and ate.

The soup was hot and thick and filling. By the time he finished it, he wanted to curl up and sleep again. Brunet said grace after eating with him, made him wash his face and hands as though he were six years old, and helped him lie down again on his side to take the pressure off his wound. Charles was sliding into sleep when Père Le Picart appeared beside his bed.

"*Maître,*" the rector said, almost whispering. "Are you awake? Your cousin has come to see you."

Charles's eyes flew open and he looked up in dismay.

Le Picart tilted his head very slightly back toward the door.

"He says he's on the point of leaving Paris. He also says he went to the Novice House and—as we expected—was refused permission to see Amaury de Corbet. He asked me if *you'd* seen de Corbet, and I said you had. He knows that you are not well, but I didn't tell him you were attacked. Let that remain unsaid." His voice rose. "And so, *maître*, I've reminded your cousin that he must speak quietly here and leave promptly. Will you see him?"

Charles sighed. "If you'll help me sit up again. When I look up from this angle, I feel as though my eyes are going to fall out."

Le Picart raised him against the pillows and frowned anxiously as Charles grimaced with pain. "Can you do this?"

"Shhh!" Charles glanced toward the infirmarian's chamber beyond the altar. "If you make a fuss about me, I think Frère Brunet might sit on me like a hen with an ailing chick."

"Uncomfortable for the chick." Le Picart grinned at him and looked toward the outer door. "You may come," he called, and went into the little chamber where Brunet mixed his medicines.

Charles watched Charles-François de Vintimille du Luc march down the room, the long wig bouncing on his shoulders. "*Bonjour*, Charlot."

His cousin made him a stiff bow. "I am sorry you're unwell."

"It's no great matter. I understand you're leaving Paris."

Charles-François's stare was cold. "Your rector says you've seen Amaury. I, of course, was turned away. What did Amaury say to you?"

"Nothing you don't already know. That he's wanted to join the Society for a long time and is glad to be where he is."

"Balls. And who was watching him and listening when he said so?"

"Only he and I were in the room."

Charles-François glanced in the direction Le Picart had

gone and lowered his voice. "So they know you've become base enough to report to his superiors. You turn my stomach, all of you!"

Charles squinted against the light, as though if he could see his cousin better he could make sense of what he said. "What are you imagining, Charlot? That the Society is so desperate for men that we hold them prisoner? Far from it, I assure you."

"Amaury is a nobleman. You're always looking for nobles, everyone knows that's why you have colleges. You—"

"We have colleges, you idiot, because we teach! Most of our students are not noble, and many are poor."

"Oh, yes, that's your public face. But I know more." He slapped at one of the big, braid-trimmed pockets on the front of his coat and glared triumphantly at Charles. "Much more."

"What do you mean?"

"You'll see." The little man's black eyes glittered as he leaned over the bed. "Did Amaury tell you that besides abandoning his military honor, he also abandoned his betrothed wife?" His voice rose with every question. "Or is he already too corrupted to care?"

"Betrothal is not marriage."

"If his father had been alive, he'd never have done it!"

"His father sounds like something of a tyrant."

"Tyrant! But of course you think so. Jesuits are always undermining true authority. And why? Because you want to be the only authorities!"

Charles sighed and let his eyes close. And suddenly remembered how he'd put an end to a shouting match with his cousin when he was ten years old. "Charlot," he said sweetly, eyes still shut, "go soak your head in the ox trough."

The swish of a cassock and the soft sound of footsteps on the rush matting came toward the bed. "I fear we don't have an ox trough," the rector's voice said. "But no matter, since you are leaving now, Monsieur de Vintimille du Luc. You can see that your cousin is tired and must rest."

Charles opened one eye enough to watch the confrontation.

Charles-François turned to stare at him. "Oh, yes, I'll leave you to your lies and secrets. But your time is short. Remember that." He strode down the row of beds, the rector on his heels.

Charles drifted into restless sleep. But he kept startling himself awake, thinking that his cousin was still talking at him. *Your time is short, you can't hide in your nest of lies and secrets. Remember that, remember . . .* The peasant woman pressed the musket's barrel hard into his back and the gathered soldiers egged her on. *Shoot, woman, he's a coward Jesuit . . .* Then Père Dainville was behind her, gazing sadly at him. There was a body at his feet, and Charles saw that it was the English scholastic Henry Wing. *How can I absolve you,* Dainville said, *until you stop the killing?*

"No," Charles cried, "he only fainted, he can't be dead!"

"Hush, lie still, you're dreaming."

Charles blinked up at Brunet, whose face was dim in the evening light as he slipped an arm under Charles's shoulders and lifted him enough to let him drink from the cup he held. "No, don't turn away, drink every drop. There, that's right."

Charles felt himself laid gently down again and then felt something blessedly cool on his forehead. Then the rector was there, shimmering in brilliant daylight.

"Why is he worse again?" Charles heard him say.

"The wound's more tainted than I'd thought. I've cleaned it again, and what I gave him will make him sleep. Sleep will help."

Charles dropped through the sound of murmured prayer back into blackness. He slept through the coming and going of light, woven inexplicably with dreams, voices, and people bending over him. Père Thomas Damiot came, and Père Jouvancy. At one point, he opened his eyes to find the English scholastic peering anxiously at him.

"You're not dead," Charles croaked, his mouth so dry he could hardly make words. "I told him so."

"Dead?" The pale blue eyes widened and the young man crossed himself. Then he looked over his shoulder and whispered in Charles's ear, "She said to tell you she's praying for you."

Charles turned his head from side to side on the pillow. "No. She wouldn't."

He fell back into sleep, where the woman who wouldn't pray for him, the woman with the musket, was waiting to curse him and the rest of the soldiers into the depths of hell. The next time he woke, the infirmary was dark except for the small sanctuary light on the altar. He lay staring at it, afraid to move in case the dream phantoms came at him again out of the night. Slowly he realized that the stab wound wasn't aching and that the air felt cool around him. He turned his head as light shone in the doorway of the infirmarian's small chamber.

"Frère Brunet?"

"Ah, you're better, *maître!*" He put a hand on Charles's forehead and nodded. "Thanks be to God, your fever broke near midnight, and your skin's still cool." Brunet put his candle down, lifted Charles on his arm, and held a cup to his lips. "Drink, you've sweated enough for a team of horses."

Charles drank gratefully and lay back again. "What day is it?"

"Monday morning. The clock just rang four."

"How long have I been here now?"

"Since Wednesday night."

Slowly, Charles pieced the days together. "My cousin was here."

Brunet nodded. "On Saturday. But then you grew worse again, so you probably don't remember much since then."

"Père Dainville? Is he buried?"

"He is. In Saint Louis, as near the altar as we could get him. With enough big white candles for the ceremony to chase away every shadow in the church."

"I wish I'd been there."

"I know. But he was greatly loved and he's gone where we all hope to go." Brunet sighed. "No need to worry for *him*, at least."

Charles look sharply at the infirmarian. "Are you worrying for someone else?"

Brunet frowned and folded his arms across his broad chest. "I don't know that I should tell you."

"*Mon frère!* You can't say so much and not tell me. Do you want me to lie here and worry and be on your hands longer than I might?"

"I'm thinking maybe you *should* stay here." Brunet's face was oddly grave. "But yes, fretting's bad for you, so I'll tell you. It's that scholastic."

"Wing?" Charles grabbed Brunet's sleeve. "The Englishman? What's happened to him?"

"No, no." Brunet tsked and patted his patient's hand. "Not him. Oh, what's the man's name? That one who's sour as a Spanish lemon."

Sour as a lemon? "Maître Richaud?" Charles said.

"That's him. He's disappeared. No one's seen him since Friday."

Chapter 10

THE FEAST OF ST. NARCISSE, WEDNESDAY, OCTOBER 29, 1687

Charles was still in the infirmary, but better than Frère Brunet had expected him to be so soon. The afternoon was mild, windless and sunny, and Brunet had let him out into the garden to sit on a sheltered bench. Charles leaned contentedly against the garden wall, listening to the sounds of the boarding students' after-dinner recreation coming from the Cour d'honneur. Though it was the day's quiet recreation hour, bursts of laughter and occasional shouts rose in the still air.

Then the sound of someone coming made him lean carefully forward to look along the side of the infirmary building. The Englishman, Maître Henry Wing, hurried through the garden and stopped in front of him, holding out a book.

"Are you better, Maître du Luc? I've brought your Saint Augustine. Someone came from the infirmary during dinner to say you needed it, and I was sent to bring it to you."

"Thank you, *maître*." Charles took the copy of extracts from *The Confessions* and laid it on the bench. Brunet had finally given him permission to read and he'd decided on St. Augustine, that saint's thought being less eye-crossing to follow than St. Thomas's. "Yes, I'm much better."

Without waiting to be invited, Wing plumped himself down on the bench beside the book. "I've been wondering where you come from? Your accent is strange."

Not stranger than yours, Charles thought, smiling at the Englishman. "I come from Languedoc. That's the south of France," he added, seeing that Wing was about to ask.

"Oh. I'm English, you know."

"Yes," Charles said, straight-faced. "I do know. From Saint Omer, I understand." He smiled ruefully. "I've been to Saint Omer."

"To the Jesuit college?"

"No. I fought in the Netherlands war. I was in the battle of Saint Omer in seventy-seven."

Openmouthed, Wing examined Charles from head to foot. "You fought?"

Charles nodded patiently.

The Englishman shook his head in astonishment. "So you were a *soldier*?"

Charles eyed Wing, wondering if he was slightly simpleminded. "Yes."

"I could never do that."

"You should thank God you've never had to."

"Oh, but He knows I couldn't. Everyone knows that. That's why I fainted after that man attacked you. I thought he was going to kill me, and I was too afraid even to run." Wing shrugged, and his smile returned. "My sisters are the brave ones in the family. I've always been a coward. I don't mind, but my father does."

It was Charles's turn to study his companion in astonishment. Wing had said he was a coward exactly as he'd said he was English, simply offering information. But of course, his Latin was heavily accented. Perhaps he hadn't said what Charles thought he'd heard.

"*What* did you say?"

Wing laughed merrily. "My Latin accent's as bad as yours, isn't it? I said I'm a coward." He looked up at the last yellow leaves on the chestnut tree towering over them. "What a beautiful day. I'd heard it rains all the time in Paris. Like in Saint Omer. And in Yorkshire, that's where my family lives. He sobered. "I miss them, but I was glad to leave England. Too many people hate Catholics there; it's very frightening. I thought that when we got King James, him being Catholic, it would all be better. It's not, but God must have a reason, don't you think? Maybe I'll understand more about it from studying theology. Did you know I'll be going with you to the Novice House on Wednesdays and Fridays for the Saint Augustine class? I went this past Friday with poor Maître Richaud." Wing leaned toward him. "Have you heard he's disappeared?"

"The infirmarian told me no one's seen him since Friday. So he disappeared after the two of you came back from the Novice House?"

"Yes. He left after dinner and never returned." Wing shuddered and looked around the garden. "I wonder if that man who attacked you got him. Do you suppose he's going around killing Jesuits?"

"If he is, he's going to be a very busy murderer." Wing missed the sarcasm, and his round face grew even more alarmed. Charles hurried to reassure him, "That was only my joke, *maître*. There's no reason to think that Maître Richaud's disappearance has anything to do with the man who attacked me." But there was equally no reason to assume it didn't, Charles thought. It was hard to imagine that Richaud, a stickler for the letter of every law, would have just walked away on his own. If someone else had lured or forced him away, that boded very ill for Richaud, indeed.

"Well," Wing said dubiously, "I hope you're right." He gave Charles a guilty look. "I shouldn't say this, since Maître Richaud may be dead, but I'm not at all sorry he won't be going with us to the Novice House."

"Why?"

"He made it clear that he doesn't approve of me. I think it was because of the girl."

Charles turned toward him on the bench and grimaced as his wound protested. "What girl?"

Wing reddened. "On the way to the Novice House, she— the girl, or young woman, I should say—came out of the book-shop, that one with the sign of the saint playing with the dog. She'd heard what happened to you in the chapel and she wanted to know how you were."

"She did?" Charles felt warmed and pleased. "A thin young woman with very dark blue eyes?"

"Almost blue-purple, yes. Aren't they pretty? She said she's been praying for you. But Maître Richaud was very angry with me because I stopped and answered her question. He went on and on about how wrong I was to let a young woman talk to me in the street. But I think it would have been very rude to ignore her," Wing said indignantly.

"It would indeed have been rude. Maître Richaud does not like women. And you weren't talking to her alone, he was right there with you. You did nothing wrong."

"No. I didn't really think I had. But being scolded always confuses me." Wing rose from the bench. "So do you think you'll be allowed to go to the Novice House on Friday? I don't want to go all that way alone like I did this morning! We could walk very slowly and I'd carry your satchel for you."

"That's kind. But it depends on Frère Brunet giving me leave."

"I'll pray he does! God bless your recovery."

The Englishman left and Charles went slowly back into the infirmary, his small store of energy gone. He put his book on the table beside his bed and was asleep almost before he was lying down. When he woke, bells were ringing for Vespers and the light was fading. As shadows gathered in the long room, he thought about Richaud and hoped that somewhere the crabbed scholastic was alive to watch the evening come.

Feet thumped down the stairs from the student infirmary, and Frère Brunet came in with a candle. "Evening's starting to rise so early now, I thought you'd like some light for your book, *maître*."

Charles pushed his pillows against the white plaster wall and slowly and carefully sat up against them. Brunet put the candle in a wall sconce above the bed and laid a hand on Charles's forehead.

"How do you feel?"

"Much better, *mon frère*. I was lying here wondering if there's any news of Maître Richaud."

"Not one little morsel. All anyone here knows is what Frère Martin's said a thousand times now, that Maître Richaud went out the postern door just after Friday's dinner—the boys were still playing in the courtyard. He told Frère Martin he had permission to go on an errand. But when the rector asked about that, no one had given him any permission."

"Do you think he's dead?" Charles said bluntly.

Brunet crossed himself. "I don't see what else there is to think. You know how he was about breaking rules. Everybody in the college—especially us lay brothers—knows, since he was always telling everyone exactly *how* they were breaking them." He gave Charles a sheepish look. "I shouldn't speak ill of him, since he might well be dead. But the man was a sore trial."

"You're not the only one who thinks so, *mon frère*. But I hope he's not dead." He grinned at Brunet. "Maybe God is just seeing to it that Maître Richaud has some—um—salutary experiences."

Brunet returned the grin. "I hope so, if he's coming back!" He went into his herb room beyond the altar, and Charles opened his Augustine. But instead of reading, he stared at the soft, worn pages and thought about Richaud, and about Wednesday night's attack. A dead intended novice, a nearly dead scholastic, and now a disappeared scholastic. Was it possible that someone actually was after random Jesuits? Charles gave up all pretense of reading and skeptically examined that thought. Jesuits had been hated for one thing and another almost since the Society's founding. Charles had never really understood why, except that they were a young order created for a new time and the church's new needs. They didn't live like most of the older orders, safely behind cloister walls. Nor did they wander like the old friars. Jesuits lived in colleges and Professed Houses and Novice Houses, working in the world, including the social and political world. Their presence in the political world angered many people. Charles himself disliked political tangles, but political life was human life, and wherever human souls were, there Jesuits *had* to be, if their work was to help souls. It was only logical. If God was everywhere, shouldn't his servants be everywhere, also?

But for more than a few Frenchmen and others, the answer to that was a resounding no. The sternly critical Jansenists, fellow Catholics, found the Society of Jesus too tolerant and lax in its teaching. The Gallicans, who wanted France and its church to be free of all non-French influence, accused Jesuits of wanting to put both church and king under the pope's thumb, and of being in every way too international. Some Gallicans carried their thinking to such an extreme that they seemed to think God Himself was French. Charles sighed and picked up his book again.

But when the bell rang for supper, he was reading the same page for the third time. He suddenly remembered the sentences that Père Quellier, the St. Augustine teacher, had quoted on Wednesday.

"The mind commands the body and the body obeys instantly."

Definitely true, because he'd told himself to pick up the book and open it, and he'd done exactly that.

"The mind commands itself and meets resistance."

Even more true, because he'd read the page in front of him three times without gleaning any idea of what it said. Well, he told himself, he hadn't read much, but he'd gotten some thinking out of his effort at studying. He looked up with relief as Père Brunet came bustling in with his supper. Brunet plunked the tray down on Charles's lap and they said the table grace and crossed themselves. Then Brunet cleared his throat and put his hands on his wide hips.

"I don't suppose you've heard the news," he said, obviously waiting for Charles to say no.

"What news?"

"Maître Richaud, God save him."

Charles put down his spoon and stared at Brunet. "Dead?"

"Seems so. Somebody found his cassock. Blood-soaked. The other side of the river, somewhere between the old temple and Saint Martin's abbey."

Looking in horror at each other, Charles and Brunet slowly crossed themselves.

"Why do they think it's his? There are plenty of Jesuits in Paris."

"Stands to reason, doesn't it? It's a Jesuit cassock and, so far as anyone knows, there's no other Jesuit missing in Paris. A monk of Saint Martin's found it this afternoon and took it to the Professed House. The Professed House rector knew, of course, that Maître Richaud had disappeared, and he sent the monk on here. Père Le Picart says that little tin medal of Saint Jacques Richaud wore on his rosary was with the cassock, though the other medal he wore, the little silver one of the Virgin, wasn't there. But silver—no one would leave that, would they?" Brunet shook his head. "Well, he's in God's hands. Eat, now, or you'll be on *my* hands for who knows how long!"

Charles started slowly on his bean and turnip soup, but he could hardly eat for thinking of Richaud. No matter how unloved, Richaud hadn't deserved this. Frère Brunet went on standing by his bed, seemingly lost in thought.

"Now what was it?" he said suddenly. "Armand? No. Grand? It was something like that, like the college's name." He frowned and ran his tongue around his teeth. "Almost like it, but something else."

"What are you talking about, *mon frère?*"

"What's happened to Maître Richaud. It's put me in mind of something else. A Jesuit that disappeared. Years ago now and I can't quite remember the name."

Charles broke a piece from his bread. "Do you mean Père Dainville's nephew?"

"That's it!" Brunet said in surprise. "How did you know?"

"Père Dainville mentioned him. That last day, on the way to Notre Dame des Champs. He said his nephew was never found."

"He wasn't. Went out from the Professed House one day

and never came back, never a bit of him found. Père Dainville hardly ever talked about it, but it haunted him, I know it did. Though it's mostly forgotten now. I'd never have thought of him myself except for what's happened to Maître Richaud. Ah, well." He shook his head and turned away. "Poor old lemon face."

Chapter 11

THE FEAST OF ST. FOLLIAN, FRIDAY, OCTOBER 31, 1687

Thursday was drenched in rain, but Friday dawned clear and mild and at midmorning, Frère Brunet reluctantly let Charles out of the infirmary.

"I want you back here after dinner. And mind you go *slow* to the Novice House. And let that Englishman carry your satchel. Understood?" He eyed the volume of St. Augustine. "Including that book under your arm. It's as big as a wheel of cheese and as heavy."

"Yes, *mon frère.*"

Charles started toward the vestibule, but Brunet fussed along beside him.

"And fasten your cloak, mild though the day is."

Charles fastened his cloak and pulled the outer door open. "*Oui, maman* Brunet."

Brunet tried to glower, but his mouth twitched toward laughter. "Go on, before I change my mind. And you'd best remember I've got a heavier hand on me than any *maman!*"

Thinking of his mother and doubting that, Charles made his way along the garden path and through the adjoining court to the Cour d'honneur. He felt almost well and heady with freedom at his escape from the sick chamber. Maître Henry Wing and Frère Martin were waiting for him at the postern door. Instead of opening it, Martin congratulated him on his recovery and showered him with admonitions to walk slowly and be warm and sit down if necessary. Wing put Charles's Augustine in the extra satchel he carried and slung it over his shoulder with his own. As Martin finally let them out into the street, Marie-Ange LeClerc, the baker's little girl, burst from the bakery door on the other side of the postern and nearly knocked Charles off his feet as she hugged him around the waist.

Charles winced, and Wing tried to pull her away. "No, don't, you'll hurt him!"

She let go of Charles's waist and clung like a crab to his sleeve. "Oh, *maître*, they said someone was dead, and I knew you were stabbed, and I thought it was you!"

Charles stroked her curly hair and pulled her little coif straight. "No, *ma petite*, far from dead, as you see." He gently disengaged himself. "I'm all right."

She looked somberly up at him. "But Père Dainville died. And that monk came with the bloody cassock. Other people have died; so could you."

Charles said in surprise, "You saw the cassock? But how? Why?"

"I didn't *see* it. It was in a bag. I was at the bakery door when the monk came to your postern, and I heard him tell Frère Martin what he had. It's Maître Richaud's cassock?"

"Perhaps," Charles said carefully, with a warning look at Wing.

"Do you think whoever killed him—the Jesuit who wore it—do you think he's the same one who stabbed you?"

Charles looked at the ten-year-old in dismay. Gossip had

moved even faster than he'd expected. "The police will have to find that out, Marie-Ange. It's nothing for you to worry about."

Her eyes told him what a stupid thing he'd just said. "Why shouldn't I worry when—"

"Marie-Ange, *what* are you doing?" Mme LeClerc hurried from the bakery. She grabbed her daughter by the back of her bodice and pulled her away from Charles. "Bothering Maître du Luc in this way—you are too big to behave like this! Dear Blessed Virgin! I tell her and I tell you, too, Marie-Ange, you make the baby Jesus weep! I'm sorry, *maître*, she knows better, but there, what they know and what they do are as far apart as light from dark." While Mme LeClerc talked, she retied her daughter's coif, repinned one side of her white apron bib to her blue bodice, and wet a finger to rub a smudge of flour off the little girl's cheek in the time-honored way of mothers. "And soon there will be another to worry about, as you know." The baker's wife gave a light slap to her belly, which swelled under the apron worn high beneath her breasts. "I've said it before and I say it again, be glad you're a Jesuit without children to plague you." But she hugged Marie-Ange tightly to her side as she said it.

Charles smiled at them both. "Madame, I hope you are well. We're praying for you and the baby in the college. But now I must go on my way or we'll be late."

But Mme LeClerc was frowning at Wing. "I've seen you passing. You're the Englishman," she said accusingly. She eyed Charles. "I heard you had one."

Wing, whose French was shakier than his Latin, looked uncertainly from her to Charles.

Charles didn't want to cope with the ancient tangle of French and English relations. "Maître Wing comes from our college of Saint Omer. He can't be trained as a Jesuit in England, you know, because they have no Catholic schools. English Catholics have a hard time now."

Torn between suspicion of an Englishman and sympathy for a Catholic bedeviled by Protestants, Mme LeClerc said grudgingly, "Then good luck to him. But you keep an eye on him, *maître*. What's his name?"

Wing understood that. "I am Maître Henry Wing, *madame*," he managed to say.

New suspicion flared in her brown eyes. "Henri? Henri?! Your parents named you that? Don't they know that Protestants are the fault of that English king Henri, the one who loved his cock more than he loved the church? If he hadn't wanted one new wife after the other, there wouldn't *be* any Protestants, now would there?"

"Oh, but, *madame*, yes, there would," Wing said earnestly. "*Our* Protestants are King Henry's fault, but *yours* here in France are the fault of a Frenchman, Jean Calvin."

Marie-Ange had wiggled from under her mother's arm and was squinting up at Wing, trying to understand his French. "You mean Monsieur Calvin wanted a new wife, too?"

Swallowing laughter, Charles said firmly, "No, Marie-Ange, there are other reasons for being Protestant. But we must go now or we'll be late."

Mme LeClerc's face softened. "*Maître*," she said to Charles, "we are all sorry you've lost the good Père Dainville. And that other one, whose cassock they brought to you," she added punctiliously. "But Père Dainville—" Her eyes glistened as she smiled. "I think everyone in the *quartier* loved him. He was a saint. Once, years ago, just before this daughter of mine was born, he came by our shop and saw me trying to lift a basket of bread to the counter. I was so big with child I couldn't bend over. He was already old then, but he came into the shop and set me aside without a word and lifted it for me. He was always doing things like that—oh, not just for me, for everyone."

Charles thought of the people in the chapel on Wednesday night, watching with Père Dainville's body and praying for him. "I know. He was greatly loved."

Mme LeClerc nodded. "That other one, though—well, the *bon Dieu* alone knows the heart, but I don't think that his heart was much use to anyone." She eyed Charles. "Or to himself," she said shrewdly. "For that one, women were the snakes in Eden, I am certain he never even—"

The baker's voice drowned out whatever she was going to say. "Beatriiiice! Marie-Aaaange! Are you going to let the devil make a suburb of hell in the oven and burn the brioche?"

"Oh, holy saints, and he was finally asleep, you know how he works all night!" She ran into the shop, pulling Marie-Ange with her.

Charles and Wing went on up the hill, and Charles was shocked to find how breathless he was after the short slope between the bakery and the turn onto the rue des Cordeliers. He halted by the building wall across from The Saint's Dog. "I need a moment to breathe, *maître*. I'm more unmanned than I knew."

The narrow street was full of black gowns: short-gowned University students and long-gowned professors coming and going from the Sorbonne's west entrance around the corner beyond where the Jesuits stood. Carriage drivers roared warnings to pedestrians and to carriages coming from the opposite way, Cordeliers being wide enough for only one equipage at a time. After the infirmary's quiet, Charles felt stunned by the din of voices, feet, wheels, and hooves ricocheting off the tall stone and timber houses along the street.

Wing stood between him and the traffic, anxiously searching Charles's face.

"It's all right," Charles said, grateful but feeling like he'd traded one nursemaid for another. "I'm only weak after so many days in bed."

The Sorbonne's chapel bell rang the quarter hour and Wing peered at Charles. "Can you walk now, *maître*? I don't think Père Quellier will be forgiving if we're late."

Charles, who was watching the stream of short-cloaked men going in and out of The Dog, grunted agreement. "I wonder if some new book's just out," he said, as he made his feet start walking again. "They're doing a brisk business over there."

"Could we stop and see on the way back?"

"Well—we shouldn't—" Charles looked at Wing's eager face. "But perhaps we could. Do you have any money?"

"A little. Left from my journey from Saint Omer. Père Le Picart said I might need to buy a book or two for my studies."

"Well, if you'll excuse my saying so, I noticed when we spoke with Madame LeClerc, that your French is—um—a little hard to understand. There's a new book just out, called *The Art of Good Pronunciation*, by a Monsieur Hindret. I saw it several weeks ago in The Golden Sun—that's another bookshop down toward the river. We could see if The Dog has it. You might find it useful."

"Oh, I'd like that! French is the hardest thing I've ever tried to learn. Why do you have so many letters no one ever pronounces? I mean, how in God's name does anyone here ever learn to spell?"

Charles laughed. "I'm no expert, I grew up speaking mostly Provençal. But I'm told that those letters we don't pronounce now used to be pronounced a long time ago."

"But then, why are you saving them? Why not just drop them?"

They talked about language the rest of the way to the Novice House. They were very nearly late, but Père Quellier had heard about the attack on Charles and didn't seem to mind. He asked Charles politely if he was well and then plunged into the session. Wing proved a much more congenial fellow student than Richaud had been, and Charles felt a new respect for the round little Englishman's mind. He was outwardly timid—though sometimes as blunt as a child—but he was sure of himself in debate and bold in his thinking and questioning. Charles could see that Père Quellier was pleased with his new pupil. When they stood to take their leave, the priest clapped Wing approvingly on the shoulder before turning to Charles with questions about the attack in the chapel and about Richaud.

"We heard about the attack on you almost at once. And then Maître Wing and poor Maître Richaud said more about it on Friday. And now Maître Richaud is gone." Charles noticed that Quellier didn't say dead. "I thank God," Quellier continued, "that you are recovering so well. But many in this house are wondering if the man who attacked you was the same man who killed our poor Paul Lunel. And if the same man has abducted and apparently killed Maître Richaud."

"Why do you say 'apparently'?" Wing asked him.

"Because," Quellier said, turning a professorial eye on Wing, "his cassock and rosary were found, but so far as I know, his body has not been. You must always examine the logic of your assumptions."

Charles was thinking about Paul Lunel. "Père Quellier, many of us—many Jesuits—are thinking that Monsieur Paul Lunel's murder, and the attack on me, and Maître Richaud's disappearance have happened because we are—or almost were—Jesuits. If I may ask, have you ever heard anything about Monsieur Lunel or his family that might make someone want him dead for reasons that have nothing to do with the Society of Jesus?"

Quellier frowned, considering Charles's question. "No, I don't think so. His father, who died last spring, was a judge in the *Parlement* of Paris. He had great respect for the Society, but his widow does not. The family town house is in the rue Jean Tison across the river, near Saint Germain-l'Auxerrois." He looked thoughtfully at Charles. "What about Maître Richaud? Is his family from Paris?"

"I believe so. But I don't know for certain."

"Well, I will continue to pray that he is alive and will return to Louis le Grand."

With remonstrances to keep their wits about them on the way home, Quellier opened the study door. "Oh, Maître Wing," he said, as they went out, "you are to come on Tuesday morning to make up the Saint Augustine sessions that Maître du Luc and Maître Richaud attended before you joined us. And we will have to find a time for you also, Maître du Luc, to make up what you missed during your recovery."

The scholastics went down the stairs to the long gallery. As they passed its tall windows, Charles looked out at the garden, hoping to catch a glimpse of Amaury de Corbet. But the young men walking and murmuring to themselves as they memorized passages from their studies were too alike in their cassocks and hats to be recognized from a distance. A lay brother let them out into the street. As he started to close the door, a black-coated boy of thirteen or so dove between Charles and Wing and slipped inside like an eel. The door banged shut on the lay brother's sharp admonishment and the boy's indignant protest.

"I wonder who that was?" the Englishman said, looking at the door.

"One of the young lay servants," Charles said. "Didn't you have them at your novitiate? They're poor boys hired for menial tasks, who get lodging and food and some teaching in return."

He looked back over his shoulder, wondering suddenly if the boy could be the one La Reynie had mentioned, the son of one of his servants.

"Oh. Yes, we had them at my Novice House, I'd forgotten." He looked happily up at Charles. "That was a very good class, didn't you think?"

Charles agreed, and they started down the dusty rue du Pot-de-Fer, unpaved beneath the trees leaning over high garden walls. Two small boys with feathers in their hats passed on sedate ponies, a groom walking between them and keeping a firm hand on the reins. A cart full of rosy bricks trundled by on its way to a building site, and several servants were coming back from the nearby market with full baskets. At the mouth of a narrow lane between tall stone houses, barking dogs, a girl's distressed voice, and raucous male laughter made Charles and Wing stop and look down the lane toward the noise. A slender woman in a black and green gown was backing away from two men in workmen's rough woven coats and breeches, who were closing on her with taunts and grins. From behind a garden wall, a small dog was barking hysterically at the voices.

"Leave her alone!" Charles strode down the lane, leaving Wing standing in the street and begging him to come back.

Charles managed to get between one of the men and his quarry, but the other had the girl by the wrist. As she cursed and tried to pull away, her thick green scarf fell away from her dark hair, and Charles saw her face and recognized Mlle Rose Ebrard. The man he'd thwarted ran at him, and Charles shifted slightly and stuck out a foot. The man fell flat, the breath knocked out of him.

"Leave her, I said!" Charles thundered at the second man and drew himself to his six feet and more, feeling how tired he was and how sore his back still was, and praying that his size would be intimidation enough and he wouldn't have to grapple further with either of his opponents. To his relief, the man holding the girl let her go. Then he helped his fellow up, cursing Jesuits in general and Charles's private parts in particular.

Charles drew the girl away and hurried her back to the street, hoping he could finish this heroic little rescue without falling on his face from exhaustion. But even more, he wondered what Mlle Ebrard had been doing alone in the lane.

"Are you all right, *mademoiselle*?" Charles said, halting to catch his breath as they reached Wing. "Walking down a narrow deserted way like that is unwise for a woman out alone in Paris. Unwise even for a man, at night."

Rose Ebrard readjusted her scarf in silence. She seemed embarrassed, and as wary of the two Jesuits as of the men who'd accosted her. Charles wondered again what she'd been doing. Surely she wasn't afraid of him and Wing, especially with Wing fussing like a nurse with a nursling.

"Oh, *mademoiselle*, you must have been so frightened!" the Englishman said, hovering close but not daring to touch her. "I thank the Blessed Virgin you're safe. I *always* tell my sisters she won't forsake them, and it's true! Here, lean on me," he begged, in a sudden burst of daring. "I'll explain to my superiors."

"For the *bon Dieu's* sake, stop fussing!" she said, waving him away.

Wing's face fell. "Oh. Was I? I'm sorry." He gazed wistfully at her. "Forgive me, *mademoiselle*, I always think people are as frightened as I would be."

"Never mind." With an obvious effort, she smiled at him. "You're right, I was frightened." She glanced gravely at Charles and he saw that she meant it. "Thank you both for helping me."

"Where were you going?" Charles asked.

"Where? Oh, I thought the lane was a shortcut. To the market."

"That lane's a dead end. The nearest market's back the other way. Toward the Foire Saint Germain, where the roads come together."

"Is it?" She shrugged at him. "I seem to have lost myself, then. But I'm new here, I still don't know where things are."

"So am I, *mademoiselle*," Wing said. "I find Paris most confusing."

"It is, isn't it? Well, since I've missed my way to the market, I should go home now. May I walk back with you? If you're going back to the rue Saint Jacques, that is."

"Of course you may," Wing said eagerly, and the three began walking slowly toward the rue de Vaugirard, Mlle Ebrard in the middle.

Glad for his hat brim shading his face, Charles eyed her empty market basket. "But won't your aunt scold you for not bringing back whatever it is you were going to buy? Of course, there's a much closer market on the rue Saint Jacques by the old wall. Just steps from The Dog."

"Oh, yes, I know." Her blue-purple eyes were wide and guileless. "But my aunt wanted needles. She said the best needles are at the Saint Germain market."

"I see," Charles said. "Are you sure you don't need to go and find them?" Needles, he was thinking. A quick-witted choice of something a pair of celibate men might know nothing about. But Jesuits learned to mend small tears in their clothing when they were novices, and Charles knew that it was the needles at the market by the old St. Jacques gate, not the St. Germain market, that were some of the best in Paris.

"Your aunt should send a maid with you," Wing was telling

her earnestly. "At home, my mother would never let my sisters go out alone when we went to York."

"My aunt is not rich. She has few servants. I think the book business is not doing as well as it was when my uncle was alive."

"Which reminds me, we want to stop at The Dog and buy a book," Charles said. "A small help, but a little something."

"You'll be welcome, *maître*." She looked ahead of them. "That's the rue de Vaugirard we're coming to, isn't it?" Her voice took on a mocking tone. "Since it's a busier street, shall I walk meekly aside? Or behind you? Otherwise, it may look like the two of you are wandering the streets with a woman."

Charles wondered at the sudden bitterness of her words. "We aren't required to shun women, you know."

"I know. Forgive me." She sighed and her long black lashes veiled her eyes. Then she looked up at him. "How often do you come to the Novice House? Do you go to visit someone there?"

"We go on Wednesdays and Fridays, *mademoiselle*," Wing said, eager to offer her something she would like, even a mundane answer to her question. "Not to visit, to study Saint Augustine."

"How did you know we were at the Novice House, *mademoiselle*?" Charles said absently, feigning absorption in watching three men throwing dice.

Her eyes flashed at him blue and sudden as a kingfisher. "Someone told me the Novice House was there. So I just assumed that's where you'd been." She turned to Wing. "Saint Augustine is the one who prayed for chastity, is he not?" she said, smiling into his eyes.

Wing gulped and blushed to the roots of his fair hair.

Charles bit his lip to hide his grin and keep from further embarrassing the Englishman. "Why do you ask about that prayer in particular?" he said mildly. "Does it seem to you a bad idea?"

"That depends on who is praying."

"But, *mademoiselle*," Wing said, "should we not all—" He yelped and skipped nimbly aside as two dogs in his path began quarreling over a bone.

"No," Mlle Ebrard said tartly, as though he'd finished his sentence, "Not all of us should."

Wing stared at her in confusion.

"Chastity is not the same as celibacy, you know, *mademoiselle*," Charles said.

"True." She blushed and walked faster.

Charles's questions were multiplying with every word she said. Matching her pace, he asked mildly, "Did you see that boy who just made it to the Novice House door as we came out? He nearly knocked us over."

"What's that you say? This traffic is making it hard to hear, I think." She made a business of shifting her empty basket to her other arm and walked a little faster.

The rue de Vaugirard was indeed full of noise. Peasants walking and driving two-wheeled farm carts were on their slow, tired way back to their villages after bringing goods to market before dawn. A religious procession in honor of St. Follian, whose day it was, made its way toward the city gate, the saint bucking on his canopied platform as the chanting clergy who carried him tried to avoid puddles and dung. Charles and his companions crossed themselves as the procession passed, then jumped back against a wall as two young riders turned out of a side street and galloped through the congestion, using their riding whips to clear a path. The priests stopped chanting and bellowed heaven's curses after them.

"Saint Follian?" Wing said doubtfully, when procession and pedestrians had sorted themselves out. "I don't think we have him in England."

"All I remember about him," Charles said, "is that robbers killed him and he lay unfound for months. Why that made him a saint, I don't know."

"That's like poor Maître Richaud," Wing said. "Since someone must have waylaid him."

"I doubt our Maître Richaud will be made a saint for it," Charles responded, watching Mlle Ebrard, who was walking ahead of them now, as straight-backed as a soldier. The servant boy he'd asked her about had come running from the rue du Pot-de-Fer, the road in front of the Novice House. The dead-end lane where they'd found her was only steps from the Novice House, and the rue du Pot-de-Fer was the only way into that lane. When Charles had asked her about the running servant boy, she'd avoided his question, but he was willing to bet that she'd not only seen the boy, she'd seen him and Wing come out of the Novice House, and that she'd turned down the lane to avoid them.

Post hoc was not *propter hoc*—one thing coming immediately after another didn't mean that the two things were connected. But it also didn't mean that they weren't. But *if* they were, what had she been doing on the road in front of the Novice House? And why would she try to avoid him and Wing?

Chapter 12

When they reached The Dog, Mlle Rose Ebrard stopped. "Do you still want to come in and buy your book?"

Charles looked at Wing, who nodded eagerly, and the three of them crossed the rue St. Jacques to the bookshop. As they mounted the few steps to the open door, they were assailed by what sounded like a score of small tapping hammers, a landslide of small rocks, and a woman's exasperated cries.

"You cursed little *pigs! Now* look what you've done!"

"Oh, Blessed Virgin, not again." Mlle Ebrard cast her eyes up and ran to the foot of a narrow staircase at the back of the shop.

The sound of little hammers grew louder as two brown and white goats clattered down the stairs and slipped past her. A half dozen more followed and fanned out in the shop, nibbling at paper and books and customers' coat skirts. A furious woman flew down the stairs after them, black ribbons flying from her headdress and her skirts gathered recklessly high. With a shriek, she caught one of the goats by its scruff.

"Give me that, you little devil!"

Charles saw that the goat had torn a page from a book dropped by a startled customer. Shaking the goat, the woman pulled at the paper until the goat swallowed it and bit her. She shrieked and let go her hold, and the goat ran out of the shop, bleating indignantly. As she stood huffing and nursing her finger, a tattered elderly woman appeared on the stairs, white hair flying around her coif as she brandished a stout stick.

"Leave my beauties be, you old plague!" The goatherd thumped down the stairs and started gathering the rest of her herd.

Charles and Wing, along with two other customers who had prudently gathered their coat skirts close, stayed where they were against the walls. Two small goats, one white and one pie-bald, came to examine the Jesuits. One nibbled at Wing's cassock and the other, with something already in its mouth, stretched its neck toward Charles. He rescued the appalled Wing from the white goat's attentions and was gently pushing away the one delicately tasting his own skirts, when the goatherd reached them and smacked the piebald goat smartly on its rump. Startled, it dropped what was already in its mouth and leaped to join its fellows at the shop doorway.

Charles picked up what the goat had dropped and saw that it was a piece of cheap brown leather. Part of a book cover, he realized, seeing letters stamped on the leather. *Cabine* was all that was readable. He looked thoughtfully at the stairs. The goats had been upstairs, and booksellers often kept their more questionable stock—pornography, usually—on the floor above the open shop. He looked at the other two customers, wondering if they'd been up there before he came in. One of them had gone back to browsing the tables, but the other was unhappily examining his coat front. Mlle Ebrard was listening resignedly to her scolding aunt. The older woman stalked back up the stairs and the girl started toward Charles, but was stopped by the customer frowning at his coat, who complained loudly that a goat had eaten one of his buttons. Charles quickly slipped the torn piece of book cover into the breast of his cassock in case it had come from upstairs. No reason to embarrass the girl. What her aunt sold wasn't her fault.

Wing sidled closer to Charles. "Why were those goats in here, *maître?*"

"Ah. Right. You said you grew up in the country."

"Yes. We didn't have goats. We had cows. But not in the house. And certainly not upstairs!"

"The goatherd was delivering milk to the bookstore owner, who lives upstairs."

Mlle Ebrard, who had joined them and heard what Charles said, burst out laughing. "Goats like to climb, Maître Wing. Which means that city people who want fresh goat's milk can get it easily, without going down and up the stairs themselves. They call out from a window and the goatherd drives the goats upstairs, milks one, and drives them down again. My aunt— Madame Cheyne—uses goat's milk on her face, she thinks it's good for her complexion." She cast a dark look at the stairs. "But it's not. Now, what book did you want?"

"Monsieur Hindret's new book on French pronunciation," Charles said.

She went to a table against the wall, sorted through the scatter of books on it, and brought back a small, cheaply bound volume. Wing dug coins from his nearly empty travel purse, she gave him the book, and he and Charles took their leave. At the door, a pair of men coming in shoved their way rudely past the two Jesuits. Wing protested, but Charles hushed him and watched the men go straight to the stairs.

"I would have moved aside; they had only to ask," Wing said indignantly, as they went down the steps. "The old one caught me on the ankle bone with his stick! Why do you suppose they went up there?" His pink face cleared. "Oh. Do you suppose they went to get some of the goat's milk?"

Charles looked to see if he was joking, but the little Englishman was serious. "I doubt it's goat's milk they're after. If you'd give me your arm, *maître*, I'd be grateful. I'm very tired."

They went slowly down the hill, and when they reached the college, Charles rang the bell with relief.

"Your Monsieur La Reynie's been here," Frère Martin said to Charles as he closed the door behind them. "And from what I hear," he murmured, glancing at Wing and dropping into French, "he's put the fox among the chickens. I'd keep my head down, if I were you, *maître*."

"Why? It's not my fox."

"And when did the chickens ever care whose fox it is?"

The bell began to clang for dinner as the two scholastics went through the street passage. As they turned toward the fathers' refectory, Charles saw that Wing was frowning, his lips shaping words as he walked.

"What were you talking about?" he said in Latin. "Do we have chickens at Louis le Grand?"

"I have a feeling I'm the chickens," Charles said, and urged the bewildered Wing up the refectory steps.

The fox, at least, was not in the refectory, and Charles ate the lentil stew with an appetite. But by the end of the meal he was so tired, he thought he might simply fall on his face in his plate and go to sleep. He was glad Frère Brunet had ordered him to return to the infirmary. Wing walked him there, saw him inside, and put his satchel beside the bed. Before Wing reached the infirmary door, Charles was stretched out and asleep. It seemed to him that he'd only just closed his eyes when Brunet woke him.

"I'm sorry, *maître*, I told him you needed the rest, but no, he says, you have to go to him now. When they're done with you, you're to come straight back here, do you understand?"

Blinking, Charles got up from the bed and ran his hands through his hair. "When who's done with me?"

"The rector and whoever's with him in his office." He twitched Charles's wrinkled cassock so it hung straight. "Smooth your hair down. There."

He shoved Charles's outdoor hat into his hand and Charles, trying to wake up, trudged out into the bright afternoon. Midday recreation was still going on in the main courtyard, and he had to pick his way among boys sitting on the grass around its edges, reading and playing board games. As he tripped over a game of French Kings and sent two of the counters flying out into the gravel, a pair of his former students came running across the gravel calling his name, in spite of the proctors.

"*Maître*, you're well!" Walter Connor, wry and black-haired and Irish, skidded to a stop in front of Charles, grinning from ear to ear.

"We've been very worried," Armand Beauclaire said earnestly, arriving behind him. He pushed his thick brown hair out of his eyes and peered at Charles. "But they wouldn't let us into the infirmary. Who attacked you? Did you see him?"

"I don't know who it was, and no, I didn't see his face," Charles said carefully, wondering how much gossip they'd heard. And spread. "But you needn't worry. Our doors are even better guarded now."

"Oh, we're not worried," Connor said. "We hope he *will* come back, so we can catch him!"

"Don't be silly," Beauclaire said. "Maître du Luc was a musketeer, if he couldn't catch him, how could we?"

"I could try," Connor said stubbornly.

Beauclaire smiled wistfully at Charles. "We miss you in the

rhetoric class, *maître*. But Père Jouvancy says you'll help with the summer ballet, is that right? I hope so, because it will be my last one before I finish here."

"I will certainly be helping with it," Charles said. "I trust that Père Jouvancy is putting in good parts for both of you as he writes the ballet *livret!* And I'll tell you something I've already told Père Jouvancy—the company of the learned saints I'm reading these days doesn't make up for the lack of your rhetoric class's company."

"We're better company than saints?" Connor bowed ironically. "My father will like to hear that!"

"But he won't believe it," Beauclaire told him, and they shoved at each other, laughing, while Charles tried to keep from his face how much he missed them and missed teaching.

"I'm sorry, *messieurs*, but I'm expected elsewhere. Go back to your games, there's still some time. God and Our Lady keep you."

Charles's smile faded as he went toward the main building's back door, wondering what was so urgent that he couldn't finish his nap. When he reached the *grand salon*, he stood for a moment outside the rector's door, gathering his wits and listening to the murmur of voices beyond the oak planks. Then he knocked, was bidden to enter, and went in to find Père Le Picart and a Jesuit he'd never seen sitting on either side of the empty fireplace.

"Come and stand here, Maître du Luc." Le Picart's face was expressionless.

Charles stood between the chairs, where both men could see and speak to him easily.

"Père Paradis," Le Picart said to the stranger, "this is Maître Charles du Luc."

Hands folded at his waist, Charles bowed.

"This is Père Alain Paradis, *maître*. He is assistant to the superior of our Paris Province."

Charles's eyes widened. A high-ranking official from the Provincial's office who wanted to see him? Trying not to show how much that thought alarmed him, Charles bowed again and the youngish, olive-skinned Jesuit slightly inclined his head. His beak-nosed face gave away nothing, though the narrow black eyes were bright with interest. For a long, uncomfortable moment, no one spoke. Charles licked his dry lips and looked at Le Picart, whose sigh was visible but unheard.

"You have been the subject of some discussion these last days," Le Picart said.

Charles's heart sank as he went hastily through the list of his sins. This summons would not be about a minor sin, and he couldn't think of any recent major sins.

"You may remember my telling you in the infirmary," the rector went on, "that Lieutenant-Général La Reynie said he was going to Fontainebleau."

"Yes, *mon père*," Charles said, even more mystified. "I remember."

"We now know why he went." Le Picart looked at Charles as though Charles had just announced he was becoming a Protestant. "The *lieutenant-général* has asked the king to request the Society of Jesus to authorize your help in finding the man who killed Paul Lunel. And who, as Monsieur La Reynie thinks, attacked you—and possibly our missing Maître Richaud as well. The king approved his request and asked Père La Chaise to pass it on to the Provincial for approval. Which he did, and which brings Père Paradis here."

Trying to hide his welter of feelings at this news, Charles

stared down at his folded hands. He was furious at La Reynie for recalling him to the king's notice. But he was also straining at the leash to be let loose to hunt the killer. Schooling his face, he raised his eyes to meet the scrutiny of the two men.

"May I ask if a decision has been reached, *mon père?*"

Le Picart sighed and nodded to Paradis. "Explain to him, please."

To Charles's surprise, the Provincial's assistant smiled slightly. "Père Le Picart has met with our Provincial about this matter. There are many questions here. First, you are not a fully professed member of the Society. You are only a scholastic, still in formation, and it is highly irregular for someone in your position to be allowed to do what the king has asked. In the normal course of things, someone in your position should not have come to the king's attention at *all*."

Charles started to defend himself, but Paradis held up a warning hand. "I know what you have done in the past to help Lieutenant-Général La Reynie. I also know why you came to the king's attention—I know what happened at Marly last summer and why it happened."

Charles kept quiet. The king had ordered those present on that June night at the palace of Marly to say nothing—ever—of what had happened. Lieutenant-Général La Reynie knew what had taken place because he'd been there. And the rector knew, because Charles and La Reynie had told him. And also because the king had written to Le Picart and sent a substantial gift to the college.

Paradis went on, "I know that you did not seek the king's attention last June. Nonetheless, the Marly event and the fact that you have assisted the chief of the Paris police on other occasions, all within not much more than a year, have given you something of a reputation for seeking notoriety. As your rector has already told you, that could compromise your future. Self-aggrandizement is not an acceptable trait in a Jesuit."

"Self-aggrandizement, *mon père?*" Charles said quietly. "The first time I helped the police, I was threatened into it by Lieutenant-Général La Reynie. On the two other occasions, I had permission from my Jesuit superiors."

"Permission perhaps somewhat after the fact, as I understand it."

Charles was silent.

"However, to be fair," Paradis went on, "we also know that you have proved yourself unusually good at discovering . . . things. And that you are trustworthy and discreet."

That surprised Charles into a startled look at the rector, which Paradis pretended not to see.

"We could have referred the king's request to Rome," the assistant Provincial said. "Which can be tantamount to burying it, even though it comes from King Louis. But we have not done that because there are worthwhile reasons to consider on the king's side of the question." Paradis looked at Le Picart, who took up the narrative.

"Like all of us, you are well aware, *maître*, that there are factions, especially in Paris, that not only dislike the Society of Jesus, but actually see us as threats to the French church. But the king sees us as *guardians* of the church and the throne, and he hates disorder almost as much as he hates any threat to his power. He has learned that there is a new wave of extreme Gallicanism in Paris, especially in the legal professions—the nobility of the Robe, as they like to call themselves. They have become even more strident about saving France from all non-French influence. At least, that's how they see their efforts."

That phrase, the nobility of the Robe—meaning the group of astute men who bought and held important legal positions as high-level notaries, lawyers, and judges—brought Père Dainville and his story of refusing to go into the law vividly to mind for Charles.

"And so, these Gallicans cannot seem to grasp," Le Picart was saying, "that our Jesuit obedience to the pope does not make us any less loyal to France and the French king." The rector shook his head in exasperation. "As I'm sure you know, there are, indeed, Jesuit Gallicans! They are reliable men who understand that the pope wields political power that can be misused." Le Picart and Paradis exchanged knowing looks. "I have never heard," Le Picart went on, "that papal infallibility covers politics. These Gallican gentlemen even say that the Society of Jesus is a threat because its men are from all over the world. It offends and frightens them that French Jesuit institutions could have Italian or German rectors. The Gallicans even believe that if Père La Chaise were to die, we would force a Spanish Jesuit on the king as his confessor. Never mind that everyone knows very well that French monarchs choose their own confessors! But our Gallicans see Spain as the source of all evil, and they're convinced that Jesuits work for the king of Spain as much as for the pope." Le Picart shrugged unhappily. "I suppose some of that is because our founder, Saint Ignatius, was Spanish. There are always men who see conspiracy in every pot."

Paradis spread his long slender fingers on the arms of his chair. "You must be wondering why we are telling you all this, *maître*. Père La Chaise has told us that the king is afraid that this murder and these attacks on Jesuits might be seen by the public as part of this new Gallican unrest. He fears that would feed the unrest always simmering here in Paris. The king wants the killer quietly found and quickly executed. And the same for the man who perpetrated the attacks, if the killer of Paul Lunel is not responsible for those."

Charles waited, hardly breathing.

"So." Le Picart sighed heavily. "Père Paradis has informed me that our Provincial, the head of our administrative province, wishes you to do what His Majesty has asked." He sounded as though he were informing Charles of an incurable illness. "As for your Jesuit future, I simply do not know. We will work that out somehow." He shifted unhappily in his chair. "You know that I see and even applaud the talent you have for uncovering wrongdoing. It is a talent that might even indicate your future, if we had a place for it. But we do not."

"*Mon père*, do not make it sound worse than it is," Paradis said briskly. He leaned toward Charles. "If notoriety dogs your future Jesuit path, Maître du Luc, you might consider the missions. Those assignments are normally coveted plums, but I think something might be arranged."

Charles coveted a mission appointment like he coveted being chased by Turks while riding a lame mule. "Could it at least be a mission to somewhere warm?" he blurted unhappily, before he could stop himself.

To his surprise, Paradis smiled. "I think we can find you a warm mission, if it comes to it."

"And there's something else we must remember," the rector said, suddenly leaning forward in his chair. "Before we consign Maître du Luc's future to the other side of some ocean, let us remember that Jesuits often act for their monarchs. Yes, I know," he said, glancing at Paradis's frown, "professed Jesuits, not scholastics. Nonetheless, that is worth keeping in mind. I've even heard that during a crisis in Germany, a Jesuit went briefly about the ruler's business in disguise, dressed like a courtier! And did the Society throw him out? Or exile him to Tibet? No! Were the ruler and the man's superiors and even His Holiness grateful? Yes! We are to find God in *all* things, and politics are part of God's world. So why should political necessities make us act like a gaggle of old virgins afraid of the touch of a man's sleeve?"

He crossed his arms militantly and sat back.

Charles bowed, amused by the image, but moved by Le Picart's obvious concern for him.

"Unusually well said, *mon père*," Paradis's eyes danced, but his face was very straight. "Though we must also remember that anxious virgins often turn out to be wise virgins. There were some in the Society who loudly questioned what the German Jesuit did. But I agree that guiding a realm to justice is something like guiding souls. Risks must be taken."

Le Picart was looking gravely at Charles. "Père Paradis and I have spoken much. What would *you* say to the king's request, if your own response were all that mattered?"

Charles's mouth was suddenly so dry that his tongue stuck to his teeth when he tried to speak. He tried again. "I would wish to obey the king."

Le Picart, well aware of Charles's dislike of Louis, raised a skeptical eyebrow.

"I would also wish to obey my Jesuit superiors," Charles replied to the eyebrow.

"To my ear," Paradis said mildly, "both of those wishes sound rather tepidly felt."

"They are not tepidly felt, *mon père*," Charles said carefully. "But I have also another reason for wanting the killer found. It was most likely seeing the body of poor young Paul Lunel that caused Père Dainville's apoplexy and death. Père Dainville was my confessor and a man greatly loved."

Paradis said, "What about the attack on you? And your missing fellow scholastic? It seems very possible, even likely, that the same man is responsible. Is that not also part of your desire to bring him to justice? Wanting vengeance is very human."

Charles looked bleakly at his superiors. "Part of me wants vengeance, yes. But I've been a soldier, I've killed men and they've tried to kill me. What I truly want is justice. Simply exacting a death for a death only creates more death."

Le Picart and Paradis traded looks and Le Picart closed his eyes briefly. Then he opened them and said, "Very well. As your immediate superior, I tell you that in response to the king's request, you are assigned to assist Lieutenant-Général La Reynie when and if he asks for your help. Especially in questioning our men in the Novice House and here in the college. You will do only what being a Jesuit allows you to do more quietly—and perhaps thoroughly—than the police. You may be present when Jesuits or their families are being questioned. Though neither you nor Lieutenant-Général La Reynie may say to anyone that you have been authorized by the Society to help the police. You will act only when La Reynie asks you for help. Understood?" His gray eyes were like steel.

"Understood, *mon père*."

"When La Reynie does require your help, you have leave to come and go as necessary. However, you will not compromise your vows, or neglect your studies or other responsibilities. You will talk to no one except myself, Père Paradis, and Lieutenant-Général La Reynie about what you are doing. If a Jesuit questions you, send him to his superior. If anyone else questions you, refuse an answer. So. That is what you are asked to do," Le Picart said. "But you know that a Jesuit may refuse an order he considers immoral. Therefore I ask you plainly, will you do this? Think before you speak."

"I don't need to think, *mon père*. I will do this."

All three sighed, whether in relief or resignation, Charles

was beyond knowing. He swayed a little on his feet and the rector's face furrowed with compunction.

"Bring that stool, *maître*. I should have remembered that you are still recovering."

Charles had hoped for dismissal, but he went to the small stool a little beyond Paradis's chair and picked it up. As he bent, the piece of book cover he'd taken up from the floor in The Dog slid from the breast of his cassock. Paradis leaned forward and picked it up.

As Charles put the stool down where he'd been standing, he saw that Paradis was frowning and turning the scrap of leather over in his hands. Then he looked hard at Charles, with no spark of friendliness in his face.

"Where did you get this?"

"I picked it up from the floor of a bookshop up the street. Maître Wing bought a book, *mon père*," he said to Le Picart, "on our way back from the Novice House."

Paradis said, "This was just lying on the floor?"

Charles told him about the goats. "I put that little piece into my cassock to throw away. I thought it might be from the cover of something illicit being sold upstairs, since that's where the goat had obviously gotten it." He looked at Le Picart. "I thought that if Mademoiselle Ebrard saw it, she might be embarrassed. She's newly come there to live with her aunt, who owns the shop," he explained to Paradis. "It's not her fault if her aunt is selling pornography upstairs, which I suspect that she is."

Paradis had handed the piece of leather to Le Picart. The rector examined it and handed it back, seeming as mystified as Charles was by the visitor's sudden change of mood.

"Pornography?" Paradis laughed harshly. "Yes, I suppose you could call it that."

"But what is it?" Le Picart demanded.

"I will take it with me and compare it, to be sure. But I am already fairly sure that it is from the cover of a recent edition of the *Monita Secreta*."

Charles and Le Picart looked at the little fragment in Paradis's hand as though it were a scorpion. The *Monita Secreta*—Secret Instructions—had long been banned in France. Written in Latin at the beginning of the century, by a dismissed Polish Jesuit furious at the Society of Jesus, it was the origin of many of the falsehoods about Jesuits. It had been declared a forgery almost at once, by non-Jesuit as well as Jesuit scholars, but the poisonous thing had gone through dozens of editions all over Europe and was accepted by many as absolute proof that the Society of Jesus was plotting to rule the world.

"But how can you tell that this is part of a *Monita* cover?" Le Picart said. "It only says *Cabine*."

"The Provincial's office keeps track of editions. I think this is from a recent edition—it's the same leather, the same color and method of curing, the same lettering. The *Monita*'s title is sometimes changed. I think this scrap of leather came from an edition called *Le Cabinet jesuitique*, written in French and printed in Cologne in 1678." He looked at Charles. "What's the name of the shop where you found this?"

"The Saint's Dog," Charles said sadly. "It's just up the rue Saint Jacques." He was thinking of Mlle Ebrard. If her aunt was secretly selling *The Jesuit Cabinet* upstairs to improve the bookshop's fortunes, both women were facing serious trouble.

Chapter 13

Charles spent all of the next day, Saturday, waiting for a summons from La Reynie in the gaps between the festival Mass for the Feast of All Saints, the additional special Mass offered for Maître Louis Richaud that he might yet be found safe and unharmed, and trying to read St. Thomas in his chamber. But no word came from La Reynie and Charles ended the day feeling edgy and deflated.

On Sunday, as he shivered in the thin sunshine on a bench in the deserted Cour d'honneur, an unread book in his lap, the back of his neck prickled coldly—the sign that someone was too close behind him. He jumped to his feet and turned, arms up to defend himself. Lieutenant-Général La Reynie stood there, his mouth open in surprise and his silver-headed stick half-raised to fend Charles off.

"I've told you, don't come up behind me like that!" Charles said. "Ever since the army, people coming too close make me want to strike first and question later."

"If you were armed, I'd take that very seriously."

"Bear in mind that an ex-soldier doesn't need a weapon to

do you serious harm," Charles shot back. La Reynie blinked in surprise. "Sometimes," Charles muttered, picking up the book he'd dropped, "I fear I really will strike out at someone before I realize there's no threat."

"I'll bear that in mind. Meanwhile, I hear you've been ordered to help me, after all."

"You *hear*?" Charles said wryly. "I think you heard that news at Fontainebleu."

A slow smile spread over the *lieutenant-général*'s face. "I had good 'hunting' there this autumn."

"And I was the quarry."

"Quite a nice 'bag,' if I may say so."

Charles gave up and smiled back. "Why do I always lose these sparring contests?"

"Because they're with me." La Reynie jerked his head toward the street. "Come. My carriage is waiting."

"My orders don't include simply roaming over Paris with you."

"They do include helping me with questions where Jesuits are concerned. So come."

Charles followed him out to the rue St. Jacques. "What Jesuits?" he said, as La Reynie climbed into the low, red-wheeled carriage.

"I'm stretching the category a little. I want you with me while I talk to Maître Louis Richaud's family. Your presence may encourage them to talk. Or—as I rather suspect—may anger them enough to make them even more indiscreet than they've already been. I sent their neighborhood police *commissaire* to do it, but *la famille* Richaud threw him out."

The lackey shut the carriage door and climbed up onto his rear perch, and the carriage moved off down the hill.

"The *commissaire*, being a promising young man," La Reynie

continued, "came to me and suggested I use that little judgment lapse on their part to my benefit. They are going to discover that they'd rather talk to me than visit the Châtelet."

Charles grinned. "Your *commissaire* does sound promising." He looked out the window and saw that they were turning off St. Jacques by the little church of St. Yves and heading for the Place Maubert. "Where do the Richauds live?"

"Near Saint Victor's abbey. There's only a sister and a brother, it seems. The brother works in the woodyard by the river."

Charles turned from the window. "They're poor people?"

"Very, my man says."

Charles was silent, staring at the rich coverings of the carriage seats and thinking about Maître Louis Richaud. It had never occurred to him that the scholastic came from poverty. It had been obvious that Richaud came from a modest background, but Charles had imagined him from some careful family of competent artisans, comfortable enough in a small way. Not that he'd ever thought much about it, because Richaud had been only a sour and vindictive minor presence in his life and best avoided. The carriage had turned and turned again, and was moving east along the river now, toward the turreted stretch of the old wall and the St. Bernard gate. The river was white-capped, and the gulls trying to fly against the wind looked as though they were hovering in midair.

"We'll go to the house," La Reynie said, as they passed the gate. "The Richaud brother won't be at the woodyard on All Saints."

The carriage rattled over the rough road along the wall, and Charles gazed across the spreading woodyards at the tower of St. Victor's church showing above the abbey walls. He wondered if Richaud, growing up here in the abbey's shadow, had thought of becoming a monk there. Or had he wanted only to get as far from these poor beginnings as he could?

La Reynie peered from the window beside his seat. "We're nearly there." He put his head out, started to call to his driver, and got a mouthful of wig in the river wind. "Stop!" he yelled, spitting out strands of hair. "We'll get out here."

The road was uncrowded on this holiday, and the driver stopped the carriage without the usual outcry from other carriage drivers and pedestrians. La Reynie and Charles descended and stood looking at the narrow shabby houses along both sides of the road. A few people sat on their front steps, in spite of the chill, and a flute was playing somewhere. A worn and stained chemise and a pair of men's breeches flapped loose from the small leafless tree where someone had put them to dry, and a shrieking little girl raced barefoot after them, her uncoifed brown hair flying behind her.

"Which house is the Richauds'?" La Reynie called to the girl.

"There." She pointed beyond where the laundry had come to rest and leaped to catch the chemise by its tail out of a bush. Then she pulled the breeches from a small thicket—of thorns Charles thought, from the ripping sound the garment made—and trudged back across the road. "He's drunk," she said warningly as she passed them.

The two men picked their way across the badly paved road and around unpleasant puddles. The plaster-and-timber house the little girl had pointed at leaned tiredly against the old house on its left. La Reynie swept a glance up its front wall and tapped at the door with his stick. An indefinable roar came from somewhere above them. He squinted up at the windows again and tapped harder.

A window opened on the top floor and a man who might have been Richaud's twin nearly fell out of it. "What?" He hung over the ledge, gazing at them through half-closed eyes until someone pulled him back into the room and slammed the window shut. Heavy shoes clattered down bare stairs and a haggard woman who looked at least forty wrenched open the door.

"What do you want?" she demanded.

"I am looking for Maître Louis Richaud," La Reynie said genially. "Are you perhaps Mademoiselle Richaud? His sister?"

Her frown turned wary and she stared at them without speaking. Behind her, the man who'd opened the window lurched down the stairs and pushed her aside to glare at La Reynie and Charles.

"You, I suspect, are Louis Richaud's brother," La Reynie said less genially. "The one who pitched my *commissaire* out the door."

The man opened his eyes wider and crouched a little, looking from one of them to the other, like an animal uncertain from which direction an attack might come. The woman stepped in front of him and folded her arms across her filthy apron bodice.

"What's it to you who we are?" she said belligerently.

"I am the head of the Paris police," La Reynie said, smiling widely. "The two of you threw my *commissaire* out of your rooms. If you don't want to go to the Châtelet for that, you will answer my questions."

At that, the drunk rushed him, swinging thin arms with muscles like ropes. La Reynie and Charles sidestepped, and La Reynie grabbed the man by the front of his shirt and shook him. "Where is your brother?" he shouted.

The man shrugged and breathed brandy fumes into La Reynie's face. The woman pulled her brother free.

"You want to know where's Louis?" she shouted back at La Reynie. "Ask *him*," she pointed sullenly at Charles. "Louis went to the Jesuits. Why come here to ask about him?"

Charles said mildly, "Has he been to visit you?"

She spat at his feet. "Louis? Come here? Jesus himself is about as likely to visit."

She reached up and shoved stringy dark hair under her coif with hands stained a muddy blue color. The same color was deep under her fingernails. Charles turned to look at the man, who had slid down the house wall and was sitting on the ground, apparently going to sleep. His hands were in his lap, stained like his sister's, and his nails harbored the same color. With a wave of guilt, Charles realized that the dark color under Maître Richaud's fingernails, which had always disgusted him, wasn't dirt, but dye.

"*Mademoiselle*, how did Louis go from being a dyer to being a Jesuit?"

"We all worked with our father in the dye works. It was down by the river. But Louis—by God's long cock, Louis was hopeless. All thumbs, couldn't hold a stirring stick the right way up, couldn't tell green from red! My father beat him till he screamed. For that and for running away, but it was no use. You'd think the brat could have done something to earn his keep and pay me back for raising him. I raised him, me. I was ten years old when he was born. My mother, oh, she was too good for a poor dyer's wife. Hardly out of childbed after having Louis, and ran off with a bargeman." She cast a bitter look toward the river. "Died not long after that, we heard, and served her right."

Charles grimaced. "And Louis tried to run away?" He was suddenly full of pity for all three of the dyer's children.

"How far can you go at six? He'd sneak away from work. The priest kept finding him in the church trying to steal the

Gospel book. Worth something, those books, but Louis couldn't even manage that much. The stupid old priest thought Louis kept taking the book because he wanted to read, so he taught him how. Lot of good that did the rest of us. All it did was make Louis brag even more about being better than us and everyone else on God's earth."

So that had been the beginning, Charles thought. Reading had been the small opening that let Louis Richaud out into a different world. That world must have come as a godsend to Richaud, as both boy and man. Why then, he wondered, had the man always seemed so joyless, gone to such lengths to dislike everyone and everything? La Reynie's voice startled Charles out of his musings.

"I want the truth, woman! Has Louis been here? Have you seen him anywhere? He's missing and no one knows where he is."

The woman paled under the dirt on her face. "You wouldn't bother with people like us just for 'missing.'"

"All right. Your brother may be dead. We don't know. We're trying to find out."

"Dead?" Her mouth trembled and Charles thought for a moment that some hidden well of feeling had been touched in her. But she only hugged herself, as if she'd suddenly felt the cold wind that was blowing, and went back into the house.

The thin mournful sound of the flute they'd heard earlier followed La Reynie and Charles at they returned to the waiting carriage.

"Did you believe her?" La Reynie asked Charles, as the carriage turned.

"About not having seen him? Yes. And if you should find a body and wonder if it's his, look at the fingernails. He has dye under his just like those two."

"A good observation. I only wish we had a likely body. Then we could be done with at least that question." He frowned at Charles. "I think that I'm about to have a worse coil to solve. When I leave you at the college, I'm going to your Provincial's office."

Charles returned La Reynie's resigned gaze with a sinking heart. "Why?"

"Your Provincial's note said they think that the *Monita Secreta* is being circulated in Paris again." La Reynie's gaze sharpened. "Why do I suddenly think you know more about this than I do?"

Charles sighed. "Because I do." He told La Reynie how and where he'd found the fragment of cover.

"Of course it *would* be you who'd find the thing. Oh, well, at least it's not another murdered man."

The carriage pulled up at Louis le Grand's postern and the lackey sprang down and opened the door for Charles.

"When you talk to the women at The Dog," Charles said, "please remember that whatever the owner may be doing, the young one has nothing to do with anything illegal. She's only just come to live there and, well—"

La Reynie laughed. "And she's young and pretty. Yes, I'll bear it in mind. Out with you, now, I'm going home for once. I doubt I'll need you tomorrow. Besides other things—including an argument I've been avoiding about the cost of candles for the street lanterns—I'm going to see the abbess at Notre Dame des Champs. I want to ask more questions there, and look again at that well chamber before her workmen go in there on Thursday. So I won't need you tomorrow. Soon after, though."

Charles got out of the carriage and watched it roll away up the hill. All the saints were witness that he needed to study, after his time in the infirmary and the time he'd just spent with

La Reynie. But the saints also knew that he'd hoped that the *lieutenant-général* would turn out to need him tomorrow, after all. *So*, he asked himself with a sigh, as he rang the postern bell, *does that mean you're insincere about wanting to be a priest? Should you accept La Reynie's old offer to join the police?* With that uncomfortable thought, he went into the college and slowly climbed the stairs to his books.

⊹❧ *Chapter 14* ☙⊹

To Charles's disappointment, Lieutenant-Général La Reynie didn't come looking for him on Monday. On Tuesday, during the recreation hour after dinner, Charles was in the library, in the small room reserved for consulting books considered dangerous or rare. He'd asked for the library's copy of *Le Cabinet jesuitique*, and was standing with it at the little reading room's tall, small-paned window to have better light. When Frère Brunet had released him back to his own chamber on Saturday, it had been with strict orders to come straight back if the wound opened, or his fever came back, or a long list of other unhappy developments. None of those had so far happened, but the more he read of *Le Cabinet*, the sicker he felt. He was reading the "fourth directive" of the forged Secret Instructions for Jesuits. In it, the vengeful author purported to tell Jesuit confessors how to gain political power for the Society.

"In order that ours undertake well the direction of princes and aristocrats, they should thus steer matters so that it appears that the direction

tends to the good that the princes believe in. But little by little . . . the directions should aim at political governance."

Charles stared helplessly at the page. How would anyone unacquainted with the Society's real rules know that this was false? Even the language sounded like the language of Jesuit documents, using the customary *ours* to refer to Jesuits. But the content would be even more confusing to outsiders. Most Catholic princes, including Louis XIV, had Jesuit confessors, and anyone with easy access to a ruler was regarded with uneasy suspicion. Charles knew how hard King Louis's confessor, Père La Chaise, worked to influence his royal charge for good—or to at least lessen some of the harm the king could do. But Charles had also seen how easily enemies twisted La Chaise's fallible efforts into a Jesuit quest for political power at court.

"Hah! I told him!"

Charles jumped and turned around, nearly dropping *Le Cabinet.* An elderly Jesuit sitting behind him with an enormous book was grinning broadly. He slapped a hand down on the table.

"*That* settles the Manicheans!" the old man crowed. "I knew I was right." He shut the book with a bang, earning himself more reproving looks from the other readers and the librarian, and shuffled out.

Trying to remember which heretics the Manicheans had been, Charles turned back to the window and found his place again in the *Cabinet.* Disconsolately, he turned the page. This book was libel, not heresy. But its effects were as destructive and even harder to counter, since so many people over the years had taken it for Gospel truth. He started reading the next "directive," about how the Society should creep into the affections—and purses—of rich widows, but it was so disheartening that he quit reading and stared out at the garden in front of the library.

The college's ancient grapevine hugged the stone wall as though it might be shivering in the chilly sunlight. The vine made him think of Père Dainville, who'd loved unearthing the school's history. Dainville had told him that the Cour d'honneur had once been an enormous garden with vineyards stretching to each side, a remnant of the vineyards that had covered the Left Bank for centuries. Thinking about that made Charles recall the illuminated manuscript page he'd stopped to look at downstairs. The brightly colored old drawing showed King Louis IX—later St. Louis—riding along a Paris street as someone emptied a chamber pot over his head. Charles wondered what had happened to the figure at the window upending the pot—and how long it had taken to get the smell out of the king's thick fur-trimmed robes. Now, after reading *Le Cabinet*, he wondered if the stink of lies this little book had poured over the Society of Jesus could ever be washed away.

From the Cour d'honneur, the bell clanged for the end of recreation. For Charles, it was the signal to go to the street passage to meet students from the older boarders' Congregation of the Holy Virgin who were this week's almsgivers. The Congregation was a social and spiritual organization, active in all Jesuit schools and in many parishes, and one of its functions was regular charity. He picked up his outdoor hat and his cloak and took his book to the librarian, who would lock it away again in a sturdy cupboard. Then he went down the library's new grand staircase and out into the mercifully windless day. Instead of going through the fathers' garden, he went the quicker way through the day students' court. Though there were nearly three times as many day students as boarding students, Charles had little contact with them, since they didn't live in the college or eat there. Now, as they flooded into the court after dinner at home or in lodgings, Charles watched them curiously. Their courtyard, like the others, had its proctors to enforce discipline, but strict discipline was harder here because of the day boys' sheer numbers. The proctors called for silence as the boys lined up at classroom doors but sensibly settled for a muted murmur of talk.

Like the boarding students, the day students wore long black scholar's gowns, many green with age and some—on the youngest boys of nine or ten—nearly trailing on the ground. Unlike the boarders, these were mostly the sons of the middle and lower bourgeoisie. There were some scholarship boys from poor families, but most of these boys' fathers were respected guild members, middling merchants, or legal men on the lower rungs of the law's hierarchy.

When Charles reached the covered passage between the day court and the Cour d'honneur, he found a huddle of day students standing with their heads together, their black hats and gowns making them look like some exotic tree. They were talking eagerly and looking at something in their midst. They didn't hear him at first, but when they did, they gasped audibly, turned like duellers at bay, and then bowed and made speed into their own court. Charles judged their ages at seventeen or eighteen, just the age when the college's hold was thinning to the breaking point. He wondered what they'd been looking at, considered stopping them to find out, and then didn't. He well remembered being a seventeen-year-old schoolboy, more than ready to cut the strings holding him to his teachers and their endless discipline.

When Charles reached the street passage, the half dozen boarders who'd gathered there to help distribute alms greeted him eagerly. Several were the same age as the day boys, and he wondered whether they, too, were chafing under school discipline. The *cubiculaire* waiting with them nodded at the baskets on the passage floor. "The clothes are there, *maître*. Père Damiot entrusted Monsieur Connor with the alms purse. A good walk and a blessed afternoon to you."

As Charles thanked and dismissed him, laughter rose beside the postern, where some of the boys were listening to Frère Martin.

"So maybe you can choose yourselves brides this afternoon," Charles heard Martin say, his bass voice shaking with laughter.

"But they're orphans," a spotty-faced boy from Normandy said, indignant and offended. "My father would never let me marry a girl without a name."

"They have names," Walter Connor retorted. "Their parents are not unknown, just dead. The girls at the Miséricorde live there because they no longer have any family to take care of them."

"So you'll be glad to marry one of them, I suppose?" The Norman boy, Jacques Honfleur, shrugged disdainfully at Connor. "Not surprising from an Irishman."

Anger turned Connor even paler than he normally was, and Charles put a hand on his shoulder.

"Enough, Monsieur Honfleur," he said, eyeing the Norman. "It's unwise and unkind to be disdainful of bereavement. As these alms we're giving should remind you." He pointed at the biggest basket. "You may carry that to help you remember. Monsieur Beauclaire, you may carry the small one."

Redly furious, Honfleur picked up his basket.

Beauclaire hefted his and said, "What's in them, *maître*?"

"Clothing. The twin daughters of a man from one of our men's Congregations of the Holy Virgin died of a fever a few weeks ago. Their father has given their clothes for the orphans at the Miséricorde, so we're taking them along with the purse your student Congregation has filled."

Connor looked at Charles. "Does the father have other children?"

"No, he doesn't."

"Ah, the poor man!" Connor crossed himself and moved toward the postern. The others, chastened, made way for him to go first.

Frère Martin opened the door, looking ruefully at Charles. "Sorry, *maître.* I made too much of a joke about them going to a house of girls."

Charles nodded his agreement, but leavened it with a friendly clap on Martin's shoulder. He chivied his flock into the street and took his place at the front of the group.

"Remember now," he said, "we are to go quietly through the streets. Little talking, and no shouting or gawking or making a spectacle of ourselves. *Habes?*"

"Yes, *maître,* we have it." The chorus of adolescent voices sounded a little like an unmusical choir, some treble, some wandering up and down the scale, and one—an Austrian boy's voice—that was nearly as deep as Frère Martin's and seemed to startle its owner every time he opened his mouth.

They set off southward, climbing the slope of the rue St. Jacques toward the city wall, As they passed The Dog, Charles looked for Rose Ebrard and wondered if La Reynie had been to the shop yet. And how long he would have to wait before La Reynie next wanted his help. As he led his group through the St. Jacques gate market, he wondered anew, as he passed the needle seller's booth, what Mlle Ebrard had really been doing on Friday outside the Novice House.

Beyond the old gate, they turned to their left on a footpath that followed the outside of the lichened wall. Connor, walking beside Charles, reached up and plucked a yellow flower growing out of the gray stones. Sensing Charles's eyes on him, he looked up.

"I like yellow, *maître*. Do you? It was my sister Mary's favorite color. My older sister. She and my younger sister died two years ago. Mary was always my favorite—people said we were like twins." He put the flower in the buttonhole of his coat, beneath his black gown.

Charles asked Connor more about his sister, letting the other boys draw ahead. Then Connor fell silent, the path turned south, and he and Charles caught up with the rest. Beauclaire was arguing with Honfleur, rebutting Honfleur's argument that Normans were superior to other Frenchmen. Since they were being reasonably quiet and not warring with anything but words, Charles left them to it. He was half Norman himself, but he had no desire to weigh in on the unpleasant Honfleur's side.

Beauclaire suddenly stopped arguing and looked at the narrow lane they were passing. "*Maître*, may we go down this way? I know it doesn't look like it goes in the right direction, but it turns."

Charles peered into the unprepossessing lane, little more than a dirt-and-grass path and lined with small badly kept houses, ragged gardens, and crumbling garden walls. "Why do you want to go this way, Monsieur Beauclaire?"

"Because I like its name." Beauclaire's eyes were dancing with a glee Charles had learned to distrust in the year he'd taught him. "Do you know what it's called?"

Everyone, including Charles, shook their heads.

"It's called Talking Flea Street! So may we, *maître*?"

"How do you know that? And how do you know it turns in the right direction?" the skeptical Connor said.

"Maître Richaud told me."

Charles was glad to see that the mention of Richaud's name provoked no reaction from any of the boys. So far, then, the scholastic's increasingly ominous disappearance had been kept from the students. He fixed Beauclaire with a warning eye. "Do you swear it goes in the right direction?"

"On my grandfather's bones!"

"Your grandfather's bones aren't here to swear on, but we'll trust you."

Beauclaire led them joyously into the lane. A shabbily dressed woman peered from an open door, and a few ragged children wandered in the dust and mud.

"It looks like a good place for fleas," Connor said to Beauclaire. "I didn't know you liked fleas so much."

"I don't like them," the bass-voiced Austrian said morosely. "They keep me up at night and not because they are talking!"

"Have you told your *cubiculaire*?" Charles said. "The college is always fighting fleas, and the sooner he knows your chamber has them, the sooner he and the lay brothers can do something."

"He knows. They put down herbs, but the fleas think they're love philtres and have more little fleas. On Saturday, a brother brought in a white fleece so the fleas could jump onto it and get killed. Almost none of them jumped. They are not stupid, your French fleas."

Everyone laughed at that, and Charles let them, since there were few people around to hear their rowdiness.

"See, *maître*?" Beauclaire pointed triumphantly to a sharp bend ahead of them that turned the lane southeast, the way they needed to go.

Charles started to nod and then jumped back as a long, thin pig raced across the lane in front of him, pursued by a child with a stick. As pig and child galloped through the weed-choked yard at the side of a small, dilapidated house, the pleasantly pungent scent of herbs long gone wild drifted in their wake, reminding Charles of his mother's herb garden. With a sigh for the warmth of Languedoc and the nearness of another Paris winter, he started the boys walking again.

It was only a short way to the Miséricorde. Charles rang the bell at the gate and an Ursuline nun slid the small grille open. Seeing Charles and the gowned students, she opened the gate and came out to meet them. The nun was very young but dignified beyond her years in her short black veil and white habit.

"Bonjour, messieurs." She smiled at the suddenly shy group of boys and looked questioningly at Charles.

"Bonjour, ma soeur. I am Maître Charles du Luc and I've brought these students from Louis le Grand to offer alms for your orphans."

He nodded at Connor, who stepped forward and gave her the purse and made his short rehearsed speech on behalf of the Holy Virgin Congregation. Then Honfleur set his basket inside the gate and Beauclaire put the smaller one down beside it. Everyone bowed to the nun, and she curtsied in return.

"We are most grateful. As our girls will be." Beyond her, several half-grown girls stood under a nearly leafless chestnut tree to whisper and stare at the boys, who were staring in return. "May the *bon Dieu* richly bless you for your charity." The nun glanced over her shoulder at the girls and, with a knowing smile at Charles, drew the gate closed.

"Well done," Charles said to his flock. "Except for the staring."

That brought what he could only call giggles. Swallowing his own laughter, he turned them back toward the college. Just inside the walls, as they were passing the St. Jacques market, they moved aside to let a carriage go past toward the river at a walking pace. The boys spotted a tumbler who'd cleared a space for himself among the market stalls, and Charles, glad to rest for a moment, let them watch. He kept an eye on the street. To his surprise, the slow carriage stopped, its window was lowered, and Lieutenant-Général La Reynie's face appeared, looking back at him. The *lieutenant-général* lifted his chin and Charles went closer.

"I need you," La Reynie said. He glanced at the huddle of entranced students. "I'll stop at the college." He put the window up and the carriage moved on. With a frisson of excitement, Charles gathered the reluctant boys and shepherded them toward the college.

Chapter 15

When Charles and the students reached the postern, the carriage was parked a little way up the hill, in front of the church of St. Étienne des Grès. Frère Martin opened the postern wide, and Charles gathered the boys in the street passage for the short prayer that always ended an almsgiving. Replete with fresh air and the city's sights and sounds, they joined heartily in the "amen."

"That was well done, *messieurs*," Charles said. "Put the baskets back in the porter's room and then wait here."

As the baskets were put away, Charles beckoned Martin closer to the postern. "Will you call a *cubiculaire* to see them to their chambers? I have another task, *mon frère*."

"Ah," Martin said knowingly. "I saw the carriage waiting when I opened the door. I know whose it is, too. God go with you both!" He lowered his voice. "Some are still saying it was a demon attacked you. Me, I know better. No one's said they smelled sulphur in the chapel, and you always do smell it if a demon's about."

"So it's said." Charles smiled at him and hurried to the carriage. As he got in, La Reynie tapped his stick on the ceiling and the pair of black horses moved off toward the river.

"Where are we going?" Charles said.

"To the Lunel house across the river."

La Reynie and Charles braced themselves as the coach bounced in and out of a pothole. Charles retrieved his hat from the floor.

"Have you been to The Saint's Dog about the book cover?"

"Oh, yes," the *lieutenant-général* said disgustedly. "We found an interesting selection of Dutch pornography. Including that scurrilous little piece about Madame de Maintenon and the king that keeps cropping up. Such a very upright woman can have had no idea what she was in for when she married King Louis." He carefully brushed pastry crumbs from the cascade of ivory lace at his neck. "Forgive me," he said. "No time for a proper dinner."

Wondering how often La Reynie ever found time for a proper midday dinner, Charles said, "Did you find *Le Cabinet* in the bookshop?"

"We did not. Not so much as a torn page."

"But the goat can't have brought that scrap from outside. It would already have eaten it."

"I agree. But damned if we could find it. We went through everything in the cellars, we had floorboards up, we went through the attic and out onto the roof. Not one single little Secret Instruction."

"What did Madame Cheyne say?"

"She owned to the Dutch trash. What choice did she have? Pleaded her poor widowhood and having to make money any way she could, and on and on. But she swore on the name of every saint and relic she could think of that she didn't have, had never had, had never even heard of *Le Cabinet jesuitique*."

"And Mademoiselle Ebrard? What did she do?"

La Reynie grinned at him. "She's not exactly pretty—wonderful eyes, though." He laughed at Charles's chilly expression. "Oh, come, nothing wrong with caring what becomes of the girl. She was upset, of course. And I agree with you, I don't think she knew anything about the books being sold upstairs. Or about *Le Cabinet*."

"Good. But what will happen to Madame Cheyne now?"

"She is at liberty for the moment. We're giving her a long rope, so she can at least lead us to whoever brings her the Dutch books. And who knows, perhaps she'll slip and do something to prove she lied about *Le Cabinet*. Though if she lied, she must be keeping the copies down her bodice and under her skirts! Not a search I care to undertake."

The carriage braked suddenly and both men were thrown forward. This time it was La Reynie's hat that fell off—and nearly his wig. He yanked it back into place and leaned out of the window.

"I think someone's carriage has broken down," he said, craning his neck. "Or maybe it's just traffic." He shrugged and pulled his head in. "God only knows what we're going to do about Paris traffic. Coachmakers keep selling carriages and there's no more room for the cursed things. Well, I suppose it gives me more time to tell you what I want to do at the Lunel house."

As he talked, the carriage started moving again, though slowly, toward the turrets of the Petit Châtelet. The squat little fortress had guarded the Petit Pont from the time when the bridge was the only southern way across the Seine and the whole city huddled in the middle of the river on the Île de la Cité. The snarl of carriages, pedestrians, and pack animals crawling toward the Petit Châtelet suddenly unwound itself, and the carriage rolled through the narrow echoing gate and onto the short bridge.

"So," Charles said, "I gather that the Lunel boy's mother and brother are back from the country now."

"Just arrived. I had the neighborhood *commissaire* watching for me, and he sent word. I'm going to have out of them why they made no response to the message that Paul Lunel was missing."

"But"—Charles frowned and shook his head—"surely you don't think the mother or the brother had anything to do with his death?"

"Only if their coming home to try to find him might have prevented it."

The carriage passed the Louvre and turned into the rue Jean Tison. It stopped in front of a marble façaded *porte cochère*, the high and wide double doors that barred the courtyards of the wealthy. Before Charles and La Reynie could get out, someone started consigning La Reynie's driver to hell or worse.

Charles looked incredulously at the police chief. "Either I'm going mad or that's Maître Beauchamps!" Pierre Beauchamps, dance director of the Paris Opera, was the most eminent dancing master in France, probably in all of Europe. He was also Louis le Grand's dancing master, and Charles had worked on two Louis le Grand ballets with him. Charles climbed quickly out of the carriage and found Beauchamps standing in front of it, threatening the driver with his ebony walking stick.

"What are you trying to *do*?" he shouted at the driver. "My legs are no longer what they were, but there's no need to take them off entirely!"

"Then get out of the way, *mon vieux*," the coachman said, laughing and eyeing a very pretty and very young woman who stood close to the wall of the Lunel courtyard, biting her plump red lip and bubbling with laughter.

"Old? You call me *old*?" The fifty-six-year-old Beauchamps swelled with insult until Charles thought his midnight blue coat might split at the seams. "Have some respect for your betters, you mud-born lackey! I'll report you! Not that our La Reynie will take any notice of what a carriage driver does; he lets them unpeople Paris with their driving. But if you care to dismount from your seat, I'll show you who's old and who's not!"

"No need for that, Monsieur Beauchamps." The *lieutenant-général* stepped forward and bowed low to the dancing master. "I assure you that La Reynie is taking notice, even as you speak."

Beauchamps squinted at him. "What? Who—oh, it's you? You sat there and let this man all but run *over* me? You see?" Beauchamps said triumphantly to the driver. "I told you he'd be utterly indifferent!"

Struggling as hard as the girl to keep his countenance, Charles caught Beauchamps's eye and nodded gravely. Beauchamps was as demanding, and even more autocratic, than La Reynie, and Charles watched gleefully to see who would come out on top in this encounter. It was the young woman who came out on top. She lifted her orange and white striped skirt above the cobbles and came to Beauchamps's side. "Don't upset yourself, *maître*," she said soothingly, taking his arm and looking up at him with warm brown eyes.

"I'll thank you not to treat me like your grandfather, *mademoiselle*," he snapped, but Charles saw that he tucked her arm close to his side.

"Come, now," she cajoled, "you are going to give me a lesson, and I'd rather not be shouted at every moment simply because you do not have this poor coachman to shout at."

"Hmmph." Beauchamps glared at La Reynie, who smiled affably back at him. "Well, *mon lieutenant-gèneral*, since you are not hurrying to take the hide off your rogue of a driver, what *are* you doing here?" He raised an eyebrow at Charles, whom he'd hitherto ignored. "And you, Maître du Luc. Are the police already at such a loss over my poor neighbor's murder that you must find their answers for them? Again?"

"Your neighbor?" Charles and La Reynie said, almost in concert.

"Of course, my neighbor. I live just there." He pointed at the next pair of courtyard doors. Not quite so impressive a pair as the Lunels', but harbingers of a solid and comfortable town house behind them. "And before you ask me, I knew Paul, the dead boy, only slightly, and the brother, Alexandre, and the parents only to bow to in the street. The father, as you no doubt know, is dead."

La Reynie said, "And how did you know that Paul Lunel is dead?"

Beauchamps cast his eyes up to heaven. "Have you no servants? The Lunel servants told mine, of course. They said you'd been to the house with the news."

La Reynie nodded. "And what else do you and your servants"—he glanced at the girl—"and your friends, of course, know about this Lunel family, Maître Beauchamps?"

Beauchamps also looked at the girl, who drew herself up and turned her head to look from one eye at La Reynie, like an annoyed bird.

"May I know your name, *mademoiselle*?" the *lieutenant-général* said.

"Forgive me," Beauchamps said. "Monsieur La Reynie, Maître du Luc, may I present Mademoiselle Marie-Thérèse de Subligny? A heavenly dancer. And a new ornament to the Opera. I am giving her some extra teaching."

La Reynie eyed her and bowed slightly. "I congratulate you, *mademoiselle*. Few women dance on the professional stage. Did you perhaps know Monsieur Paul Lunel?"

"Paul?" She shrugged slightly. "No."

La Reynie kept watching her. "You call him by his Christian name. So you know the family?"

The girl managed somehow to draw dignity visibly around herself, which told Charles that she must be a very good stage performer.

"Monsieur Alexandre Lunel comes to see me dance," she said. Her eyes dared the men to draw the obvious conclusion from that. "But I have not seen him lately. I only knew that his brother was dead because Maître Beauchamps told me."

"Ah. I am surprised indeed that you have not seen Monsieur Alexandre Lunel lately. How could he stay away?" La Reynie's tone made his assumptions about her relationship with Lunel very clear. Charles wondered if the mostly straightlaced *lieutenant-général* disapproved of her dancing on the Opera stage. Nearly all female courtiers performed in court ballets, but the Opera was another thing altogether.

Her eyes flashed with anger, and Beauchamps, with the air of someone slamming a door before it was too late, said quickly, "Monsieur Lunel is a very busy man with many friends. He is a prominent young lawyer. Soon, no doubt, he'll be a judge, and being busy is part of being a successful man. Like Mademoiselle de Subligny, I also have not seen him lately."

"How well did you know Monsieur Paul Lunel?" La Reynie asked him.

Beauchamps sighed a little. "When he was small, I caught him climbing my wall to watch a dancing lesson through the windows. After that, I sometimes let him come inside to watch. He had his own dancing master, but the master used his stick freely to correct mistakes, and poor Paul didn't like him much. He learned little from that tyrant."

"He never saw *you* use your stick?" Charles couldn't resist saying.

"I never used it on him. Paul was a good boy with a good brain. I liked him." He sighed. "He had the makings of a good dancer." From Beauchamps, the accolade had the feeling of a eulogy. "But he would never have matched your young Bertamelli," the dancing master said, smiling suddenly at Charles.

"And how is Bertamelli?" Charles asked. "Is he well? Are you pleased with him?"

Michele Bertamelli, a fourteen-year-old from Milan, had been Charles's rhetoric student and a spirited dancer in the college ballets. Now—partly owing to Charles's help—he was Beauchamps's youngest Opera dancer.

Beauchamps sighed rapturously, as though seeing a holy vision. "He's magnificent. Simply magnificent. I could fall at his feet, his technique grows so exquisite. At least, I could fall at his feet on the days when I am not considering killing him for one thing or another."

Charles grinned. "A familiar set of choices where Bertamelli is concerned. Please give him my greetings and say that I am glad to hear such a good—well, mostly good—report of him."

Seeing that the diversion to dance threatened to go on, La Reynie looked at Charles and nodded toward the Lunel gates. Charles ignored him.

La Reynie, exasperated, said, "If we are through with Opera business, is there anything more you can tell us about the Lunel family, Monsieur Beauchamps?"

"Nothing. I wish you luck. Paul Lunel's killer deserves to hang. Or worse." He bowed, Mlle de Subligny looked down her nose at La Reynie and curtsied like a duchess, and they went together to Beauchamps's double doors.

La Reynie pulled on the bell beside the Lunel *porte cochère*. After a long wait and another pull that nearly wrenched the rope from its mooring, steps sounded on the cobbles.

The inner shutter was lifted from a small grille and round eyes peered at them. "Who's there?"

"Lieutenant-Général La Reynie. Open the doors."

The shutter banged back over the rectangle, bolts slid, and the right-hand half of the big door was pulled back. They went into the courtyard and the very young groom bowed awkwardly and looked around the court, as though hoping to see someone who would tell him what to do next. To Charles's surprise, La Reynie said kindly, "The next thing, *mon brave*, is to take us to the door."

With a grateful look, the little groom scuttled across the cobbles, leaving his charges to exchange grins and follow. The imposing house of honey-colored stone was straight across from the double carriage doors, flanked by a carriage house with open doors on one side and a stable on the other, into which another groom was leading a sweated bay horse. The boy pounded on the house door as though he were a siege army. A fat red-nosed man, wearing a suit of good black cloth that proclaimed him a high-ranking indoor servant, flung the door open angrily. When he saw the visitors, he composed himself with an obvious effort and the boy fled toward the stables.

"*Bonjour*, Monsieur La Reynie," he said, bowing. He seemed not to see Charles.

"My companion and I must speak with your master," La Reynie said, and waited until the man had bowed very lightly to Charles. "I judge, by the fact that a carriage is in your carriage house and the horses are being stabled, that he has returned. Please tell him that I am here, and Maître Charles du Luc also."

"I regret, *mon lieutenant-général*, that I cannot do that. As you say, Monsieur Lunel is only this moment arrived from the country. With his mother. They are fatigued from their journey.

And they are in mourning, as you well know. They are seeing no one."

"Do they not care who killed their son and brother? Whether they do or not, they will see me. Go and tell them."

Stiff with offense, the man left them on the step and disappeared into the house. La Reynie pushed the door wider with his stick and went in, Charles behind him. The high-ceilinged foyer with its floor of red and white patterned stone was full of light. They heard a door close, and then voices approached from beyond the dark red velvet curtain between the foyer and the next room.

"It can't be helped." The light tenor voice sounded tired and resigned. "Of course I must see him."

"But the other——"

"Never mind. Bring them in and go back to work. I'll see to this."

The servant pushed the curtain aside and exclaimed in anger when he saw La Reynie and Charles standing in the foyer.

"As your master just said," La Reynie told him, "never mind. We have taken the liberty of not waiting on your doorstep, Monsieur Lunel," he said, raising his voice.

A stocky, strong-featured man of about thirty pushed the curtain aside and stood framed in the archway. His suit and coat of mourning black were wrinkled, and his dark brown wig was windblown. With a look that sent the furious servant quickly away through a side door, the young man said, "Monsieur La Reynie. You must forgive my servant Laurent. He was very fond of my brother and cannot seem to pull himself together." He bowed, ignoring Charles as the servant had done. "How may I help you?"

La Reynie stepped aside and presented Charles with a flourish. "This is Maître Charles du Luc. He and I have come to speak with you about your brother."

Lunel gave Charles the slightest of nods. To La Reynie he said eagerly, "You have found his killer, *mon lieutenant-général?*" His strained face was lit with hope.

"I regret, no, *monsieur.* I must speak with you, and with *madame*, your mother. The more I know about your brother, the better chance I have of finding his killer."

Lunel hesitated. "And may I ask what Maître du Luc's part is in this?"

"But surely that is obvious, *monsieur.* Your brother was on the verge of being a Jesuit novice. Maître du Luc and his brother Jesuits have, in a way, lost a brother, too." La Reynie smiled as though he had explained everything. "May we go now to your mother?" He moved toward the gracefully curved stairs.

"I will go first and warn her," Lunel said quickly. "She is devastated by my brother's death and may be lying down."

"But of course." La Reynie stood aside and watched Lunel mount the stairs. Charles half expected him to follow, but the *lieutenant-général* stayed where he was. When Lunel was out of sight, he said softly to Charles, "After we are settled and talking, excuse yourself to the privy. Have a look around, especially down here. Say you're lost, if someone sees you. See what the servant who dislikes us so much is doing. And who those belong to." He flicked a glance at the outdoor cloaks and the amber-headed stick on the foyer's side table.

"You suspect the servant?" Charles said softly.

La Reynie shrugged. "More information is always better than less."

Lunel's returning footsteps sounded. "My mother invites you to come up."

They followed him up gracefully curved stone stairs to a light, welcoming *salon*. A faded woman in her fifties lay half reclining in a chair covered in green velvet, a soft gray blanket spread over her black skirts. Her son made the introductions, Charles and La Reynie bowed, and she inclined her head to them.

"Forgive me for not rising. As you see, I am something of an invalid just now." Her oval face was pale and lined but showed the remains of beauty. She kept her eyes on her folded hands, and Charles had to strain to hear her low voice. "What do you want to know about my darling Paul?"

"Were you happy when he decided to become a Jesuit, *madame*?" The *lieutenant-général* pulled up a small footstool and sat as near her as courtesy allowed.

Lunel had withdrawn beyond his mother's chair. Charles remained standing near the door, where he could watch everyone.

"I will be frank with you. No, I was not." Mme Lunel picked up a snowy handkerchief lying in her lap and smoothed its lace edges. "But my husband had given him permission to enter the Society of Jesus, and it was not for me to prevent him. His going was a great grief to me. Poor Paul, he could have gone any time since last April, but he waited, hoping, I think, to win me over to his plan. But that he could never do. I told him so, and he decided to enter with the new novice class in October, after the feast of San Rémy."

"May I ask, *madame*," La Reynie said, "what your objection was?"

A small muscle moved in her cheek and she looked briefly at him. "If you have a son, do you want him to be a"—she looked down—"a religious?"

"Not greatly. But I hope for his happiness."

Charles heard the small catch in La Reynie's voice, though

he didn't think the others did. Even if they had, they wouldn't know what Charles did, that the *lieutenant-général* and his son were estranged.

"I did want his happiness," she flared. "But do children necessarily know what their happiness is?"

No one spoke, and a tense silence grew.

Finally, La Reynie said, "I know that word reached you that Paul did not arrive at the Novice House. Why did you not come back to Paris and search for him? It seems you made no response to that news at all."

Madame Lunel looked reproachfully at Alexandre. "Word did not reach me that Paul was missing. Only later, that he was dead."

La Reynie was also looking at Alexandre Lunel. "And why was that?"

Lunel averted his gaze. "It was my fault," he said disconsolately, "and I've been doing penance for it ever since, I assure you. I—well, I confess I also was not pleased with Paul's decision. I wanted him to go into the law, like me. Like our father. I took it badly when he chose his own path. Seventeen seemed so young and I felt—oh, I don't know—rejected, I suppose. Which was very childish of me." He glanced at Charles. "I found his 'vocation' hard to credit, but who am I to say whom God is calling?"

Charles nodded uncomfortably, thinking of Amaury de Corbet and his own doubts about Amaury's vocation.

Lunel went on. "When I learned that Paul hadn't arrived at the Novice House, I thought—no, to be honest, I hoped—that he'd changed his mind."

One of La Reynie's black eyebrows was climbing steadily as he listened. "You never feared that some ill fortune had come to him?"

"I should have, I see that now. But a strong, healthy, peace-able young man who sets off in daylight to go a short way—what could happen to him? I thought he'd gone to some friend's house to, well, hide for a little. Because of the embarrassment of changing his mind. He always minded what people thought of him."

"So you saw him go?" La Reynie said.

"No, not even that. He said he didn't want me there when he left; he refused my company on his walk to the Novice House. He said it would make going too hard for him, even though he wanted to go. So I went to stay with friends to let him have his way. I went with a very heavy heart, I can tell you."

"Oh? Who did you stay with?" La Reynie said, as though the answer didn't much interest him.

"A good friend who lives a little way south of the city. The family name is Coriot."

"Didn't your servant know where to find you? Why didn't he send you word there instead of sending to the country?"

Lunel smiled sadly. "I forgot to tell him I was going there first. I was only there for two days and then I went to Chaillot, to our mother. That's where I found the message from the Novice House about Paul's absence. It was addressed only to me, and when I read it, I thought that my brother's nerve had failed him, that he had come to his senses and was lying low with his own friends until his embarrassment passed and he could come home and admit his mistake. I didn't tell my mother because I didn't want her to get her hopes up. I—I'm sorry." He looked pleadingly at his mother.

"I knew how she would worry if I couldn't tell her where he'd gone." His shoulders slumped. "I will blame myself all my days for not telling what I knew. If I had, it might have saved his life." His sudden look at La Reynie and Charles was full of anguish. "After it was discovered that he'd been killed, I sent to everyone I could think of, asking if he'd been there. But no one had seen him. Where *can* he have been those three weeks? And why, dear God, *why* would anyone kill a boy like Paul?"

His mother finally looked up, but there was no warmth in the look. "Softly, Alexandre. You thought you were acting for the best. We can't change things."

La Reynie waited a decent moment and then said to Lunel, "I want a list of the families you contacted, a list of Paul's friends."

"Of course. Though I don't see the good of that now." He went to a bureau with an intricate crisscross pattern of black and gold in its dark wood and took a quill and paper from a small compartment.

"*Madame,*" Charles said, "if I may ask, why did Paul's father not send him to Louis le Grand, if Paul had some inclination toward the Society of Jesus?"

The sound of Alexandre Lunel's quill scraping suddenly across his paper drew everyone's eyes. He muttered in exasperation, examining his pen. Then he smiled an apology over his shoulder. "Your pardon. I didn't see that the point was gone."

As he rummaged for another one, his mother replied, gazing out the window across from her chair, "When Alexandre here was a child, he was sickly, his eyes were weak. He could not go to school, so we hired a tutor for him. My husband felt that his education was very good, and decided to have the same for Paul. So they both stayed at home and studied. My husband had found a Jesuit tutor to teach Alexandre but was persuaded to try a young layman to tutor Paul. Which worked out very well. Though Paul was disappointed not to have a Jesuit. He'd heard so much about your missions," she said to Charles. And added, "He had a silly idea of doing something like that after—"

"That's everyone I can think of," Alexandre Lunel said, cutting her off and holding out his list to La Reynie.

"My thanks, *monsieur*." La Reynie tucked the paper into his coat pocket and looked from under his brows at Charles.

Belatedly reminded of their agreement, Charles said, "If you will excuse me for a moment? I must—um—" To his annoyance, he felt his face grow red.

Mme Lunel glanced at him with distaste. "Just go down the stairs and beyond the red curtain," she murmured.

Her son started to object, but Charles ignored him. When he reached the foot of the stairs, he noticed that the cloaks and the walking stick were still on the side table. He listened for a moment at the velvet curtain, then pushed it aside and went into the passageway beyond. There were closed doors on either side of it and what looked like an outside door at the end. It opened onto a cobbled court walled by two short wings of the house. There was a covered well in one corner, a privy house in another, and an arched wooden gate across from the door where Charles was standing. The court was strewn with evidence of the Lunels' return from the country: a scattering of barrels, an enormous basket of autumn vegetables, hothouse fruit in straw-lined wooden frails.

Two coatless young men came out of the door in the left-hand wing, laughing and talking. When they saw Charles, they fell abruptly silent, staring at him in obvious dismay. Surprised and wondering who they were—by the lace on their shirts, they weren't servants—Charles smiled amiably and wandered into the courtyard, pretending an interest in the vegetables. Instead of any courteous greeting, one of the pair muttered something to the other, and both turned to go back inside. Then someone pounded on the gate. The man who'd spoken ran to open it, and a half dozen brown and white goats trotted in, followed by the same old woman Charles had seen at The Dog.

"Ah, I see you're getting goat's milk," Charles said to the man, as though they'd been introduced. "Do you live here with Monsieur Lunel?"

"We're helping him get settled," the young man said curtly, pushing a goat away from his shirt cuff. "Madame Lunel needs the milk. She isn't well."

He urged the old woman and her goats toward the door he'd come from, but the goats were more interested in the hothouse fruit at Charles's feet. He leaned down to push one away from the basket, and it captured his swinging rosary in its mouth.

"No, no, not that!" Half laughing, he pulled the rosary out of reach. "I refuse to tell the clothing master that a goat ate my rosary, *ma chère.*"

The goatherd shook off the young man who was trying to get her into the house. Standing still, she watched Charles stroking the head of the marauding goat. Her small brown face was a tangle of lines, but her black eyes were sharp and knowing.

"*Grandmère*, quickly, we haven't all day. Come and get the pail." The young man pulled at her arm, and the strap of the coarse linen bag she carried slipped from her shoulder.

The bag dropped like a stone and a big wheel of dark bread fell onto the cobbles. Cursing the man, she picked it up, stuffed it back into the bag, and hauled the bag back onto her shoulder. Then she darted across the cobbles to Charles and grabbed his hand. She turned it over and traced its lines with a finger. Charles tried to pull away, but her grip tightened.

Her eyes closed and her long dirty nails dug into his palm. She swayed slightly and her eyes closed. "Follow the dead, find your death." She was half singing, her voice thin and high. "Follow the dead, find your death."

No one moved. Then she opened her eyes, blinking irritably at Charles as though he'd been standing in her way, and herded her milling goats toward the door in the house wing.

Chapter 16

Charles stood in the street, looking fearfully up at the night sky as showers of falling stars plunged toward him. Then, between one breath and another, all the lights in Paris died, and the darkness was thick and silent. Terror overcame him. He felt night creatures slinking past his cassock skirt, and clouds billowed around him in a wind he couldn't feel. Then a door straight in front of him burst open and light brilliant as fireworks outlined a woman with a musket. She cried out in triumph and fired. But the bullet never reached him. Instead, a cassocked man with a sword in his hand ran at him. The man was Maître Richaud. He was laughing and a trail of blood was dripping from his cassock. His sword was aimed at Charles's heart. Charles screamed and twisted wildly away.

"*Maître*, wake up! You're dreaming, hush now!"

Breathing as though he'd been running, Charles flinched away from Père Thomas Damiot, his neighbor across the corridor, who stood over him holding a candle.

"You screamed, you were dreaming." Damiot put the candle down on the stool beside Charles's bed. "Here, let me untangle you." He pulled the twisted bedcovers back into place and straightened them. "Do you want a drink?"

"Please." Charles wiped sweat off his face with his sheet. "I woke you? I'm sorry."

"It's a little after midnight; I was already waking from my first sleep." Damiot went to the copper pitcher on the table. "Are you fevered again?"

"No. I don't think it was a fever dream." He took the cup Damiot handed him and drank gratefully. "But it was nearly as odd. I dreamed all the stars were falling. And then the street lanterns went out and then—" He caught his breath as he remembered the woman with the musket, the woman at the Battle of Cassel. "—and then Maître Richaud tried to kill me with a sword," he finished, and put the cup down beside the candle.

"Maître Richaud? One cannot imagine him knowing what to do with a sword," Damiot said dryly. "But you have more reason than most of us to scream at a dream like that, since someone tried to run you through so recently."

"Well, not to run me through, exactly. It was only a knife."

"Only?" Damiot cast his eyes up. "The reply of an intrepid soldier, *maître*. According to Frère Brunet, the knife nearly served to do the job."

Charles turned his face away, seeing the woman again. "Hardly intrepid."

"Are you sure you're all right now?" Damiot said.

Charles nodded abstractedly. "*Mon père*, what have you heard people saying about Maître Richaud's disappearance?"

"Here in the college? Most think he's been murdered. Possibly by the man who attacked you and killed our almost-novice. And you must admit, his bloody cassock being found does suggest a violent death."

"In my dream his cassock was dripping blood. But he was

laughing." Charles hesitated over what he wanted to say. In dreams, after all, logic came and went like flickering light. "The dream made me wonder if the cassock was meant to be found, meant to suggest a violent death?"

To Charles's surprise, Damiot didn't laugh at him. "I suppose it's possible. If that's the case, it would suggest he's been kidnapped. But why would anyone snatch Maître Richaud? No one's asked for ransom, at least not as far as I know. And if the college *were* asked for one . . ."

He and Charles looked sheepishly at each other.

". . . would we pay to have him back?" Charles finished for him.

"I can think of better investments to make, I must confess. Though not wanting him back doesn't mean I want him dead."

"No." Charles sighed. "But if he is dead, why hasn't his body been found?"

"Any number of reasons. It could be in the river or hastily buried or sold to the anatomists."

"True enough." Charles sat up enough to lean against the wall. "Another question, then. We joked the other day about the village witch. But do you believe in witches?"

Damiot didn't even blink. "Witches," he said consideringly. "Did you dream about them, too?"

Charles shook his head.

Damiot moved the candle and cup to Charles's small table and sat down on the stool. "Well, it depends on what kind of witches you mean. There are different kinds, you know." He squinted at Charles. "If you're looking for one, it's a little safer to do that now than it used to be. Witchcraft's not a crime anymore, at least not the white witch kind. Legally, it's just fraud. Only sorcery's a crime—calling up the devil and so on."

"What I'm talking about," Charles said carefully, "is the kind of woman I remember from the villages around my father's land. The wise-woman, the herb-woman who cures sicknesses—"

"—and gives love philtres and delivers babies and reads the future." Damiot was nodding. "Or pretends to read the future. Half the peasants in France, here as well as in the south, would die without the help of those women in sickness and childbirth. Of course I believe in them! Every village priest believes in them. Around here, most village priests help choose the next one when the old one dies."

"Does Paris have women like that, too?"

"Of course. All the poor neighborhoods have them. But everyone consults them. Which infuriates the University physicians." He smiled ruefully. "My mother swears by her favorite wise-woman."

"Does she think the woman can see the future?"

Damiot frowned. "Where is all this leading, *maître?*" When Charles remained stubbornly silent, Damiot said, "The Bible mentions witches. And wiser men than I have believed they can tell the future. Under God's will, of course. So yes, my mother listens to her favorite wise-woman. Now. Why are you asking all this?"

"Because of what an old woman with a herd of goats said to me yesterday."

"Goats? Ah. Was she a little, wizened woman? With a big canvas bag?"

Charles nodded.

"That was Hyacinthe." Damiot smiled. "My mother's witch. Can you imagine a more unlikely name for a goatherd? My mother also buys goat's milk from her."

"Well, this Hyacinthe grabbed my hand and went into a sort of trance. I didn't like what she said." He repeated the woman's words.

Damiot's black eyebrows drew together. "I wouldn't much like that, either," he said soberly. "What do you think it means, 'follow the dead, find your death'?" He looked sharply at Charles. "You did find a dead man."

"Yes. But it was his death, not mine." Charles looked down at the coarse brown blanket. He couldn't say what was really worrying him about her words. When she'd said them, he'd thought, of course, of the murdered Paul Lunel. Since then, however, when he repeated the words to himself, they took him into his memories of Cassel. But he'd long ago found the bodies in the ruined cottage and was still alive. And how could the old woman know anything about Cassel?

When Charles said nothing more, Damiot frowned and said, "I think there's something you're not telling me. Whatever it is, *maître*, don't dismiss what the goatwoman says. Perhaps she's done you a good turn with her warning, because I suspect—no, you don't have to tell me—I suspect that you are doing what you usually do and looking for that boy's killer. Hyacinthe has a reputation for these sudden 'seeings.' She claims the Blessed Virgin talks to her, which is one reason my mother believes her. And one reason you should, too." He stood up and stretched and picked up his candle. "If I leave you now, will you be all right? Can you sleep again?"

"I think so. Thank you for coming to pull me out of my night terrors. And I won't forget what she said." Charles slid down under the covers. *"Bonne nuit, mon père."*

"May the holy angels defend you through the rest of the night." Damiot turned to go. Then he turned back. "There's something else I should tell you about the goatwoman. It will help you take her seriously, which I'm not sure you're doing yet. Last Saint Nicholas Day she told my uncle—my mother's brother—that he'd die before the Epiphany. He spent the rest of December feasting and dancing and laughing at her. He collapsed and died two days before the Epiphany."

"Oh, yes, that should definitely help me go back to sleep." Charles turned over with his back to the door.

When Wednesday's sun rose, it stayed hidden beyond a damp gray sky. As Charles was leaving breakfast, a lay brother brought him a message from La Reynie, telling him that the Novice House rector had agreed that Charles could come and question the novices from Paris who had known Paul Lunel or his family even slightly. Since it was also the day when Maître Henry Wing was going there to make up the St. Augustine sessions he'd missed, he and Charles set out for the rue du Pot-de-Fer together.

The still air had thickened with mist, and as they walked up the rue St. Jacques, the mist beaded on their cloaks like tiny pearls and found its cold way under their collars. Carts were hauling loads of wood up from the quays for householders' winter fires, and an old clothes seller calling, "Old cloaks, better than none!" was striding down the hill, his long pole hung with cloaks braced on his shoulder. As Charles and Wing turned right, past The Dog, Charles lifted his head and sniffed like a beagle.

"Chestnuts?" he said hopefully, and sniffed again. "No, it's just someone's fire. I thought I smelled chestnuts roasting, but I suppose it's still too early for them." He looked to see if La Reynie had someone watching the bookshop in the hope that Madame Cheyne would give herself away, but if a man was there, he was well disguised or well hidden.

Wing was also looking back at the bookshop, but not, from the expression on his face, watching for police. "Do you think we'll see Mademoiselle Ebrard today?"

Charles looked sharply at him. "I doubt it. Why?"

The Englishman blushed furiously under his hat. "She's nice."

Charles let a moment go by. "Yes. I believe you find her pretty, too," he added, to see what the Englishman would say.

Wing's pink face and defiant glance made Charles think of an offended piglet. "God makes beauty, Maître du Luc," Wing said stiffly. "Why shouldn't we admire it?"

Admonishing each other in charity was part of a Jesuit's obligation toward his brothers. And when the brother Jesuit was as innocent as Wing seemed to be, the admonishing might be downright urgent.

"Jesuits are supposed to admire female beauty cautiously, Maître Wing. To say the least." Charles wished he could make it clear that he spoke from personal knowledge of caution's failure and not from a Richaud-like urge to chastise.

Wing was silent, watching his feet walk.

Trying to sound offhand, Charles said, "Did you—um—know girls before you entered the Society?"

Wing sighed. "Hardly any other than my sisters. We lived quietly and the Yorkshire countryside isn't a very social place." He looked up at Charles. "May I tell you something?"

Charles nodded and the Englishman moved closer. "I've never kissed a woman," Wing breathed. "Except my mother." He looked down, hiding under his hat brim. "I dreamed of Mademoiselle Ebrard last night."

Oh, no, Charles thought. *Now what do I do?* What he wanted to do was to shove Wing out of the Society of Jesus and back into the ordinary world, at least until Wing knew how to kiss a woman and whether doing it mattered to him. But before Charles found something to say, Wing surprised him.

"Oh, well. It's not the first time I've dreamed about women. My confessors always say it's just part of being a religious. But it makes what Saint Augustine says about love very interesting, don't you think? I mean, when he prayed for the gift of chastity, but didn't want it 'yet.' I think that was before he was a monk—I suppose I should have done that, too."

Relieved, Charles listened with half an ear as the Englishman mused about St. Augustine's private life. Beneath the appearance of listening, Charles thought about the Ebrard girl, but not in the way of Maître Wing's dream. Since he'd found the fragment of *Le Cabinet jesuitique*'s cover and learned that The Dog sold Dutch pornography upstairs, Charles had wanted even more urgently to know what Mlle Ebrard had really been doing on Friday in the lane near the Novice House. He didn't believe the story about shortcuts and shopping for needles. What he was reluctantly wondering was whether she was helping her aunt distribute *Le Cabinet*, or the Dutch books. Or both. He didn't think there was a bookshop near the Novice House. But she might have been delivering books to customers' houses.

And if she is, his coldly logical inner voice said, *will you turn her in? Or are her eyes too pretty?*

If she's delivering illegal books, Charles growled silently back, *she's probably doing it because her aunt is forcing her—maybe her aunt is threatening to turn her out if she refuses. I want to find out before La Reynie does and warn her. She has enough trouble. At the very least, she'll have nowhere to live if her aunt goes to prison.*

As the scholastics approached the Novice House, a boy ran out of the narrow cleft beside its church, his legs flashing and black jacket tails flying. On an impulse, Charles reached out a long arm and caught his collar. "Hold up, flying Mercury, for one small moment!" Charles turned the boy to face him. "I am Maître Charles du Luc. A friend of Lieutenant-Général La Reynie. Are you the son of his maid?"

The boy wiped his sweating face. "I am, *maître*." His face clouded and his green-hazel eyes grew worried. "Is there trouble? Is my mother ill?"

"No, no, nothing like that. What's your name?"

"I'm Michel Poulard."

"Well then, Michel Poulard, will you do something for me?"

The boy eyed him. "What would that be, *maître*?"

Approving that wariness, Charles said, "I imagine you see most of what goes on around the Novice House. If you see anything odd, anyone coming or going who shouldn't be there, I want you to go immediately and tell the rector. Tell him I asked you to do that. Will you?"

"Yes, *maître*."

"Oh, and another thing, Michel," Charles said casually, "I suppose books get delivered to the house, don't they? For the novices to use?"

"Books?" The boy's slender body was suddenly very still. "Why do you want to know about books?"

"I thought you might have seen them delivered, that's all."

"I haven't seen anything like that. I have to go now, I have an errand." He took to his heels as though they really had sprouted Mercury's wings and turned down the lane where Mlle Rose Ebrard had gone.

Wing turned anxiously to Charles. "He's going down the lane where you rescued Mademoiselle Ebrard. You don't think she's there again and needs help, do you? Should we go and see?"

"Of course not! You heard the boy, he just has some sort of errand there." Charles hoped fervently that he was correct, and that Rose Ebrard was behind The Dog's downstairs counter, selling blameless books.

Wing followed Charles to the Novice House door but kept looking over his shoulder.

"Listen," Charles said, "if I'm not here at the door when you leave, that will mean I'm still busy with Père Le Picart's errand and you'll have to go back alone." That was the explanation Charles and the rector had agreed would be given to Wing for Charles's going to the Novice House. "If that happens," Charles said sternly, "don't go down that lane looking for Mademoiselle Ebrard. Just go straight back to the college."

Wing looked mulishly at Charles and said nothing.

"Maître Wing," Charles said, "there are plenty of men who would happily set on a lone religious for fun." Especially one who looks as defenseless as a piglet, he didn't say. "Do you want to cause trouble—and unseemly notoriety—by getting yourself attacked?"

Abashed, Wing shook his head. "I'll go straight back. I promise."

A lay brother answered the bell, and Wing nodded to Charles and started along the gallery to the stairs.

The brother looked impatiently at Charles. "Where are you going?"

"I am Maître du Luc. The rector is expecting me."

The brother told him how to find the rector's office and hurried away, muttering to himself about fleas in the martyrs' rooms. Which sounded ominous, Charles thought, grinning, if you didn't know that most Novice Houses had sleeping chambers named after Christian martyrs. Before he reached the rector's office, he met the rector coming toward him.

"I think you must be Maître du Luc," said the slender, balding, graying Jesuit. His downward-sloping brown eyes were tired and preoccupied. "The brother put his head in on the way past my office and said you were here. I am Père Guymond, rector here. I remembered your name when Monsieur La

Reynie's message came to me early this morning. You asked permission to see our Amaury de Corbet, I believe. And how did you find him?"

Charles chose his words carefully. "He seemed well, *mon père*. And glad to be here."

"Good. I think he is very glad to be here." Guymond sighed. "Our Provincial has told me of the task you've been given. It was I who identified poor Paul Lunel's body. Be assured that I am grateful to have you asking questions here instead of the police. You are young and no doubt remember that novices—especially new novices—are easily upset. Indeed, this murder has been a blow to all of us. If you'll follow me, I'll take you to the room we've set aside for you. It's out of the way, which will help to keep our peace undisturbed."

Charles followed him into the garden he'd seen through the gallery windows and toward a long building across the courtyard. The garden was checkered with paved paths and low-hedged flower beds, and in a vegetable garden near the other end of the building they were approaching, several young novices were harvesting cabbage. Charles looked for Amaury but didn't really expect to see him. He found it hard to imagine the proudly noble Amaury doing anything with cabbages.

"That is our refectory," Guymond said. He turned toward a door at the refectory's north end. "And this we call the Little Room." He ushered Charles into a room not really so little, but with a good bit of its floor taken up with tools, boxes, and storage barrels ranged against the white plastered walls. "I've put you here," he said apologetically, "for privacy, and also because we dine early. If you're still busy at dinnertime, this will make it easier for the novices to eat as soon as you're finished with them."

He ducked under a huge ham hanging from a beam, and

closed and barred the heavy door leading into the refectory, shutting out soft footfalls, an occasional clattering, and the muted voices of table setters and kitchen workers. Then he pulled two chairs close to the small table positioned just inside the half-open courtyard door. "If you need anything, or need to speak to me, send someone from the refectory to find me. Unless something urgent comes to light, no need to see me before you leave."

Charles thanked him, and the rector withdrew. Charles took quill and paper from his satchel and sat down to wait for the first of his novices. Within moments, a gangling boy of sixteen or so stuck his head around the open door. At Charles's nod, the boy came in, closed the door, and stood awkwardly before him.

"*Bonjour, maître.*" The novice's big hands, folded at his waist, clutched each other as though one of them might escape. "I am Monsieur Étienne du Bois."

"Sit, please," Charles said, smiling. He needed these young men to talk freely, and standing at attention before even such a lowly superior as himself was not going to encourage that.

Du Bois stumbled over his feet and fell into the other chair. Charles pretended not to notice. "We are trying to find out more about the unfortunate Paul Lunel, who was to have been a novice with you. You have already been told that he didn't arrive on the entrance day and was later found dead. I have been asked to talk to some of you who say you knew him or his family before you came to the Novice House."

"Me? I didn't—well, not exactly, only my—I mean—" He shut his eyes, gulped air, and untangled his words. "I didn't really know him, *maître*. But I told the rector that my mother knows his mother."

"Ah. I see." Charles thought for a moment about Mme

Lunel. "Do you know how his mother felt about her son becoming a Jesuit?"

"My mother said that Madame Lunel didn't like it. Oh, Madame Lunel is very devout," the boy said earnestly. "She and my mother used to go to church together on feast days. But Madame Lunel doesn't like Jesuits. She's a—" He frowned anxiously. "A Galliard?"

Charles couldn't help laughing, and du Bois blushed. "I think you may mean that she's a Gallican," Charles said. "Does that sound right?"

The young face cleared. "That's it! But *Gallic* just means French. Doesn't it?"

"It can. But these days *Gallican* means someone who doesn't want any non-French influence in France."

"Oh. But why doesn't Madame Lunel like Jesuits? Jesuits are French."

"Not all Jesuits are French. Yes, I know, it's complicated. A Gallican wouldn't want the Novice House or Louis le Grand to have rectors who might be Italian or Spanish or German Jesuits."

"Oh. Do you mean we're going to have a new rector? I don't mind. As long as he's not English. He'd make us drink beer."

"I didn't mean that. Never mind," Charles said desperately. He asked everything he could think of, but the devotion of Paul Lunel's mother and her bewildering Gallican sentiments was all he got. From the next novice, he learned only that Paul Lunel had been tutored at home, rather than going to a college—which he'd already known. And that the deceased Monsieur Lunel *père*, a well-respected judge, had been famously stern with his sons, brooking no rebellion from their future as legal men who would carry on the family name in the nobility of the Robe.

The third novice, Jean Renier, auburn haired and with the pure profile of a classical statue, was as self-possessed as a courtier and as voluble as the lawyer he had decided not to be. He had shared a dancing master with Paul Lunel, but had apparently had no curiosity about him. After a few minutes, Renier launched into a discourse on the wildly unlikely motives of Paul Lunel's killer and how the killer could be found, and Charles got rid of him as quickly as he could.

The fourth and last novice, Monsieur Pierre Lyon, was built like a small bull. He explained that his family's town house was near the Lunels' on the rue Jean Tison. But he had only *no* to say to Charles's questions. Charles was about to give up when Lyon said shyly, "Please, *maître*, may I say something else?"

"Of course. What is it?"

"I—we've heard here about the scholastic named Richaud who's missing from Louis le Grand."

Charles nodded. "Do you know him?"

"No, I don't *know* him. It's just that you're asking us about Paul Lunel, and that made me remember that I saw Maître Richaud once at the Lunel house."

Charles studied the boy. Lyon seemed stolid and undemanding. Not, Charles thought, someone likely to dramatize himself.

"When did you see him? And how did you know it was Richaud?"

"It wasn't very long ago, only at the end of September, just before I came here. The Lunels live across the street from my father's house and as I was riding home, I saw a Jesuit come out of the Lunel courtyard. That's why I noticed, you see, because I could tell by his cassock that he was a Jesuit and I was about to enter the Society. The man he was walking with called him Maître Richaud. I was a little surprised, because they were laughing loudly together, and I thought Jesuits were supposed to be quiet in the street. When I heard he'd disappeared, I remembered seeing him. I've been praying he'll be found safe and well."

Laughing? Richaud? "Can you describe him?" Charles said.

"He was shorter than the other man—small and thin. He had his hat on, of course, but I could see that his hair was dark. And he had a narrow face."

"That does sound like him. It's well that you're praying for him. We're all hoping he'll soon be found unharmed."

"But you're not expecting it."

Startled, Charles reappraised the little bull yet again. "The longer he's gone, the harder it is to expect it."

The novice rose and started to make his bow, but Charles stopped him.

"Did you recognize the man with Maître Richaud?"

"No. It wasn't Paul Lunel's older brother. But he was about the same age as the brother. I suppose he was one of Monsieur Alexandre Lunel's friends."

The bell had begun ringing for the novices' dinner, and Charles thanked the boy and dismissed him. He put his notes and quill into his satchel and let himself out into the garden, keeping to the path under a line of chestnut trees beside the wall, since he was going against the silent tide of the household coming across the garden toward the refectory. As he approached the main building, the rector came to meet him.

His former friendliness gone, Guymond held out the book he was carrying. "Do you know what this is?"

Charles took the small book and read the title stamped on its leather cover: *Le Cabinet jesuitique.* He returned Guymond's grim look. "Yes. I do. Where did this come from, *mon père?*"

"From inside the mattress of your friend Amaury de Corbet."

Chapter 17

"No," Charles said flatly. He handed *Le Cabinet jesuitique* back to the Novice House rector. "Amaury de Corbet would never have this poison in his possession. Who found it? Who says it's his?"

Bridling at Charles's vehemence, Pere Guymond said, "A lay brother found it. Some of the mattresses were stuffed with new straw yesterday, and new herbs were put in to fight fleas. When the brother reached into Monsieur de Corbet's mattress to put in the herbs, he found the book and brought it to me. Before you ask, we keep no copy of this anywhere in the Novice House. Nor have I ever before found one here."

"I'm sorry to tell you that this book is again circulating in Paris, *mon père*. I discovered that by chance last week. The Provincial knows of it and so does Lieutenant-Général La Reynie."

"God save us. That's the last thing we need. But if the book is circulating, that would seem to make it even more likely that Monsieur de Corbet brought this with him. Even if someone else hid it in the mattress, Monsieur de Corbet surely would have felt it through the new straw in the night. You know how thin a novice's mattress is."

Charles smiled wryly. "I do know how thin they are, but if

Monsieur de Corbet felt something uncomfortable in his mattress, he would probably just move to a different position. He's spent ten years in the army and navy. I served in the army and I can tell you that even Jesuit novice beds are better than what he's used to. In any case, if the mattress was emptied and restuffed, others obviously had the chance to put something inside."

"Possibly. But I think you say all this because Monsieur de Corbet is your friend. You have no proof."

"Forgive me, *mon père*, but neither do you have proof." Charles braced himself for an indignant reply.

But Guymond only said, "Come, let us walk. We'll call less attention to ourselves." They walked on toward the main building, brushing occasional wet yellow leaves from their cassocks. "Even if Monsieur de Corbet did not bring this into our house," the rector said, "someone did. Someone who lives here, because no one else could reach the novice chambers, especially his."

"Where is Monsieur de Corbet's chamber?"

"On the top floor, at the far end of the building from the street entrance. It's one of the Martyr chambers, the one called Miki, after the Japanese martyr."

"Ah. Yes, I heard one of your lay brothers talking about fleas in the martyrs' rooms. Who shares the chamber with Monsieur de Corbet?"

"Only two others, since Paul Lunel never arrived. The head chamber novice is Monsieur Joliot. And the other—" Guymond closed his eyes, trying to remember. "I can never remember his name. To myself, I call him the lawyer. He's—"

On a hunch, Charles said, "Monsieur Jean Renier?"

"Yes, that's him." The rector looked sideways at Charles.

"Interesting that you knew who I meant—since, so far as I know, today is the only time you've spoken with him."

"Once was enough." Charles grinned. "'The lawyer' describes him perfectly. I'd hardly opened my mouth before *he* was questioning *me*. I could hardly shut him up. I wonder if you could send him off to Rome and make a canon lawyer out of him."

The rector sighed and lowered his voice. "I've had that very thought. Unfortunately, he has to finish his novitiate first. Why is talent so often annoying?" Guymond shook his nearly bald head as though shaking off flies. "I simply don't understand this book being here at all! A novice has taken no vows. If he changes his mind, if he wants to leave for any reason, he is free to do so. He has no need to convince anyone that terrible things are true of the Society of Jesus. And a novice who wants to be here would never bring this book in. What would be the point? Besides all that, you surely remember how impossible it is to keep anything hidden in a Novice House."

"An especially aggrieved novice might be spiteful enough to try to damage the Society and urge others to leave with him. This book could be used for that. Though, as you say, keeping it hidden long enough for that would be difficult."

"I cannot, of course, read anyone's mind. But I would say, from past experience, that the second-year novices have been here long enough to be fairly sure of their choice. And the new ones haven't been here long enough yet to lose their first fervor."

"I doubt that the guilty person is a novice," Charles said flatly. "No, I don't say that to protect Monsieur de Corbet. I say it because this book may have been brought here because someone *knew* it would be found. Wanted it to be found."

"But why?"

"The book is already making you look askance at your novices. You say your lay brother looked through it before he brought it to you. If he's literate enough, he's probably wondering about what he read."

"You're saying that someone wants to destroy trust among the men here? Trust and even vocations?"

"That's what I'm saying. We also don't know how long this copy has been here. Monsieur de Corbet's mattress may be only its most recent hiding place. And we don't know if this is the only copy."

Appalled, Guymond stared at Charles. "No. We don't."

"May I ask what you're going to do, *mon père*?"

"It was found in Monsieur de Corbet's bed and I will talk to him first. He's still the most likely culprit. If he's guilty, I'll dismiss him. Either way, I will notify the Provincial. And Lieutenant-Général La Reynie, since this trash is illegal to possess or distribute in France."

"Monsieur La Reynie already knows *Le Cabinet jesuitique* is circulating in Paris. But he needs to know you found it here." Charles hesitated. "*Mon père*, may I be present when you question Monsieur de Corbet? I ask because I have been charged by La Reynie with asking questions in our houses that might help to find Paul Lunel's killer. In addition to Lunel's death, a Louis le Grand scholastic has disappeared, as I am sure you know. And I, myself, was attacked. And suddenly, this book is among us. I cannot help but wonder if all this destruction—and effort at destruction—go together."

"A devilish thought." Guymond crossed himself. "Yes, you may listen while I question Monsieur de Corbet. But you may not speak unless I give you leave. Agreed?"

"Agreed, *mon père*."

"Then I will call him from the refectory."

The rector and Charles went into the gallery, where Guymond stopped a lay brother.

"*Mon frère*, be so good as to go to the refectory and send Monsieur Amaury de Corbet to me, in the Chapel of Saint Ignatius."

"Yes, *mon père*."

The brother hurried out into the garden, and Charles and Guymond went along the gallery to a range of rooms bordering the south side of the front courtyard. In the small Chapel of St. Ignatius, Guymond knelt before the painting of the saint above the altar and prayed with his head in his hands. Charles knelt, too, and prayed that Amaury would be able to clear himself of any knowledge of *Le Cabinet*. He got up as the lay brother who'd been sent for Amaury entered the chapel. He was alone. The brother waited until the rector looked over his shoulder and rose to his feet.

"*Mon père*, Monsieur de Corbet is not in the refectory. I'm told that he was taken on an errand with the provisioner. I wasn't told when they would return."

Swallowing frustration, Guymond thanked the brother and dismissed him to dinner. Then he turned to Charles.

"Talking to Monsieur de Corbet will have to wait until he returns. Shall I send you word when he comes back?"

"Yes. Thank you, *mon père*."

The rector returned to his prayers and Charles made his way to the street door.

Out in the rue du Pot-de-Fer, he turned toward the college, but as he passed the narrow cleft beside the Novice House door and the church, his steps slowed. He thought about the running servant boy he'd stopped, Michel Poulard, and wished he'd asked the boy if he knew Mlle Ebrard. Because Charles strongly suspected that she'd been talking to the boy in front of the Novice House on Friday, before she'd ducked down that dead-end lane. And a short while ago, the boy had disappeared down that same lane. But what connection could there be between Rose Ebrard and a thirteen-year-old servant boy? No matter how hard he tried, the only connection Charles could think of was books. And the boy had grown suddenly wary when Charles had mentioned books. Hoping against hope that he was wrong about all that, Charles started walking again.

No matter how much you hope, his pessimist inner voice said, *she still has a bookselling aunt who ignores the needles in her neighborhood market and sends her willing niece to buy them at the market near the Novice House. Do they even sell needles at that particular market?*

Charles said dismissively back, *Of course they sell needles there; everyone needs needles.* But he turned around and strode down the rue du Pot-de-Fer in the other direction, toward the market.

The market was near the abbey of St. Germain, where four streets came together. It was was loud with hawkers and bargaining buyers and reeked of fish. Charles gave a wide berth to the fish cart parked at its center and bristling with fins and tails, and started inspecting market booths. But after a few minutes, he realized that even if he didn't find any needles, there might be a regular needle seller who happened to be absent. He approached a pair of basket-laden maidservants and asked if there were ever needles on offer.

"Oh, no," the older one said, when she and her friend had finished looking him up and down and giggling. She had a scatter of pockmarks on her cheeks, but her dimples and dancing black eyes made her still comely enough. "Not at this market. Why, do you want to sew your own cassock?"

"We do sew our own cassocks."

That sent both girls into fresh giggles, especially the other one, whose lush roundness Charles was trying not to notice. "Oooh, I'd sew it for you," she teased, and let her eyes stray appreciatively over him again. "But you'd have to take it off."

He nearly choked on the stifled urge to tease back, which pretty girls still roused in him, and bowed slightly. But his twitching mouth belied his attempt at clerical dignity, and he gave up and smiled at them as he moved quickly away. His smile died as the cold prickling that told him he was being watched spread down his spine, and he turned abruptly. No one was behind him. Pretending that something had bitten him and scratching his calf, he let his eyes wander over people and booths and shadows beneath the trees . . . and came to rest on Rose Ebrard.

She was standing on the path between the row of booths. Her back was to him, and he went quickly behind a small booth selling ribbons, where he could see what she did without being noticed, even if she turned. But as he stopped at its corner, the prickling returned. He spun on his heel, but again, no one was behind him. But a short black cloak was swirling out of sight around the booth's other side and Charles went after it. He saw three men, all wearing short black cloaks, walking quickly toward the city wall. Two were wigless, their own straight hair showing under black hats. Dressed entirely in black—even to their stockings—they looked almost like priests. *Dévots*, Charles thought, laymen and laywomen who went to all the church's services, gave selflessly to the poor, and sometimes lived an almost monastic life, though most of them had families, and the men often had businesses. Most of the men were also members of one or another Congregation of the Holy Virgin, the same kind of congregation the Louis le Grand students belonged to. Indeed, all Congregations of the Holy Virgin were directed by Jesuits. So why would a *dévot* be covertly watching a Jesuit? Charles was uneasily certain that one of them *had* been watching him. But if he went after them, he'd lose Rose Ebrard, and every instinct was telling him to keep watching her.

He went back to the corner of the ribbon booth. She was still there, but farther along the path now, looking at something to her left instead of at the booths and their piles of apples and onions. Charles followed her gaze. And found himself looking at Amaury de Corbet, who was carrying a deep basket and standing with lowered eyes behind an older Jesuit. Charles frowned and looked beyond Amaury, thinking that the young woman must be looking at something else. But when Amaury and the other Jesuit—the Novice House provisioner, Charles guessed—went to another booth, she followed them. When they stopped, she stopped. Charles's thoughts tumbled over each other as he tried to rearrange his assumptions. Until what sounded like a goose hissed at him and he jumped.

It wasn't a goose, but a woman, the ribbon seller whose booth he was hiding behind. "Who are you spying on, Jesuit?" she spat, leaning over the booth's side.

"Not spying," he said vaguely, watching Mlle Ebrard. "Well, actually, yes, but—"

The woman leaned farther toward him. "Get away from here!"

Mlle Ebrard suddenly moved and Charles went after her, absently signing a blessing at the startled ribbon seller.

At the abbey's wall, the pathway turned sharply right beneath tall, ancient lime trees overhanging a short stretch of the wall. On either side of the path were smaller stalls and goods spread on the ground. Trying to stay in the trees' shadow, Charles kept the girl and the two Jesuits in sight. Then the provisioner stopped before a woman selling a rainbow of different-colored apples and pears, with Amaury behind him, his eyes still modestly on the ground as befitted a novice. Standing at a tallow chandler's booth near Charles, Mlle Ebrard watched the novice as intensely as an animal about to spring. Charles moved a little to see more of her face. Its longing abruptly enlightened him and made him catch his breath. He wondered if Amaury could possibly be unaware of her burning gaze. Or if, perhaps, he was all too aware and his stillness was meant to be his armor. Even as other people in the market turned to watch a shouting group of men chasing a fleet-footed pickpocket, Amaury went on staring at the ground, lips moving as he prayed or recited Scripture, just as novices were supposed to do when sent to carry burdens at the market.

Charles didn't see what more Rose Ebrard could do, unless she was willing to draw the anger of the provisioner and make trouble for Amaury. Whatever was going on here, Charles didn't want that kind of trouble for either of them. And he had his own grim questions for Mlle Ebrard. But as he started toward her, the provisioner turned to put his purchases into Amaury's basket and saw Charles, whom he recognized from the Novice House.

"Maître!" The provisioner smiled eagerly and beckoned Charles to him.

Amaury de Corbet, hearing the Jesuit title of *maître*, looked up. He gave Charles a slight and surprised smile. Then he saw Mlle Ebrard, and his eyes widened to fill half his face. The provisioner saw nothing, too busy asking Charles in discreet Latin about the murder of Paul Lunel. Charles feigned avid response, willing to turn handsprings if it would keep the provisioner from noticing his novice. Because now Amaury was looking at Rose Ebrard the same way she was looking at him.

Charles fell back on what his mother called his talent for talking the horns off a brass goat. In likewise discreet Latin, he spoke in lengthy rhetorical flourishes, all the while shifting his position and forcing the other man to shift with him until the provisioner's back was turned to Amaury. Still talking, Charles saw out of the corner of his eye that Mlle Ebrard had moved face-to-face with Amaury and was talking even faster than Charles.

Charles realized almost too late that the provisioner was about to take his leave and that when he turned, he would be looking straight at his novice, who was now listening to Rose Ebrard as though she were the only being in the world. Charles twitched his leather satchel off his shoulder, twitched it again as it fell, caught his quill case as it fell out, and closed his hand around it. Everything else spilled onto the ground around the provisioner's feet.

"Oh, *mon père*, I am so sorry, forgive me!" Charles cried, exclaiming and fussing and deploring his clumsiness as he bent and tossed the quill case hard at Amaury's feet. The startled novice bent to pick it up, as Charles knew he would, since novices learned very quickly to retrieve anything that fell to the ground. Amaury picked up the case and carefully dusted it off, and the provisioner anxiously smoothed a wrinkled page in the copy of St. Augustine Charles had forgotten to take out of his satchel. Charles darted quickly aside, as though picking up something else that had fallen, and said under his breath to Mlle Ebrard, "Go! Or he'll be in trouble. Wait for me beyond the market."

She vanished into a clutch of passing housewives. Amaury, still seeming like a man in a dream, handed the quill case to Charles and looked back where she'd been. But he found only empty air and turned in bewilderment to Charles. Before the novice could speak, the provisioner bustled up to them and handed Charles the St. Augustine. With a warning look at his friend, Charles stowed the book in his satchel, thanked the provisioner, and said good-bye. He left Amaury standing as though he'd never moved, holding the basket, eyes on the ground, lips moving silently. Whatever the man's prayers had been before, Charles was sure that now they were wrung from a divided heart. And more trouble was waiting for Amaury at the Novice House. Charles hesitated, torn between going after Rose Ebrard and returning with Amaury to face the rector. But Charles's feet seemed more decisive than his head and took him purposefully out of the market toward the city wall.

Chapter 18

Charles half suspected that Mlle Rose Ebrard wouldn't wait for him. Not after what he'd seen. And she surely wouldn't wait if she was responsible for *Le Cabinet*'s presence in the Novice House. But as he neared the wall, the sun finally emerged from the clouds and poured a stripe of light down the stone, and a woman's blue scarf blossomed against the gray. Relieved that she'd waited for him, Charles hurried toward her. She watched his approach unsmiling.

"Well?" she challenged him, when he reached her.

"Not well at all, I think, *mademoiselle*. From what I saw in the market."

The fight suddenly went out of her. "No. It isn't."

Charles looked quickly around for somewhere more private to talk. He should not be standing in the street in talk with a woman. And he didn't want this conversation overheard, which meant they could not go to the college or The Dog. But if they went anywhere else more private and were seen, that would create worse scandal. It would have to be the street, but at least the street noise would help cover what they said.

"Shall we walk, *mademoiselle*? As though I'm simply escorting you home? If you could look as though you need escorting, that would help."

"There's much I need, but I don't need that." But she walked docilely enough at his side and Charles stole covert glances at her set face.

"When Maître Wing and I found you in the lane by the Novice House," he said, "were you there because of Amaury de Corbet?"

"Yes."

"And you were talking to Michel, the Novice House servant boy, I think."

She frowned suspiciously. "I am not obliged to answer you. You have no authority over me."

"None at all."

She quickened her pace, but Charles matched it. They walked in a strained silence. Except for Charles's sharp-tongued inner voice. *You have no authority over her, that's true. But you are certainly obligated to report attempts at secret communication with a novice.*

Charles rolled his shoulders uneasily under his cassock. *Fifty other people saw them just now. That's hardly secret communication.*

With elaborate weariness, the voice said, *Use the brain God gave you.*

Charles looked sideways at the young woman. "I think you were asking the boy about Amaury. Perhaps asking him to give Amaury a note from you? And then, when the Novice House door opened, the boy ran to keep the lay brother from seeing him talking to you. And you ran to keep Maître Wing and me from seeing you."

The girl sighed. "All right, if you know so much already. I did write a note. But the boy never delivered it. When I saw him again, he said he'd been too afraid of losing his place there and had put the note down the latrine. I'm only telling you this," she went on, "because Amaury has spoken of you. Many times. I almost told you the day we met at Louis le Grand, when you said your name. And yesterday, your cousin, Monsieur de Vintimille du Luc—the one whose ship Amaury served on—came to see me at The Dog."

"Yesterday?" Charles said in mingled surprise and dismay. "I thought he'd left Paris."

"He'd gone to the country, to my father's house—what used to be my father's house—to look for me. Someone told him where I was and he came to the shop. He wanted to know if I'd seen Amaury."

Hoping this didn't mean that Charles-François would come back to Louis le Grand, Charles said, "I thought that you recognized my name when we met, but I couldn't imagine why. Mademoiselle, my cousin told me that Amaury had planned to marry but withdrew from the betrothal. Was he betrothed to you?"

"Yes." She was quiet for a moment, then surprised him by saying, "Until I met you, I hated you. Since it was your being a Jesuit that started Amaury on this mistaken path of his."

"I knew nothing about that. Until I saw him in the Novice House, I'd seen and heard nothing of him for ten years."

"But you lived in his mind all that time. He would have gone to be a Jesuit years ago, if his father had died sooner." Charles started to speak, but she shook her head at him. "Wait. Last Christmas, Amaury got leave from his ship and came home and asked me to marry him. We'd grown up near each other. In the country, between Paris and Vincennes." Her eyes flashed at him. "If you're thinking I'm not worthy to match with nobility like the de Corbets, you're wrong. They have land, but little money, and my father was a well-off and respected merchant. When Amaury asked me to marry him, I thought he'd gotten over wanting to be a religious." Her voice sank. "Gotten over the things that haunted him."

"Things from the army?"

"Yes. But that's his story to tell if he wants to, not mine. Then his father died suddenly in early spring, and that ruined everything. Amaury came home and broke our betrothal. He confessed to me that while his father lived, he'd been afraid to disappoint him, afraid to refuse what every nobleman is supposed to do—fight and beget sons to carry on his name. He said he loved me and that he'd thought that with me, he could put aside his wanting to leave the world and turn wholeheartedly to another life. But when his father died, he'd realized he couldn't," she finished bitterly.

Charles snorted. "Well, if he thinks being a Jesuit is leaving the world, he's an idiot."

"He's an idiot about a lot of things. But I love him," Mlle Ebrard said despairingly. "I'm not giving him up without a fight; you should know that. No matter what you or anyone else says. Not just because I want him, but because I know he's wrong about himself! He's trying to give his whole life up to guilt, now that his father's gone. And he still loves me; I saw that in his face just now in the market."

"So did I," Charles said. "So did anyone who looked at the two of you. And so would the provisioner, if I hadn't distracted him." He looked at her curiously. "If you'd made sure the provisioner saw what was going on between you and Amaury, you could have ended his career as a novice by nightfall. Why didn't you?"

Her look was full of disdain. "You've obviously never loved anyone."

A small rueful sound escaped Charles, and he looked away. But he felt her eyes on him as they walked.

"Forgive me," she said softly. "I see that you have. Then you must know that I would cut off my hand rather than harm him or cause him pain!" She wiped tears away with her scarf. "I don't suppose you'll believe me, but if he really had a vocation, if God had really called him to your Jesuit life, I would die rather than stand in his way. But he doesn't have a vocation. God hasn't called him, I'm sure of it! Amaury is only hiding in your Novice House. From his guilt about what happened in the army. What kind of offering is that to God?"

Charles flinched inwardly at that echo of his cousin Charles-François's bitter accusation. *You're a coward hiding in your safe Jesuit nest.* "One may offer suffering to God," he said.

"But is suffering a vocation? Amaury is trying to twist his ordinary devotion into a—a shroud! That's not a vocation, that's refusing God's gift of life!"

Chastened by her blunt clarity, Charles watched a pair of ravens pecking at something squashed in the street. In the Jesuit rules, there was a list of things that barred a man from becoming a Jesuit. One thing was "An intention that is not as right as it ought to be for entrance into a religious institute but is mixed with human designs." In Amaury's case, "human designs" might well include trying to twist guilty self-hatred into Christian humility and penance. In his own case, he'd been wrestling with his army guilt, God knew. But he'd also been sure that he had a vocation to help souls—and in doing that, to come as close to God as he could. But his cousin Charles-François's visit had forced him to see how deeply he'd buried his guilt over the peasants' deaths at Cassel—and made him wonder miserably if that guilt should perhaps have disqualified him.

Charles used his elbow to fend off a maidservant's market basket full of beets and cabbages. "If your father is so well off, why are you working for your aunt here in Paris? Did you run away to be near Amaury?"

"When we met, I told you that my father had died. He was

killed in August on a trip to Italy, on the route merchants used to call the Murder Road." She sighed and hugged her cloak tightly around herself. "After my poor father died, I found out how his affairs really stood. Everyone thought he was near to being wealthy. And he had been, but then we learned that one of his two ships had gone down on the way to New France, and that he'd had other losses, some on bonds for loans he couldn't collect. There was almost nothing left for me. When my uncles met to decide what to do with me, I persuaded them to let me come to Paris and live with my widowed aunt at The Dog. They can't marry me off profitably now that I'm poor, so they didn't really care what I did." She smiled wryly and shrugged. "My aunt is a trial, but at least I'm in Paris."

Charles was about to ask her what she planned to do next to get Amaury back, when three grave-faced men dressed in black, the same three he'd seen in the market, stopped beside him.

They bowed and the oldest man gazed sadly at Charles. "We are Gentlemen." He gave the word an audible capital letter. "Think, we beg you, on what you are doing. Go quickly to your confessor." His glance brushed Rose Ebrard, who was staring openmouthed at him, and fled back to Charles. "A Jesuit must spurn women like this one. You are somewhat young—a scholastic, I suspect, and not a priest. But that cannot excuse you. Think on this. For the good of souls and Christian society." He and his comrades bowed and paced solemnly away.

Mlle Ebrard said angrily, "Who are they? Did you hear them? 'Women like this one' indeed!"

Charles looked after them in disgust. "They're called Gentlemen of the Professed House. That's the name for laymen from the Congregation of the Holy Virgin overseen by Jesuits who live at our Professed House. Some of these Gentlemen see themselves as everyone's moral guardians. And some of them are terrified of women." He sighed. "Those three will go to Louis le Grand to tell my rector that I am on my way to hell in the public street for talking alone to you."

She tossed her head and straightened her tight-fitting, orange jacket that matched her skirt. "I know that those congregations do good things. But men like that must make God blush!"

"I hope so. *Mademoiselle*——" Charles hesitated, but he had to ask. "What are you going to do now about Amaury?"

She met his question with her own. " Are you going to warn them about me at the Novice House?"

"I don't know. Have you sent other notes to Amaury?"

"No." Her chin went up and her mouth was a firm, tight line.

"But you'll go on fighting us for him."

She stepped in front of Charles, forcing him to stop. "Of *course* I will go on fighting," she said fiercely. "No matter what you and the rest of them do. And if you accuse me to them of trying to get him out of there, I'll deny everything and say that you pursued me with talk. So be warned."

To her further anger, Charles's mouth twitched toward smiling. "Oh, I'm feeling very warned about many things," he said. "Between those three Gentlemen and you. Please, will you walk?" He tilted his head toward two avidly watching Franciscans who had stopped near them. "It's bad strategy to let your campaign become notorious before it has to."

"Stop laughing at me." She turned on her heel and walked quickly ahead of him.

He caught up with her. "Mademoiselle, we may be enemies in this." *Though I rather think we are not*, he thought, but wasn't ready to say aloud. "But there is one thing I beg you to tell me. Did you give someone at the Novice House a copy——or copies—of *Le Cabinet jesuitique* from your aunt's bookshop? Are you distributing copies of it for her?"

"No." She stared at him, mystified. "She hardly ever offers to have books delivered. And the only person from the Novice House I've ever spoken to—besides Amaury just now—is the servant boy, and I certainly never gave him a book. I doubt he can read."

"I imagine he can, he gets teaching in return for his work. Well, that's one question answered. Here's another. Is your aunt selling *Le Cabinet jesuitique* upstairs at The Dog?"

A flush crept up the girl's throat and she kept her gaze determinedly on the street in front of them. "I know what's upstairs. Is this *Cabinet* one of those Dutch books?"

"Have you seen a book with that title among the Dutch books?" Charles countered.

"I don't remember a title like that. But I don't—I try not to look at them. My aunt doesn't make me sell them. But she says that if The Dog doesn't have them, someone else will make the profit. She's trying to make a living for us both, and the shop hasn't done so well since her husband—my mother's brother—died."

They moved aside to let a string of porters go by, bent under carrying frames loaded with bales of cloth.

"Mademoiselle Ebrard, do you swear by the Virgin that you are not helping your aunt distribute *Le Cabinet jesuitique?*"

Impatience flared in her deep blue eyes. "Yes! How many ways do I have to say it? Why does it matter so much?"

"Because *Le Cabinet* is an illegal and poisonous book full of clever lies about the Society of Jesus, and someone in Paris is selling it. I was sure it was your aunt." Charles's tone grew lightly ironic. "And if she were, what a stroke of luck that would be for you. *Le Cabinet* might well persuade a Jesuit novice that he'd made a bad decision."

Her eyes were as cold as a Paris winter. "I mean to win Amaury back, but not with lies."

She put a pleading hand on Charles's arm. "*Maître*, if I know that Amaury has no business in your Novice House, surely God must know it!" She tried to laugh. "I wish I could send God a note! Because I need a miracle. I'm so outnumbered—there are so many of you—so many Jesuits—standing between me and Amaury."

"He's taken no vows. He can leave if he wants to. We don't keep anyone in the Society who doesn't want to be there."

"But so long as he tells himself he has a vocation, and is surrounded by men with vocations, he will want to be there. And I know that your Society always wants nobles."

They were nearing the rue St. Jacques. Behind his calm face and carefully lowered eyes, Charles was in turmoil. He doubted Amaury de Corbet's vocation as much as the girl beside him did. He'd seen the way the two looked at each other, and he knew what it was to look at a woman like that and lose her. He also thought that Amaury needed time and refuge for enough penance to help him leave the Battle of Cassel behind. But a man could have those things without having a religious vocation. On the other hand, Charles told himself, who was he to pronounce for certain on another man's vocation? And who was this girl to pronounce on the vocation of a man she wanted for herself?

What am I to do? he flung at God. And waited, hoping against hope that the Silence would come to him now, there in the street. Instead, he heard something crack like a musket shot. It came again, and terror flooded Charles. The world around him was suddenly a battlefield and he smelled death. He grabbed Rose and shoved her against a building wall, covering her with his body to shield her. His heart pounded and sweat poured from him as he heard gunfire and screaming. His closed eyes showed him a flood of stumbling, bleeding men. The blood smell and his own acrid fear were sharp in his nostrils as something hit his shoulder. He tasted salt and knew that he was weeping, not for pain, but for life gone, for failure, for death . . .

"Let go! Let *go* of me!"

Something went on thudding against Charles's shoulders and he heard a growl of angry voices. He opened his eyes. The guns had stopped. Rose Ebrard stopped pounding at him with her fists and pulled hysterically away as his hold slackened. A workman built like a barrel, with sweat-soaked black hair plastered across his forehead, grabbed Charles by the throat and bounced his head off the wall.

"You false rotten cleric, that's the last girl you try to take!"

"Move away! Me, I'll teach him," a bigger and broader workman said, planting his feet and flexing hands the size of skillets. A rumble of approval rose from the half dozen bystanders.

"No, leave him," someone else said in disgust. "He's not worth what you'll bring on yourself! He's a Jesuit, can't you see his cassock? He belongs down the street there. Take him there and they'll see to him, never fear." The first man started dragging Charles toward the college.

Charles tried to wrench himself free. "I wasn't trying to harm her. I was trying to protect her. I heard——" He looked in bewilderment at the ordinary Paris street. "I thought I heard shots and screams and——I thought we were about to die."

"That's likely, in broad daylight. You come, too, *mademoiselle*, and tell the priests what this scum in a skirt tried to do."

But Mlle Ebrard was watching Charles and shaking her head doubtfully. "I think he's speaking the truth. He frightened me, but there *was* a loud, sharp sound. I heard it, too. But I didn't think it was a shot."

"Oh. I know what that was." The youngest and smallest man grinned at her and hefted an enormous mallet. "It was me, *ma belle*, splitting cobblestones with my mallet. It makes a crack like the coming of doom, maybe that's what he heard."

"Yes. Yes, that was it." Charles looked at Mlle Ebrard. "Forgive me. I meant no disrespect. I was afraid for you. Sometimes—I—" His face was hot with embarrassment. "Since the army, if there's a loud sound or someone comes too close behind me, I"—he glanced at the workmen and shrugged—"sometimes I think there's danger when there's not."

The workmen looked at each other and then at Charles, but now there was a kind of understanding in their eyes. They moved away, muttering among themselves. Charles looked up at the gray sky, feeling both relieved and shamed. A breath of wind chilled his face, and he realized it was wet with tears. So those, at least, had been real. He stumbled with sudden weariness and braced a hand on the building wall. God knew this grief that haunted him was real—grief for that day at Cassel, for failed courage and deaths wasted. Grief without end, it seemed. How could he be so arrogant as to think that he knew what Amaury de Corbet should do with his own grief?

The silent question hung in the cold air, without complaint, without hope, and the Silence came. Between one breath and another, it was there and gone again. *Charles. Nothing is wasted, not even death.* The words splintered into blinding clarity in Charles's heart.

When he could see again, he felt so light that he looked down at his feet to see if they were on the cobbles. The clarity seemed to lie over everything. The gray wall under his hand glinted with small points of silver. A swirling cloud of crows blackened the sky and left it seeming almost white. A fold of Rose Ebrard's tawny skirt blew against his cassock, burning like sunset.

"Are you all right?" she said hesitantly.

He wasn't sure whether moments or years passed before he straightened and turned to her. "I think finally I am."

Her eyes narrowed. "What happened just now?"

"Listen," he said, leaving her question unanswered. "When I talked with Amaury, I, too, doubted his vocation. I will find a way to talk to him again. But only he himself—and his superiors—can finally judge. That will take time. Are you willing to wait? For whatever his decision finally is?"

Hope made her eyes shine. "I can wait."

Chapter 19

Charles went back to the college and across the Cour d'honneur to the chapel. He signed himself with holy water from the font and went to St. Ignatius's altar on the side wall. He sank to his knees and covered his face with his hands. *Nothing is wasted, not even death.* He said the words to himself over and over. Not yet asking what they meant, but drawing them around him like a cloak. He knew from experience now that the gift in the words would push him further than he wanted to go. But not yet. So he let himself just rest there beneath the painting of St. Ignatius. Until a different voice—not the Silence, though perhaps the saint—reminded him of what he'd promised Rose Ebrard. That promise pitted the Jesuit rules he tried to live by against the new clarity in his heart. That flat contradiction made him look up uneasily at Ignatius, whose austere face gave so little away. But perhaps there were no contradictions. *Nothing is wasted,* the Silence had said. *Not even death.*

"I don't believe in Amaury de Corbet's vocation," he said silently to Ignatius. "But I *do* believe in my own. Amaury gave me the chance for my vocation, my right life, when he saved my life at Saint Omer. How can I not do what I can to give him back his right life?"

How arrogant, Charles's acid inner voice said. *So you've already forgotten the story about Père Dainville. Will you never learn to leave things to God and your superiors? Who are you to say Amaury doesn't have the life that's rightfully his?*

Charles ignored the voice and held out open hands, pleading for the saint's understanding. *We're linked, Amaury and I. That day at Cassel, we became more than brother soldiers.* Ignatius would understand that, Charles thought; the saint knew all there was to know about soldiers. *Don't you see? Amaury and I became like those unfortunate children born with their bodies grown together,* Charles said. *Only we're joined by death, not birth, by the deaths we were too afraid to prevent. And by the guilt that's grown in us since. If a surgeon tries to cut apart two children born monstrously together, they always die. It's like that for Amaury and me. The suffering for what we failed to do at Cassel can only end for both of us or for neither.*

Angry shouting pulled Charles rudely back to the outer world. It was coming from somewhere beyond the chapel's always-open north door. The noise grew louder and he got to his feet, crossed himself, and went hastily out into the courtyard. But the shouting was coming from a small Mary chapel built against the big chapel's east end, the meeting place of the day students' Congregations of the Holy Virgin. Two courtyard proctors running toward the Mary chapel converged with Charles at its door.

Inside, they stopped short, trying to make sense of a chaos that Charles had never expected to see in a consecrated place. At the front of the Mary chapel, a quartet of boys stood faced off against two furious Jesuits. Most of the other fifty or so boys—all aged seventeen or eighteen, by the look of them— were still kneeling on the stone floor, but some had drawn away and stood by the walls, their faces white with shock. Others, though, grinned broadly as they watched.

"But King Philip is *Pater Noster* to you," the best-dressed boy, obvious leader of the troublemakers, jeered at the pair of Jesuits facing him. The proctors started toward him.

"Wait," Charles said softly. "We need to hear more." The day he'd taken the shortcut through the day students' court, he'd seen this boy in the center of the huddle of students, holding whatever the others had been looking at.

Apparently oblivious of Charles and the proctors standing by the chapel door, the ringleader said tauntingly, "You always teach us that we must speak the truth. So we'll pray to your Jesuit *Pater* again!" He threw back his head like a crowing cock and his supporters joined in.

> *"Philippe, you're king of everyone,*
> *we won't be mute, we won't be dumb.*
> *We'll confess to all just who we are,*
> *We're your dear sons, to us you are: Our Father!"*

The *Monita Secreta*, Charles thought, with a tired sigh. The blasphemous *Pater Noster* had been printed at the back of the copy he'd read in the library. He nodded grimly to the proctors, and the three of them strode up the single center aisle. The priest who'd been faced off with the boys saw them coming and grabbed for the ringleader's arm. But the boy twisted easily away and skipped backward a few paces, now singing the blasphemous prayer to a street tune while his *confrères* laughed and shoved the priest and his assistant away. The gleeful singer didn't know anyone was behind him until Charles's hand closed on his arm and twisted it behind his back.

"Out," Charles said through his teeth. "And shut up." The boy yelped and struggled, but Charles gripped his shoulder and sank his fingers hard into the young muscle. "Another word, any more struggle, and who knows? Frère Brunet may be working on your dislocated shoulder."

"You can't," the captive snarled. "It's against the rules. You're not—"

"You are deficient in grammar," Charles said sweetly. "I *shouldn't*. But I *can*. What's your name?" The boy didn't answer, and Charles's fingers dug deeper. "Your name!"

"Ow! Louis Poquelin."

The proctors and the priest's young assistant—whom Charles recognized now as a teaching scholastic—had subdued the ringleader's three lieutenants and were marching them out of the chapel. Charles recognized the student with red hair—red hair was unusual in the college—as another of the day boys he'd seen when he'd crossed the day students' court. Keeping a grip on his own captive, Charles scanned the faces of the remaining boys in the Mary chapel, his gaze lingering on those who were still grinning and had obviously enjoyed the rebellion.

"*Mon père,*" he said loudly and distinctly to the priest, who was dusting his hands after delivering the last of the three conspirators to the proctors. "Please keep your Congregation here. Don't let anyone get rid of anything. They're all going to be searched. Someone will come to help you."

The disheveled priest nodded and turned to his now-silent flock.

As Charles, the proctors, and their captives crossed the Cour d'honneur, Charles saw the rector's face briefly at his office window. When the little cavalcade reached the *grand salon*, Père Le Picart was there waiting for them.

"I heard the noise," he said. "What has happened?" His gaze went from student to student.

The proctors looked at Charles. "Blasphemy, for one thing, *mon père,*" he said. "In the Mary chapel where these boys' Congregation of the Virgin was meeting." He turned his captured student over to the proctor who had only one boy in his charge. "*Mon père*, will you send proctors to search the other Congregation members? They're all still in the chapel." He lowered his voice. "I think that these we've brought—and probably others, too—have been reading *Le Cabinet*."

Le Picart looked as near cursing as Charles had ever seen him. "How? Students aren't allowed it in the library."

"But day students are free to go where they wish and buy what they can out of school hours. They were taunting the priest with the King of Spain *Pater Noster* from the back of the book. And several days ago, I saw at least two of them—the one there with red hair and Monsieur Louis Poquelin beside him—showing something to an avid huddle of boys."

The rector's face was rigid with anger as he turned to the proctors. "*Mes frères*, you may leave these malefactors with us. Please find a third brother and go back to the Mary chapel. See that every boy takes off his scholar's gown and turns out the pockets of his coat. And any other hiding place there may be in his clothing. Any books you find, bring to me. Along with their owners."

"Yes, *mon père*."

The older proctor raised his eyebrows at Charles, who nodded and took charge of three of the captives. The other scholastic took charge of Poquelin, who seemed to be the rebellion's ringleader. The proctors went to carry out the rector's order, and the rector knocked sharply on the office door of Père Montville, who was in charge of day students. Le Picart was about to knock again when the door opened. The skullcap Montville wore for warmth had slipped sideways, and he was blinking and stifling a yawn. His good-natured round face was apologetic. He bowed to Le Picart.

"Forgive me, *mon père*. I confess I had fallen asleep. Last night I fear I played my poor violin somewhat late. At the Professed House, you know, because—well, I'm sure you didn't come to hear about my struggles with music. Come in, come in." Belatedly, he saw the little crowd behind Le Picart, and his sleepy blue eyes opened wider. "Oh. Oh, dear. Come in, everyone."

The rector, who had patiently waited out the flood of talk, went into the cramped office without explanation. Charles and the other scholastic herded the four boys in and lined them up in the shallow alcove across from Montville's desk, there being nowhere else to put them. Montville placed a chair, facing the alcove, for the rector. Then, pushing his skullcap straight, he sat down behind his desk and waited for Le Picart to tell him why his office was full of people. Le Picart told Montville what he knew and then nodded at the scholastic from the chapel. The pale scholastic, obviously holding himself rigidly in check, bowed to the rector.

"The older *externes*' Congregation of the Holy Virgin was meeting in the small chapel," he said. "I am, as you know, *mes pères*, assigned to help with that congregation. We were all reverently kneeling, beginning the meeting with prayer. But as we began the *Pater Noster*, these four students started bellowing blasphemy and taunting us. The devil never sleeps!"

The young man's clasped hands were shaking and his knuckles were white. He was scared, Charles realized, perhaps even more frightened than angry at what he'd seen and heard. The four boys kept their faces carefully blank, but their eyes gleamed with satisfaction.

"And what exactly was this blasphemy?" Montville said.

The scholastic flinched and swallowed. "I hardly like to say, *mon père*."

"I don't suppose you do. But you must."

"It was a blasphemous rendering of the Our Father." The young Jesuit was almost whispering. "It was addressed to Philippe, the Spanish king. These—creatures—were laughing at us, they said that this blasphemy is the secret Jesuit *Pater Noster*."

The rector looked at Charles. "And where," he demanded of the shaken scholastic, "did they find this so-called *Pater Noster*?"

"I don't know, *mon père*. Perhaps they made it up themselves. Though I hate to think their depravity goes so deep." The scholastic turned suddenly to Charles. "You also heard it, *maître*."

"I did. They didn't make it up." Charles looked inquiringly at the rector, who slightly shook his head. Not naming *Le Cabinet*, Charles went on, "They got it from a book."

"Search them," the rector said.

Charles started with Poquelin. He made him take off his scholar's gown, which had no pockets, and then his new-looking coat of rich brown wool. Charles went through the two pockets on the coat's front and found only a few coins and a broken quill.

"Pull up your shirt," Charles said.

It was Poquelin's turn to look shocked. Charles thought he was going to resist, but then he shrugged, tugged his shirt free from his breeches, and pulled a small book out of his waistband.

Charles took it, saw that it was indeed *Le Cabinet jesuitique*, and handed it to the rector. Montville leaned to see its cover and his mouth fell open.

"Where did you get this?" Le Picart said to Poquelin, so quietly that the hair stood up on Charles's neck. "How long have you had it?"

When Poquelin didn't answer, Charles said, "Monsieur Poquelin, on Tuesday, I saw you and your friend here with other boys in a corner of the passage between the day students' court and the main court. You were holding something, and the others were gathered around looking at it. I think it was *Le Cabinet.*"

"Is that true?" Le Picart's voice rumbled like thunder and all four boys flinched. "You have not only read this filth yourself, you have corrupted others with it?"

Charles almost felt sorry for the boys. In his time at Louis le Grand, he'd learned that Le Picart could be the gentlest and most perceptive of men. He'd also learned that the rector's sense of right and truth was formidable, and that he had no use for lazy men or lazy half-truths. Or for fools, Charles thought with a sigh, seeing that Poquelin had thrust up his chin and was staring fixedly into the distance, acting for his own enjoyment the captured hero of a romance undergoing interrogation.

"Search the others," Montville said in disgust, putting the copy of *Le Cabinet* on his desk. As though distance would make it less objectionable, he pushed the book away from him with a finger, raising a small cloud of dust.

Charles and the other scholastic searched the remaining three and came up with several illustrated pages torn from Dutch pornography, a small crumbling cake, a ruined quill, and a slingshot. Another copy of *Le Cabinet* was under the red-haired boy's shirt.

"What's your name?" Montville said curtly, as the book was put with the first one on his desk.

As the boy mumbled his name, Montville sneezed, and all Charles heard was "Jacques." Sighing, Montville told the scholastic to take the two boys who had not had copies of *Le Cabinet* to wait in the *grand salon.* "Sit and think of what you've done," he said darkly. "Pray for the Virgin's forgiveness for desecrating her chapel and failing in the service you owe her and the college."

The scholastic took them away and Montville turned his scowl on the red-haired boy.

"Where did you get this book?"

But Jacques proved as mulish as Louis Poquelin. Montville and the rector fired questions at the pair of them, while Charles wondered how the boys had even known about the old anti-Jesuit libel. From their families? But why would a Jesuit-hating family send boys to Louis le Grand? On the other hand, even Protestants sometimes went to Jesuit schools, because the education was good. Charles's stomach growled, and he realized sadly that he'd missed the midday meal again.

"—but your own father is a Gentleman of the Professed House," Le Picart was saying to Poquelin.

"And he's *so* very pious, *so* very superior," the boy mocked. "My father is a true *tartuffe*."

Charles stared at him. *Tartuffe*. Poquelin. He looked questioningly at the rector.

The rector nodded wearily. "So, Monsieur Poquelin, you share the opinions your father's illustrious cousin Jean-Baptiste Poquelin put forth in his play *Tartuffe*?"

"Yes, and he was exactly right!"

"We educated little Jean-Baptiste Poquelin, you know," Le Picart said. "Before he went out into the world and called himself Molière."

"Of course I know that. He was here at Louis le Grand, he knew Jesuits, he knew the Congregations, he saw everything, that's why he could write *Tartuffe* and expose you all! And now his cousin, my poor father, is the biggest hypocrite in the most important Holy Virgin Congregation in Paris, the so very holy Gentlemen of the Professed House. You're all—" Poquelin's face worked, but Charles guessed that he couldn't quite find the courage to call Le Picart a hypocrite to his face.

"What your father's cousin Molière saw and understood," the rector said evenly, "was that piety can indeed cover its opposite. It often does. But that does *not* mean—and Molière never said it meant—that to be pious is to be a hypocrite. For all your years with us, Monsieur Poquelin, I see that we have not taught you to think logically. Which is a pity, because your time with us is ended." The rector's words rang like hammer blows on a steel sword. "If you agree, Père Montville?"

"With regret. And sadness. But yes, I certainly agree."

Louis Poquelin's chest swelled with martyred satisfaction.

Montville sighed and looked at the boy whose surname Charles hadn't heard. "You, on the other hand, *monsieur*, do not surprise me so much. We dismissed your brother some years ago for similar reasons. But your mother begged us to take you, in spite of him. She will be heartbroken to see you go the same way."

"The same way?" Charles said.

"His older brother fell into freethinking. Their mother is a devout woman who gives generously to the Ursuline nuns' charities. And to ours."

"*That's* why you want me to stay," the boy said triumphantly. "So you can have more of her money than she'll give you if you throw me out."

"Monsieur Coriot," Montville said wearily, "you have put yourself beyond all chance of staying. I only want one thing of you. Where did you get your copy of this book?"

Startled, Charles blurted out, "Coriot? Is that his name?" Montville nodded impatiently, and Charles said, before Montville could return to his questioning, "Where do you live, Monsieur Coriot?"

"South of the walls. Why do you—"

Montville cut him off, repeating his question about the book.

Charles watched Jacques, thinking that he was surely the

younger brother of the man Alexandre Lunel had been staying with when his brother Paul disappeared. Which might well mean that this Jacques had known Paul Lunel.

A sharp rap came at Montville's door.

"*Now* what?" Montville glared at the door. "No doubt someone has come to say that there's a squadron of Huguenots and Lutherans at the gate. Oh, well, *entrez!*"

The serenely placid lay brother who stuck his head in looked as though Luther himself, resurrected and battering down the door with a Bible, wouldn't bother him. "A Gentleman of the Professed House to see you, *mon père*," he said to Le Picart. "Monsieur Louis Poquelin. He wants to complain about someone."

A hastily smothered sound escaped Charles, and the rector looked thoughtfully at him.

"Tell Monsieur Poquelin to come in," Le Picart said.

The rector and Charles and Montville looked at the Poquelin son. But young Louis seemed not at all bothered by the news that his father was there.

"When your father comes in, you will stay there in the alcove and hold your tongue," Le Picart said. "I will tell him what has occurred."

"I promise you I will not hold my tongue if you lie!"

Le Picart regarded him sadly. "When have you ever known one of us to lie?"

"It says so right in that book—and it's my book, I want it back, you can't keep it! It says Jesuits lie all the time, it says—"

"If you insist on believing idiocies, have the decency to keep them to yourself," Le Picart said.

Poquelin shut up—in sheer surprise, Charles thought. The elder Poquelin came in and bowed so humbly that he had to twist his neck to look at the rector. As Charles had feared, Poquelin was the man who had chastised him in the market.

The rector stood. "I was about to send for you, Monsieur Poquelin."

Poquelin, who had not noticed Charles or the two boys standing back in the alcove, bowed even farther toward the floor. "Ah. So you know, then, about your unfortunate sheep," the newcomer intoned. "I am glad. One must stop these things at the very beginning if young men are not to be lost. Though in one so long under your tutelage, I would have thought—ah, well. But I am a humble man and it is not for me to judge." He folded his plump hands together and straightened a little to smile sadly up at the rector. "Have you beaten him?" he said hopefully.

The rector frowned in confusion. "I haven't beaten anyone. I've only just discovered what he's done."

Poquelin drew himself almost to a normal posture, and Charles saw his eyes gleam. "I know that Jesuits don't like to do the beating themselves. I would be glad to offer my humble services. Though that would be almost too much honor, *mon père*, allowing so humble a Gentleman to thrash a Jesuit for having— um—concourse with a strumpet in the market. If you insist, of course, I can only do my duty."

Père Le Picart, momentarily speechless, gaped at Poquelin. The two students were listening round-eyed. Charles sighed inwardly and tried to think how to deal with this without saying more than the boys and Poquelin should hear.

"What Jesuit are you talking about, *monsieur*?" the rector demanded.

Charles stepped out of the alcove. "He means me, *mon père*."

Chapter 20

"You?" The rector's tone was mildly inquiring, but the look on his face was anything but mild. "And what were you doing in the market, Maître du Luc?"

"Returning from the Novice House, *mon père*. I happened to see our neighbor Mademoiselle Ebrard." Charles widened his eyes and held the rector's gaze. "I gave her your message for her aunt."

"Message? What—oh, of course." Relief at Charles's quick invention softened the rector's expression. "Well done, *maître*. Well, Monsieur Poquelin, it seems you have been too hasty. There was nothing untoward in what you saw."

Poquelin's face fell. "No? Nothing?" he said plaintively. However gravely this Gentleman's son and namesake had misjudged his teachers, he had judged his father with a nice exactness: a pious hypocrite, a *tartuffe*, indeed.

"Nothing," Le Picart repeated. "And for the good of your soul, I must tell you that you have done a respectable young woman—indeed, a devout young woman of quality—a grave discourtesy in speaking of her as a strumpet. But I am sure you will not fail to include that in your next confession."

"Oh. Of course. It was a mistake. I only thought—women, you know—"

"And so," the rector said over the elder Poquelin's gabbling, "as I said, I was about to send for you. Père Montville will tell you why."

Montville, startled into speech, cleared his throat. "Yes. I— he—we—" He tried again. "As you may know, *monsieur*, I am in charge of our day students." He looked toward the alcove. "Step forward, Louis Poquelin," he said, pointing at the boy. The father jumped as though he'd been scalded and turned around to gape at his son. "I am expelling your son Louis from our college for blasphemy and discourtesy." Ignoring the elder Poquelin's pop-eyed dismay, Montville told him what had happened in the chapel. "After so grave an offense, we cannot keep him and allow him to infect others. I hope that you will be able to show him the error of his ways and that he may finish his education somewhere else. We will, of course, pray for him. You may take him home now. I will send a formal letter of dismissal."

Courteously and gravely, Montville rose and opened his office door, leaving the silenced father and the triumphant son no choice but to go. Montville escorted them out and Charles went quickly to Le Picart, leaving Jacques Coriot still in the alcove.

"*Mon père*," he said in the rector's ear, "will you assign me to escort Jacques Coriot home? I think that he may have known Paul Lunel. Alexandre Lunel was staying with a family called Coriot when Paul disappeared. I'd like to talk to Jacques."

"Yes. A good thought." Le Picart smiled slightly. "But do try to stay away from strumpets."

Charles grinned and stepped back to his place as Montville returned to the office.

"And now we come to you," Montville said, stopping in front of Jacques. "I do not think you are as deep in blasphemy and error as your friend. I beg you to think about what you have done, and pray to the Virgin for forgiveness." He sighed. "Monsieur Coriot, this book that you think so revealing was proved false as soon as it appeared more than seventy years ago. Think about that." He waited for a response, but there was none. "I will send for someone to see you home. And I will send a note to your poor mother."

"Perhaps, Père Montville," Le Picart said, as though it had just occurred to him, "Maître du Luc could see Monsieur Coriot home."

"That will do very well." Montville nodded at Charles. "Wait a moment while I write." He went to his desk and wrote a brief message to Mme Coriot, folded it, and handed it to Charles. "You may tell her that a formal letter of dismissal will arrive shortly." He tried once more with the boy. "Have you anything to say, Monsieur Coriot, before you leave for good?"

"Only that I thank God that I have finally learned the truth about you."

Montville shook his head sadly. "God go with you and help you to see your errors."

The rector tilted his head at the door, and Charles propelled the rebel out of the office.

"Exactly where do you live?" Charles asked him, as they reached the street.

"South, as I told you. On the rue Saint Jacques. I don't need to be taken there like a child!"

"Don't you? Then why the ridiculous charade in the Congregation chapel?"

"We were only telling the truth we learned from those books. Which you've stolen because they show you for what you are. I want mine back!" The boy was looking angrily at Charles instead of watching where he was going, and Charles put out a hand to keep him from walking into the rats dangling from a passing ratcatcher's pole.

"You Jesuits make everyone think you're so holy," the boy spat at Charles. "But your hearts aren't set on God, they're set on power—over everyone, over the whole world!"

Passersby were staring. Some nodded vigorously and one man egged the boy on.

"For your own credit as a gentleman, Monsieur Coriot," Charles said, "try not to yell in the street. And try to use your brain instead of your emotions for a moment. No sane man wants power over the whole world." Though Charles supposed there would always be less-than-sane men who did want such power. Perhaps even some Jesuits, but that didn't make *Le Cabinet* true.

"Of course you *say* that. Jesuits are clever; you make jokes, you make things easy for your penitents, you even make studying pleasant. So no one sees that under it all you're following your secret instructions! You and your Spanish and Italian and English and God knows what else kind of Jesuits—want to make our French church and France itself the pope's slaves and your own!"

"Monsieur Coriot," Charles said, "is it really impossible for you to hate the pope and the Society of Jesus and still be courteous in the street? Or does your newfound 'truth' require you to cease being an *honnête homme*?"

Coriot drew back as though Charles had struck him. An *honnête homme* was, among other things, a man of breeding who knew how to behave, and to be accused of not being one was a serious judgment.

"Of course I am an *honnête homme*," the boy muttered. "Coriots are nobles of the Robe—good lawyers and judges—for generations back." He shut his mouth with a snap and stalked beside Charles for perhaps a dozen paces. "More than that," he hissed, "we are Frenchmen. With our last breath we will protect France from the pope and the king of Spain and foreigners."

Charles shrugged. "You are telling me you are a Gallican. Which is not the same thing as a Frenchman. And even Gallicans differ, you know. Some Jesuits are also Gallicans. The king's confessor, Père La Chaise, is a Gallican." Charles shook his head as the boy opened his mouth. "Don't bother telling me that Jesuit Gallicanism can only be a pose."

"Of course it's a pose! Everyone knows your Society of Jesus forces Jesuit confessors on the king so they can help the pope!"

Charles laughed outright. "I take it you have never been at court, or you would know that no one forces anything on Louis the Fourteenth."

Coriot thrust out his chest, trying to look knowing and succeeding only in looking very young. "Control over the good of my soul the Holy Father may have. But not control over the affairs of France!"

"That does seem to settle the pope. But what about the king of Spain?"

Coriot tripped over a loose paving stone. "You're only taunting me."

"I am seeking information."

"Ha."

The silent stalking resumed, and Charles saw that they had almost reached the St. Jacques market. Finally, unable to resist lecturing someone not only older, but a teacher, the boy burst out, "Jesuits want the king of Spain to rule France because your Ignatius of Loyola was a Spaniard."

Trying not to let his mental eye-rolling show, Charles said, "I don't follow you. What you say isn't even logical. I mean, my mother is Norman, but that doesn't make me want a Norman king. Besides that, our French king is more than a little Italian. If the king can be a little foreign, why not the Society of Jesus?"

Before Coriot could refute that, a series of crashes, shouts, and curses came from the opening in the walls where the St. Jacques gate had been. Charles walked faster, craning his neck to see what had happened. Three carriages had collided and a horse was screaming. The way through the walls was completely blocked.

"Oh, no," Charles said, "not another carriage accident. And that poor horse has gone down."

"There's no way through there," Coriot said eagerly. "You can leave me to go on alone; it's a much longer way, taking the other road and connecting back to the rue Saint Jacques."

Disabusing him of that hope with a look, Charles took him by the arm. He steered him to the left around the gathering gawkers, to a place in the wall where the work of demolition had started. As they picked their way over the old stones to a small street leading south, Charles weighed the questions he wanted to ask Coriot. He decided to get the least important out of the way first.

"Monsieur Coriot," he said, "don't think that questions about *Le Cabinet* are over. You will have to tell the police where you bought it. If you tell me now, it will go easier with you later."

"The police?" The boy seemed to shrink. "But—I didn't buy it! I—I found it."

"You surely don't expect me to believe that. Are you going to tell me that Monsieur Poquelin found his copy, too? Where were all these illegal books lying out, waiting to be found?"

"I don't have to tell you."

"You'll have to tell someone, I assure you. But if you don't want to answer that question, we can speak of something else. I think you must have known Paul Lunel. Tell me about him."

Charles heard Jacques Coriot's sudden intake of breath and turned to look at him. The boy's face was white and miserable.

"So you did know him," Charles said flatly.

"I knew him a little. My brother told me that Paul was found murdered."

"Yes. He was. Tell me about Paul."

Coriot's lips trembled. "There's nothing to tell. He was stupid. Old-fashioned. Deluded. Stubborn." He grew louder with each angry word. "Paul abandoned—" Coriot shut his lips, obviously struggling with himself.

"Abandoned what?" Charles said, feeling carefully toward what he suspected was the answer.

But the boy shrugged and turned his head away. "Everything. There's nothing else to say about him."

"Who do you think killed him?"

"I don't know. He'd never harmed anyone!"

Charles matched his companion's steps in silence, every sense alert. Hating himself for the necessity, he said coolly, "So your friend abandoned you and went to be a Jesuit. And you've learned to hate Jesuits. Did you kill him for that? And for turning his back on you?"

The boy spun toward him and tried to slap his face, but Charles caught his arm. Coriot struggled against Charles's hold. "How dare you say that!"

"You yourself have been saying this afternoon that finding out the truth is all that matters. Don't you want Paul Lunel's killer caught?" Warily, he let the boy go, grateful that the only passersby were stolid, home-going peasants, too tired from coming to the city markets before dawn to care about the little scene. Coriot stood at bay, breathing hard.

"I think you loved him," Charles said quietly.

"Not love, not like a girl!"

"That's not what I mean. I mean that he was your friend. Perhaps the rare kind of friend who's your mirror, your other self. Yet he decided to go where you couldn't follow him or even see him. He abandoned you. People older than you have killed because of that."

The boy pressed his shaking lips together until he could speak. "I felt like he was killing me. But how did you know?"

"I've had friends, too, *mon brave.*"

That brought tears, and Charles pulled his handkerchief from his sleeve and held it out.

"I'm sorry," Coriot said, using it and handing it back. "I'm sorry I tried to strike you."

"Well, one should not strike a man for pushing for the truth. But I did push you."

"Do you believe me, that I didn't kill him?"

"I do. But I need to know who did kill him. Did he have enemies? I take it he was not such a Gallican as you are."

"No. He was—" Coriot glanced suddenly down the lane on their left. "Ah, no, here they come!"

A half dozen goats were trotting toward them up the lane, followed by the goatwoman called Hyacinthe. Charles and Coriot moved quickly to the side of the street, where another lane branched to the right.

"I seem to see those goats everywhere," Charles said, watching a tiny kid trotting awkwardly beside its mother. "That's Talking Flea Street they're coming from, isn't it?"

"Yes. How did you know? My father rents out a house there. The street's run-down, but it's cheap. There's even some pasture left farther along, that's why the goatwoman lives there."

The goats were turning toward the city, as though they knew

their way, and Hyacinthe was murmuring to herself and scrabbling in the heavy bag she carried. As she drew out a hunk of black bread, she looked up and saw Charles. She froze, staring at him, and then ran at him with her stick poised like a sword.

"I told you!" Her voice was a high-pitched sing-song. "I tell you again. Follow the dead, find your death!" The whites of her faded eyes showed and she seemed to be looking through Charles.

Coriot and Charles backed hastily into the weeds. "Calm yourself, Grandmère," Charles called, wondering what it was about him that set her off. Maybe, he thought wryly, she didn't like Jesuits, either. The first time, he'd taken her words as warning, but maybe they were a threat. More likely, though, she was only crazy, like so many poor and lonely old women.

She retreated into the midst of her goats, like a lord surrounded by his protecting ring of retainers, and went on her way, eating bread. Which made Charles remember again that he'd missed midday dinner. He doubted he'd be offered anything at the Coriot house, given his errand.

"We go this way to get back to the rue Saint Jacques and my house," Jacques said, starting down the steeply sloping right-hand lane. "What was the goatwoman talking about?"

"Who knows?" Charles shrugged. "I think the poor old thing imagines dangers everywhere."

The sloping lane took them back to the rue St. Jacques, and then it was a short walk to the Coriot house, which was set back from the road a little north of Notre Dame des Champs. Which started Charles wondering, for what seemed like the hundredth time, why Paul Lunel had been killed in Notre Dame des Champs.

"Stop a moment, Monsieur Coriot," Charles said. "Did Paul Lunel stay in your house during the time everyone thought he was in the Novice House? On your soul, I want the truth."

"No, *maître.*" Coriot seemed puzzled by the question. "He never stayed here, though his brother, Alexandre, did. He was with us when Paul went to the Novice House. Then Alexandre went to his mother in the country."

Charles thought of something else. "Do you know if Paul liked to go and pray in Notre Dame's crypt?"

The boy shrugged and sighed. "He stopped talking to me about those things."

Coriot rang the bell hanging beside the gate, and a servant opened it. In the cobbled court spread before the old stone house, two young men in black legal robes copiously trimmed with black ribbons were mounting their horses. The man nearest the gate, who was red haired and freckled like Jacques, recoiled when he saw the boy and Charles.

"Jacques!" the man called. "What are you doing here so early? And with him?" He pointed his chin at Charles.

"They've tossed me out." The boy's tone wavered between bravado and apology. To Charles, he said, "That's my brother Victor."

"Have they? Good." Victor Coriot adjusted his hat to a fashionable angle over his lushly curled wig. "It's about time. I have a case at the Palais. Go in to *Maman.* She'll moan at you about being thrown out, but that's a small price to pay for being quit of Louis le Grand." Ignoring Charles, he and his companion rode toward the gate.

Well, Charles thought, it was easy enough to see where the younger brother had learned his extreme Gallicanism. Charles stepped into Victor Coriot's way, keeping an eye on the horses and ready to move fast if he had to. Victor Coriot swore and reined his big white gelding to a stop.

"A moment of your time, Monsieur Victor Coriot," Charles said. "I know that you are a good friend to Alexandre Lunel.

Do you have any thought about where his younger brother spent the three weeks between his expected arrival at the Novice House and his death?"

Charles saw the lawyer's spurs move, and he reached up and caught the gelding's bridle. The confused horse danced and laid its ears back, and Victor Coriot and Charles locked eyes.

"No," Victor Coriot said curtly. "Move out of my way."

Charles didn't move. "How did you account for his being killed in Notre Dame des Champs's crypt, so close to your own house?"

"Why should I account for it? I was not his keeper."

"You cannot spare even a thought for your friend Alexandre's murdered brother?"

"At least the poor boy is saved from being one of you." He put spurs to the horse again, sending Charles to the cobbles as the bridle was ripped from his hand. As Charles picked himself up, the other lawyer followed Coriot through the gate, smiling with satisfaction and looking neither right nor left.

Chapter 21

When the college bell rang for supper, Charles was the first arrival at the scholastics' table in the fathers' refectory. He stood behind his chair, waiting for the others and trying to keep himself from biting into the table's loaf of bread by going over what had happened at the Coriot house. Jacques Coriot had fled into the house while Charles was picking himself up from the courtyard pavement. Charles, seething with anger at the boy's brother, and still having Père Montville's letter to deliver, had pounded on the house door. A hatchet-faced maidservant had opened it and refused him admittance. Mme Coriot was with her son, she'd said unhappily. Charles had thrust the letter at her, adjured her on her hope of salvation to deliver it, and trudged back to Louis le Grand.

Behind him, the refectory slowly filled. All the scholastics except Maître Placide Du Pont and the Englishman arrived, grace was said, and the evening reading from the life of St. Ignatius began from the lectern. Charles was trying not to gulp his soup and eat more than his share of the bread when Du Pont hurried to the table.

Glancing at the reader, he said as quietly as he could, "Have any of you seen Maître Wing?"

The scholastics exchanged anxious looks and shook their heads.

Cold with apprehension, Charles put his spoon down and beckoned Du Pont closer. "He went with me to Père Quellier at the Novice House this morning, but he was supposed to come back here on his own. I had to stay on an errand."

"Do you know for certain that he returned?"

"No, I don't."

"So you are the last of us to have seen him."

"If he didn't return, yes, I am. I told him to go straight back here by the way we'd come. He couldn't possibly have gotten lost!"

"I agree. Will you come with me, please?"

But Charles was already on his feet. Père Le Picart had not come to supper and they finally found him in the dark chapel, praying before the main altar. While they waited for him to finish, Charles prayed hard that Wing was only lost. The soft movement of cloth recalled Charles as Le Picart got stiffly to his feet, the altar's candlelight gilding his thin face.

"What is it?" The rector's shadowed eyes went from Du Pont to Charles. He glanced around the empty nave. "Tell me here. We are private."

Du Pont said succinctly, "Maître Wing seems to be missing, *mon père*."

Le Picart drew in a sharp breath. "God forbid. Where have you looked?"

"Everywhere he might be. Everywhere I could think of, at least. None of the theology scholastics have seen him since the morning." Du Pont looked at Charles.

"You know that he was going to be coming back alone after his extra session with Père Quellier," Charles said. "He promised me that he would come straight back by the way we'd gone, the only way he knew. I never thought to check that he was back. I should have."

Le Picart made no response to that. "Go to the police *barrière*, Maître du Luc, and—no, it's late, the *sergent* may not be there. Go straight to our *commissaire* and bring him to my office. He will have heard the happenings in the neighborhood during the day and may be of some help. I will also send for Lieutenant-Général La Reynie." To Du Pont he said, "Check Maître Wing's room again, also the library, the latrines—in case he is ill—and the other small chapels. I've heard that his devotions wander all over the college." A smile twitched at the corners of his mouth, but his eyes were full of worry. "And Maître du Luc, when you return with the *commissaire*, send him on to me and stop at the bakery. Ask the LeClercs if they've seen Maître Wing. I've also heard that he wanders to the bakery and that Marie-Ange slips him little morsels. And we all know that Madame LeClerc keeps a good watch on the street."

Charles and Du Pont bowed and left the chapel, nearly running. The neighborhood's police *commissaire* lived in the Place Maubert, a few minutes' walk from the college. As Charles went, running in reckless earnest in the small dark streets where there were few lanterns and no one around to see him, he hoped that the *commissaire* wouldn't simply send his *sergent*. The *sergent* was slow and stolid, and Charles's gut told him there wasn't time for that. But when he reached the *commissaire*'s house, his heart sank. At night, people often took their problems straight to the house, and the lantern-lit courtyard was full of shouting, arguing people. The *sergent*, threatening both sides indiscriminately with his stick as he tried to keep order, turned with relief to Charles.

"What is it, *maître*? So long as it's not families, I'll do anything you want if it'll get me away from this! We've got a girl who's slapped her mother-in-law over a stolen frying pan, and a sister-in-law who's come after the girl with a knife, and the husband, intelligent soul—who was the only other witness—has slunk off to some tavern."

"I'm almost envious," Charles said, half smiling. "I'm afraid we have something worse. Another missing Jesuit. The rector begs Commissaire Tourette to come quickly to his office."

The *sergent* grimaced. "Leaving me with these squawking hens. Ah, well. I'll go and tell him." A grin split his big, good-natured face. "You want my stick while I'm gone?"

Charles laughed and the *sergent* plodded through the furious women, shaking his head and his stick at every question. Charles drew back into the courtyard shadows, but not before a bedraggled matriarch holding a gnarled hand to her face spotted him and came at a waddle.

"You tell her, *mon père*, she'll never go to heaven treating me like she does! Honor your mother, it says! And your mother-in-law, too. I only borrowed her filthy frying pan and that's another thing. Dirty?! You've never seen—"

She was still in full spate several minutes later when the *commissaire* came out of the house in his official black robe and hat. He nodded at Charles, set the matriarch briskly aside, and made for the courtyard doors like a man sighting freedom. Charles glanced over his shoulder at the abandoned *sergent* and saw that the outraged woman had cornered him and was starting over with her story.

A wind had begun to blow again from the river, tangling cloaks and sending the reaching fingers of winter down collars. Commissaire Tourette jammed his hat more securely down on his wig. Charles reached up to secure his own hat and realized he'd rushed from the refectory without it. As they walked, he told

Tourette all he knew about Maître Henry Wing. When he finished, the man pulled a wadded handkerchief from his coat pocket, honked into it, and shook his head.

"I hate this wind. Well, I've been praying you wouldn't lose another one. But it seems God's not hearing me. Has anyone found this one's clothes?"

Charles felt his stomach twist at the *commissaire*'s bluntness. "No. Not that we know of. That may be to the good."

But Tourette's assumption that Wing was dead hung in the air like fog. When they reached the bakery, Charles sent Tourette on to the college postern and knocked on the LeClercs' door. No one came. Charles tried to peer through the crack in the shutters. The shop was dark, but light showed from the room next to it. He was about to knock again, when an approaching light glimmered.

"Who's there?" a deep male voice bellowed.

The baker, Charles thought, realizing he'd only seen the baker, whose name was Roger, twice in all the time he'd been at Louis le Grand. Not surprising, since bakers did much of their work at night, but it was Mme LeClerc Charles wanted to see.

"It's Maître du Luc from the college," Charles shouted back. "I must speak with you and your wife."

The bar on the door thudded as the baker set it aside, a key grated in the elaborate lock, and Roger LeClerc held up his candle and glared at Charles. "You'll have to speak with me. What?"

"Forgive me for disturbing you, *monsieur*," Charles said. "The rector sent me to ask if you or Madame LeClerc have seen our English scholastic Maître Wing today. He's missing."

LeClerc blinked at Charles, frowning, but before he could answer, his wife's voice called, "Who is it, Roger? If it's not the police or beggars or students, bring him in, I haven't seen any-one all day and what am I to do, be as silent as a turnip because of a baby?"

Charles's eyes opened wide. "Has the baby come already?"

LeClerc shook his head and sighed like a storm gust. He opened the door a little wider and Charles saw the worry in his face. "It's trying to come but it's too early. She's had hell since the afternoon."

"Roger, bring whoever it is inside and shut the door, I am freezing!"

Reluctantly, the baker let Charles in. Marie-Ange put her head around the door between the shop and the room next to it, and when she saw Charles, she ran to him and hung on his arm. Her father started to pull her back, but Charles smiled over her head at him.

"It's all right, *monsieur*." He looked down at the little girl. "How is your mother, *ma petite?*"

Her brown eyes were wide with fear. "It's hurting her so much. I don't know how to help her. She—"

"*Maître!*"

The three in the shop jumped and looked toward the inner doorway. Charles, at least, was reassured by the volume of Mme LeClerc's impatient shriek.

"I can hear that it's you, *maître*, come in, don't mind my old Roger, he thinks I'll break if anyone looks at me, but if no one comes to talk to me, I tell you I will die of boredom just to spite you all—that is a joke, Marie-Ange. But come in here, all of you, if you don't want to find a madwoman in the morning!"

LeClerc rolled his eyes and shrugged. Marie-Ange seized Charles's hand and dragged him into a large, square room with whitewashed walls, warm from its big fireplace surrounded by cooking utensils. Mme LeClerc lay back on pillows in the large bed, under a faded green quilt. The green bedcurtains were wound tidily around the bedposts and a picture of the Holy Family was tacked to the wall above the bed. There was a table, a bench and an armchair, a tall cupboard, and several old chests. Beyond the hearth, a small bed stood in a shallow alcove.

Mme LeClerc's round face was pale and sweating, but she smiled at Charles across the hillock of her belly and held out her hand to him. "You see me as God made me," she said, tucking a swath of curling chestnut hair under her white linen cap. "Well, not exactly, perhaps, but . . ." Her eyes closed and she grimaced in pain. "Ah, blessed Saint Anne, enough! Roger, I've said it before and I say it again, the furnishings for marriage beds are green because green is the color of fools and here you see what happens to one of the fools in the bed!" Another spasm shook her.

Charles looked anxiously at the baker. "Has the midwife been?"

"Yes. She's coming back tonight. She says the baby may come or may wait." The man's tired face softened a little. "Marie-Ange asked your porter Frère Martin for a tisane from the infirmarian. I said how would a Jesuit know what to give a pregnant woman, but whatever he sent gave her some ease and I'm grateful." He sighed and rubbed his drawn face. "As for what you asked me—no, I've not seen your Englishman today. And my wife and Marie-Ange have been only in the chamber there."

"Have you lost Maître Wing?" Marie-Ange said, pouring water into a cup. "I hope not, I like him."

"Wing?" Mme LeClerc drank a little as Marie-Ange held the cup to her lips. "That English Henri, like the old king? Hah. If that one's gone off somewhere, I can imagine where. To put some other poor woman in this plight."

Charles stared at her and then laughed out loud. "No, *madame*, truly, not this Henri." He patted her hand. "I will pray for you, *madame*, and that the little one waits his time. Or if not, that you'll both be well and strong."

"Tell Père Le Picart to pray, too," Marie-Ange demanded, tucking more of her mother's newly escaped curls under the cap again.

"I will. Whatever else we can do," he said to the baker, "I trust you will ask us." He signed a cross over Mme LeClerc. "My mother always said, *madame*, that Saint Anne is listening to every woman in childbed."

In spite of the spasm of pain showing on her face, Mme LeClerc's dimples flashed. "Of course she is! That's what a woman needs, a little good conversation and all is well!" Then she closed her lips hard together and Marie-Ange stroked her belly, her face full of worry.

Charles and the baker backed out of the room.

"I'll go for the midwife if she's not here soon." The baker looked back at the bed. "Please pray hard for her."

"I will. God be with you all tonight."

Charles went out into the street and the bar thudded back into place across the door. The wind struck cold on his face as he started toward the college postern, and he prayed that wherever Henry Wing was, he was alive and warm enough. And that the coming baby, and the woman bringing him into the cold world, would both be well.

Suddenly, the wind leaped up the rue St. Jacques like a wild thing, and the street lanterns creaked on their hooks and chains, their candles flickering, guttering, going out. Charles was suddenly back in the dream that had made him cry out and wake Père Damiot. The wind sounded like the breath of a hunting animal as it tossed and worried the one lantern still lit, making shadows spin like the leaves coming down from the trees. As the shadows closed around Charles, it seemed to him that they were full of faces: the goatwoman's face, the face of the peasant woman at Cassel, the face of his cousin Charles-François, Amaury's face and Wing's and Richaud's. Then Père Dainville's serene face flashed past him and the shadows calmed and the wind drew back. But the evil dream went on. A door opened and a man came striding out to kill him. Charles ran.

"God's tears, *maître*, what's come to you?" La Reynie shouted. "Get back here!"

Charles's feet faltered and he looked over his shoulder. *"Mon lieutenant-général?"*

"Of course it's me! Come back!"

Charles went slowly to the postern. "Forgive me. I—I thought—" He shook his head. "I don't know what I thought." He looked at the street in a daze, the wind whipping his hair into his eyes.

La Reynie led him to the postern and into the passage. He stopped under the passage lantern and peered anxiously at Charles.

"What happened out there?"

Charles shook his head. "The wind—the lanterns went out and it was like a dream I had. I thought I saw faces . . . the goatwoman and—"

"What goatwoman?" La Reynie said sharply.

"It wasn't really her, only shadows—"

"Which goatwoman?"

"The one called Hyacinthe. She's old and"—Charles shrugged—"just an old woman. She lives on Talking Flea Street, out beyond the wall."

"Has she told you something?"

Charles stared at him. "How did you know?"

"She's a seer," La Reynie said grimly.

Charles felt his skin crawl. "Surely you don't believe that!"

"I believe what I see. I've seen what she says come to pass."

"What she said made no sense. She said, 'Follow the dead, find your death.' She's said it twice—the first time was when I saw her in the Lunel courtyard, which I told you about."

"You didn't tell me she'd said something to you!"

"It didn't seem important. And the other time was this afternoon by Talking Flea Street. She said it again, and shouted at me to stay away. I suppose she's just a mad old woman."

"Who frightened you enough that you ran when you thought you saw her face just now in the street."

"I was a little bewitched by shadows and my dream," Charles said impatiently. "That's all."

"*Bewitched* is exactly the word. Listen to me. The woman warned you against finding. And you *are* searching—for a killer. Everyone in the Latin quarter knows that her words are not to be brushed aside."

The *lieutenant-général*'s flat certainty about that, coming after Père Damiot's, settled over Charles like a cold mist, and he could find nothing to say.

La Reynie nodded with satisfaction. "Good. You've heard me. You've been a soldier and no matter what you are now, you haven't forgotten how to protect yourself. So be on your guard. Now. I've seen Père Le Picart and the *commissaire* and heard about your missing Englishman, and we'll search for him. I was also called to your Novice House this evening." He eyed Charles sourly. "The Novice House rector is breathing fire at me because of *Le Cabinet*. As though I have enough men to keep every illegal book out of the city."

Irritably, he flicked a speck of dirt from the breast of his tobacco-colored coat. Charles saw the blue shadows under his deep-set black eyes and wondered, as he often had before, when La Reynie went home and slept.

"The Novice House rector told me he suspects your friend de Corbet of bringing *Le Cabinet* into the house," La Reynie said. "Though de Corbet swears the copy of *Le Cabinet* is not his and refuses to say anything more. I got the strong impression that de Corbet is acting more like an offended noble than a Jesuit novice learning humility."

"The Novice House rector was going to let me be there when he talked to de Corbet," Charles said. "But he never sent word."

"He tells me he did, late this afternoon, but you weren't here. I wanted to take de Corbet to the Châtelet for a little talk, but the rector suddenly shifted his ground to play father hen and refused to give up his chick. I didn't press him. We agreed that you would walk with the novices tomorrow morning to their country house at Montrouge. You are to talk with de Corbet about the book during the walk. You are also to eat dinner with them there, he says, and then come back to the city on your own. He has sent a note to your rector about it." La Reynie glowered at Charles. "I tell you now that if you don't find out what your friend knows, he *will* find himself at the Châtelet."

Charles bristled. "And I tell you what I've already told the Novice House rector. Amaury doesn't know anything about that damned book. However lacking he may be in Jesuit humility, he's the image of the old stories' 'perfect knight.' I didn't know him well in the army, but everyone knew that his word was his word, and that honor probably meant more to him than his hope of heaven." He eyed La Reynie balefully. "And yes, if Père Le Picart permits, I'll walk with them and find out what I can."

"Père Le Picart sends his permission through me."

Charles eyed him skeptically.

"For God's sake, *maître*, even I know not to lie about a Jesuit rector." La Reynie grinned. "Except in exceptional circumstances. No, no," he said, laughing at Charles's look, "he really did say that. I'm *not* noble, but my word is still good."

"It had better be," Charles said back. "I doubt talking to Amaury at the Châtelet would be any use to you. If he says he didn't bring in the book, he didn't. What might be of more use is talking to Michel Poulard, your maid's son who's a servant at the Novice House. I think he knows a good deal about everything that goes in and out of that house."

"And how do you know that?"

Charles didn't want to tell La Reynie about Rose Ebrard and Amaury. He smiled blandly. "Just a thought."

La Reynie sighed. "Someone needs to have a useful thought about all this. Because I seem to have none. Your missing Englishman—would he go off on his own? Would he run away from the Society?"

"He might go off on his own for some reason that seemed good to him, but not for long. I can't imagine him running away."

"Is he a bold man?"

"Far from it," Charles said. "He told me straight out that he's a coward. Can you imagine a man actually saying that? And the night I was attacked in the chapel, he fainted."

La Reynie frowned in disbelief. "What use do you have for someone like that?"

"Jesuits don't do much hand-to-hand fighting," Charles said lightly, not wanting to talk about courage.

"Yourself always excluded. Well," the *lieutenant-général* said, "when you return from the country tomorrow, come to my office and tell me what de Corbet said. And anything else you learn." He sketched a bow and went to the postern. "Oh," he said, as he waited for the porter to open the door. "I nearly forgot—Père Le Picart says you needn't go to his office. He tells you to go to your books. A *bonne nuit* to you."

The thought of trying to digest St. Thomas reminded Charles of his interrupted supper and how hungry he still was. Thinking that even if he couldn't face martyrdom in some mission, he ought to be able to at least manage a little fasting, he started toward the stairs to his chamber. Then he turned back and went outside and across the court to the chapel. The nave was in darkness, the only light from the sanctuary lamp and a pair of candles on the altar. A lay brother sat beside the street door, and a few neighborhood people were kneeling among the benches. Charles knelt at the main altar. St. Ignatius's altar. The long day had seemed as clamorous as a battle, and the chapel's silence and the darkness washed over Charles like a baptism of peace.

But the silence didn't last long.

"Maître?"

He turned and saw Mlle Ebrard standing behind him.

"I heard that the Englishman is missing," she said very softly. "I came to light a candle for him."

Charles rose and crossed himself, and they moved away from the altar. "Did you see Maître Wing today, after you returned to The Dog?" he asked her.

"No. And I'm worried about Amaury. If someone is taking Jesuits . . ."

"Amaury is never out alone. I'm sure he's safe. I'll see him tomorrow." He told her briefly about walking to the house at Montrouge to ask Amaury about *Le Cabinet.*

"Oh, I'm glad! And will you talk to him about—other things?"

"If I can."

"Where is this Montrouge? How can I see you when you return, and hear what he said?"

"It's south from the Novice House, thirty or forty minutes' slow walking," Charles said, remembering the somewhat indirect route. "But when I return after dinner—they eat early—I'll be coming straight up the rue Saint Jacques to the college. I'll stop in The Dog around noon or so, and we can talk a little as though you're helping me find a book. Yes?"

"Yes. Thank you," she breathed, and withdrew into the dark nave.

With a sigh, Charles left the chapel, thinking about how much penance he was going to owe when all this was over. He had permission to help La Reynie, but he didn't have permission to talk repeatedly in private with women. And he certainly didn't have permission to persuade a novice out of the Society. But he had a vocation to help souls. And what did one do when what souls needed was not what rules demanded? Which led him to such a tangle that he went gratefully to his chamber and the relative simplicity of St. Thomas Aquinas.

Chapter 22

By morning, the wind had died, leaving Paris sunlit and cold. The college clock was striking eight as Charles huddled into his cloak and started up the rue St. Jacques. Then he turned back and pushed open the bakery door. The air was heady with the smell of fresh bread, but Marie-Ange was alone at the counter with her head on her arms.

"*Ma petite?*" Charles said anxiously, going in. "How is your mother?"

She lifted her head. "Oh, *maître*, she had a terrible night." Her small face was gray with exhaustion. "She has pains and more pains, but the baby doesn't come. The midwife came last night just after you left and she's still here."

A long groan came from beyond the closed door into the other room. Wincing, Charles went to Marie-Ange and smoothed back her tangled, uncoifed hair. "I am praying for her, I promise you. For all of you. I'll come back later to see how things are."

She wiped away tears and gave him a watery smile, and he went back out to the street with a heavy heart, remembering his mother's sufferings in childbed with her last child, who hadn't lived. When he turned the corner by The Dog, Mlle Ebrard was standing in the bookshop doorway. She smiled at him and he nodded, but neither spoke. He could feel her eyes on him as he passed the shop, but when he looked back, she was gone.

At the Novice House, he was taken to the Hall of St. Joseph, where the novices were waiting to set out for Montrouge. Cloaked, hatted, and carrying their small leather satchels, they stood quietly, waiting for the rector, Père Guymond, to give them the signal for leaving. When Amaury de Corbet saw Charles, he smiled uneasily but made no move to approach him. The rector immediately began assigning companions. These were mostly groupings of three, but there were a few pairings of an older Jesuit and a novice, including Charles and de Corbet.

The long line of groupings followed the rector from the hall and along the gallery to the street door. Charles and Amaury were last. Out in the rue du Pot-de-Fer, everyone lowered his eyes and lifted his long, heavy cloak to keep it from the street dirt and from tangling with his companions' cloaks, and the line set out slowly and in absolute silence. Amaury's lips were moving in silent prayer—one of the prescribed things to do while walking—and he didn't notice the gurgle of laughter behind them. Charles looked over his shoulder and saw the young and fleet-footed servant Michel Poulard pacing in their wake. Holding a bundle of kindling on his shoulder with one hand, he mimed holding his cloak away from the dirt with the other. He saw Charles watching him, returned his grin, and vanished down the passage beside the chapel.

Still smiling, Charles returned to the business at hand. There would be no talking at all, he knew, until they passed the tax *barrière* beyond the city. Not that the silence had anything to do with the toll for bringing goods into Paris, but by the time the *barrière*—a small manned booth—was reached, there would be fewer people on the road to be edified by the novices' strictly disciplined behavior. It had been much the same in his own novitiate in Avignon and, he supposed, was much the same in all Jesuit Novice Houses. But he wanted urgently to talk to Amaury and could hardly contain himself as they made their dignified way along the rue de Vaugirard. But even when they reached the *barrière* and turned left to skirt the walled gardens of the Luxembourg palace, silence was kept until the paving gave out and the road became a dirt track. Then the rector raised his hand and his flock stopped.

"You may speak quietly to each other. Remember, however, the rules of behavior you have learned."

The group moved off again, and quiet conversation began.

Amaury said, without looking at Charles, "So are you here to question me about the book?"

"I am."

"I told him the truth," the novice said curtly. "I will not rub my honor in the dust, begging to be believed." The way he shut his mouth made Charles think of a helmet's visor falling.

"I believe you," Charles said. "I told him that. And I understand why you're insulted at being told to prove that you speak truth. Listen, Amaury—I'm sorry, I should call you Monsieur de Corbet now—the rector *wants* to believe you. Otherwise, he would not have asked me to speak with you. Do you know what *Le Cabinet jesuitique* is?"

"I know it's a forgery, a libel on the Society."

"It's also illegal to possess or distribute in France. The head of the police is determined to find out where it's coming from this time—it shows up periodically—and stop it. He's threatening to take you in to the Châtelet for what he calls 'a little talk.'"

"He wouldn't!" Amaury's face, already ruddy from the cold, flamed with outrage.

"He would. So think of the dishonor of *that*. You're noble, yes. So am I. But other things matter more in the world now. It's 1687 and the great knight Roland and the rest of them are dead. Long dead."

"My father would kill you if he heard you say that!"

"So would mine, probably. But they're both dead, too. So tell me about the book." He held the novice's eyes. "And then tell me about Mademoiselle Ebrard."

Amaury de Corbet went as white as altar linen and then as red as a maple leaf. "She's none of your business!"

"Shhh. She's none of your fellow novices' business, either. But she thinks you are still *her* business. The book first, though." Charles smiled dangerously. "Unless you're going to disobey your rector and refuse to talk to me. Which will mean making the acquaintance of Lieutenant-Général La Reynie."

Amaury turned a cold stare on Charles. "How dare you threaten me! What's happened to you? You don't even sound like a Jesuit!"

"Nor do you," Charles said. "But you have some excuse, since being a novice is only the beginning of being a Jesuit. Do you really not understand that by putting yourself in the Novice House, you've made yourself a Jesuit first and a noble second?"

Frowning blackly, Amaury watched his sturdy shoes appear and vanish beneath his cassock on the dusty track. "What do you want to know?"

"You say you didn't hide the book in your mattress, that you'd never seen it until the rector showed it to you. So tell me how it could have come there. The rector and La Reynie need another track to follow."

Amaury shook his head helplessly. "How can I know? I make my bed every morning and have never felt anything in the mattress but straw. But I'm out of my chamber most of the day, so I suppose anyone could have come in and unpicked the stitching and put the book there." He looked sideways at Charles. "The rector also accused me of stealing a needle and thread to stitch the end of the mattress cover after I'd put the book in."

"Does someone in the house dislike you enough to do this?"

"If someone does, I don't know it. I can't think why they would. Whether you believe it or not, I've done my best to behave as we're told. And I barely know anyone in the house."

Charles thought about that and they went a little way without speaking. The rector led the group to the right, onto another unpaved track that led straight south, through harvested and autumn brown fields. Pleased to be in the countryside in spite of the cold, Charles watched a wide-winged hawk soar above them as he tried to imagine a novice waiting for Amaury's chamber to be empty, leaving whatever thing he was supposed to be doing in the strictly scheduled day, finding needle and thread, unpicking the mattress cover's stitching, thrusting the book into the mattress straw, stitching the cover closed, and leaving the chamber before anyone discovered him. And getting the book out again would be just as tricky. Putting the thing in and getting it out repeatedly beggared belief. Chosen as a hiding place by anyone but Amaury, the mattress cover simply made no sense.

But beyond that certainty, Charles found he couldn't go. *Well,* he told himself, *leave it for now. Let it settle. There's still the other thing to say.* He looked at the pair of men ahead of him, a very young novice listening respectfully to a gray-haired senior. To lessen the chance of being overheard, Charles bent down and made an unnecessary adjustment to his shoe, which forced Amaury to stop and wait politely.

"There," Charles said, straightening and seeing that the pair in front was far enough away. "Now, what about your former betrothed?"

Amaury tensed as though Charles were suddenly holding a weapon. Which in a way, Charles thought ruefully, he was.

"Mademoiselle Ebrard is a fine—a devout—young woman," Amaury said stiffly. "She is guilty of nothing. You have no right to even speak of her."

"You didn't know until the day at the market that she was in Paris, did you?"

"No."

"When you saw her standing in front of you, what did you think?"

"What do you want? Why are you tormenting me? Go away!" Amaury veered angrily out of the line toward the front and the rector.

Charles caught a fold of his cloak. "Wait. Please. I beg you."

Reluctantly and staring straight ahead, he dropped back into place beside Charles.

Offering up a quick plea for the right words, Charles said, "What I am going to say to you, I say as a man who owes you his life. And as the man who shares the memory and the guilt of that terrible day at Cassel." With a sense of stepping off the edge of something, he finished, "And as one longer in the Society who is concerned about your vocation. And about you."

Emotion moved across Amaury's face like wind over water, but he said nothing. Ahead of them, Charles saw rooflines coming into view and knew that his time was nearly up.

"If I'm wrong, I'm wrong and you will tell me later. Amaury, I ask you to think hard about why you're here. About the possibility that you're hiding in the Novice House." Charles winced at the echo of what his cousin had said to him. But he made himself go on. "I think you're haunted beyond bearing by that day in the army. I think you're confusing your need for forgiveness with having a religious vocation. I think you're turning away from Mademoiselle Ebrard for all those wrong reasons."

"And what about you? You just said you carry that day and its horrors, too. If my vocation is tainted, so is yours, and it has been for years now!"

"I didn't enter the Society because of that day at Cassel. I entered because I wanted to come as close to God as a man can—whether God forgives me for that day or not. And that's something I've rarely told anyone, in the Society or out of it. But yes, I've carried that day, and those deaths, for all these years. And with them my certainty that I am a coward. I *was* a coward that day. If I hadn't been, I'd probably be dead. But we're never allowed to know what would have happened. Only what we can choose now." Charles had stopped in the road, and the passion of his words held Amaury motionless, listening. "Here's what I've learned," Charles said. "Nothing is wasted. Not even death. You don't have to go on sacrificing yourself now because you didn't sacrifice yourself then."

A tremor swept the long length of Amaury's body, but he said nothing.

"Rose Ebrard loves you," Charles said softly. "I saw your face in the market and I know that you love her. She knows and I know—and I suspect your superiors in the Novice House will soon know—that you have come here to do lifelong penance. What good is that to God? Or those peasants at Cassel, long dead and at peace? What good is that to the Society? God is love, not guilt. And not pride."

"Pride?" Amaury said bitterly. "I haven't the pride of a worm."

"Wrong. You've been too proud for ten years to let anything—not God, not Mademoiselle Ebrard—come between you and your guilt. You and your soiled honor."

"Damn you to hell!" Amaury said distinctly, not bothering to keep his voice down. He strode away toward the rest of the line, which was far ahead of them now.

Charles stayed where he was, watching the novice's heels raising small storm clouds from the dusty track. Then he hurried to catch up with the others. He ached for Amaury's unhappiness. But he didn't regret what he'd done.

Within its walls, the rambling stone country house was surrounded by gardens, small groves of nearly leafless trees, and a few gnarled grapevines dropping their broad leaves. Wide stubbled fields where hay and wheat had been harvested stretched beyond the walls, and sheep and cows grazed under the brilliant sky. The Montrouge house was a beloved place of recreation and rest for the novices and the older Jesuits who taught and supervised them. But days there began with a quarter of an hour's spiritual reading, and the novices took the books they'd brought out of their satchels. Some found places on the grass and under the trees and others walked, holding their open books. Charles saw Amaury go hurriedly to the far side of the stretch of grass. After the reading there would be the silent morning examination of conscience, and when that was done, dinner at a quarter to eleven.

When the novices had settled to their reading, Père Guymond summoned Charles to a small room where sunlight fell through a new, large window and gleamed on the floor's polished oak.

"Why was Monsieur de Corbet cursing you as we arrived here?" Guymond said, without asking Charles to sit.

"I goaded him," Charles said frankly.

"He was very stiff when I admonished him for it. I do not like this determination to take offense that I am suddenly seeing in him."

"Whatever may come of that, *mon père*, I am certain that he had nothing to do with bringing *Le Cabinet* into the Novice House. I've questioned him closely, and I believe what he tells me. Someone put the book where it was found, but it was not him. And he's very offended that you doubt his noble word of honor. As you well know, that's grounds for a duel in the world he comes from."

"He's no longer in that world. And cursing anyone, let alone a fellow Jesuit, is forbidden."

Charles was politely silent, wondering if this sincere and stern man ever looked anything but tired. Though how could a man in charge of novices—and by that charge, responsible for the Society's future—look anything but tired?

Guymond frowned. "If you really did goad him, perhaps you should ask his pardon."

"Willingly," Charles said. "But about the book, what are you going to do?"

"I cannot simply take your word for his innocence. You are his friend. I don't say you are lying. I do say you may be too trusting. I must pursue the matter with him until I am certain." A small bell rang somewhere in the house and Guymond stood up. "That's the ring for the examination of conscience. I must go. You may do as you choose until dinner, *maître*."

Charles went out into the garden, where most of the novices were still walking or sitting as they made their examination of conscience, called the *examen*, and he realized he'd have to wait until after it to make his apology to Amaury. He'd meant to make his own *examen*, but instead he went toward a gate beyond the mostly bare flowerbeds and let himself out into an autumn-bleached meadow. He wished he'd been able to convince Guy-mond that Amaury had nothing to do with *Le Cabinet* being found in the Novice House. But he'd done his best. And if he was wrong about Amaury's vocation, then Amaury was going to have to learn humility. And that he could do nothing about.

Trying to remember how long it had been since he'd been footloose in the real countryside, he wandered slowly toward a wooden fence and leaned on it, watching cows drowsing under a huge oak. Cows, sheep, and goats, he thought, growing drowsy himself. He wondered idly if the goatwoman brought her flock to the Novice House. Ignatius had charged all Jesuit superiors to take great care of their men's health and there might be someone at the novitiate who needed goat's milk . . .

Charles jerked awake as behind him another bell was ringing. He retraced his steps reluctantly toward the house. When he reached the refectory, the places beside Amaury were taken, and during the meal, Amaury avoided Charles's eye. Talking was permitted, but Charles ate his mutton silently, while an elderly priest beside him cataloged all the reasons why the ancient fragment of cloth preserved in Chartres Cathedral was certainly a piece of the Virgin's nightdress, worn for the holy birth of Christ. Charles bit his tongue along with his mutton, to keep himself from gravely asking the old priest's opinion of the reputed slice of our Lord's holy foreskin at Chartres, which was reverenced by women wanting, or about to have, babies. That unkind temptation set him to praying sincerely for the safety of Mme LeClerc and her baby, and for Marie-Ange and M. LeClerc.

When dinner ended, Amaury went quickly from the room before Charles could disengage himself from his talkative neighbor. As Charles went to look for the novice, the click of billiard balls began from the upper floor. Wishing he could go up and join the game, Charles went through the house and garden and finally found Amaury in the small bare chapel, kneeling before the altar. Charles waited patiently just inside the door, but Amaury was rigidly still, his long back bowed and his face hidden in his hands. After half an hour, Charles left him, found the rector, and said he would make his apology when he went next to the Novice House. Then he took his leave and started back to Paris.

At least, he thought, letting himself out onto the dusty track from the gate to the road, he'd shaken Amaury de Corbet momentarily out of his grim submission to novice discipline and, God willing, made him think again about what he was doing. Walking briskly, eyes mostly on the dirt track at his feet, Charles prayed his way north, working through his worry over Amaury and Maître Wing and Mlle Ebrard and Mme LeClerc. As he turned east toward the rue St. Jacques, the most direct way back to the college, he remembered guiltily that he should also pray for the vanished Richaud. But as he started his prayer, he realized that a footpath he was passing would take him a shorter way to the rue St. Jacques and started down it.

Except for a man walking some way ahead of him, the path was empty. The man looked up at a flock of squawking crows, and the midday sun lit his profile beneath his stylishly cocked hat brim. It took Charles a moment to realize what he was seeing. Then he broke into a run.

"Richaud! Maître Richaud, is it you? Stop!"

The man glanced over his shoulder and fled around a turn in the lane. When Charles reached the lane's end at the rue St. Jacques, Richaud—or the man who looked like him—was gone. Charles stopped in confusion. The profile and meager body were very like the missing scholastic's. But this man wore a wig and layman's clothes, a short cloak over gray breeches.

Charles thought suddenly of Richaud's drunken brother and wondered if that was who he'd been chasing. There was a family resemblance between the two, and Charles could easily imagine the brother running from a pursuing Jesuit.

He shook his head and went on north toward the city wall. A little way ahead, he heard outraged female cries rise beyond a stone wall running along the road. Charles put his foot on a projecting stone, caught the wall's top with his good arm, and pulled himself up. Three nuns with rakes and hoes were chasing the man in the short cloak and gray breeches across their neatly laid-out convent garden and calling him names nuns were rarely suspected of knowing. Thinking that if the fleeing man was Richaud's brother, he must have some unusually urgent reason to run, Charles jumped over the wall, passed the startled sisters, and put on a burst of speed. His quarry reached the wall on the garden's far side and was up and over in a flash. Which made Charles doubt even more that this was the missing scholastic, because he couldn't imagine the Richaud he'd known being so fast and agile.

Charles pulled himself up onto the wall, half fell from it to a narrow road, and picked himself up. There was no one in sight except a small girl leading a donkey and a farmer driving a dung-laden cart. But then he saw a swath of bushes thrashing and trembling on the slope beyond the road. He leaped across the road and climbed quickly and quietly up a dry water channel, watching the moving bushes as he went. He was almost at the top of the slope when a stone rolled under his foot and he went down. On the little ridge above him, the man broke from cover and disappeared again. When Charles reached the top, the narrow path there was empty and the man was gone.

Charles strode along the path, keeping an eye out for his

quarry and feeling more and more confused. If the man he was chasing was Richaud, then Richaud was neither dead nor being held captive. So why had his bloody cassock and his rosary been found? Why hadn't he returned to the college? Had Richaud simply walked away from the Society of Jesus? But if that was what he'd wanted, why not go through the procedure for leaving? Like Charles, he hadn't yet taken final vows. The vows taken after the two novice years contained a promise to make final vows at some time in the future, but the promise could be broken. The Society wanted wholehearted commitment.

A honking, dust-raising gaggle of geese was being driven toward Charles from the lane on his right, and he drew aside to let them pass. He recognized the lane as Talking Flea Street and realized that he was half fearing and half hoping to see the goatwoman again. No matter how much he tried to dismiss her cryptic prophecy, it haunted him. She'd begun to seem always there in the shadows of his mind, muttering and shouting and singing her warning. *Follow the dead, find your death.*

Charles walked determinedly down Talking Flea Street. Jacques Coriot had said she lived somewhere on it. The man he'd chased was gone. But her he could maybe find and make tell him what she'd meant, and have done with this nonsense. A woman in one of the first houses, spreading wet laundry on bushes, glanced at Charles and turned away. Two children drawing in the lane's dirt looked up fearfully and edged away from him. Not from him personally, Charles suspected, but from anyone unlike themselves, anyone not poor, who might wring more coins or unwilling obedience from them. Wishing he had something to give the children, he walked on, searching the gardens and waste ground for the little herd of goats.

As he passed the garden where the pig had run when he'd walked down the lane with his students, two crows flew low over his head and dived at something on the ground. Because he liked crows—and wasn't unwilling to put off finding the goatwoman—he stopped to watch them. A third crow was waddling through the overgrown garden with something shiny in its beak. The shiny thing flashed in the sunlight as the fortunate crow with the treasure hopped closer to him, and the other two crows swooped again, trying to snatch it. Then all three crows fled into the air as a hawk's shadow stooped from the sky above them. The fortunate crow dropped its treasure, and Charles bent down and picked it up. It was a small silver oval, a medal of the Virgin, finely worked with a surround of tiny lilies. He held it up and turned it to catch the light. Unless his memory played him false, he was looking at the missing medal of the Virgin that Maître Richaud had worn on his rosary, or at least at its twin.

Charles looked up at the house in the abandoned garden and the equally decrepit houses up and down the lane. Crows picked up small shiny things and flew away with them. The medal could have come from anywhere. It seemed too valuable a thing to have come from these houses. He started down Talking Flea Street again, thinking that he could show the goatwoman the medal and ask her if she'd seen it before. And if she'd seen the man who looked like Richaud. Above his head, the crows were suddenly back, a half dozen of them this time, raucous as boys let out of school. He looked up and pain bloomed in the back of his head. The sunlight dazzled into fireworks and went out.

Chapter 23

THE FEAST OF ST. WILLIBRORD, FRIDAY, NOVEMBER 7, 1687

Charles's sense of touch returned before his sense of sight. And his sense of smell, unfortunately, came with it. He felt damp straw under his cheek and tried to turn his head away from the reek of mold. But turning his head made it sing with pain, and he sank back into oblivion.

"*Maître?*"

Something scrabbled at Charles's cassock skirts and a crack opened in oblivion. He thought he heard a voice. But it was blurred and seemed to be speaking a language he didn't know.

"*Maître . . .*"

The voice whispered on unintelligibly and Charles inched away from it, heard someone groan, and went back to sleep. The next time he woke the crack was wider and the voice had switched to blurred but recognizable Latin.

"*Maître*, please, wake up. It's morning, he'll be down soon." Fingers scrabbled again and pulled hard on Charles's cassock. "It's me, Henry. Oh, dear, are you dead?"

Charles groaned and opened his eyes. He was in complete darkness, lying on his side in stinking straw. The back of his head felt as though a horse had kicked him, and his stomach lurched when he tried to move.

"Oh, thank you, blessed Mary, thank you, Saint George! I was so afraid you were dead, *maître*. Can you hear me?"

"Wing?" Charles managed to say. His mouth was dry as a March drought.

"How did they get you?" Wing said.

"Who?" Speaking was an enormous effort, and Charles felt himself sliding back into blessed unknowing.

Then he seemed to be in something that rocked. Wing was there, too, because he was still talking, and Charles thought gratefully that someone must be taking them home in a carriage.

"*Maître, please!* You have to wake up before he comes down."

The fingers pulling rhythmically at his cassock pulled harder and pain clutched his head like claws. "Stop that!" Charles demanded.

"You're awake." Wing heaved a sigh. "Good."

Charles opened his eyes to see light coming in around broken window shutters. His hands were tied painfully behind him and he swore as he shifted on the straw to look at Wing. "Dear God, what happened to you?"

The Englishman's face was bruised and one side of his mouth was so swollen, Charles wondered that he could talk at all.

"He hit me," Wing explained, seeing Charles's expression. "But when he brought you in last night, I knew that everything would be all right. You were a soldier; you'll know how to get us away. But you have to think of how to do it quickly." His blue eyes were round and trusting. "Because when they're tired of hitting us, they're going to make Maître Richaud kill us."

Charles closed his eyes and tried to make sense of that. Until footsteps sounded and someone kicked him in the side.

"Wake up, Jesuit."

Charles half opened his eyes. *"Bonjour,* Richaud," he said wearily. "I suppose I should no longer call you *maître.*"

"Very clever. You always have to be so much cleverer than anyone else. But I'll still be charitable. Here."

Charles cried out as cold water hit his face. Then he tried to lick all the drops his dry tongue could reach. He heard Wing reacting to the same treatment. Then a cup was shoved against Charles's lips and he drank thirstily. The water was fetid but wet, which was all that mattered. A little revived—though more consciousness brought more pain—Charles stared up at Richaud.

"Why so kind? And what are you doing here?"

"I have to keep you alive for a while yet. I'm here because I've come to my senses."

Charles stared at him. "What do you—" He licked his lips, trying to manage his still dry and stumbling tongue. "—mean, 'come to your senses'?"

A triumphant smile spread over Richaud's narrow face. He reached into his coat pocket. "I mean this." He dangled a small book in front of Charles.

Charles couldn't see to read the book's cover, but he didn't need to. *"Le Cabinet jesuitique."*

Richaud burst into crowing laughter, the first laughter Charles had ever heard from him.

"Clever to the end, aren't you?" He kissed the little book and put it back into his pocket.

Charles stared at him in horror, *"You?* You brought *Le Cabinet* into Louis le Grand and the Novice House?"

Richaud smiled enigmatically. "God saw to that."

"But you know the book's a forgery, every Jesuit knows that! If you've come to hate the Society of Jesus for some reason, why not just leave, for God's sake?"

Richaud leaned close over Charles. "You know that no one just leaves the Society! If you leave, they harass you, they hunt you, they'll kill you if they can, so you won't tell the world their secrets!"

"That's insane," Charles said flatly.

"That's the devil speaking in you!" He shoved Charles hard down into the straw. "The Society bewitched me," he shouted. "I thought they saw who I really am and what I can do. But I was wrong, they saw that my wit was far above theirs and they were envious. They hid me away and made me tend to dirty linen! They'll suffer for that now! I was too smart for them," he said, his eyes going from Charles to Wing, as though inviting them to share his glee. "I learned the truth and got away, and God has told me to spread the truth about Jesuits everywhere. God has meant that to be my greatness all along. He let me become a Jesuit so that He could enlighten me. And through me, the world."

"And where do Maître Wing and I fit in your plan for enlightenment?"

"Nowhere. The Englishman is too stupid and you're too far gone in the Society's evil. The world will be rid of two more Jesuits." The ex-scholastic gazed at the wall beyond Charles as though a vision hovered there. "You will be gone, du Luc, and I will be left in the place of honor. His dark eyes glittered. "The last shall be first!"

A chill crawled under Charles's skin. Wing started to argue with Richaud, but Charles moved a warning foot against him and shook his head.

"I see, Monsieur Richaud," Charles said respectfully, hoping that submission might forestall the violence he felt simmering in the man. "God has told you to do this alone? A great responsibility."

"Prophets bear a greater burden than anyone else," Richaud said matter-of-factly, turning from his vision and picking up the cup from the straw. "But God has given me handmaids to help me sow the good seed."

"Maids?" Charles said carefully. "Women?"

Richaud spun around from putting the cup on a table. "How dare you, you unclean lecher! Of course I don't mean women! But you'd like that, wouldn't you? I've seen the way you talk to women, I've seen them fawning over you. I've seen you with the baker's wife! And that little girl, she's the worst, she hangs all over you and you like it! I've begged the rector to get rid of you, but no, you're his favorite, aren't you?" He came back and stood over Charles. "But no more! It's his turn to weep! I won't fail this time."

Appalled understanding flooded Charles. "This time?"

Richaud patted his pocket. "This time."

Charles swallowed, trying to make himself say what he knew. The words came out in a whisper. "It was you in the chapel gallery. You, my brother Jesuit. You stabbed me."

"And fooled you all, didn't I? None of you even imagined it might have been me. It was so simple. I took off my shoes and left them at the top of the north stairs. I made a few silly schoolboy noises. And up you came like a little lamb."

"But why? Why, Richaud?"

"Because you can't leave anything alone. You found Paul Lunel's body and brought La Reynie and his people swarming over the Carmelite crypt. I keep—"

"Are you telling me you killed Paul?"

"Killing Paul was unnecessary. I'm not stupid. As I was saying, I keep my copies of *Le Cabinet* there in the well chamber, until I need them." He shrugged. "I thought if you died, La Reynie's attention would be on you. Because you're his little *mignon*, his handsome little pet, aren't you? Just like you're the rector's pet."

Charles let that go. "But the knife—no Jesuit has a knife!"

Richaud bent over him. His foul breath made Charles turn his face away. "You're too stupid to live. Have you forgotten that I saw you slavering over that woman from the bookshop? The very day your beloved Père Dainville died. I saw you from the porter's room. Where students have to leave weapons at the start of the term. I had a nice choice of knives."

"I heard you running in the gallery above me," Wing said suddenly. "But no one else did because you were running in your stockings."

Richaud looked at him in surprise. "Well, a glimmer of intelligence. It was so easy. The north stairs end away from the light, near the courtyard door. I only had to run down them, slip my shoes back on, and act like I'd just come in from the courtyard."

"You're right about one thing, Richaud," Charles said. "We've all underestimated you,"

The ex-scholastic gave him a sly smile. "Envy always underestimates brilliance." He turned his back on them and picked up his hat from the table. Pulling it well down over his straggling brown wig, he went out by the back door.

Charles tried to sit up, gritting his teeth against nausea. "It's our chance. Come on, help me."

Wing lay where he was, shaking his head. "He's only gone out to piss."

"He puts on his hat to go and piss?"

"He's terrified someone will recognize him."

The light from the open door made Charles's head hurt more, and he squinted at the Englishman. "How did you get here? *Why* in God's name didn't you go straight home from the Novice House?"

"I did. I mean, I was going there. But I got lost. Then someone told me another way, but I ended up at a market and that's when I saw him."

"Richaud?"

Wing nodded eagerly. "But he was wearing what he's wearing now and I wasn't sure it was him. So I followed him till I was sure and then caught up with him. He told me he was hiding from the secret, powerful Jesuits who wanted to kill him. I told him Jesuits wouldn't kill him, but he said I was stupid and naive. Then he said that because I'd seen him, they'd try to kill me, too, but if I came with him, I'd be safe." The Englishman sighed and glanced at Charles. "I said no, but he grabbed my arm and showed me a knife in his other hand, and I went. I was afraid. How did he get you, *maître*? I thought you'd be too shrewd for him."

"Unfortunately, I wasn't, I saw Richaud and chased him. I lost him and he came up behind me and hit me on the head. Listen, these helpers of his, these 'handmaids,' do they come here?"

"Oh, yes, you'll—"

The door scraped open and Richaud was back. He ignored his captives and busied himself making a fire on the small hearth. Then he took a loaf of bread from a bulging satchel beside the hearth, and threw ragged pieces to Charles and Wing.

"How are we supposed to eat?" Charles said, lifting his tied hands behind his back.

"Like the animals you are." Richaud took the wine he'd

heated for himself, the rest of the bread, and the satchel, and went upstairs.

"Like this," Wing said. He twisted on the straw and picked up the bread in his teeth.

It was a tedious business, and by the time Charles had eaten—the smaller the piece grew, the more difficult it became to eat and the more straw came with it—his head was pounding and another need was demanding his attention.

"How are we supposed to piss?"

Wing, sitting up now and leaning against the wall's peeling plaster, called out, "*Maître!* I mean, Monsieur Richaud! Please, we need to go outside."

Charles was wondering how much longer he could hold out when Richaud finally came downstairs.

"Get up, then," he said, standing over them. "And don't make noise out there or you'll be dead sooner rather than later."

Wing managed to get to his feet, but Charles's headache was too blinding and he fell back on the straw. Richaud untied Wing's hands and let him pull Charles up. Then he herded them out a low back door into the wildly overgrown garden.

"You first," he said to Wing.

Wing started wading through the overgrown garden to its crumbling wall. Though his hands were still tied, Charles launched himself at Richaud, knocking him to the ground and falling on top of him.

"Help me!" Charles yelled, and Wing came at a run. But he was too slow, and Richaud heaved Charles off with surprising strength and pulled a long knife from under his coat.

"Stop! Don't move, he has a knife," Charles cried, and curled into a ball as Richaud kicked him savagely in the thigh.

"Shut up! Get back inside, crawl if you have to, you scum," Richaud hissed at Charles. "You, too, Englishman."

To Charles's surprise, Wing ignored him and helped Charles up. "You have to let him piss, too," he said sternly to Richaud. "It already smells bad enough in there. And you have to breathe the air just like we do."

"Get away from him." Richaud made a feint with the knife at Wing, who ducked and clapped a hand over his mouth, trying not to cry out, his momentary courage gone. With a swing of the knife, Richaud warned Charles not to move. Then he retied Wing's hands and ordered Charles to turn around.

"Go piss," he said, when Charles's hands were free. "Make any other move, make a sound, and this one's dead." He went to Wing and stood behind him with the knife at the Englishman's throat.

Charles limped away through the undergrowth, telling himself that he would have a chance to try again. When he was relieved from his body's clamoring, he limped back, breathing deeply because he'd remembered from the army that sometimes breathing was almost as good as eating. He filled his lungs with cold morning air and the faint scents of herbs like rosemary and mint rising from plants long gone wild and crushed underfoot.

Richaud and Wing stood exactly as Charles had left them. Richaud ordered Charles to stop and turn around. Charles turned slowly, eyeing the length of rope dangling from Richaud's free hand.

"Walk backward to me," Richaud snapped at him. When Charles reached him, Richaud started retying his wrists. Wing started complaining that his rope was too tight and Richaud's hands stilled. Charles felt him turn to look at Wing. "Stand still and shut up," he muttered at the Englishman.

Charles glanced over his shoulder. Wing was still wriggling and complaining and Richaud was looking at him instead of at what he was doing. Charles pulled one wrist slightly higher than the other and managed to hook a thumb through a loop of rope. He had to bite his cheek to keep from crying out as the rope was tightened on his thumb joint, but he went meekly back inside with the satisfaction of having given himself a small weapon.

Inside, however, more trouble was waiting. Two well-dressed young men whom Charles had never seen before stood beside the fireplace. One had stripped off his gloves and was impatiently slapping the table with them. The other had pulled off his wig and was swearing as he tried to brush a fat brown spider off it.

Richaud flicked a glance over them as he herded his captives back to the straw. "What kept you?"

The man with the gloves ignored the question. "Is all ready for us?"

"Yes, no thanks to you. Since you leave me to see to everything."

The men glanced indifferently at the scholastics, as though they were chickens trussed for sale in the market.

"Go up." Richaud waved his hand magisterially at the staircase. The man with the gloves mounted the stairs, but his companion stamped on the spider and then went to the hearth to peer into the jug of wine.

"This should be steaming, *mon cher* Richaud. Heat it and bring it with you." He shook out his wig, put it on, and took the stairs two at a time after his companion.

Richaud, swearing resentfully under his breath, went to the hearth and poked up the fire to warm the wine. On the floor above, the two men talked in low voices and there was a volley of thuds as something fell to the floor.

Richaud took the wine from the fire and glanced at the Jesuits.

"If you move from the straw or make noise to attract attention from the road, I'll kill you now instead of later." As he stamped upstairs, Charles began straining against the rope around his wrists, softly telling Wing what he'd done outside. The Englishman prayed and Charles patiently twisted the rope, biting blood from his lip to stop himself yelling from the pain in his newly healed stab wound. But the knot refused to slip.

Finally Charles shook his head. "It's not working."

"Then we should both pray."

Their prayers were short. As Charles had learned on the battlefield, when death seemed likely, there was surprisingly little to be said, and that little was simple enough. "Oh, God, make haste to help me." And if one could manage it, "Not my will, but thine be done . . ." Though, more often it was, "Save me, God! And I will do this and that and this other thing for you, I swear it . . ." When their prayers were done, quiet talk and purposeful noises from the upper floor told them that the three men were absorbed in whatever they were doing.

Wing snuffled the air like a forlorn piglet. "You smell like rosemary," he said softly. "From the garden. That's nice. It smells bad in here."

Charles smiled at him, wishing that the two of them were likely to live long enough for their friendship to grow. Then feet clattered down the stairs, and the two young men appeared, dressed now in coarse, dirt-colored coats, ragged breeches, and their own tousled hair instead of wigs. They carried tall, conical baskets on their backs. Richaud, carrying the wine jug, was talking at them and wagging a finger.

"Remember, when you've delivered the books to the private customer first, then the bookshops, come straight back. Stop in some working man's tavern for a joke like last time, and you will bitterly regret it."

The men with the baskets rolled their eyes at each other. "Filthy dyer's brat," the one who'd had the gloves muttered as they went out, just loud enough for Richaud to hear. Which made Charles wonder again why the two put up with Richaud's assumption of authority as much as they did.

Richaud kicked the door shut so hard that the flimsy walls shook. Then he sat down beside the hearth, poked savagely at the fire, and picked up the wine jug. No one spoke. Charles feigned sleep, trying to ignore his aching head and his hunger. Finally he fell asleep for real, and woke with his head aching less. Beside him, Wing was sitting up, tensely watching Richaud, who was staring drunkenly back at him. From the light, Charles thought it was late afternoon, and was surprised he'd slept so long. Richaud suddenly blundered to his feet and out the front door, and Charles saw from the outdoor light that the day was as far gone as he'd thought. He heard the sound of Richaud's water on the wall and voices passing on the road. Wing got out the start of a shout for help before Charles could shut him up.

"He's going to kill us!" Wing whispered. "He's drunk, and when he's drunk, he's terrible!"

"Hush!" Watching the door, Charles turned on his side and moved his wrists against the rope, trying again to feel if he'd been able to defeat Richaud's tying even a little.

Bewildered and near tears, Wing watched him. "What are you doing?"

Softly, Charles told him. "It could still work. Ah—I think—"

Wing wasn't listening. "He's been drinking all the time you were asleep." The Englishman's battered face was rigid with fear. "He got more wine from upstairs."

Richaud came in and slammed the door behind him. "I heard you yell, damn you!" He ran at Wing, and it was a mercy he was so drunk, because the kick he aimed at the Englishman shattered a half-broken chair into firewood. Richaud came at Wing again. Desperately working at the rope, Charles rolled away, got his back against the wall, and drew his feet under him. Richaud rained blows on Wing, but Wing managed to get a leg up and kicked his tormentor savagely in the belly.

Richaud bent double and staggered backward, retching and coughing.

Charles crouched and hurled himself bodily at Richaud. They went down, Charles's weight pinning Richaud to the floor.

"Get up," Charles yelled at Wing. "Get out of here, find help!"

"Don't bother," a voice said calmly.

The small round pressure against Charles's backbone made him go limp and absolutely still. Someone kicked him off Richaud, and Charles found himself looking up into the hard eyes of Alexandre Lunel.

Chapter 24

For once in his life, Charles had no words. Everything he thought he knew about Richaud and his conspiracy collapsed into confusion as he stared at Alexandre Lunel.

"Richaud's drunk again," Lunel said to someone else. "I can smell him from here. Take him outside and empty a bucket over him."

The other man dragged Richaud through the back door, and Lunel pointed at the straw with his pistol. "Get back there."

Charles rolled back onto the straw beside Wing. He stared in bewilderment at Lunel.

"You're part of this? Surely you don't take Richaud's ravings seriously."

"His ravings make him eminently usable."

"But *Le Cabinet*—a man like you must know that it's a libel, a forgery! Educated men have known that since it first appeared."

"Jesuits have *said* that since it appeared. As of course they would."

Charles fought hopelessness. Finding a way to escape from Richaud had seemed possible. Alexandre Lunel was another matter altogether. "I begin to understand," he said. "You're a

Gallican like your mother. Neither of you wanted your brother to be a Jesuit."

"Shut your filthy mouth about my brother!" Lunel raised a menacing hand but let it drop as the other man pushed a soaking wet Richaud back into the room.

Almost past surprise, Charles saw now that the other man was Victor Coriot, the lawyer who'd nearly ridden him down in the Coriot courtyard. And whose family, according to young Jacques, owned a ramshackle house on Talking Flea Street— this ramshackle house, no doubt. Richaud came toward the pile of straw, shivering and whimpering, and Charles braced himself for another attack, but Richaud stumbled past and up the stairs.

Victor Coriot laughed. "That gets rid of him for now, anyway. I could almost thank you for that, du Luc."

"Don't bother, Monsieur Coriot," Charles said grimly.

Lunel looked questioningly at them. "I thought I'd told you, Alexandre," Coriot said. "We met when Jacques was expelled from Louis le Grand. Du Luc brought him home. My young brother is shaping well for us," he added proudly.

"Shaping well for your Gallican conspiracy, I take you to mean," Charles said with ironic courtesy.

"Of course," Coriot made him a mock bow. "We're going to get the Jesuits out of France. And for good, this time. Henri the Fourth got you out years ago, after your student Jean Châtel learned at Louis le Grand to kill kings and tried to kill Henri. But then old Henri let you creep back. This time you won't. And France will finally be free to be French."

Charles dropped his irony. "Jean Châtel was an insane fanatic. And so is your dupe, poor Richaud."

"*Poor* Richaud?" Alexandre Lunel reached the straw in two

strides, anger radiating from him. "He's a Jesuit. No Jesuit deserves compassion."

Coriot shook his head at Lunel. "Softly, Alexandre. As for you, Maître du Luc, 'poor Richaud' has beaten you and probably starved you. Not to mention trying to kill you at your college. Why in God's name feel sorry for the creature? Unless you're just exhibiting your piety."

"Because he's twisted beyond helping himself," Charles said doggedly. "And you're using him, like using a simple-wit."

"Oh, he's very sane about Jesuits," Coriot laughed. "And he has no scruples, which you must admit is useful in desperate enterprises. But surely an ex-soldier knows that."

"How do you know I was a soldier?"

"My little brother Jacques told me. He says all the boys at the college admire you for it."

Lunel made a disgusted sound, and a face like someone about to be sick, and went to the hearth. He crouched down, put his pistol beside him on the floor, and started to rekindle the dead fire. Coriot watched him for a moment and then shrugged and went upstairs, swinging the empty wine jug by its handle. As Lunel got the fire going with flint and tinder, Coriot came back with the jug, now full by the careful way he carried it, and poured it into the small iron pot at the edge of the fire. Lunel pulled bread out of a bag and gave some to Coriot. Twilight was showing now around the shutters, and the fire filled the decrepit room with shadows. Charles and Wing tried not to watch the men eat and drink.

Wing sighed suddenly and murmured, "Is it Friday?"

Charles thought for a moment and nodded.

"I'm so hungry. But it's a fast day," the Englishman said. "Even if we were at Louis le Grand, we'd still be hungry."

"Not this hungry."

The men by the fire looked toward them, and Charles quickly closed his eyes. When nothing happened, he looked at Wing and mouthed, *Need to piss?*

"Nothing *to* piss."

"Pretend." Charles sat up. "Please, *messieurs*. We need to relieve ourselves." They would untie his hands for that and that gave some chance where now there was none.

"Do it in the straw," Lunel said indifferently.

"I'll take them. It stinks enough in here." Coriot got up and pulled Wing to his feet and kicked at Charles. "Get up."

Charles hauled himself to his feet. His hands were untied, and he made his way to the garden wall. It was nearly dark and—if Charles remembered right—there would be no moon. Trying to think how to use that to advantage, he looked desperately for a loose stone he could pry from the wall. Not that one small stone would do much against three men and a pistol, but it could add a little weight to the scholastics' side of the scales. If Coriot turned toward Wing, Charles might be able to throw a stone and bring him down silently. But all the stones small enough to throw or hide were solid, and if he bent over to search the ground, Coriot would see him.

Charles started to turn from the wall. Then something rustled on the other side of it and he looked up. A white, staring face glimmered in a gap in the stones and was gone. Charles strangled a cry, unsure if he'd seen a man or simply a phantom conjured from hunger and exhaustion.

Back on the straw, once more securely tied, a wave of despair washed over him. Wing curled up and took refuge in sleep, and Lunel and Coriot took their bag of food and their jug and went upstairs. Charles lay open-eyed, in case one of them came back. His exhausted mind was dark with confusion and fear. No one knew where he and Wing were. Even if the glimmering face at the garden wall had been someone from the nearby houses, the poverty-hardened neighbors wouldn't risk themselves against armed men for strangers. Charles's eyes wandered over the decrepit room, and he thought of the peasants hiding in the cottages out-side the Cassel wall. They had died in a place not unlike this. There would be some symmetry to his death, if he died here. More than that, he dared not claim, but the thought comforted him.

He listened for a moment to the low murmur of voices upstairs—mostly Lunel's voice, he realized. It was Lunel he was most afraid of. *Yes, afraid,* he told his oddly quiet inner voice, in case it was about to comment. *As afraid as I was of the soldiers who enjoyed killing at Cassel.* With the arrival of Lunel and Coriot, what had seemed a deluded plot spawned by Richaud's feelings of ill-use had become far more ominous. Charles knew that Coriot was dangerous enough, but Lunel was something else, something more. A Gallican dislike of Jesuits was common. But to the point of conspiracy and murder? And Lunel had hidden his feelings so well when Charles and La Reynie went to his house—to protect the conspiracy, Charles supposed, since La Reynie had already known that copies of *Le Cabinet* were surfacing.

Charles shifted miserably on the straw. It was dark now, no light around the shutters, only the small fire that made the shadows blacker. Feet clattered down the stairs, and Lunel and Coriot went to the fireplace.

"It's freezing up there," Coriot said, building up the fire and holding his hands to it.

Lunel pulled the only somewhat whole chair nearer the hearth, and Coriot sat down on the stool Richaud had put there. Charles gathered himself for one last effort to buy time. *Time for what?* his inner voice said dispiritedly. *I don't know,* Charles said. *For God to make up His mind, maybe.*

"You both must be very anxious to hang," he said to the men by the fire.

They ignored him.

"You probably won't hang for bringing *Le Cabinet jesuitique* into France and circulating it. But you will most definitely hang, if you kill Maître Wing and me."

Coriot drank from the jug and passed it to Lunel. "Oh, we're not going to kill you," he said airily. "Richaud's going to do that."

"If we're going to die, then you won't mind what you say to me. Are you still keeping your cache of *Le Cabinet* copies at Notre Dame des Champs? Men must be working in the well chamber by now. What are you doing about that?"

There was no answer. Charles decided that a wild lie couldn't hurt and might help. "I might as well tell you," he said, "this house is being watched. Lieutenant-Général La Reynie knows where I am."

"Liar," Coriot said, but he looked anxiously at Lunel.

"Don't be a little girl," Lunel said back to him. "If La Reynie knows where he is, why hasn't he come? He knows nothing."

Beside Charles, Wing stirred and opened his eyes. "Shhhh," Charles said softly, as another thought came to him. He raised his eyebrows at Wing, who stared back in confusion. Hoping Wing would follow his lead, Charles heaved a mock sigh. "That's always the way with plotters, Monsieur Lunel. You think no one else can plot. So much the worse for you." He broke off and gasped in terror, staring at the window with the shutter hanging on one hinge. "Oh, Blessed Virgin," Charles wailed, "it's back, God save us!"

Wing took his cue. He screamed, staring at the window. Coriot spun toward the window on his chair.

"What is it?! What did you see?" He stood up. "Did you see it?" he demanded of Lunel.

"No." Lunel drank from the wine jug. "Sit down."

But Coriot strode angrily to the pile of straw. "What do you mean, 'It's back'?"

"The demon," Charles quavered. "It was black and had a rope around its neck."

"What? No! Are you sure?" Coriot's eyes were huge.

"We're clerics, of course we're sure," Wing said impatiently.

Coriot glanced uncertainly at the window. "I think I did see it, out of the corner of my eye. But I thought it was white."

Wing rubbed his leg. "It couldn't have been white," he said pedantically. "And Maître du Luc is mistaken about the rope. But he's right about the color. The demons the devil sends to fetch murderers' souls are always much blacker than the usual ones. You must be very stupid not to know that." Wing gazed at Coriot with the disdain of a professor for a hopeless student.

Everyone jumped as slow heavy steps sounded on the stairway. Coriot backed slowly away, his face distorted with fear.

"Get back up there, Richaud; you're drunk, you've caused enough trouble," Lunel bellowed. "I've had enough of your insolence. Come down here and I'll shoot you for a useless lump of dung." He picked up his pistol and began ramming shot into the long, engraved barrel.

Richaud clumped unsteadily to the foot of the stairs. "What did *I* do? You're not worthy to hand me my shoe, but I've been humble. I've done everything for you: I've gotten the books into Louis le Grand, I've carried them here, I've supervised your young idiots, I've single-handedly taken these two hell-bound Jesuits, *I'm* the one who's been chosen—"

Hardly looking at Richaud, Lunel leveled the pistol and fired. In shot-deafened silence, the four men watched Richaud crumple to the floor and balance for a moment on his knees, as though he would pray. Then he fell onto his side, blood bubbling from his mouth, and was still. Moving only their eyes, Charles, Wing, and Coriot watched Lunel pull a cloth from his pocket and rub at the pistol.

"A cleric," Victor Coriot whispered. "You've shot a cleric. Oh, God, what—"

"What God? The one in whom you don't believe? Stop acting like a child and help me get him out of here. And you can thank me that there's one less Jesuit."

The two men dragged Richaud out the back door of the cottage. Charles felt Wing quivering on the edge of hysteria.

"Keep quiet," he hissed. "Pray. For Richaud's soul and for us. I'm going upstairs. And when you hear our captors coming back, if I'm not here, keep them out somehow."

The Englishman clasped his hands so tightly they were bloodless, rested his face on them, and began the prayers for the dead. Hoping Wing had taken in what he'd said, Charles braced his back hard against the wall and rose to his feet. He forced himself quickly up the stairs. There were two small rooms, one unused and stinking of mice. The other stank almost as much, but it had a straw pallet and blanket on the dusty floor. A large leather satchel lay empty by the pallet, a small, tapped wine barrel stood in a corner, and a stack of *Le Cabinet jesuitique* stood on the floor under the shuttered window. Wishing his hands were loose so he could pick up a book and hide it in his cassock, Charles did the next best thing and kicked a copy into the darkest corner where there was already a small pile of refuse. If he and Wing died, at least there would be evidence, a book here to be found. If, of course, anyone looked. He was barely back downstairs and on the straw before Lunel came in from the overgrown garden.

Wing cocked an eye at Lunel and started talking. Trying, Charles thought gratefully, to keep him from noticing Charles's breathlessness.

"Well, *monsieur*, did you see more demons out there? Go and look again, then. The devil usually sends at least a dozen to take killers to hell. You don't really deserve a chance to save your soul, but I suppose I'm honor bound to tell you that if you change your mind about killing us, the demons will go away."

Lunel, wiping his hands on the cloth from his pocket, paid no attention. Wing ran out of words as Coriot came back, sweating and white with fear.

"Alexandre," Coriot said, "are you mad? We can't just leave him hidden out there. He'll be found; we have to bury him."

"Then bury him."

Coriot stood openmouthed for a moment and then went back outside. Lunel went back to the fire. Charles began to murmur his own prayers for Richaud, and Wing joined him.

"Shut up!"

They flinched and opened their eyes to see Lunel standing over them. He struck them both across the face and backhanded them for good measure. "Why are you praying for Richaud? Especially you, du Luc. Didn't he tell you that you owe your knife wound to him?" Lunel went to his chair and sat, staring into the fireplace.

Charles lay still. Wing groaned and was sick into the straw. The back door opened and Coriot burst in.

"Come and help me, damn you! There's no shovel."

"Get one," Lunel said, without looking at him. "We have three graves to dig."

Shaking his head and close to tears, Coriot went out by the front door.

Lunel, haloed by the firelight, turned his pistol this way and that, making the light flicker redly along the silvery barrel. Charles watched him, aching all over and half wishing the man would just shoot them and finish this.

"Why do you hate Jesuits so much?" he said.

A visible tremor went through Lunel's body. "Because I'm a good, free-thinking Gallican noble of the Robe. Why else?"

"Few Gallicans hate Jesuits to the point of torturing and killing them." Charles felt Wing move convulsively beside him and leaned gently on him to keep him quiet.

Lunel turned his head and looked at Charles. Even in the tricky firelight, his eyes looked dead. "Torture? You don't know the meaning of the word." The even, flat hopelessness of his words were like a miasma of death spreading on the air.

Charles waited. "You've been tortured?" he said carefully.

The dead eyes stared through him. "Oh, yes." Lunel lifted the pistol and laid it alongside his cheek as though to comfort himself.

Charles swallowed. "When?"

"Do you want to gloat over me, Jesuit?" Lunel made to rise, but his body sagged and he sank back onto the chair. He raised the pistol and pointed it at Charles. "I was tortured by day and I dreamed it all over again at night. I turned into a puling little wraith. But everyone thought I was only more sickly than before." His arm dropped and the pistol hung from his hand as he picked up the jug and drank, turning it nearly upside down to drain it. Then he slammed it down onto the hearth, and pottery shards sprayed around the fire.

Charles tried to get enough spit in his mouth to speak again. *Shut up, keep quiet, are you mad? Leave him alone, do you want to die here and now?* Charles felt almost sorry for his terrified inner voice. *No, I don't want to die,* he told it. *But at the very least, if he's talking, he's not shooting. And if he talks long enough,* Charles thought, *something may change, something . . .*

He said, "I think you're telling me that a Jesuit tortured you."

Lunel spat on the floor. "The good Père Grandier. My tutor. Oh, yes, my tutor, he was certainly that." His raucous laughter bent him double so that his face rested on his knees.

"What did Père Grandier do?"

Lunel stared furiously at Charles. "Don't mock me. You *know* what he did! You do the same, they all do, that's why I had to save Paul! He wouldn't listen, he didn't believe me. Oh, God, he wouldn't listen. He was so young, so beautiful, and he didn't believe me." Lunel struggled for breath, as though he'd been running.

Charles felt sick. "And what happened?"

Lunel wrapped his arms around himself. "Grandier was big. Like his name. Bigger than you. Too big to fight. I was small, not very well, not strong."

"What did he do to you?" Charles asked again. He was sure he knew, but if the man would say it, he might be somehow eased and less dangerous.

"He used me. He used me like a girl." Lunel turned his head from side to side like a tormented beast. "And when I was big enough, I killed him."

"*Killed* him?" That Charles had not expected. "But—you were a child. How could you hide his body? Or was he found? Did your parents know?"

As Lunel straightened and looked at Charles, a log broke in the fire, and new flames leaped behind him. Seeing the man outlined in the halo of flame removed Charles's last doubt. But his certainty brought no triumph, only a leaden sadness.

"I was fifteen," Lunel said, "big enough to hide him. No

one knew. No one *will* know, because I'm going to kill you, too. I have to."

"Alexandre." Charles held his gaze. "Tell me what happened to Paul."

Something like a sob escaped the man and he looked away. "Tell me."

Lunel looked defiantly at him. "Why not, then? You'll be telling no one. Paul wouldn't listen. Don't you see? I had no choice! I made him think I'd left Paris, that I wasn't going to stand in his way any longer. But I went after him and I caught him before he got to that cursed Novice House. I brought him here. I thought if I talked enough, if I told him everything, he'd understand. I showed him *Le Cabinet*, I read it to him, I told him he could help us. But nothing made any difference. Then he got free somehow. He'd guessed where we stored the books, because he knew they weren't here in the cottage. I thought he'd go there and that's where I found him, in the well chamber in Notre Dame's crypt."

"What made him think the books were there?"

Lunel laughed harshly. "Because I myself had taken him there. Oh, God knows I didn't want to, but my father made me. He knew that my strangely vanished tutor had taken me there often, to see the old paintings still visible on the wall. That was the reason Grandier gave my father, but he really took me there to use me—a deep, deserted chamber, thick walls, thick door." Lunel shuddered. "So my father made me take Paul there to see the paintings. Paul liked them, but he was fascinated by the old well." Lunel put the pistol in his lap and covered his face with his hands. "We agreed it was a good place to hide things," he said through his fingers. "Paul said that if he ever had a treasure to hide he'd take out the rubble and put his secret treasure in the well and no one would ever find it." Lunel laughed hysterically. "But there was already a secret there!"

"You put your tutor's body in the well."

"It was the only place. I told you, he was big. I was fifteen, but I couldn't carry him up the stairs."

"And Paul?"

"I only wanted to save him." Lunel spoke so softly that Charles could hardly hear him. "He was too angry about the books to listen. I—I shook him." Lunel looked beseechingly at Charles, as though trying to make sense of his own words. "I shook him and his neck snapped—I heard it and let go and he fell back against the wall. I didn't mean to kill him."

Charles was racked with pity and horror. But he made himself go on. "And then you went to get a shovel. Something to help you clear rubble from the well and hide Paul's body there."

Lunel jumped to his feet. "No, not in the well, there are other places in the crypt!" He began to shake. "You think I would put Paul with that evil Jesuit? Curse you, I'll kill you for saying that!" He grabbed his pistol and lunged unsteadily at Charles. Wing screamed and rolled to the wall. Charles drew both knees to his chest and kicked Lunel in the groin. Lunel howled and bent double. With his last strength, Charles got to his knees between Lunel and Wing.

Lunel, still clutching himself, leveled his pistol at Charles. Both cottage doors thundered against the walls and the apparition from the garden wall flew at Lunel, wailing like something out of hell, a swarm of creatures shouting and crowding behind her. She raised both arms and a swarm of black things flew through the firelit air. Lunel went down, but his pistol was still trained on Charles and a shot cracked and roared. Charles toppled gently into the straw, wondering why there was no pain. *Follow the dead, find your death,* he heard or thought he heard. His last thought was that his death was easier than he'd expected.

Chapter 25

The face hovering over him when he next opened his eyes was not God's, or at least not any face of God his imagination had ever conjured. This face was scowling and yelling orders, and its plumed hat was awry.

"Bring more light, damn you! Now!"

A lantern swam into view and Charles squeezed his eyes shut against its glare. God gave orders. But He was unlikely to need a lantern. Or a hat, for that matter. *Ergo*, this loud, angry man could not be God. Given that every part of his body hurt, this seemed to Charles an admirable feat of logic.

An ungentle hand brushed his hair back from his face. "Look at this," a different voice said with quiet menace. "May Lunel's soul feed all the devils of hell."

"Lunel—" Charles couldn't follow a thought very far, but far enough to find a welter of feelings about Alexandre Lunel. "He told me—"

A cold wet cloth sponged his face and cut off his words. A cup of water was held to his lips. Charles opened his eyes. His cousin Charles-François de Vintimille du Luc was down on one knee in front of him, holding the cup like a one-armed worried mother. Lieutenant-Général La Reynie was peering anxiously over his shoulder at Charles.

"How do you feel?" Charles-François said gruffly.

"Alive." Charles's head cleared enough for him to realize how astonished he was. "Charlot? What are you—how in God's name did you know I was here?"

Behind Charles-François, someone else leaned down into the lantern light. "He didn't. But I did." The goatwoman peered at Charles from her web of wrinkles.

Charles blinked at her in confusion. "I thought I'd found my death. Like you said."

She picked up his hand, turned it over and gazed at the palm. Without comment, she put it down again. "Well, it's me you can thank for feeling alive. I was looking for one of my goats. I saw the two of you pissing on the wall out there, and the man keeping watch. So I went to find the girl, and then we found His Highness here." She jerked her head at La Reynie. "That's why the other one's dead, not you."

"The other one?" Charles's head swam as new horror gripped him. "Maître Wing?"

"No, no, I'm here."

Charles twisted, grunting at the pain, and saw Rose Ebrard sponging Wing's battered face. Wing was gazing at her as though the battering had been worth it.

Charles decided that he was dreaming all of this.

"All's well," the girl said, smiling at Charles. "Much better than you know."

Thinking that if this wasn't a dream, it must be fever, Charles sank back onto the straw. "Is the gunshot wound very bad?" he asked his cousin faintly.

"Bad enough," Charles-François said. "He's dead."

"What? Who's dead?"

"The man who was about to shoot you."

"Alexandre didn't shoot me?"

"He didn't." Lieutenant-Général La Reynie knelt beside Charles-François. "Your cousin here shot him first. And now we have to get you and Maître Wing home."

Charles ignored him, staring at Charles-François, who looked everywhere but at Charles.

"Charlot? You saved my life?" Charles thought he was going to cry, but then he started to laugh. "I would have thought you'd offer the man your pistol if he missed me the first time."

His cousin grunted and shrugged and said something indistinctly.

"Thank you," Charles said gravely.

With the air of a man swallowing gall, Charles-François looked him suddenly in the eye. "You were trying to save *me* from something at Cassel. I never admitted it, but I knew it. So we're even now."

La Reynie started to slip an arm under Charles's shoulders to pick him up.

"No, wait," Charles said. "Richaud's here, he's dead. His body's in the garden. And the books—"

"Richaud? Well," La Reynie said in surprise. "I kicked in the back door, but I didn't see a body out there. We'll look. I've seen the books upstairs, though."

"And Alexandre Lunel killed his brother, Paul."

"Ah." La Reynie withdrew his arm and sat back on his heels. "That I didn't know, either."

"And there's another body. At Notre Dame des Champs, in the old well. Alexandre killed him, too."

"You seem to know everything. The abbess's workmen took what's left of a body out of the well this morning. It's nothing but bones now. Bones wearing a Jesuit cassock." La Reynie was quiet for a moment. "Are you sure Alexandre Lunel killed the man? He would have to have done murder very young."

"He said he was fifteen. The man was his tutor. His name was Grandier."

Charles was suddenly too exhausted to explain further, but La Reynie was no longer listening. He was looking toward what was left of the open front door. Loud male voices were approaching, but it was a boy carrying a wriggling white goat kid who came into the room.

"I have her, Hyacinthe!" He put the little goat down beside the goatwoman. "Well done, Michel," La Reynie said to the boy. "Come outside now and help me by keeping a watch on the carriage." He got up and piloted Michel outside, and Charles-François went with them.

Charles stared after them. "That was Michel Poulard, from the Novice House. What's *he* doing here? I don't understand—"

"Let it be," the goatwoman said soothingly, as the baby goat butted against her skirt. She gathered it into her arms and cuddled it, looking down at him. "I told you, I saw you and went to find the girl." She nodded at Rose, who was still sitting with Wing. "She saw me earlier and said she was looking for you."

"You said you'd come to The Dog, *maître*," Rose put in. "When you didn't, I was worried. So I walked up the rue Saint Jacques, hoping I'd meet you, and saw Hyacinthe."

The goatwoman nodded. "That's right. So when I saw you here later, I went to the bookshop and told her and the rest of them where you were. Then we saw His Highness here"—she grinned at La Reynie—"getting into his carriage down at the college. And the girl ran down the street screeching at him like a scalded cat. And so we all came to get you. In the carriage." Hyacinth pursed her lips thoughtfully. "First time I'd been in one. I liked it." She gently pulled a straggling lock of her hair out of the tiny goat's mouth. "When I saw you pissing, I was looking for this little one," she said to Charles.

Charles struggled for words. "Then—maybe it's the little goat I have to thank for being alive."

A surprised smile spread across Hyacinthe's face. "Well. So you do see how things touch each other. I wondered." She nodded as though he'd passed a test and leaned close to him. "So I'll tell you something else." She looked into his eyes for a long moment. "That's why you can never find the beginning of a thing and close it in your hand. Or the end. Never. All's moving, always moving, like water, like air."

With that, she withdrew to the side wall. She put her empty canvas bag down on the floor and settled beside it, as contented and self-contained as one of her goats. Wondering vaguely what she was waiting for, Charles put her words away to think about when he was better able to think. All he could think of now was how much he wanted someone to take him and Wing home. But not yet, he sighed to himself, as the loud voices he'd heard before came closer, and he recognized his cousin's military bellow.

"Hold your tongue, you cur! If you haven't something to hide, why run from us?"

Charles-François and a man in a floppy brown hat dragged Victor Coriot into the cottage, holding him between them as he struggled and begged. La Reynie came behind them with a shovel in his hand.

"I didn't kill him," Coriot howled, as his captors shoved him across the room toward the door to the garden. "I didn't kill anyone, I've done nothing!"

"Then why were you creeping toward this house in the dark with a shovel?" Charles-François growled.

"Would this have something to do with the body outside?" La Reynie asked Charles, holding up the shovel.

"No doubt. Lunel ordered Coriot to bury Richaud. Coriot

went for a shovel. But he's telling the truth; he didn't kill Richaud, Lunel did."

"Burying the murderer's handiwork is a good road to the gallows," La Reynie said grimly. On his way to the back door, he swore and kicked something aside. "Will someone pick these up? Every copy has to go with us as proof."

"I will." Rose Ebrard got up from the straw. Charles closed his eyes and a short, blessed quiet fell. Then Mlle Ebrard was stooping over him. "When La Reynie comes back in, I'll ask him to let us take you home," she said softly.

Charles opened his eyes. "Pick what up? What did he mean?"

"Books." She nodded down at the stack she'd gathered. "Those books you've been so worried about."

La Reynie, who had returned alone while Wing was speaking, stopped beside the goatwoman.

"Hyacinthe," La Reynie said, "can you read?"

"What use would I have for that, *mon lieutenant-général?*"

"The books Mademoiselle Ebrard is holding came out of your bag."

"But yes, surely they did."

"Why?"

"Has all this coil addled your wits? The books came *out* of my bag because they were *in* my bag. They fell out when I hit the man with it."

"Don't trifle with me, *ma bonne femme. Why* were they in your bag?"

"Because I must live, like everyone else. I get good money for carrying books to those that want them."

"Who paid you this good money?"

"Him." She jerked her head toward Alexandre Lunel's body, lying now by the front door and covered, Charles thought, with the blanket from the bed upstairs. "Sometimes the one you just dragged past paid me, but mostly him." She sucked her teeth. "They won't pay me now."

"You got your books here?"

"Not here. At the big Lunel house. I sold them milk and came away with books." She smiled at Charles. "You saw me. Your wits aren't working, either, but you have some excuse."

"I did see her," Charles said, looking up at La Reynie. "The day we talked to Lunel. While I was downstairs, she came to the back courtyard with the goats. I told you that a young man who didn't seem to be a servant let her in."

"You did?" La Reynie frowned at him and shrugged, rubbing his tired face.

"Monsieur La Reynie," Rose Ebrard said firmly, "do you think Maître Wing and Maître du Luc could go home now?"

"What?" he said distractedly. "Yes, of course they can go home. I will go with them and then come back. Monsieur de Vintimille du Luc is staying here till my men arrive to take charge of Coriot."

The goatwoman picked up her goat and her bag and looked questioningly at him.

"You can go, too," he told her. "I know where to find you."

"Do you, Your Highness?" She laughed and shuffled out of the cottage.

La Reynie called Michel Poulard and his coachman in, and the two of them helped Wing to his feet. La Reynie and Rose supported Charles, and they made their way slowly outside. When Charles and Wing were settled in the carriage, La Reynie went back to the cottage and the coachman climbed onto the driving box. Then La Reynie and the man in the floppy hat returned and La Reynie got into the carriage. Michel shut the carriage door and climbed onto the narrow perch at the rear.

The other man handed the stack of books to Rose Ebrard, who put them with more books on the carriage floor.

La Reynie leaned toward the window. "You and Monsieur de Vintimille du Luc will stay with the prisoner and the bodies until my men arrive?"

"We will." The man in the brown hat looked at Mademoiselle Ebrard. "And then I'll be back."

The voice brought Charles bolt upright in spite of his weakness and bruises. *"Amaury?!"*

"Yes, it's me," Amaury de Corbet said back, laughing. "No, no more questions now. Rose will tell you."

But Charles was beyond asking anything more. It seemed only a moment later that someone touched him gently on the arm. Beside him, Wing was stirring and making complaining noises as he moved. The carriage had stopped, and in the glow of a street lantern Charles saw Frère Martin and Père Le Picart at Louis le Grand's open postern door. La Reynie got out and went to them.

"These two will mend," Charles heard him say. "But I grieve to tell you that Richaud is dead."

Then Wing and Charles were helped from the carriage and set on their feet. Rose helped Charles to the postern.

"Yes, Amaury has left," she said softly, in answer to Charles's half-framed question. "He'll come and see you." Her eyes were shining in the lantern light. "Thank the Blessed Virgin that you and Maître Wing are safe. And that Amaury is safe." Reaching up, she gently touched his bruised cheek. "Thank you." She walked briskly toward the bookshop.

In the street passage, Frère Martin exclaimed over the scholastics' battered faces and sent a younger lay brother running ahead to warn Frère Brunet. Then he picked up a lantern and led them to the infirmary, the rector helping Wing and La

Reynie keeping a tight hold on Charles. Brunet met them at the door. He put the scholastics to bed, bathed and salved their cuts and bruises, and fed them watered wine and hot broth. Through it all, La Reynie and Le Picart got in his way, made urgent suggestions, and exasperated him with questions until he shooed them out. Then he extinguished the candles, leaving only the infirmary altar lamp and the sconce candle beside his own room alight, and went to his bed.

Wrapped in peace, Charles sank gratefully into sleep to the rough music of Wing's contented snoring.

Chapter 26

Maître Henry Wing was sleeping. Frère Brunet had given him something to ease the pain of his bruised face, and he was once again snoring peacefully. Charles was sitting up against pillows, watching his cousin Charles-François stride martially toward the infirmary door. Charles-François looked back, lifted his arm in a half salute, and was gone. Charles closed his eyes. Of all the astonishments of the last few days, his reconciliation with Charles-François came close to astonishing him the most. He had never expected the two of them to come to any mutual acknowledgment of what had happened at Cassel. Had never expected his cousin to stop blaming him for the loss of his arm. Charles lay savoring the lightness of having that accusation lifted from him. And, of course, Charles-François was no longer angry about Amaury de Corbet. That story Charles had not yet heard in full, but he thought he was about to, because Frère Brunet had told him that another visitor was expected.

He drifted back to sleep and was half in a dream, laughing as he watched his cousin Pernelle playing with her little girl Lucy, when he realized that someone was standing by his bed.

"Charles? How are you?"

"Better, Amaury," Charles said, opening his eyes. "I hoped you would come. Sit down."

Amaury de Corbet pulled a stool close to Charles's bed and sat. "You were right," he said.

"Was I?"

"You know you were. And I think this is the first time I've ever been truly glad to be proven wrong." He grinned ruefully at Charles. "As the Novice House rector would tell you, humility seems to be a virtue whose acquaintance I have yet to make."

Charles started to laugh, but it hurt too much. "Well, don't expect me to instruct you. My rector might say much the same thing about me." Charles studied the man beside him. Amaury was carrying the same floppy brown hat he'd worn the evening before, and his brown coat and breeches were shabby and ill-fitting.

"Not a sartorial success, am I?" Amaury said. "The clothes belonged to Monsieur Cheyne, Rose's aunt's dead husband. As you see, he was fatter than I."

"You left the Novice House in nothing but your shirt?"

"I left in my cassock."

"What made you leave so suddenly?"

Amaury's face reddened. "The rector called me into his office again," he said, not looking at Charles. "The martyred Saint Laurence was not more thoroughly grilled over his fire than I was with questions about that cursed book. And he'd asked me all of them before! No matter what I said or swore or explained, Père Guymond kept at me, refused to believe me, refused to take my word of honor that I knew nothing about it." He shook his head helplessly. "It went on and on, and finally, I knew that if I didn't leave, I was going to hit him. So I left."

"Just walked out?"

"I went to The Dog and told Rose I'd been an idiot and asked her if she'd still marry me." He grinned suddenly and looked at Charles. "She said she couldn't accept a proposal from a man in a cassock. She fetched her aunt, and the old dragon rooted through a chest and found me some clothes. Then I asked Rose again, and she said yes. And I sent my cassock back to the Novice House. By little Michel Poulard. He'd followed me to The Dog, trying to get up his courage to tell me that he'd put the book in my mattress."

"Michel put it there?" Charles gaped at Amaury.

"Yes. That goatwoman supplies goat's milk to the Novice House infirmary. Michel said she was in the kitchen courtyard when he was refilling mattresses with new straw. A book fell out of her bag, and he picked it up. It seems he loves books and, well, he stole it without even looking at it. He had to hide it quickly, so he pushed it into the mattress cover, as far down into the new straw as he could. But then he was told to go and work in the garden and had no chance to take the book out before the mattress cover was sewn shut again. Michel heard the rector accusing me—Père Guymond's accusations and my denials got louder and louder—and he saw me leave. He was very upset that I'd been accused of his crime. But even more upset, I think, about losing a book he never even got to read. So he was there at The Dog when the goatwoman arrived, and he came with us to rescue you."

"And my cousin—I couldn't believe it when I opened my eyes in that cottage and saw him looking so worried about me."

"Yes," Amaury said, laughing, "he arrived at The Dog when I was down on my knees before Rose. It was one of the few times I've ever seen him speechless. He'd come to tell Rose he could do nothing more and was going back to his ship." Amaury's expression sobered. "I was glad to have a chance to make things up with him."

Charles nodded. "When you all burst into that cottage, it was like the armies of heaven descending on evildoers."

"A rather ragtag army of heaven."

Charles grew grave. "That's twice you've saved my life, Amaury. How am I ever going to repay you?"

"Ever since you tried to do what I failed to do at Cassel—bring my men back under control and save those wretched peasants—I've been in your debt past ever getting out." Amaury swallowed hard and looked down at his clasped hands. "You seem somehow to be able to live with what happened that day. But I still don't know what I'm going to do with my guilt about it."

A stillness gripped Charles. *Tell him*, the Silence said.

"What is it, Charles?" Amaury said anxiously. "Are you in pain?"

Charles shook his head slowly. "No. No, it's—" He pulled himself farther up on his pillows. He opened his mouth to do as he'd been told and then shut it. Waiting, just in case. *In case of what?* his blunt inner voice said. *In case the Silence changes its mind.* His inner voice laughed so loud, Charles thought that Amaury must be able to hear it. *Liar*, it said. *You're afraid Amaury won't believe you. You're afraid he'll think you're crazy.*

"Shut up!" Charles said out loud.

Amaury looked at him in bewilderment. "I didn't say anything."

"No, sorry, I know you didn't." Charles sighed. Amaury was going to think he was crazy. But Charles knew he had no choice. "Listen," he said. "I'm going to tell you something I've only told one other person. You asked me how I manage my guilt about Cassel. It's haunted me, as it does you. I've tried to bury it. And to bury my certainty that I was a coward that day and am maybe a coward at heart. Then Charles-François came. He accused me of all of that, and of bearing the blame for your entry into the Novice House." Amaury opened his mouth to protest. "No, please, just listen." Charles looked away and fixed his eyes on the crucifix across from his bed. "Sometimes, not often, something I call the Silence speaks to me."

"Do you mean God?"

Charles held the question off with a raised hand. He'd never wanted to answer that question, lest he seem to claim too much. "A few days ago, in the street, I had one of those strange waking dreams of being back on the Cassel battlefield. And in the midst of it, this Silence said, 'Charles. Nothing is wasted. Not even death.' Not even death, Amaury. Not even the terrible deaths of those peasants we failed to save. Or the death of the soldier they killed. God wastes nothing."

Amaury was holding his breath, and his deep-set dark eyes seemed to burn as he stared at Charles. He reached out and gripped Charles's hand so hard that Charles nearly cried out. "Do you swear that what you tell me is true? It happened? You heard those words?"

"It's true. And I told you because just now the Silence said, 'Tell him.'"

Amaury bowed his head onto their linked hands. He made no sound, but Charles felt his tears like a tiny river running through his fingers. A deep and silent peace wrapped both of them.

That evening, long after Amaury had gone, Wing woke up, seeming much restored, though his bruised face was painful to look at. Brunet brought their supper of boiled beef and bread, and as they ate, sitting up in their beds, they talked. "There's something I haven't told you," Wing said, looking across at Charles. "About what happened in the cottage, at the end."

Charles, who had a mouth full of bread, raised his eyebrows. He wondered if it was something about the medicine Brunet had given him that made the Englishman look so bright-eyed.

"Remember that you thought you'd been shot? When you came to yourself after everyone had come into the cottage?"

Charles nodded.

"That was because, just when Alexandre Lunel was about to shoot you"—Wing tried to suppress a grin and failed—"you fainted."

Charles's mouth opened, and he dropped his spoon into his soup. "I did not! I've never fainted in my life!"

"You have now. It made me feel better about fainting in the chapel." Wing smiled sweetly.

Charles scowled at the wall. Then his indignation crumbled and he fell back on his pillows in a fit of helpless laughter and spilled his soup. When he could speak, he said, "So you and I are even. And I'll tell you something, as well. When I was first in the army, an older man said to me, 'Only stupid men are never afraid.'"

"Neither of us is stupid," Wing said seriously, and came to help him mop up the soup.

Two days later, on Tuesday, the feast of the soldier St. Martin of Tours, they were released from the infirmary, their faces still garishly colored by healing bruises. Late that afternoon, they went to the college's *grand salon*, where Père Le Picart had summoned a council. They stood quietly aside on the faded rug, watching the last comer, Père Paradis, assistant Provincial of the Paris Jesuit province, settle himself in the circle that already included the Novice House rector Père Guymond, Père

Pinette the Professed House rector, and Lieutenant-Général La Reynie. Père Montville was busily making sure that the offices around the *grand salon* were empty, and that the doors leading out of the *salon* were shut and guarded by proctors. Then he nodded to the rector of Louis le Grand, who took his own seat and gestured Charles and Wing forward.

Le Picart's sea-gray eyes went slowly around the circle. "I have summoned you," he said, speaking in French for La Reynie's sake, "with the approval of our Paris Provincial, whose assistant represents him today." He nodded politely to Paradis. "The recent deaths of Paul Lunel, intended Jesuit novice, and Louis Richaud, former Jesuit scholastic, concern all of us. As does the coming to light of a Gallican conspiracy against us, and the appearance in Paris of that troublesome forgery, the so-called Jesuit Secret Instructions—this time as *Le Cabinet jesuitique*. The more we understand about how these unhappy events are related, the more vigilant we can be in the future. To better protect our men, and to prevent the so-called Secret Instructions from circulating.

"I have said that this matters to us. But it matters also to those who come after us." Le Picart's face was as somber as the November afternoon's gray light. "Lies may be silenced. But lies once heard—or read—are always repeated. As they are repeated, more people believe them and they grow louder. We know, of course, that our enemies are always ready to believe lies. But the simply credulous and ignorant are easily convinced. For the sake of the Society of Jesus and for the sake of truth, the Secret Instructions' lies must be stopped from spreading."

He looked at La Reynie and then at Charles and Wing. "These two scholastics nearly lost their lives in this affair. You see from their faces how ill-used they were in their captivity.

Thanks to their courage, and to Lieutenant-Général La Reynie and several others, they are alive and can tell us much we would not otherwise know. They will speak and Monsieur La Reynie will also speak. Then these three will withdraw and leave us to consider as Jesuit heads of houses what should be done to lessen the risk of the so-called Secret Instructions appearing again in Paris. Maître du Luc, you may begin."

Charles bowed, marshaling his thoughts. He and Wing had been strictly charged to be brief.

"As you know," he said, "three weeks ago the late Père Dainville and I found the body of the intended Jesuit novice Paul Lunel in the crypt at Notre Dame des Champs. He disappeared on the day he should have entered our Novice House. When we found him, he was newly dead but had been three weeks missing. Soon after that, I was attacked here in the college chapel. By Maître Louis Richaud, I learned later, who was himself later killed by one of his fellow Gallican conspirators. Then, when I was somewhat recovered from my wound and allowed to go out again, I happened to pick up the torn piece of a book cover from a bookshop floor." Charles smiled at the Jesuits in the circle. "I picked it up only because Jesuits pick up trash when they see it. I meant to throw it away, but when I returned to the college, I was summoned to speak with Père Paradis, who had come because of the murder of Paul Lunel. As we talked, I happened to drop the scrap of leather. Père Paradis recognized it as being from the cover of *Le Cabinet jesuitique*. We assumed it was being sold at The Saint's Dog, the bookshop where I'd found it.

"Soon after I was attacked, Maître Richaud disappeared from here. We thought that he, too, had been murdered. And then Maître Wing disappeared." Charles looked at Wing, who took up the narrative.

With a new dignity, the Englishman told them about seeing

Richaud, following him, and being kept prisoner in the Talking Flea Street house.

"Poor Maître Richaud seemed to have lost his wits," Wing said, speaking French slowly and carefully. "He told me he wanted to leave the Society of Jesus, but that if he left openly, we Jesuits would kill him. He said he ran away and left his bloodied cassock to be found so we'd think him dead already. He said this conspiracy about the book was his, but it was clear the others were using him. Then Monsieur Alexandre Lunel, the real ringleader, killed him."

Le Picart looked questioningly at Paradis, who nodded slightly.

"I will tell you," Le Picart said to the circle, "that the unfortunate Richaud was indeed unsettled in his mind. To my shame, I failed to see how deeply unsettled. He had grown very angry at the Society of Jesus and very suspicious of everyone. I knew that he was thinking of leaving and, frankly, I thought it might be for the best. I did not know that he already had *Le Cabinet* in his possession.

"Until Richaud began his theology studies last month, he was a *cubiculaire* responsible for provisioning boarding students' chambers. Another scholastic, in his second year as a *cubiculaire*, has recently come to me and said that at the end of the summer term, Richaud found a copy of *Le Cabinet* in the chamber of a boarding student. That student finished his education and left us in August, and so is no longer under our jurisdiction. Richaud confiscated the book, supposedly to turn in to me. But it's safe to assume now that he kept it and read it. *Le Cabinet*'s lies about how we treat Jesuits who leave the Society inflamed his disordered feelings beyond sanity. Through two of our day students, Jacques Coriot and Louis Poquelin—both now dismissed—Richaud joined Victor Coriot's Gallican conspiracy, a conspiracy of extreme virulence. I think that Richaud fled the college when he did because he feared being discovered as Maître du Luc's attacker." Le Picart sighed and looked at Wing and Charles. "Have you more to say?"

They told what they'd seen and learned in the cottage, and Charles wound up the tale.

"Alexandre Lunel was uncompromisingly Gallican. He was fiercely against the pope's interference in France and the French church and fiercely anti-Jesuit. But he had other reasons for hating Jesuits. Tragic reasons." Charles sighed and shut his eyes for a moment, wishing he didn't have to tell the next part of the story.

"Alexandre was sickly as a boy. His father, who was not at all anti-Jesuit, hired a Jesuit tutor for him, Père Grandier. For years, this tutor would take Alexandre to the well chamber in Notre Dame des Champs, where he repeatedly sodomized him. Finally, when Alexandre was fifteen, he killed Grandier and hid the body under the rubble in the old well there. He was horrified when his younger brother, Paul, wanted to join the Society of Jesus. Alexandre was convinced that in a Jesuit house, Paul would suffer the same fate. So Alexandre kidnapped him and kept him prisoner in the cottage while he tried to dissuade him. He even read *Le Cabinet* to him. But Paul refused to be convinced. He also saw the comings and goings of the conspiracy, and thought he knew where the copies of *Le Cabinet* were being kept. He managed to escape and went to see if he was right. Alexandre found him there, in Notre Dame des Champs's well chamber." Charles sighed and shook his head. "They argued and Alexandre was beside himself with rage. He shook Paul so hard he broke the boy's neck. He said he didn't mean to kill him, and I think that was the truth."

An appalled silence fell. The noise of shouts and carriage wheels and trotting horses from beyond the antechamber's great double doors seemed to come from another world. To Charles's surprise, the famously cold Père Pinette dropped his face into his hands.

When Pinette finally looked up, his rigid control was gone, leaving his face pinched and drained of color. "I remember Étienne Grandier. He disappeared in 1672 and we never knew what happened to him. We finally assumed that he was dead." His voice was barely audible. "I was not the Professed House rector then, but I knew him. And I wondered about him." He looked pleadingly around the circle. "I thought he shouldn't be a tutor. But I said nothing. God forgive me."

"Many Jesuits here at Louis le Grand knew Étienne Grandier," Le Picart said heavily. "What most of you do not yet know is that he was our Père Dainville's nephew. He disappeared and was never found."

Charles stared unseeingly at the floor, remembering Dainville's story of his nephew. He was glad Dainville didn't have to know why Grandier had disappeared. Then he found himself thinking that now, Dainville did know.

"I think the rest of this is mine to tell," La Reynie said. "The workmen cleaning out the old well in Notre Dame des Champs's well chamber found a huddle of bones in a Jesuit cassock. So Alexandre Lunel's story is confirmed. And copies of *Le Cabinet* that the conspirators had not been able to remove were found in the well chamber, tucked into a long wall niche that had been blocked with a loose but very heavy stone. Victor Coriot is imprisoned in the Châtelet and has given us names of other conspirators. We don't have all of them yet, but some of those we have will hang along with Victor Coriot." La

Reynie looked at Le Picart. "Coriot's brother, Jacques, and young Poquelin, the other student you dismissed, I've left to their mothers. Who, I think, will keep them on very short leashes."

"What about Hyacinthe, Lieutenant-Général?" Charles said.

"Oh, yes, Hyacinthe." La Reynie snorted with laughter, and the others in the circle looked askance at him. "Hyacinthe, the goatwoman, was one of the conspiracy's book couriers. And a clever choice, because a more unlikely courier would be hard to imagine. She did it purely for money. She can't read, she wouldn't know what *Gallican* means, and she doesn't hate Jesuits. Indeed, our two scholastics here owe her their lives." He looked at Père Guymond. "She had copies of *Le Cabinet* in her bag when she went to the Novice House with her goats. She wasn't told to leave any there, but one copy fell out of the bag and a young servant who's just learned to read picked it up. He only wanted a book to read. But he was afraid it would be taken from him, so he hid it in the new straw of a mattress he was stuffing." La Reynie grinned. "I'm not going to arrest either him or Hyacinthe."

Wing spoke up. "I've been thinking about her. And what a nice classical touch it was—like Fate in a tragedy, you know—that she knocked Alexandre Lunel to the ground with a bag full of *Le Cabinet jesuitique!*"

Le Picart and the other Jesuits frowned at the frivolous interruption and Charles gave Wing a warning nudge.

"What?" the Englishman said earnestly. "It *was* just like Fate!"

Charles gave up and bit his lip, and Le Picart and Paradis indulged in a fit of coughing.

The Novice House rector was trying to make himself heard. "The *boy* put it there? Oh, no. Oh, dear Blessed Virgin. And I hounded that poor young man out of the Novice House. I must see him, I must get him back—"

"No," Charles said bluntly. "You won't get Amaury de Corbet back, *mon père*. I've seen him. He's getting married."

Guymond stared at him in horror. "But who—how—"

"I think we must leave it there, *mon père*," Le Picart said quickly. "Thank you, Monsieur La Reynie. Thank you, *maîtres*. You may withdraw now and leave us to talk together."

La Reynie got up from his chair and bowed. Charles and Wing bowed in their turn and followed him through the side door. In the postern passage, La Reynie settled his hat and gazed approvingly at Charles and the Englishman.

"Well done." He winced a little, looking at their faces. "Why do bruises always make one look recently dead just when one is, in fact, getting better? But never mind that; I thank God with all my heart that you're both alive. It took courage to keep trying to learn the truth, in spite of danger and pain. You're brave men, both of you."

Wing fidgeted and muttered something in English.

La Reynie looked at Charles. "What did he say?"

"I think he's surprised that you called him brave."

"He *is* brave. Tell him. My spoken Latin's deserted me long ago."

Charles told the Englishman what La Reynie had said. And added, "He's right, you know."

Wing looked searchingly at Charles, and then at La Reynie. Then, instead of tangling himself in the long speech of denial Charles was expecting, he drew himself up to his full unimpressive height and beamed at the *lieutenant-général*.

"You are very kind, *monsieur*," he said in French, enunciating very carefully. "I've been using that book we got, *maître*," he said aside to Charles. He bowed again and marched away toward the court as proudly as a military procession. La Reynie watched him go. Then his shoulders rose and fell in a sigh and he looked at Charles. "Gabriel has left," he said abruptly.

Charles knew something of La Reynie's long struggle with his estranged son, Gabriel. "Where has he gone?"

"Rome." The *lieutenant-général* watched a dozen teenaged boys walk past the courtyard end of the street passage. "He told me he will never come back."

The unhappy silence grew. Looking at La Reynie's rigid face, Charles wanted to offer comfort, offer something. "Do you remember," he said carefully, "that when we talked by the rose bushes, the night I was attacked, you said that perhaps you and I are two of a kind?"

La Reynie didn't look at him. "Yes."

"I think you were right."

La Reynie's mouth opened slightly, and he turned his head, staring at Charles like an actor who had forgotten his lines. Then he blinked hard and walked toward the street. "Open!" he barked, and the lay brother opened the postern for him.

Charles followed him out into the rue St. Jacques. The early November dusk had come, and people in the houses down the hill were lowering the street lanterns from their walls as the lighter with his bucket of candles worked his way up from the river.

"Do you ever miss the old darkness?" Charles said, partly to ease the other man's awkwardness. "With these lanterns, I don't notice the stars as much as before I came to Paris. I don't somehow look so far up."

La Reynie snorted dismissively. "I can live with a few less stars if that's the price of being able to walk the streets without being robbed or killed." He turned to get into his carriage.

"Wait, I've been meaning to tell you something. The last

time I talked with Père Dainville, he told me a little about how Paris used to be. He said that you deserve an assured place in heaven for what you've done to make it safer."

La Reynie made a soft surprised sound and looked at Charles over his shoulder. "Did he?"

Charles nodded.

A slow smile spread over the lieutenant-général's tired face. "Thank you." He climbed into the carriage, the waiting lackey closed the door and sprang up behind, and the carriage started down the hill.

Charles went to the door of the LeClercs' bakery. Marie-Ange answered his knock and pulled him inside. "*Maître*, come in—oh! What happened to your poor face?"

"Someone hit me. But I'm all right, everything's well."

"That's good!" She was wriggling with excitement. "We have something to show you. Papa, bring him!"

Roger LeClerc came into his shop, walking like a man escorting the king and carrying what looked like a small bundle of laundry. Solemnly, he came to Charles and peeled back the corner of the bundle's blanket. A tiny, red-faced baby stared up at Charles. Its wide, dark eyes were fringed with eyelashes as long as a doe's. Charles's heart melted and he put out a tentative finger.

"My son," LeClerc said tremulously, and the baby grasped Charles's finger.

Charles grinned at the baker. "Well done, *monsieur*! He has a good grip on him! Have you named him?"

"He is Brice Roger Auguste LeClerc." The father's attempt at formality dissolved and he grinned back.

"'Brice' is after my grandfather. The 'Auguste' part is after Père Dainville," Marie-Ange said. "Papa, let me!" She held up her arms and Charles gently withdrew his finger from the fierce little grip. Roger LeClerc carefully gave her the baby.

She stroked her brother's cheek. "*Maman* says he looks just like I did, *maître*."

"I can see that he has your eyelashes. How is *madame* your mother?"

"*Maman* is sleeping, she's very tired. But she's well."

Charles glanced at the baker for confirmation.

"Yes, very well indeed," he said. "My Beatrice did bravely."

"Thank the Virgin and Saint Anne," Charles said from his heart. He watched Marie-Ange kissing her brother on his minute nose and turned to LeClerc. "I will go now, *monsieur*. I don't want to wake *madame*. I'll tell Père Le Picart and Père Brunet that all's well. And that your son carries Père Dainville's name." He shook LeClerc by the hand. Then he enveloped Brice Roger Auguste and Marie-Ange in a careful hug and took his leave.

Outside, he walked slowly down the St. Jacques hill toward the river. It was nearly full dark now. The widely spaced lanterns were lit and the street's daytime noise had hushed. He walked slowly, thinking of all that had happened and all he'd learned. When he reached the river, he turned to the left, past the Petit Pont's fortress gate, and took a short narrow lane down to the river's edge. The Seine flowed fast and black, but even in the dark it was busy with boats and men and starred with lanterns. A late barge had just tied up a little way downriver, and men with lanterns and ropes were making it fast for the night. The clock on the other side of the Île chimed the hour, and bells from church towers joined it.

As Charles gazed at the water, the knotted mass of thought and feelings left from all that had happened seemed to float away with the river. For a while he stood blessedly not thinking or feeling at all. Then he found himself wondering idly where the Seine began, and thinking that someday he'd like to go to wherever it ended in the sea. And maybe farther than that . . .

When the November wind grew too cold, he turned back toward Louis le Grand. But he took a last look at the Seine running west under the swinging lanterns on the boats and the stars, and as he looked, he remembered what the goatwoman had said to him: that endings and beginnings can't be untangled. That they flow into human hands and out again, like air, like water. He stretched his big hands in front of him, as though he were offering something. All he had to do, then, was keep his hands open. And his heart. Because no matter what flowed into them and out again, nothing was wasted.

In each of the Charles du Luc books, I've taken readers to different parts of seventeenth-century Paris. Much of *The Whispering of Bones* takes place west and south of the old city walls. The church of Notre Dame des Champs, where Charles and Père Dainville find Paul Lunel's body, is no longer there, but its crypt still exists beneath a Paris parking lot. In the spring of 2012, I tried to visit it, but was unable to get access. There's a photograph of the crypt in *Paris in the Time of Ignatius of Loyola*, by Philippe Lécrivain, S.J.

As for new historical characters in this book, Charles's cousin—Charles-Francois de Vintimille du Luc—is real. His relationship to my Charles du Luc, of course, is fiction. But his background is fact. He was the older brother of the Bishop of Marseilles (who appears offstage in *The Rhetoric of Death*). He lost an arm at the Battle of Cassel in 1677, then became a naval officer, and in the early eighteenth century, was Louis XIV's ambassador to Switzerland and Austria. Likwise, Molière's famous play, *Tartuffe*, takes aim at religious hypocrisy—and while his relatives in this book, the Poquelin father and son, are fictional, a man named Poquelin was a member of the lay Congregation of the Holy Virgin at the Professed House in the 1680s.

The Gallicans and their desire to keep the pope's political influence out of France were also real, and were an oddly assorted lot. Many were lawyers and judges, some were anti-Jesuit, and some Jesuits—like the king's confessor, Père La Chaise—were Gallican. Past reality is never any simpler than present reality!

If you want to know more about the Paris Jesuit Novice House, read Patricia Ranum's fascinating recent book, *Beginning to Be a Jesuit: Instructions for the Paris Novitiate circa 1685* (Institute of Jesuit Sources, St. Louis, 2011). Patricia is an endlessly learned historian of seventeenth-century French culture, and has patiently answered my questions as I've created the Charles books. She found the handwritten original of instructions for the Paris novitiate in the Mazarine Library in Paris, where they'd been unnoticed for a very long time. She translated and annotated them, and included wonderful period drawings of the Novice House.

The other book that figures largely in *The Whispering of Bones* is the *Monita Secreta*—or *Le Cabinet jesuitique*, as the 1678 version I've used in the novel is called. I've wondered why so much dark mythology surrounds the Society of Jesus. All human institutions are certainly flawed and the Society is no exception. But the still widespread beliefs that the Society of Jesus was—and is—secretly scheming to run the world, or that the Society serves as "the pope's shock troops," as someone once said to me, are simply peculiar. The *Monita Secreta*, which means *Private Instructions*, was first printed in Cracow, Poland, in 1614, and pretends to be the secret instructions for a select inner circle of Jesuits about gaining inordinate power in the world. It was actually written by Jerome Zahorowski, a Polish Jesuit angry over being dismissed from the Society, and despite being immediately recognized as a forgery by non-Jesuit as well as Jesuit scholars, it unhappily proves that people in every age love a conspiracy theory. Contemporary scholars see parallels between the *Monita Secreta* and the notorious anti-Semitic *Protocols of the Elders of Zion*, which fueled the tragic anti-Semitism before World War II. Hitler, who hated Jesuits nearly as much as he hated Jews, had the *Monita Secreta* in his library. The *Monita Secreta* has gone through at least 148 printed editions, in many countries and languages, under many different titles; there was even an edition published as recently as 1996, in Moscow. These days you can also find several fringe websites warning against the so-called Jesuit conspiracy to run the world. Because Charles loves truth and hates lies as much as I do, the book became part of this novel.

Besides reading *Le Cabinet jesuitique* in the Mazarine Library in the spring of 2012, I also read the October 1687 *Mercure Galant*, the closest thing Charles's Paris had to a newspaper. The *Mercure* was published monthly as a small book, rather than as the kind of newspaper we know, and circulated all over France. When I asked for the *Mercure* at the Mazarine, a man in a blue smock climbed a long ladder to get the book from a very high shelf. The librarian brought it to me, along with a weighted silk cord for holding the fragile pages down without damaging them while I read. As I opened the *Mercure*, I was moved almost to tears. I was holding a tiny piece of 1687 Paris in my hands. I could imagine Charles, or any of the other characters, reading it, passing it around, talking about its news, singing its songs. In *The Whispering of Bones*, I made use of details that were all new and interesting in October 1687, such as white skirts with orange stripes like Mlle de Subligny's, the riddle Père Martin the doorkeeper solves, and the love song Charles hears as he stands at his window. For me, part of the joy of writing historical novels lies in inviting readers to touch the past. Another writer has said, "There are no dead . . ." When something allows the past and the people who lived there to flash into vivid and tangible life, I understand the way in which those words are true.

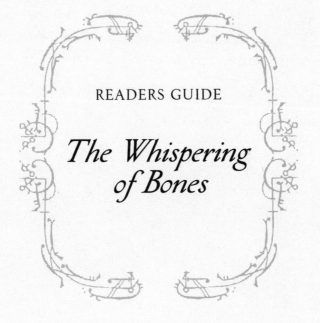

READERS GUIDE

The Whispering of Bones

DISCUSSION QUESTIONS

1. Why do you think it took Amaury de Corbet so long to become a Jesuit novice? How is discerning our own vocations affected by our emotional lives?

2. Charles and his cousin the naval commander have different understandings of courage. Are they both right? How do you understand courage?

3. What drives the Jesuit scholastic Louis Richaud to do what he does? What effect do you think his family life might have had on him?

4. Did anything you learned about the Jesuit Novice House and life as a novice surprise you?

5. Why do you think books like *Le Cabinet jesuitique* (the *Monita Secreta*) are always so popular, even when what they say has been proven false?

6. At the end of the book, how did you feel about the Lunel brothers, Alexandre and Paul?

7. What do you think will be different for Charles, now that he's no longer haunted by the terrible secret from his time as a soldier?

8. Is the goatwoman a witch or just a shrewd old woman?

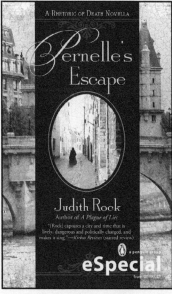

Notes

Notes